BURNING LIES

WINDSTORM
PRESS

PRAISE FOR BURNING LIES

The Gift pulled me in. This story has all the elements of an engrossing thriller—dynamic characters, secrets, suspense, sex, violence, and a believable and likeable protagonist. A very enjoyable read!

—Diana Stevan, author of *A Cry from the Deep*

JP McLean at her six-star best; she had me forgetting to get meals, up late into the night, only to wake thinking about the story where I left it. And once I read THE END she had me reaching for the next one. This book, like the first two, builds up to an exciting crescendo, so much so, that sometimes you have to force yourself to breathe.

—Pat McDonald, British crime author

PRAISE FOR THE GIFT LEGACY

66 A profoundly intelligent story of a captivating young woman whose victories and struggles with a unique gift will grab your every emotion.
—Jennifer Manuel, award-winning author of
The Heaviness of Things That Float

66 JP McLean possesses her own unique gift: the ability to bewitch her readers with her boundless imagination.
—Elinor Florence, Globe and Mail bestselling author of
Bird's Eye View

66 A deftly crafted, impressively original and inherently compelling read from first page to last.
—Midwest Book Review

66 Danger, suspense, and mystery all bundled into one perfect read.
—Urban Lit Magazine

66 An excellent read in every way—fast paced with a unique premise and wonderful, rich characters.
—Ev Bishop, award-winning author of
the River's Sigh B & B series

66 Fun ... sensual, full of adventure.
—Bill Engleson, author of *Like a Child to Home*

66 JP McLean skillfully manages to have you question what you once thought impossible.
—Island Gals Magazine

66 A compelling journey into a unique world that supernatural suspense fans will adore!
—Lisa Voisin, author of The Watcher Saga

66 It's gentle and lyric, and it's dark and hard.
—J.F. Kaufmann, author of The Langaer Chronicles

Titles by JP McLean

The Thorne Witch Novels

The Never Witch

Hexborn

The Dark Dreams Novels

Blood Mark

Ghost Mark

Scorch Mark

The Gift Legacy

Secret Sky

Hidden Enemy

Burning Lies

Lethal Waters

Deadly Deception

Wings of Prey

The Gift Legacy Companion

Lover Betrayed (Secret Sky Redux)

Novellas

Crimson Frost (A Supernatural Noel)

BURNING LIES

The Gift Legacy
Book 3

JP McLean

Burning Lies
The Gift Legacy ~ Book 3
First Canadian Edition

Previously published as *The Gift: Redemption*

ISBN
978-1-988125-35-0 (Paperback)
978-1-988125-36-7 (MOBI)
978-1-988125-37-4 (EPUB)
978-1-988125-38-1 (PDF)

Edited by Nina Munteanu
Copy edit by Nancy Wills
Book cover designed by JD&J with stock imagery provided by
Konstantin Kamenetskiy & Progressman © 123RF.com
Author photograph by Crystal Clear Photography

Cataloguing in Publication information available
from Library and Archives Canada

WINDSTORM PRESS
BRITISH COLUMBIA, CANADA
WWW.WINDSTORMPRESS.COM

This one is dedicated to you, the reader; the one who dares to believe, if only for a moment, in the impossible. For you are the one who understands that impossible is a word that should be used sparingly.

Rather than love, than money, than fame, give me truth.

—Henry David Thoreau

Chapter One

The black granite hadn't lost its lustre. I should have known it would be black, but still, it threw me. I'd expected soft white marble and cherubic angels, maybe harps for an infant's grave, but cold, stark granite?

A gentle breeze stirred the dry air.

"Emelynn, are you all right?" Mason could have passed for a bodyguard or a hit man. He kept a cautious watch over me as I kneeled at my brother's headstone and traced the engraving with my fingers. A tear escaped.

Andrew Reynolds Taylor
Beloved
March 2, 1986 ~ April 13, 1986

"Yeah," I lied. My half-brother had lived just forty-two days and I'd only recently learned of him. I didn't have siblings. Maybe that's why I didn't like referring to him as a "half." Somehow, it diminished him. But the tears weren't for the boy I never knew; they were for my father. The agony he must have suffered burying his son made my chest ache. I knew that ache well. Was it he or the child's mother, Jolene, who had the sad task of writing the epitaph? I wiped the tear away.

"Were you here? For the funeral?" Though in his early forties now, Mason would have been a teenager when his nephew died.

"Yes." Whether he spoke softly in reverence for the setting or in sadness, I couldn't tell.

Andrew would have turned twenty-five this year—just three years older than me. What would he have been like? Would we have been close?

I glanced up at Mason and he forced a thin smile. "Are you ready to go?" he asked offering me his hand. He'd forgone his usual black leather gloves; they would have drawn attention in California's late-September heat. The rest of his attire made no concession to the temperature: black slacks, black shirt and black shoes. Mason was always prepared; all of the Tribunal Novem were, especially now.

I nodded then reached for his hand. "They picked a beautiful spot," I said. Turner Acres was a small cemetery nestled in the hills northeast of Oakland. Mason helped me to my feet, a small courtesy I was both grateful for and resentful of. I brushed the grass from my capris and straightened my hideous blouse. It was a loose-fitting, multi-hued fashion misstatement, but a necessity that helped conceal the fact I wore no bra. I wasn't yet able to tolerate anything tight against the tender skin on my back.

"Yes, they did," he agreed and we strolled through the sombre grounds of the cemetery back to his Audi. The air smelled like freshly mown hay.

Mason and I had gotten to know each other better in the month since my ordeal. I now knew he'd never married nor did he have children. I'd also learned that he lived with his parents, a fact which stunned me and didn't fit with the imposing image of the leather-clad man who'd stormed into my cottage mere weeks ago. Since then, he'd been making an effort to be kind and keep his menacing tendencies in check. It was working. I was actually starting to believe what he'd said about considering me his niece since his only sibling, Jolene, had gifted me.

He looked down at the car keys in his hand. "If we ever find Jolene, we'll lay her to rest with Andrew."

Although I didn't like to think about it, Jolene had likely died as a result of giving me her *gift*. If the process itself hadn't killed her, it would have weakened her to such an extent that a bad cold could have ended her life. Sadly, half the documented cases of gifting ended in death and no one had heard from Jolene in a decade: there was little room for hope. Mason and I talked about Jolene a lot. She'd captivated my father years before he met my mother.

"Thanks for bringing me here," I said. Mason had made all the arrangements. The Tribunal's private jet had flown me directly from Vancouver to San Francisco, where he'd picked me up. We'd driven straight from the airport to the cemetery.

"You're welcome." He opened the passenger door and waited until

I'd tucked in my legs. "I'm happy you wanted to come." The door closed with a soft thunk. His gaze shifted left and right as he walked around to the driver's side. He'd been vigilant since we left the airport. It reminded me that we were never really safe—even here in the peaceful countryside.

He crammed his six-foot frame into the driver's seat, pushed in the clutch and jiggled the stick shift in neutral. "My father is anxious to meet you," he said, shifting into first. He slowly released the clutch and the car inched forward. Gravel crunched under its wheels.

We turned onto sun-faded asphalt outside the front gates of Turner Acres. I pulled my new Garmin GPS from my purse and input the cemetery's location. The GPS was a wrist-mounted model just like my last one. Unfortunately, that one was tagged as evidence in the Major Crimes Division lock-up in Vancouver. My kidnappers had known to destroy my GPS-enabled cellphone when they'd drugged me and taken me to their filthy trailer in the woods, but they hadn't a clue that the wristwatch they'd thrown into a bag with my clothes was, in fact, a GPS. It was the only time I'd been thankful for my dismal sense of direction that ensured I wore it everywhere.

"I booked you a room in Bodega Bay, although I wish you'd reconsider and stay with us."

"I appreciate all you've done for me, Mason. I'd just feel more comfortable in a hotel." I didn't mean to be difficult, but I didn't think of him as my uncle—not by a long shot. Besides, he probably lived in a dank basement apartment and I didn't want to impose on his parents.

But more than that, his family had ancient ties to the Tribunal Novem—the judge, jury and executioner for our kind. I didn't want to be any closer to them than necessary. Mason was a card-carrying member of this so-called judicial body. I learned that the night I met him … the night I'd been the unlucky focus of the Tribunal's attention.

The Tribunal had paid me a visit when they learned that I possessed Jolene's gift. They had a well-earned reputation for brutality; a fact I learned first-hand. Mason was there the night the Tribunal bloodied me and forced James Moss to read my memories. It was only after Mason and the others were satisfied that I hadn't *stolen* Jolene's gift, that they released me. I couldn't just ignore that.

After that violent encounter, I shut Mason out of my life. It wasn't until after he helped rescue me from my kidnappers that I finally understood how much I needed him. Mason was one of only a handful of people who could teach me about a facet of Jolene's gift that continued to elude me. A facet that would get me killed, if I didn't learn how to control it. So I'd swallowed my pride and forced a change of heart where Mason was concerned. It's why I was here. Well, that and also to learn everything I could about Jolene and the time she spent with my father.

The Audi's engine purred as we headed toward the San Rafael Bridge. During the long drive, Mason recounted stories about Jolene from when they were children. Jolene was eight years older than Mason. They'd grown up just north of Bodega Bay on an estate he called Cairabrae. These were happy memories for Mason, and he spoke about his childhood home with pride. "The name's Scottish," he explained. "It's been shortened, and the spelling's been bastardized, but it means dear friend on the hill." I tucked away the fact that he thought of his family home the same way I felt about my cottage.

"Jolene went abroad to study art when I was ten, first to Paris for a few years, then to Rome. She came back for breaks or we'd visit her, but we didn't have a lot of time together until she returned to Cairabrae. I was fourteen then. She would set up her easel in the solarium or out in the pasture somewhere and paint all day. Sometimes, she'd head out to the beach or down to San Francisco and fill a sketchbook. We'd ride the horses on the weekends and my friends all thought she was hot." Amusement crinkled the corners of his eyes.

I didn't doubt him. I could still picture her from our brief encounters on the beach outside my cottage that fateful summer when I was twelve. I'd only met her a few times before naively accepting her gift: a gift that altered my life's path. Mason had the same wavy hair as Jolene, but his was now flecked with grey and he kept it short, brushed back from his forehead.

"She brought her share of boys home but none of them compared to your father. When she brought Brian home, we all knew he was special and not because he was a doctor. She looked at him like he was her whole world. I think she fell for him the moment she laid eyes on him. If they hadn't lost Andrew, I'm sure they'd be together still."

And if they'd never parted, I thought, I would never have been born. But they *had* lost Andrew and Jolene lost herself. For three long years, the man who would become my father reached out to her, but she didn't reciprocate. Grief paralyzed her. Eventually, my dad met my mother, Laura. They married when she became pregnant with me, and Brian made a new life for himself. I'd only recently learned about Jolene and their son from a letter I found in a box of my father's things I'd discovered in the attic of my cottage. It had left me reeling. Neither he nor my mother had ever shared that part of his life with me. Maybe it wasn't the kind of thing you shared.

We travelled north on Highway 101. Mason kept a keen eye on the rear-view mirror, his left wrist bent over the steering wheel, his right hand loose on the gear shift. The cityscape increasingly gave way to larger green spaces, or what would have been green space if it weren't for the drought. Now the scenery was largely tan and yellow except for the deep green of trees that punctuated the gently rolling slopes.

"Why do you think Jolene felt she had to forfeit her gift?" I asked.

"I wish I knew. A part of her died with Andrew. She ran away—settled in Greece for a time. When she finally came home, we thought she'd come to terms with his death. I didn't realize she'd reached out to Brian until I read that letter you found. She must have realized that she'd lost him, too."

"I can't imagine giving this wondrous gift away. She must have been desperate."

"Jolene struggled with depression after Andrew's death. She never painted again. Mom went to great lengths to get her to stay at Cairabrae. She even cut off her trust fund. But Jolene would never stay for more than a month or two. I was away at school then and wrapped up in my own life. I think Carson Manse was the final blow. God, how I wish I could go back and reach out to her. We could have protected her."

Jolene had been running from Carson Manse at the time she gifted me. He'd been her lover and was the same man who, years later, arranged to have me kidnapped. Mason and I speculated that Carson had tried to steal Jolene's gift in much the same way he'd tried to steal mine: inside a circle of wood ash and under mortal threat to her or someone she loved. He would have tried to force her to recite an incantation that would transfer the gift to him, but somehow, she'd escaped him all those years ago. I wasn't so lucky when he found me.

"But she coped for fifteen years after Andrew's death," I said. "Surely she found some peace and happiness in that time."

"She was never the same."

"I can't decide if Jolene was terribly brave gifting me, or a coward."

"She was exhausted," Mason snapped. Immediately, I regretted my insensitive choice of words. He shook his head and softened his tone. "Her depression was never treated."

I turned to study his face. "Suicide?" I asked, shocked at the realization. That possibility had never occurred to me, but it made perfect sense. It also explained why she hadn't ensured there was someone in place to help me transition into the world she'd inexorably made me a part of. Mason shrugged and we drove on in silence.

We exited Highway 101 at Petaluma and headed west toward the coast. Half an hour later, we hit the postcard-perfect Shoreline Highway at Bodega Bay and turned north. The narrow highway wound precariously around bluffs and beaches for another fifteen miles before he signalled a turn to the right. The steep, winding road was marked "private." The nearly bald ocean cliffs gave way to pasture and sagebrush, as we climbed higher into the hills. Rocky outcrops and eucalyptus stands marked the slopes. We wound our way uphill for another five minutes before we came to a stop at the gates of Cairabrae. I recognized the Reynolds family crest on the wrought-iron gates. It also adorned the cover of the Reynolds family anthology, a leather-bound heirloom that Mason didn't know I carried in my luggage. Mason clicked what looked like a garage door opener and the big gates swung open.

We drove over a rise and Cairabrae came into view. Clearly, I'd underestimated Mason's definition of estate. Cairabrae was a sprawling two-storey stone mansion with wings on either side of a large columned entryway. Formal manicured gardens surrounded a circular drive that passed under a wide porte cochère. Outside the porte cochère, opposite the front doors, stood a larger-than-life marble fountain. It consisted of three Greek-inspired female figures standing shoulder to shoulder, facing out. Their stone dresses were wet from water that spilled from the heavy vases on their shoulders. Each of the figures held a dove in an outstretched palm.

"This is beautiful," I said, my voice filled with awe. He pulled in under the porte cochère and parked. Mason definitely did not live in a musty basement.

"Dad's had a late lunch prepared for us. I'll take you to your hotel after we eat."

"Thank you." I reached to open the car door. Mason came around and held it for me then offered his hand. I took it, once again apologizing for my frailty. Mason winced in sympathy.

I hated feeling weak. "It doesn't hurt that much." I smiled brightly as I straightened my clothes. "Avery says two more weeks and I'll be as good as new." Avery was my doctor and the closest thing to a father I had in my life. The new skin on my back hadn't hurt this much since he'd removed the bandages a week ago. But I'd been on the road since seven this morning, most of that time strapped in with my back against a seat—almost five hours in the plane and another hour and a half in Mason's car. The pressure irritated, but the skin would soon toughen up. I'm not sure the same could be said for my psyche. The horror of my ordeal still woke me some nights.

The right side of the big double-entry doors opened before Mason reached them. A man, who could only be described as a pro-wrestler, held it ajar. He was dressed in black and had biceps larger than my thighs. His neck was even thicker. All he needed was the ornate gold belt and spandex tights.

"Mason," the man said, dipping his head. His clean-shaven face was kindly but a smile wouldn't have gone amiss.

"Ryan. Where's Dad?"

"Out back. Do you have luggage?"

"No. Emelynn's not staying. Emelynn, Ryan," he said.

"Ryan." I offered my hand. He darted a glance to Mason. Was a handshake inappropriate, I wondered?

He forced a brief smile. "Nice to meet you, Emelynn." Ryan was too intense to be the doorman. He must be security.

"This way," Mason said, steering us forward.

I considered myself lucky to come from a family that was well-off, but this was well-off to the hundredth power. It was easily the most beautiful house I'd ever been in, though "house" was a misnomer: it was a palace. We stepped over the threshold into an expansive vestibule. Pale marble floors gleamed all around and a six-foot-wide staircase curved up on the left to a second-storey atrium. A round claw-foot table sat in the entrance and it was bigger than two of my dining-room tables put together. In fact, my dining-room table would have collapsed under the weight of the enormous bouquet of flowers that graced this one. A thick oriental carpet was centred under the table and a chandelier the size of an armchair lit the lofty two-storey entryway. It put me in mind of a hotel lobby.

We crossed the floor and descended three steps to a formal sitting area. The scale of the room was huge. To the right was a fireplace I could almost stand upright in, and I'm five foot seven. In the corner to the left sat a beautiful, red-lacquered grand piano. Floor-to-ceiling folding glass doors stretched across the back wall.

We strode through the room and stepped outside onto a vast covered patio, beyond which lay an expanse of pavers drenched in sunlight. Potted palms were artfully scattered about and blue water sparkled invitingly in a pool off to the left. The back lawn, cut short and faded to a crispy pale brown, stretched on for an impossible distance. Horses swished their tails in a paddock beyond the lawn.

I spotted Mason's father sitting just inside the shadow of the covered patio. He set his glasses on the table and rose to greet us. Pure white hair framed his tanned face. He smiled at me like an indulgent grandfather as Mason made the introductions.

"Dad, I'd like you to meet Emelynn Taylor. Emelynn, Stuart Reynolds."

I offered him my hand. "Mr. Reynolds." He was shorter than Mason and handsome despite the deep lines on his face.

"Stuart, please," he said, crinkling the edges of his dark eyes as he grasped my hand firmly between both of his. His hands were rough; a working man's hands.

"It's so nice to finally meet you, Emelynn. Please have a seat." He gestured to a chair on his right. I perched on the edge of it while Mason took a seat on Stuart's left.

Stuart turned to Mason. "Any trouble along the way?"

"None," Mason said.

Stuart nodded and turned back to me. "How was your trip?"

"The jet was a nice touch," I said, embarrassed at the extravagance.

He shrugged like it was nothing. "It wasn't being used today. Please, make yourself comfortable."

Mason interjected. "She's still healing, Dad."

The reminder stung, but not as badly as the whip that my kidnappers had used to persuade me to cooperate with them.

"Forgive me. Can I offer you a refreshment?"

"A glass of water?" I suggested.

"Still or sparkling?"

"Ah, still please." Tap water would have been fine. I felt like such a poseur in this palace.

"Iced tea," Mason said.

Stuart raised his hand and movement in the shadows close to the house caught my eye. A woman I hadn't noticed before moved silently behind a bar and moments later delivered our drinks. She was dressed in a black shirt and slacks, just like Ryan. Maybe she was also security. She certainly didn't look like a barmaid. Her brown hair was pulled back and twisted tightly in a chignon and she looked as fit as an aerobics instructor. She blended discreetly back into the shadows as quickly as she'd appeared.

"I'm very sorry about your run-in with Carson Manse," Stuart said. "Rest assured he'll be dealt with appropriately if he ever regains consciousness."

I could only nod. Their version of *appropriate* meant he'd be dead. You would think that would upset me. It didn't.

"What's his status?" Stuart asked Mason.

"He's still in a coma. James is keeping tabs on his condition."

"Good." Stuart turned his attention back to me. "I've taken the liberty of ordering our lunch. I do hope you enjoy salad niçoise. Maria makes the best one in California."

"Then I'm sure I'll love it."

Stuart wasn't wearing the basic black uniform. He dressed casually in a blue checked shirt, and cowboy boots peeked out beneath the legs of weathered jeans.

"Maria's your wife?" I asked.

"Maria's our cook," Stuart said. "Regretfully, my wife's in poor health and isn't able to join us."

"I'm sorry. I didn't know."

Stuart breezed over the subject. "I understand you'll be with us for a few days?"

I shot a glance at Mason. Had he told him I was staying here? "I'm returning home on Friday," I said with no mention of my accommodations.

"Good. That gives us some time to get to know one another. Next time, you'll stay longer."

I raised my eyebrows. Now I knew where Mason learned to be so presumptuous.

"You must take after your mother," Stuart said, studying me. "I don't see much of Brian in you."

My heart lurched at the mention of my father's name. "Did you know him well?"

"Yes. He and my Jolene were very close. They planned to marry right here at Cairabrae after Andrew was born."

"I didn't know that."

"Yes, well, it didn't come to pass. Terrible thing, losing a child." A shadow of his own loss crossed his face.

"How did they meet?" My curiosity burned to know every detail of my father and Jolene's time together.

"He walked into the gallery one day when she was working."

Mason interrupted his father's narrative. "The gallery was in San Francisco."

That fit. My father had worked in a clinic in San Francisco in the early eighties.

Stuart frowned at the interruption then continued. "The gallery was a cooperative where the artists took turns running the shop. After Jolene met your father, she came home lit up like the fourth of July. Jeannette knew right away." He shook his head, smiling at the memory. When he saw my confusion, he quickly clarified. "Jeannette's my wife—Jolene and Mason's mother."

"She knew Jolene was quite taken with the young man who'd admired her work. Jolene kept Brian coming back with promises of more pieces from the same artist. She strung him along for weeks before telling him that she was that artist. But by then, I don't think it was the art that drew him to the gallery. She was talented with a paintbrush, but no one likes seascapes that much." He chuckled and winked at me.

I couldn't help but smile back and told him of the painting of Jolene's that still hung in my father's study. "I remember him looking at that painting absolutely mesmerized," I said. "He never tired of it."

Stuart seemed pleased with that.

"So, Emelynn," he said, "tell me about yourself."

I knew they'd be as curious about me as I was about them, but talking about myself made me uneasy. I felt uncomfortable being in the spotlight, so I'd prepared a Coles Notes version of my life. "There's not a lot to tell. I lived with my parents in Summerset until I was twelve. Summerset's on the west coast of British Columbia," I said, describing the location of a hometown I'd learned few people had heard of.

"Just south of Vancouver. Yes, I know it," Stuart said, nodding.

Surprise registered on my face. "Well, the summer I turned twelve, I met Jolene and that October my father was killed. After the funeral, my mother moved us to Toronto."

"I'm sorry. I liked Brian very much. How did he die?"

"His float plane disappeared on its way to a fishing lodge in the Queen Charlottes. They never found him."

"That must have been difficult."

Some days it still was. My recap was finished, but they both looked at me expectantly. I wanted to tell them—I'm only twenty-two—there isn't more.

Stuart spoke, breaking the awkward lull. "If you wouldn't mind, tell me about Jolene."

"Jolene," I said, wondering where to start. "I met her on the beach in front of the cottage in the summer of 2001. She visited a few times, just briefly. She was soft-spoken. Wore a big floppy hat and sunglasses, as if she was hiding from someone. Carson Manse, I suppose."

Stuart and Mason listened without touching their drinks. "I liked her. She asked about my family and brought me feathers and pretty beach glass for the sandcastles I liked to build. The day she gifted me, she told me she had to leave soon. She said she wanted me to have something special but insisted I keep it a secret. The next thing I remember was waking up on the sand and wondering where she'd gone." I look furtively over my shoulder. The woman with the chignon stood quietly behind the bar.

"You can talk freely," Stuart said, correctly guessing the reason for my hesitation.

"All right." Did all of the staff here know about us?

I continued. "I discovered my night vision a few days later and knew then that she'd given me something special." I paused, remembering the first night that darkness didn't fall. Even though I was just a child, there was no mistaking when the night took on a blue hue and my vision remained clear as day. The miracle of it has never faded. "I didn't understand what it was, but I kept my promise; I didn't tell anyone."

"She never contacted you after that?" Stuart asked.

"No. Maybe she tried, but we'd moved to Toronto. I looked for her when the floats started, but I only knew her first name."

"The *floats*?" Mason and Stuart said simultaneously.

I stifled a laugh and not just because of the matching quizzical look on their faces; most people would think I was a lunatic in search of an asylum for telling this story. But not these two men. I had their undivided attention.

"That's how I thought of it before I knew what the gift was. It started with sleep-walking, or at least my mother thought I was sleep-walking. It was years before I figured out that I was losing gravity in my sleep and drifting around the condo. Thankfully, my mother never got a live-action view of it and, luckily, the condo was small so I couldn't float too far away."

"You could have been seriously hurt," Mason said. He leaned back to let the woman with the chignon refill his glass.

"That came later. The summer before I started university, I began experiencing the floats when I was awake. There was no predicting when it would occur, so I started packing weights around to keep me grounded. I thought I'd lose my mind. Jolene wasn't my favourite person during those years. When the floats took me unawares, I'd usually end up hurting myself." I took a breath, allowing myself a brief wallow in the torment of my awkward childhood. I now knew that the vast majority of Fliers were born with the gift. The few like me who were gifted would normally be mentored, but I'd been left on my own to figure it out.

"That's what finally brought me back to the cottage in Summerset. When I finished university, I figured there'd never be a better time to learn how to control this thing. I knew if I wanted any kind of a normal life, that's what I needed to do. The cottage was the ideal place; it's isolated and private, and my mother had no interest in returning with me. In fact, she gave me six months' living expenses for my graduation gift."

"I'm so sorry, Emelynn." Stuart reached forward and took my hand. "Please believe me when I say that my Jolene would never intentionally hurt you or anyone else. She was a gentle soul—too much so for our world I'm afraid. I have to believe she wasn't in her right mind at the time."

He released my hand and sat back in his chair. "How did you learn about the gift?"

"Foolishly, I thought I could teach myself how to control it, but I was wrong. I ended up in the hospital after a spectacularly bad fall and, fortunately for me, Dr. Coulter was on duty in the ER that night. He spotted the second lens in my eyes and recognized me for what I was. What I am," I corrected, feeling the weight of the words.

"He arranged for Jackson Delaney to take me under his wing. I thought Jackson was delusional, but who wouldn't? His impossible notions flew in the face of everything I knew about physics, but the proof was undeniable. Jackson introduced me to the local covey and, with their help, I learned about your world."

"I imagine it came as a shock," Stuart said. He had no idea.

"Mason tells me your covey is admirably loyal to you."

"Not just to me." With only eleven of us in the covey, we all knew one another. It felt like family. We were tied together by our gift and depended on one another to protect the secret and each other. We'd worked hard to develop our defensive skills and we'd proven that we could protect our own. I was enormously proud of that.

Maria arrived with our lunch, and the woman with the chignon set out wine glasses.

"The Gerty today, I think, Debbie," Stuart said, and the woman, who now had a name, quickly produced a chilled bottle of Gewürztraminer for his inspection.

"Yes, that's the one. You'll join me, I hope," Stuart said, turning to me.

At this point, I was famished and would have eaten with my fingers and stuck a straw in the bottle. But then again, I drank tap water. I nodded and Debbie poured us each a generous glass of wine. Over lunch, they asked me endless questions about my *floaty* episodes. Maria's salad niçoise really was the best I'd ever tasted. The tuna was grilled rare and the tarragon was fresh. It was after three o'clock by the time coffee was served.

"If you don't mind, Emelynn, I'll take my leave," Stuart said. "I like to visit with Jeannette after lunch and I'm sure you're tired after your trip." He stood. "Finish your coffee and then Mason will show you to your room. Feel free to use the pool or wander around and get to know the place."

"That's very kind of you, Stuart, but I think there's been a misunderstanding. I'm staying in Bodega Bay."

"Oh?" He tipped his head. "You know you're welcome to stay here. Lord knows we have enough room."

I swallowed, feeling awkward. Mason sat there like he knew nothing of my plans. Was this his way of pressuring me to stay?

Stuart must have sensed my unease. "Well, whatever you're most comfortable with," he said. "Dinner's at eight."

"Thank you for lunch," I said, pondering his dinner statement. Or was that an invitation?

"My pleasure." Stuart nodded at Mason before turning and strolling back into the house.

"Thanks for your support there, Mason."

His lips curled in a wry smile. "He's right, you know. Look at this place and just three of us live here."

Though tempted, I hadn't changed my mind. Mason didn't

understand how much it had taken to get me this far. I'd come despite the loud and insistent protests from James Moss. James had become a good friend despite not one, but two fiery introductions. He'd proven himself highly skilled in the security arena. I paid attention. "Something's not right," he'd warned. "He's trying too hard to get you to visit."

Mason's persistence that I stay at Cairabrae reminded me of James's warning. Right now, however, I needed Mason. I was only staying three days and I'd assured James that I would leave at the first sign of duplicity. That didn't do much to appease James, but I was living *my* life, not his.

"Would you like to see Jolene's room before I take you to your hotel?"

My face lit up. "Yes, I would."

"Come on then. I'll show you." He stood and led the way into the house.

Chapter Two

Jolene's bedroom, or more accurately her suite of rooms, was on the second floor. The door to her apartment opened into a wide entryway lined with louvred closet doors. I walked ahead of Mason into a bright sitting room. He crossed in front of me to open French doors to a stone balcony. A fresh breeze stirred the air. Across the room, a second set of French doors lay open to a bedroom. Mason nodded his head, urging me to go look. I glimpsed a high four-poster bed littered with pillows. I felt like a voyeur, greedily taking in every inch of the room.

"The closet and bathroom are through there," Mason said, startling me. I hadn't heard him approach. He pointed at a tall louvred door to the right of the bed. The animation I'd seen on his face earlier in the car when we talked about Jolene was gone. "Go ahead, take a look."

I pushed open the door to find a room that no one in my small social circle would call a *closet*. It was a dressing room as big as my bedroom at the cottage and full of clothing. Sweaters and T-shirts lay folded neatly on shelves, and slacks and dresses hung from hangers. Shoes, boots and purses stood at attention, perfectly aligned. I pulled open one of the numerous built-in drawers and found coils of belts in a rainbow of colours. Another drawer held layers of silk scarves.

Opposite the closet, another door opened to a bathroom. A tub big enough for four dominated the room. The toilet was in its own closet beside a large shower that had no fewer than six different spray heads. Between two narrow floor-to-ceiling windows sat a spindle-legged vanity table. Perfume bottles and toiletries were lined up like dominoes across the back, in front of its three-part mirror.

I returned to the sitting room and found Mason out on the balcony. He stared off into the distance, leaning against the stone balustrade. I followed his gaze past the white fencing that separated the manicured lawn from the fields beyond. Several outbuildings, including a massive barn, sat on the periphery of the pastures.

My voice interrupted his reverie. "Are those Jolene's things?" I couldn't imagine they'd kept them for the past ten years.

"Yes. Before we found you, we had hoped that she'd come home one day."

"She still might," I said, ever hopeful.

"She won't." He squinted into the sun. "When we learned about you, we decided to leave her things until you had a chance to go through them. Keep what you want and we'll donate the rest."

"I couldn't do that."

"Jolene would have wanted you to."

"Jolene didn't even know me."

"No, but she loved your father." He turned to me. "And she knew the consequences of her actions. If you're not ready yet, I understand. But, she *is* gone. There's no point keeping this room ready for her return. It's not healthy. We've grieved long enough."

I supposed they had. Jolene's balcony faced east, off the back of the house. I joined Mason at the railing.

"Did she leave photographs?"

"I don't know. You're welcome to stay and look . . . unless you'd rather go to your hotel?"

"No. I'd like to look around." My curiosity had gotten the best of me as I suspected he knew it would.

I heard Mason's phone buzz. He pulled it from his pocket and checked the display. "Mason," he answered, all business. "No. Don't assume anything. Follow it up." He hung up and took a deep breath then turned his attention back to me. "I'll meet you downstairs for dinner at eight."

"Is everything all right?"

"Of course," he said, dismissing my query.

"You've been on edge since you came to get me. What's going on?"

"It's nothing," he said, pushing off from the rail. Then he paused and reconsidered. "A search of Carson Manse's house turned up a few leads. We're chasing them down. It really is nothing for you to worry about. I'll see you at eight," he said, then he turned and left.

I didn't believe him. When someone says you have nothing to worry about, you usually have something to worry about, and he'd been acting wary all day.

I glanced around Jolene's room. Going through her things felt intrusive. Back in her bedroom, I sat on the edge of her bed. Sheer curtains didn't obstruct the view of the horses ambling lazily in the distant paddock. The warm air carried a tang, hinting of the ocean that couldn't be more than a few kilometres away. I kicked off my sandals, curled up on my side and pulled one of the scattered pillows under my head. It was peaceful here. When I closed my eyes, the only sounds I heard were the chirps of birds and the buzz of insects.

When I opened my eyes, it took a moment to gain my bearings. I shot upright. I hadn't meant to crash like that. My luggage sat on the floor just inside the room. Someone had brought it in while I slept and I hadn't woken. I must have been tired. My purse still lay on the far side of the bed. I pulled it over to get my cellphone. Five thirty: I'd slept for more than an hour.

I stretched then wandered out to the balcony and dialled Avery. The stones were warm beneath my feet. He didn't pick up. I left a message saying I'd arrived safely, and then I called James's cell.

"Emelynn," he answered. "Is everything okay?"

"Yes, everything's fine. How are things at the cottage?" James was staying in my guest room while I was here in California. He said he had some local business to take care of but hadn't elaborated. James rarely elaborated. He was a private investigator when he was home in New Orleans. He wasn't supposed to work cases in Canada, but he'd been doing a lot of *vacationing* in BC since my kidnapping.

"Your coffee maker died."

"Sorry. It was ancient. I'll get a new one when I get back. There's a Starbucks on the strip on Deacon," I offered. Coffee in the morning was an imperative for me.

"I'll manage. How's it going there?"

"Good. I'm standing on Jolene's bedroom balcony right now and I've already been to my brother's grave. That's two items off my to-do list. Turner Acres is nice, if you can say that about a cemetery."

"What do you think of the Reynoldses' place?"

"It's impressive. I met Mason's father. He seems nice enough. Presumptuous. I guess Mason comes by it honestly. Have you ever been here—to Cairabrae?"

"Yes."

"You don't sound impressed."

"I don't have fond memories of it. It's a beautiful estate, no question, but you might want to ask your hosts where their money comes from."

He said *hosts* with a sneer in his voice, and not having *fond memories* probably meant James had been coerced into doing the Tribunal's bidding here. James hated that the Tribunal had control over his family's special talent. All the men in the Moss family could read memories and James was the last of the sons who carried that gene. He'd vowed to not have children to prevent passing the trait on to yet another son who the Tribunal would claim and control.

"I don't think I'll poke that hornet's nest. I want their help, remember?" I said.

"Be careful. They're used to taking, not giving. And don't forget they're not the only ones you need to be vigilant of." James was referring to Carson's ruthless gang who called themselves Redeemers. We still didn't know their identities or whether Carson had told them what he knew about me.

"I will. I haven't forgotten your warnings."

"No—you ignored them."

"I did not—not entirely—and I appreciate all the precautions, but back off. I need to do this. Mason's the best chance I've got to get a handle on this thing, and you know how important that is."

"You're right—I do know how important it is—but it could have waited another month or two until you were fully recovered."

"It might have. But in a month or two, I hope to be working." My mother's graduation gift of financial support would run out at the end of October, and I needed more than the temporary work I'd picked up. I couldn't very well take time off from a new job to run around California. So, the timing of this trip wasn't up for discussion. James meant well and he'd earned my trust, but he was inflexible where the Tribunal was concerned.

I heard his frustrated sigh. "Have you returned their anthology?" he said, changing the subject.

"I haven't found the right moment yet." It was more than that though. I didn't know how my father had ended up with their heirloom, and I was apprehensive about how they'd react when I returned it.

"Will you be there on Friday when I get back?" I asked.

"I don't know yet."

I felt unsettled after we hung up. James had been a loyal friend and I felt like a traitor being here, consorting with the very group who'd terrorized his family. But it was only a means to an end and a brief one at that: get in, get what I need and get out—nothing else.

I went back inside and wandered around Jolene's room. My childhood memory of her didn't run as deep as knowing her sense of style or her tastes, however, the pastel colours throughout didn't match the image of Jolene I had in my mind. I imagined her as more of a bold-colour hippy type, and this room suggested prim and proper.

I opened random drawers in her closet, touching soft silks and fine cottons. I slid hanger after hanger along the racks, glimpsing styles that varied from casual faded jeans to tailored suits. She wore size six, like me, but she was a petite, so most of the pant legs and shirt sleeves would be too short for me. The clothing was dated, but pencil skirts never went out of fashion. Some of them would fit and maybe a dress or two. Her size-five shoes were too small.

Two full drawers were dedicated to bathing suits and that made me pause. The pool had looked enticing. If I was quick about it, I had time for a swim before dinner. I rummaged through her collection and found a backless one-piece. I grabbed a sheer beach cover-up and set my bag on the bench at the end of the bed to dig out my flip-flops. I used the bathroom then pulled my hair into a ponytail and headed down to the pool. The house felt eerily empty.

At the bottom of the curved staircase, I crossed the marble foyer, descended the three steps into the seating area and went out through the folding glass doors. The pool was on my left, beyond the covered patio. I flip-flopped my way to a lounge chair close to the sparkling water. There were several chairs to choose from and each one had a towel rolled up like a bolster on it. I tried to imagine what it must have been like for Jolene to live here. Had she known how privileged she was?

I shucked my flip-flops, removed the cover-up and walked to the pool's edge. The water temperature was somewhere between luke and warm. I descended wide steps at the shallow end of the pool and pushed off with a breaststroke. The water enveloped me, soothing the skin on my back. I kicked my feet and made a slow circuit of the pool. Floating on my back, I concentrated on getting my toes to break the surface. When my ears dropped below the waterline, the world went on mute and I relaxed in a watery cocoon. The sun had dipped behind the house and the peak of the day's heat had passed.

I swam to the far side of the pool and looked back at the house. The columns supporting the covered patio were decorated with crimson and fuchsia splashes of colour where bougainvillea vines had grown as high as the balusters on the veranda above. My gaze followed the foliage up to the balcony where a small figure sat in a wheelchair. Was that Jeannette? Squinting into the fading light, I saw a second figure. It was Stuart and he was watching me. I waved and headed for the lounge chair to towel off. I couldn't shake the feeling that I was trespassing and any minute now Ryan would bodily escort me off the premises.

I returned to Jolene's room to shower and dress for dinner. Rifling through my bag made me painfully aware that I had nothing suitable to wear in this elegant setting. I'd only brought the capris I'd travelled in and a pair of cargo pants. I also had my black yoga pants and hoodie—I wouldn't go anywhere without those, but they weren't suitable either. Maybe Jolene's closet would prove useful after all and Mason *had* told me to help myself.

My back could probably tolerate the hunter-green jersey dress I found, but I'd look like a hooker in it without a bra. The gowns were lovely but much too formal. Then I came across a knee-length black linen halter dress that looked promising. I slipped into it and glanced at my reflection in the large three-way mirror. The dress was backless and I was happy to note that the lash scars across my back had faded from red to barely pink. The hydrogel product I'd been treated with in the hospital after my rescue had worked miracles. Avery had assured me that, eventually, the scars would pale to hardly visible, much like the scars from the gunshot that had pierced my left side.

My back, however, did not need to be on display and I'd seen just the thing to cover it. Among the gowns, I'd spotted a light-as-air organza shirt that would easily double as a jacket. I pulled it on then returned to the mirror to pirouette. That was better. I stepped up to the mirror and pushed my hair back from my eyebrow. The ragged inch-long gash had healed smoothly. I had to be breaking some sort of record with the rate at which I was collecting scars. Maybe with a tan, they'd be less noticeable. If only my pale skin didn't burn so easily.

Oh well—nothing to be done about it. The mop on my head, however, could still be fixed. I returned to the bathroom and ran gel through my light brown locks to tame the curls. My hair had grown and fell halfway down my back now. I could see the red highlights my father always teased me about and didn't mind the colour so much anymore. A touch of eyeliner drew attention away from the scar above my eyebrow. Lipstick completed my sparse makeup routine. I rarely wore a scent, but Jolene's bottle of Coco Chanel intrigued me. I spritzed some in the air and stepped through the mist like my mother had taught me. Not too much, she'd warn. I dabbed a bit more behind my knees, slid my feet into my sandals, and headed down.

When I got to the bottom of the staircase, I heard voices and recognized Stuart's as one of them. A quick glance confirmed they weren't in the sunken living room or on the patio. I followed the voices and found Stuart and another man in a darkened pantry. The kitchen had to be close given the delicious aromas wafting by.

"The Pinot Grigio with appetizers and the Malbec with dinner," said the thin man dressed in black, as he repeated the order back to Stuart. His voice had a refined quality.

"Yes, and I think the Vidal with dessert. Make sure you uncork a bottle of Port as well."

At that point, Stuart sensed my presence. "Emelynn, you look lovely. Anything else?" he said to the man in black.

"No, that's all."

Stuart turned back to me. "It's a warm night. Shall we go outside?" He had traded his jeans for tan dress slacks and a brown jacket but hadn't worn a tie. He steered me away from the man in black, unencumbered by any expectation of introductions. Stuart's white hair looked wet and slicked back. On our way outside, we passed the dining room. The large table had been set for three.

Outside, he escorted me to a comfortable-looking grouping of chairs around a low coffee table. "We'll have the usual, Debbie," he said, addressing the shadows at my back. Ice cubes promptly clinked against glass. Debbie was still on duty? I wondered what drink was Stuart's *usual* and whether I'd like it. Maybe presumptuous was too mild a descriptor for the man.

Moments later, Mason joined us. He too looked fresh from the shower and wore dress slacks with a jacket—black, naturally. "Dad, Emelynn," he said. "You look nice."

I smiled my thanks wondering if he suspected the clothes were Jolene's. Debbie approached with three frosted glasses balanced on a small tray. She set one drink in front of me before handing Stuart and

Mason, theirs. She disappeared and Mason took a seat. "Cheers," he said, reaching over to touch our glasses.

I took a sip. "Martini?" I asked, taking the olive as a hint.

"Yes," Stuart said.

"I didn't recognize the glass."

Stuart cleared his throat. "I tend to knock over the tall stemmed ones. Too delicate for me. How was your swim?"

"Refreshing, thanks. You have a lovely home."

"Yes, we're very fortunate."

"Was that your wife I saw with you on the balcony?"

"Yes. She suffered a stroke and can no longer manage on her own, but the view from the balcony seems to calm her."

"At least she has that much."

"Yes, well, no point dwelling on the things you can't change." He turned to address Mason. "She asked for you today."

"I'll visit after dinner," Mason said, staring into his drink. I got the impression his mother's condition was hard on him too.

"How long have you lived here?" I asked, striving for a happier topic of conversation.

"I'm the third generation to live here. My great-grandfather built Cairabrae. My father added the stables, Jeannette added the solarium, and I had the place re-wired and re-plumbed. I imagine Mason will add his own touch when the time comes." He smiled at his son.

"I already have. The helipad?" Mason said, arching his eyebrows.

"Indeed. I'd nearly forgotten that reinforced concrete blight."

Mason shook his head as if this was an old conversation repeating itself.

"Never mind. Times change and we have to adapt. Right, Emelynn?" Stuart offered the sentiment like an olive branch.

"I suppose," I said, not comfortable adding fuel to that conversation.

"Speaking of adapting, Emelynn," Stuart continued, "You never did finish telling us about yourself. I don't believe we got any further than when Dr. Coulter put you in Jackson Delaney's care."

I'd thought they'd finished with their interrogation. Their curiosity about Jolene was understandable, but why did they have to know about me? "I'm sure it would bore you both."

"My dear," Stuart said, leaning forward. "My Jolene gifted you and we haven't seen her since. There isn't a thing about your life I would find boring."

Not since the day I learned what Jolene had given me, and what price she'd likely paid, had I felt the weight of it like I did at that moment. What had I been thinking? Jolene had given up everything for me, and her legacy was far more than night vision. It was more valuable than any physical treasure, more precious than time or truth. Jolene's gift was the incomparable wonder of flight. It was a freedom beyond comprehension except to the handful of Fliers like me who were lucky enough to possess it. The least I could do in return for her gift was give her family some answers.

I swallowed my reticence. "All right," I said, and then I told them how I learned to fly. I began with Jackson jump-starting my liftoffs until I learned how to do it on my own. "After that, I figured out how to slow and stop and land properly." I shared an anecdote about the first time I felt the force of gravity return. Recounting my experiences reminded me how far I'd come. In fact, I rarely even thought about the mechanics of flying anymore. It had already become second nature to me.

And despite my feelings about Jackson Delaney, I credited him for his role in my training, but I skipped over the fact that I'd given him my virginity only to later learn that he was married. The entire covey now knew that embarrassing tidbit and I didn't feel the need to spread the joy any further.

The man from the pantry interrupted our conversation to call us to dinner.

"Thank you, Phillip," Stuart said, revealing the thin man's name. I abandoned my half-finished martini and followed Phillip to the dining room.

They were curious about my covey, but I hadn't forgotten that Mason and Stuart were Tribunal. For that reason, I wouldn't divulge any personal details. I owed the covey my loyalty and protection.

Over the shrimp cocktail, I shared with them the covey's training efforts and how we used paintball games, and more recently laser tag, to hone our defensive skills. Mason was interested enough to ask questions about the custom laser tag equipment we used. That discussion took us through dinner.

Savoury garlic and rosemary aromas accompanied the main course, a mouth-watering crown rack of lamb served with green beans and herbed potatoes. Phillip switched out the wine glasses for new ones when the Malbec was served. Did they know Malbec was my current favourite red?

Though I didn't have a watch, it had to be well after nine by the time we finished eating and I wondered if Mason had confirmed a late check-in with the hotel.

"Thank you, Maria. It was lovely, as usual," Stuart said, as Maria made her last pass through the dining room. "Shall we?" Stuart said, sweeping his arm out for us to exit in front of him. We rounded the staircase and descended the three steps into the living room.

"Who plays the piano?" I asked. The stunning red instrument was clearly the centrepiece of the room despite its placement in the corner.

"Jeannette played until she had her stroke." Stuart sat back on a brocade loveseat and rested his feet on a matching, tufted ottoman the size of my car. "Jolene played too, but she was shy about it. Now it gets played by strangers on the rare occasion when we host a formal gathering." Stuart's melancholy was tinged with annoyance.

Phillip arrived with a collection of small glasses on a tray, and offered Port.

"Thanks, but I couldn't manage another drink," I said.

"Nor me," Mason said, waving him off. Phillip nodded and slipped away soundlessly. "Emelynn, would you like me to drive you into town?"

"I would, thank you. Can you give me five minutes?"

"Sure. I'll meet you out front."

"Thank you for dinner, Stuart."

"Don't mention it. We'll see you tomorrow."

I rushed up the stairs to Jolene's room and repacked my bag then dashed back out and almost ran over Ryan in the hall.

"Let me get that for you," he said, reaching for my bag. It was only a small carry-on and I wanted to protest, but refusal would have made for an awkward trip down the stairs.

"Aren't you ever off shift?" I asked, trying for small talk on the way to the front door. He chuckled, leaving me with the impression I'd asked a silly question.

Mason waited in the Audi out front. Ryan opened the passenger door for me then put my bag in the trunk. The trip back to Bodega Bay took almost half an hour and I peppered Mason with questions about his sister for the duration. He smiled when he talked about her. I think he appreciated having someone to tell her story to.

Moments after following a curve away from the ocean, the lights of Bodega Bay cropped up. The town catered to tourists, as evidenced by the number of hotels, inns and restaurants that dotted the main street.

Mason turned down a road toward the bay, pulled into a driveway almost hidden by a cypress hedge and parked out front of what looked like an old inn. The sign read, The Lodge at Bodega Bay.

"Mason," I said. His hand was on the door latch. He stopped and looked at me. "Thanks for telling me about Jolene."

"You would have liked her," he said, a sad smile on his face, but it didn't linger. He inhaled a cleansing breath and brightened up. "We'll start your lessons tomorrow."

"I'd like that."

He popped the trunk and retrieved my bag, and for the first time today, I was out of the car before he could offer me a hand. With my bag over his shoulder, he opened the front door of the hotel and accompanied me to the registration desk. Despite my protests, he insisted on offering his credit card. The clerk was not inclined to argue. I let it drop. It wasn't important and money was obviously not an issue for him.

When he started to walk me to my room, I stopped him. "Thanks, Mason, but I think I can find it."

"All right." He handed me my bag. "I'll pick you up in the morning."

"That's not necessary. I've organized a rental car."

"Oh?" he said. I'd caught him off guard. "Then I'll see you at say . . . ten o'clock?" I was relieved he hadn't argued.

I waved as he drove out of the parking lot and watched the Audi's tail lights disappear around the hedge.

The clerk at the registration desk held the phone to his ear. I rounded the counter and headed down the corridor toward the elevator—then straight out the back door. I quickly traversed the parking lot and threaded my way through a stand of tall eucalyptus trees that separated this property from its neighbour. A sprinkler head challenged my footing, but I made it back out to the sidewalk without drawing attention.

I walked out to the main road, crossed the street and slunk along until I spotted the crumbling asphalt apron in front of Bailey's Motel on Bodega Bay. I presented the fake ID James had procured for me and checked in.

"Welcome to Bodega Bay, Ms. Christopher." Bailey's was a shack compared to the Lodge, which Mason had picked out. It didn't even qualify as an outhouse next to Cairabrae. But no one knew I was here and that, above all else, was the most important factor. It's just for three nights, I reminded myself, disregarding the dust that clung to the faded silk palm tree pressed against the fogged glass of the front window.

Following the clerk's instructions, I took the walkway that ran alongside the aging clapboard building and up the metal staircase to the second floor. Home sweet home, I mumbled, unlocking a door at the far end. The small room was dominated by a sagging double bed and a hulking television that was bolted to a wood-laminate table. The digital clock blinked 12:00. Without even checking, I knew the cheap reproduction print above the bed would be screwed to the wall.

I was staying at a motel where guests stole stuff like this. If I didn't laugh at the absurdity of it, I'd cry. I clicked photos with my phone and sent them to Eden with the text, "It looked so much better online."

Eden was working in the ER tonight and wouldn't have her phone on, but the photos would give her a laugh on her break or maybe later when she headed home.

There were only two people in my life that I considered close enough to be sisters. They were the bookends supporting my strange life: Eden Effrome held up the Flier end and Molly Connolly held up the "normal" end. Molly knew nothing of my Flier world and without her, I feared I might drift away from any sense of normal; she grounded me.

After I checked the mattress and found no evidence of bed bugs, I felt better about the place. The sheets were thin and the towels scratchy, but they looked clean enough and relatively free of stains . . . at least large stains, I thought, eyeing what I hoped were only drops of rust on the edge of the hand towel. Morning couldn't come too soon. I fell asleep listening for critters and thieves. Neither interrupted my sleep, but it was not a restful night.

Chapter Three

The bathtub drain gurgled sporadically all night long. At one point, I'd gotten up to put a stopper in it but couldn't find one. I woke tired and wiped a wet cloth over my face, brushed my teeth and escaped Bailey's Motel without a backward glance.

By seven thirty, I was sipping coffee in the window seat of a small cafe anticipating the scrambled eggs I'd ordered. The sidewalk wasn't busy yet, but this was probably the tail end of tourist season. At least, that's what I guessed when I didn't have any trouble booking a rental car. I flipped through *USA Today* while I ate, and then strolled back to the Lodge.

The concierge happily accepted Jolene's clothes for dry cleaning and pointed me in the direction of the rental-car counter. James reasoned that if anyone knew my name and my connection to the Reynolds family, they'd already know where I was staying. There was no point wasting my new ID on a rental car they could easily trace. I found the light blue Ford Focus, dropped my carry-on in the trunk and drove north out of Bodega Bay along the twisty Shoreline Highway.

The first beach access slipped by before I was ready for it. I kept a close watch after that and didn't miss the next one. The paved parking area was visible from the highway. An old red truck with a trailer and a blue VW campervan were already parked. I chose a spot a respectable distance away, locked up, and headed to the beach. Low shrubbery and tall grasses grew in clumps along the path. Taller trees lined the upper slopes but were absent on the lower levels, close to the beach where the few trees that grew looked like stunted bonsai specimens.

Bright sunshine sparkled along the crests of the waves that crashed down on the sandy beach in a low steady rumble. Far off to my left, a black lab romped at the water's edge. A stick dangled from its owner's hand. I turned right and set a brisk walking pace on the water-packed sand close to the surf. It felt good to get my heart rate up. From here, it looked like the beach stretched on forever.

I'd been itching to get back into my fitness routine. My recovery had put me on the sidelines, but Malcolm and I were all set to re-start on Monday morning. Malcolm Perreault was the personal trainer I'd hired a few months ago. I had no doubt Malcolm would get me back into shape in record time.

The beach, as it turned out, wasn't as unencumbered as it first appeared. Steep cliffs and treacherous rock formations impeded my path and I had to turn around sooner than I wanted. It was tempting to lift off and skim across the tops of the waves like the sandpipers. Maybe tonight on my way home, I'd stop here and do just that under cover of darkness.

It was nine o'clock when I returned to my car and marked the beach in my GPS. Mason had suggested ten o'clock. I wondered how he'd deal with my early arrival.

Twenty minutes later, I drove up to the gates at Cairabrae. They were closed, with no obvious way to contact security. I got out of the car and studied the heavy gates, looking for an intercom. Without warning, they began to open, startling me. I jumped back behind the wheel and darted through the opening, fearing the gates would close before I could get through.

I crested the hill and the lovely stone facade of Cairabrae presented herself. She stood proud, her grey stone immovable against the gently waving swaths of golden grass growing on the upward slopes. I pulled under the porte cochère and parked.

Ryan quickly approached to open my door. "Emelynn, we didn't expect you so soon."

"I woke early."

He offered me a hand out. "They're in the kitchen. Debbie will show you the way." He motioned toward the front door where Debbie awaited. Ryan and Debbie were once again dressed in black and back on shift.

"I'll need your keys," Ryan said with an outstretched hand. I raised an eyebrow. "To park the car."

"Sure." I redirected the keys from my purse to his hand.

Debbie led me down a corridor to the right and pushed open a door at the end, admitting me into a large, bright kitchen. The door squeaked to announce my arrival. Stuart peered up from behind a newspaper. He was seated by himself at a small round table across the room.

Stuart set his paper aside. "Emelynn." He scooted his chair back to stand and greet me.

I raised my hand. "Don't get up, Stuart," I said, quickly closing the gap between us.

He waved off my protest. "Let me get you a coffee." He looked like a farmhand in a faded short-sleeved shirt tucked into jeans cinched with a wide belt. "Have a seat."

"Sorry to barge in," I said, eyeing Stuart's half-eaten bowl of bran flakes. I took a seat at the unassuming table. The airy room had all the hallmarks of a commercial kitchen: stainless-steel counters, a six-burner gas stove, and a long marble-topped work surface that ran down the centre of the room.

Stuart retrieved a coffee cup and filled it. Beyond him, a spring-loaded, swan-necked faucet rose menacingly above a big, stainless-steel sink. A double oven was set into the wall opposite the sink, a short distance along from four built-in refrigerators, or more likely, a combination of refrigerators and freezers.

"How were the accommodations?" Stuart asked, handing me the cup and resuming his seat.

"Fine, thank you. May I?" I asked, pointing at the jug of milk on the table.

"Help yourself," he said, and I doctored my coffee. "Would you like some breakfast?"

"No, thanks. I ate at the hotel." I took my first sip of coffee. It was outstanding. It put my coffee at home to shame. "Thanks again for dinner last night."

"My pleasure. How are you enjoying Bodega Bay?"

I complimented the pretty little town with the spectacular views of the Pacific while Stuart resumed eating. When he finished, he dropped his spoon into the bowl and leaned back in his chair. His big hands dwarfed his coffee cup.

"How's Jeannette this morning?" I asked.

Stuart frowned at my question. "She's well," he said. "As well as can be expected." His penetrating stare unnerved me.

"I'm sorry. Was that too familiar a question?" Had I offended him?

"Not at all. It's nice that you thought to ask." He looked wistful for a fleeting moment then bolted upright at the sound of a thump and squeak as the kitchen door admitted another visitor.

Mason blew into the room like a storm cloud, spoiling the calm. He wore full black leather flying gear and approached the table, pulling at the tips of his leather gloves.

"What did you learn?" Stuart asked.

"Nothing." Mason set his gloves down and poured himself a coffee. "He'd fled before we got there." He dropped some bread into the toaster and punched the lever down harder than necessary.

Stuart shook his head. "They know we're on to them now. They're running scared."

"They should be," Mason retorted. He was in a foul mood. Just how long had he been up, I wondered?

"Are you talking about the Redeemers?" I asked, hoping he wouldn't take my head off.

He disregarded my question and addressed his father. "Putting Manse out of business scattered them."

"We'll find them," Stuart said, then looked to me. "I understand you and Mason have plans today, so I'll excuse myself. Lunch is at one." He gulped the last of his coffee and rose from the table. "I'll see you then." He turned from us and headed back through the kitchen.

Lunch at one. Another compelling invitation.

Mason sat down and attacked his toast. "Maybe we should put off my lesson until later," I suggested. I didn't relish being anywhere near him when he was angry.

"No. We're both here now. Just give me ten minutes to change." He inhaled his coffee and left the kitchen.

While I waited, I scanned Stuart's newspaper. When Mason returned, dressed in jeans and a T-shirt, his mood seemed lighter.

"Shall we," Mason said, tilting his head toward the small door that led out to the patio.

"What's through there?" I asked, pointing to another door at the end of the kitchen.

"It's a service door," Mason said.

I stood, puzzling out the why behind a service door.

"For deliveries," Mason said. "There's a separate access road off the highway south of the main gate."

I suppose deliveries made sense with a house this size. Just more evidence that I didn't belong here.

We stepped out the patio door into bright daylight and strolled across perfectly manicured grass toward the white fence. The stretch of lawn was deceptively vast without a single tree or rock to give the distance perspective. When we reached the fence, we passed through a gate then paused to admire the bay horses grazing nearby.

"Do you ride them?" I asked.

Mason chuckled. "No, not these ones. They're owned by a syndicate and their trainers are particular about who handles them." He leaned on the top rail. "Are you familiar with horses?"

"I don't know the first thing about them."

"Well, these delicate beauties are high-strung, high-maintenance animals. They're treated better than a lot of people. If I ever threw a saddle on one of them, I'm not sure who'd stroke out first, the horse or the trainer." He had a good laugh at that then pushed off from the rail. "Come on," he said, turning toward a rambling outbuilding across the dirt road. He wrenched on a heavy door and it rumbled open along an overhead rail. "We'll have privacy in here."

My eyes adjusted to the light in what looked like a tack and feed storage area. The tidy space smelled of hay and sweet grass. Mason closed the door behind us. "This way," he said, leading me deeper into the building. We passed spotlessly clean but empty stalls, and rooms with concrete floors and stainless-steel tables. I recognized a wash stall that looked like a coin-operated car wash with overhead water wands. He stopped when we arrived at a corral with a hard-packed dirt floor, in the centre of the structure. I pivoted around to take in the space. It had to be a hundred feet across and thirty feet to the ceiling.

"What is this place?" It had looked like nothing more than a big barn from a distance.

"It's a rehab facility. The vets and handlers use this building, but not today." Mason walked into the corral and leaned back against the metal railing hooking his heel on the lowest rung. "What do you know about ghosting?"

Okay. Small talk was obviously over. "Nothing. It happened by accident when I was with Avery. He recognized it for what it was and tried to help. Unfortunately, his research efforts have been futile."

"By accident? How?" Mason's voice took on a suspicious tone. The last thing I wanted was Mason's attention on Avery.

"He'd been teaching me how to use my eyes to *jolt*. I got in the way and was hit by accident." The lie fell from my lips effortlessly.

"And . . ." he said, waiting for more.

The next part, I didn't have to lie about. "Avery's jolt hurt like hell, and poof," I said, turning my hands outward. "I vanished and when I touched the doctor, he started to fade too." Eventually, we both re-formed but an experience like that sticks with you. It demands explanation. An explanation only a Ghost like Mason could provide.

Mason narrowed his eyes. "What you're describing is incredibly . . . peculiar." My pulse quickened. Mason was a hair's breadth away from calling me a liar.

I jutted my chin. "What do you mean by 'peculiar'?"

"Ghosting doesn't just *happen*."

"You don't believe me." We should have waited to do this until he was in a better mood.

"I didn't say that. I said it was peculiar." He unhooked his heel and crossed his arms then took up an agitated pace, back and forth. "You said Avery has been researching it. What has he learned?"

"Not a thing. But he no longer believes Ghosts are mythical. Obviously," I added raising an accusatory eyebrow.

"Who else knows?"

"That every one of the Tribunal Novem is a Ghost?"

"No, that you're a Ghost."

"Only James Moss. But you already know that." Mason had all but told James I was a Ghost when Mason first offered to help me. But that wasn't when James found out. He actually saw it with his own eyes the night I was shot. I hadn't ghosted intentionally—I didn't know how. It might have been the shock of it or perhaps the excruciating pain, who knows, but it happened. I ghosted that night and took his sister, Sandra, with me. We escaped her captors and James brought me safely home to Avery. Just one more thing I owed James for. One more thing, Mason didn't need to know. One more lie.

"Did Manse or any of his cohorts give you any indication of how they came to know you were a Ghost?" He leaned back against the rail again.

"No. They knew that Jolene was a Ghost. They assumed I'd been gifted the trait from her, but I don't know how they learned about Jolene." Something in the set of his shoulders changed and my intuition flared. "Do *you* know how they learned about Jolene?"

"No."

I didn't believe him. He denied it too quickly. What was he hiding? "Could the information have come from someone connected with the Tribunal?" I asked.

"Could have, but it's unlikely."

"Why unlikely? There are nine founding coveys—that's a lot of people who know about us." Even if those coveys were as small as my own, it could still amount to more than a hundred people and that's not including all of their close friends and families.

"Not everyone in the founding coveys is a Ghost. Those of us who play an active role in Tribunal affairs are, but those numbers are closer to forty. The Tribunal couldn't function effectively without us, so they're very protective of us and what we do. They, more than any other among us, know what's at stake. Risking our lives risks their own. That's why it's unlikely one of us leaked the information about Jolene."

"Still," I said, "It's possible." Mason cocked his head in grudging acknowledgement of the possibility. "And why is there no information out there about us? Surely sometime—somewhere—someone witnessed a Ghost in action over the years."

He shook his head and shrugged his shoulders and, again, my intuition flared. He knew more than he was telling me. It served as a reminder that I couldn't trust him. It bothered me, but I put the irritation aside. I didn't need to know. I didn't want to be privy to any more secrets.

Mason pulled a pendant free from under his shirt and pushed away from the rail. When he got close, I saw a narrow, cylindrical container secured to the chain. He opened the tube and tapped the contents into his hand. "Do you recognize this?" he said, extending his palm. In it was a clear crystal nearly the width of his palm. I knew without touching it that it would be warm. I also knew it was six-sided and smooth with a prism capping each end. It was almost identical to mine. The difference being that you couldn't physically hold mine. My crystal was metaphysical. It existed in my soul or my mind's eye or whatever else you called that special place where memories and dreams exist. It was no less potent despite its lack of physical presence. I sensed it within me always and could draw on its power with ease. It's what I used to break free from gravity when I flew. Not another living soul knew about my crystal talisman and I wasn't about to reveal its existence now.

But I didn't need to lie. "Carson had a crystal like that. He referred to it as a replacement for the one I'd stolen from him. I think he was referring to a crystal he believed your sister might have had." Carson had hinted that the crystal was connected to Ghosts, but I didn't know how.

"Jolene didn't give you one like this when she gifted you?"

"No." Mason tipped his chin. He didn't believe me—again. "Carson's people searched my house and my car." I couldn't believe that here I was, once again, being accused of stealing one of these damn crystals. I shook my head. What the hell was the connection?

"I don't have, nor have I ever had, Jolene's crystal." I said it slowly, enunciating my words.

"Did Avery give you one?"

"No," I repeated.

Mason returned the crystal to its tube with a well-practiced move and tucked it back under his shirt. "Do you remember what I said to you when I found you glowing like a floodlight outside that trailer?"

I drew my eyebrows together in concentration. Much of what happened toward the end of the night of my rescue was a blur.

Mason continued. "I told you that you were in danger of breaking your crystal. I warned you that you were going to hurt yourself. Ron, Carrie and I had to shut you down. Remember?"

"I remember." I also remembered being furious with him. At the time, my only focus was getting my hands on Carson, and Mason had stopped me.

"Ghosts only glow like that when their crystals are supercharged. A crystal can't withstand more than a few moments at that intensity before shattering."

"So you thought I had a crystal," I said, realization dawning. "Jolene's crystal."

"We thought it had been lost in the chaos, but now you're telling me you didn't have it. Can you understand my skepticism?"

I understood all right, but I trusted my instincts on this; no one could know that my crystal was metaphysical. The only way to steer Mason away from the truth was to feed him an alternative. I had no ready explanation for the incident with Avery, but . . . that night with Carson . . . I grasped at a possibility, an edible lie. "Did you find Carson's crystal in the wreckage?"

"No. The debris was strewn over a large area."

The lie might stick if I wove the story well. I arranged my features. *Thoughtful* . . . "Is it possible I had his crystal and didn't realize it?"

Perplexed . . . "He'd wedged it between our palms during the gifting and I was dazed afterwards." *Working through the possibility* . . . "I lost track of it. I thought Carson dropped it when he fell unconscious, but maybe I held onto it." I finished my tale with a look of *astonishment* then forced myself to breathe. So much depended on gaining Mason's cooperation, and I hadn't planned on this last-minute hiccup.

Mason took a moment, weighing my words. After an interminable silence, he spoke. "I'm sorry we weren't able to recover it. Clear crystals of this size and clarity are rare, and you'll need one to ghost."

Relief flooded me. His words said he'd believed me, even though his expression hinted at reserved judgement. I didn't care, as long as he taught me how to ghost. I used his words as momentum and ploughed forward. "Do all Ghosts need a crystal?"

"Yes, without exception. Ghosts use their crystals to achieve that state. You will too."

"Can I borrow one until I can find one of my own?"

"I'm not sure you understand what you're asking. Crystals are cherished heirlooms. They're passed down from one generation to the next. Mine was given to me by my grandfather. Jolene's belonged to our grandmother. Our grandparents got them from their grandparents."

"But the number of children fluctuates from generation to generation. There must be crystals around that aren't being used."

"Emelynn," he said, flustered. "Ghosts don't *lend out* their crystals like library books, and particularly not to novices. The crystals may look indestructible, but they're not."

"Come on, Mason. We're all novices at some point. Maybe I could borrow a starter crystal until I get the hang of it."

Mason put his hands on his hips and hung his head, but I saw the smile that tugged at his lips. "You are persistent, I'll give you that."

"I'm a quick study, Mason. Show me what I need to know and I'll get out of your hair."

He looked up at me, puzzled now. "You're not in my hair. Dad and I like having you here."

That sentiment was wildly out of place. How could these people—whose only link to me was a gift from Jolene—feel connected to me? I didn't understand and I didn't feel the same way about them. How could I feel comfortable with Fliers who condoned and participated in unsavoury Tribunal deeds like coercing James's family?

But as unsettling as it was, I couldn't afford to offend Mason or

Stuart right now; not until I had the answers I'd come for and I was so close I could almost touch them. I needed Mason to teach me about ghosting. I couldn't blow it. "Thanks. That's very kind of you."

"Emelynn, I don't know what I have to do to make you understand. You're family. It's not *very kind* of us. It's what family does. Why is that concept so hard for you to understand?"

"I'm sorry, Mason. This whole extended family idea is still new to me. I'm not used to it."

"Well get used to it. It's not just Dad and me, either. The Tribunal Novem coveys have been hounding us to introduce you." Mason had told me that the founding coveys and therefore the Tribunal Novem would consider me one of their own when they learned that Jolene had gifted me. It was a consideration I didn't want.

"I'm not ready for that, Mason." Get in, get what I need, get out. Nothing more.

"You won't be able to put it off forever, Emelynn."

"Let me get a handle on ghosting first. That's enough for me to manage for now."

"For now," he repeated reluctantly. He turned and paced in a small circle, his hands still on his hips.

After a moment, he seemed to come to some conclusion. "Before we start, there are some things you need to know. Ghosting drains your energy. The longer you remain in ghosted form, the weaker you become. When you're new at this, it isn't the ghosting that's the problem, it's the re-forming. If you can't materialize, you'll eventually pass out from exhaustion."

I recognized the truth in his warning. That first time it happened to me in Avery's kitchen, it took a considerable amount of concentration and time before I was able to re-form.

"When you're learning, you need to do it in a safe environment and plan for that possibility. It's unlikely you'll be able to ghost the first time you try. When you do finally manage to ghost, it will take time to learn how to ghost and re-form smoothly."

"Okay, what else?" I asked anxious to get on with it.

"You'll also need to learn the skills necessary to move around in that form. And don't try to do it outside. When you're unskilled, even a slight breeze can wreak havoc on your ghosted form."

I looked at him expectantly.

"I think that's enough to start." Mason inhaled deeply then reached for his pendant. He opened the tube and dumped the crystal into his palm again, massaging it like a worry bead. "In order to ghost, you need to absorb the crystal." He held out his palm and carefully wrapped his fingers around it.

"That's not possible," I said, shaking my head, "unless that's a trick crystal."

"Are you always this cynical?"

"You're right. I'm sorry." Given what I'd learned in the past two months, I should know better than to question the impossible. "Please, go on."

He eyed me sharply, but held out his palm again and continued. "When you apply pressure, the crystal's walls break down. Think of it like ice on your tongue or a bite of cotton candy. The crystal itself becomes a part of you, absorbed through your pores. When you want to physically re-form, you have to coax the crystal to re-form. Watch my hand."

His fingers closed and his knuckles whitened. My gaze jumped to the muscles tensing in his forearm and then he disappeared. I swung my head around and then turned. My eyes told me that he was gone, but I could still sense him. I called out, "Mason, are you here?"

"I haven't moved," he said, his voice drawing me back around. The air wavered like it was rising off hot asphalt on a summer day, and then he was standing there with his crystal in his palm.

A smile I had no control over, stretched across my face. That was astounding. Could I really learn how to do that? God, I hoped so and it couldn't happen soon enough.

"Do you want to try?" he said, offering me his crystal.

"Your heirloom?" I asked, surprised at his offer.

He pulled his hand back. "On the condition that you follow my instructions to the letter. If you get stuck in ghosted form, there's a cot in the back. You stay in this building until you re-form then call me. Got it?" I nodded.

"And you do not supercharge my crystal." That was an easy nod. I may have done that by accident, but I didn't know how to do it on purpose.

He extended his hand again and I plucked the crystal from his palm. It felt just as I imagined it would, but it didn't have the steady thrum of energy that mine had. I raised it up to the light streaming in from the second-storey windows and rainbow prisms splayed across the walls and onto the dirt floor.

"It's beautiful," I said, twisting the crystal in the sunshine. It looked like a kaleidoscope had blown up and released brilliantly coloured jewels into the air. I stared in awe and looked over at Mason, who seemed equally mesmerized by the brilliant light show. "What would happen to me if the crystal were to shatter?"

Mason snapped his head up and looked at me with frightening intensity. He took a deep breath. "If it shatters while you're in ghosted form you'll be lost to us. You can't return to your physical form without re-forming the crystal. It's not something you want to test."

Thinking I'd come so close to that happening sent a shiver through me. "No, of course not." I shook off the horror and refocused.

The crystal was a solid weight in my hand. As a projectile, it would break a window. I couldn't imagine it would melt into my palm with a bit of pressure, yet Mason had done just that.

"Are you ready?" he asked.

I nodded and wrapped my fingers around the crystal.

"Steady pressure," Mason coached.

I squeezed my fingers and held tight, but felt nothing. I squeezed tighter. "How long does it take?"

"It's unpredictable. Keep it up." I held on tightly.

After a depressingly long time, I suggested switching hands.

"Yes, try that."

I repeated the grip with my left hand. Seconds ticked by like hours and a twinge of despair threatened. This felt a lot like my earlier struggles with flight. "Maybe Carson damaged my gift."

"Negative thoughts won't help. Keep the pressure on."

Maintaining my grip, I closed my eyes and visualized ghosting. There was no spark with Mason's crystal. Why was that? Mine was constantly vibrating, like it was a living part of me. After several minutes, I opened my eyes. "It's not working, is it?" I said, disappointed.

"No. But this is only your first attempt. I warned you it might take time. How about we take a break?"

"Already?"

"We'll try again in a couple of hours. Meantime, why don't I take you on a tour of the property?"

One failure wasn't going to deter me, but maybe focusing on something else for a while would help. "I'd like that," I said, and followed him out of the corral toward the far end of the building.

He pushed a wheeled door open and led me into a garage. Two

battered pick-up trucks and a flatbed occupied the space, but it was a recreational vehicle Mason headed for.

"Get in. Fasten your seat belt," he said, pointing to a four-wheeled toy with no doors and only a roll cage for a roof. "It's a quad," he said over his shoulder in response to my voiceless query. He opened an overhead door. While I fumbled with my seat belt, he jumped in beside me, turned the key and, without warning, hit the gas. We shot out of the garage. I grabbed the edge of my seat as he yanked the steering wheel hard to the right, spinning the wheels in the loose dirt. A dust cloud enveloped us. He picked up speed on a curving path that disappeared over a crest in the distance. "Hold on!" he shouted over the roar of the motor. He wore a playful grin that made his eyes sparkle.

As we climbed, we passed swaths of tall grass that soon thinned into clumps and then disappeared in favour of sage brush. Soon, small pines and rock outcroppings became part of the landscape and when we crested the hill, I got my first glimpse of thick stands of evergreens.

Mason spun the quad around and stopped. A cloud of dust had followed us up the hill and settled around us. "I want to show you something," he said, releasing his seat belt.

I followed him out of the quad and back along the path we'd just travelled. From here, Cairabrae's dark slate roof looked like a postage stamp on a very large manila envelope; the white fence, like fine stitching. The driveway lay like a ribbon on the rolling hills. It connected to the thicker belt of the coastal highway and beyond the road, the stunning blue Pacific beckoned like a giant swimming pool. The deafening roar of the waves was absolutely silent from here. Most surprising of all was the vastness of it. "It's stunning."

"Isn't it? This is where I come when I need to put my life back into perspective. It's amazing how many problems seem insignificant in the presence of this."

We took in our fill of the view then reluctantly headed back to the quad. Once again, he channelled his inner teenager and spun us in the dirt before continuing along the dusty trail. We didn't see another fence for miles and when we did, it was plain old barbed wire—not nearly as impressive as the white-painted fencing closer to the house.

"This is the southern edge of the property," he said, slowing down. We turned east and followed the fenceline until the trail branched off. He told me to keep an eye out for their small herd of a hundred and fifty head of cattle. "They're grazing the southern section. We should see them soon." We cut away from the fence and crested another rise. The wind picked up, stirring fresh dust into the warm air and blowing my hair into my face. Far off to the west, Mason pointed out the scattered brown forms of the herd. Satisfied that all was in order, he stirred the dust once more and took us back to the barn.

"Can we try ghosting again?" I asked, releasing my seat belt.

Mason jumped out and checked his watch. "Dad will be expecting us." It must have been close to command appearance time. How could I have forgotten?

"Afterwards, then?"

"Sure."

On our long walk back across the manicured lawn, powdered dirt settled into the sweat that the mid-day heat pulled out of me.

"You can use Jolene's room to clean up," Mason said.

I followed him through the open glass doors at the back of the house, and we parted ways at the foot of the curved staircase.

As I wound my way up the stairs, my thoughts took a negative turn. Was my gift irreparably damaged? Mason had explained that only Fliers born with the gift could give it away. Those of us who had been gifted couldn't; gifts could only be given once. It was the ultimate no-regifting policy. The only way I could pass on my gift was through my genes to my children. Carson Manse hadn't known that. And now I feared my crystal may have been compromised in that ash circle with Carson.

A fresh surge of anger welled in me and it was all directed at Carson.

Chapter Four

Jolene's balcony door was open and the sheers billowed into the room on the warm, sweet-scented breeze. I stripped off, trailing clothes from her bedroom to the shower. I got in and lifted my face into the watery spray. Heaven, I thought, letting the cool water quench my hot scalp.

After drying off, I wrapped the damp towel around myself and drifted out to the balcony. I could barely make out the trail Mason and I had just driven, though I was staring out at the very hillside. The pool lay below me to the right, its surface a perfect reflection of the sky. I heard activity on the patio below, but couldn't make out the voices. Probably Maria and Phillip getting lunch ready. It reminded me that I'd better get ready too.

I collected my wilted clothing from the floor and walked back out to the balcony. A vigorous shake in the fresh air didn't revive them enough to tempt me to put them back on. Jolene's closet came to my rescue once again. I swiped through the hangers until I found a suitable blue-jean skirt and paired it with a white halter top. Her flimsy flip-flops were too small, but they'd do for an hour or so. All I needed now was something to hide my back . . . no need to spoil everyone's lunch. Yesterday's beach cover-up was gone from the bathroom hook on which I'd left it to dry. Luckily, her closet was better stocked than a department store, and I quickly found another one.

I stuffed my dirty clothes into one of Jolene's beach bags then headed down to lunch. I crossed the foyer, took the steps into the formal living room area and walked out the folding glass doors. Stuart and Mason were engrossed in a conversation and didn't see me approach.

"... he told me Manse is being moved tomorrow," Mason said.

"Can we influence his destination?" Stuart asked.

"Carson is being moved?" I said, interrupting, and they both turned to me.

"Yes. To a nursing home in Vancouver."

"Why?"

"His condition is stable."

"But what if he regains consciousness? He'll still be locked up, won't he?"

"Emelynn, he hasn't been locked up since he left the ICU two weeks ago. The police pulled his security detail when his doctor declared him to be in an irreversible coma."

"Why didn't someone tell me?" My temper flared. "The man tried to kill me! Is it too much to ask to be kept in the loop?"

"Emelynn!" Mason countered my temper with a show of his own. "It wasn't our decision. And we just found out about the move."

I wrapped my arms around my stomach. "I need to be there. I want to see him with my own eyes."

"No!" Mason and Stuart said in a chorus.

"Neither you nor anyone else associated with us can be seen anywhere near that place right now," Mason said.

I looked at him, startled. "Why on earth not?"

"Because, if anything happens to him and you're hanging around, who do you think is the first person they'll suspect?"

"The man's a cockroach. If I could get close enough, I'd jolt him to oblivion with a clear conscience."

"Exactly my point," Mason said.

Stuart chimed in. "I appreciate he's earned your homicidal focus, Emelynn, but it's best that you're here among witnesses right now."

I turned my back to them and walked to the edge of the patio. Carson was comatose. He couldn't hurt me now. I conjured up the last image I had of him; the photo Detective Samuel Jordan showed me in the hospital. In it, Carson lay unconscious with an ugly black line of stitches across his forehead. It was the image of him I liked best. I paced to dissipate my anger. Carson Manse had changed something in me. I felt harder, meaner.

"I'm sorry," I said, returning to the table. "I overreacted."

Stuart rose to pull a chair out for me. "Understandable, in light of your history with Manse. Have a seat."

"Why were you asking about influencing Carson's destination?"

"It would be easier if he were close at hand, that's all. James Moss is monitoring Manse's medical records online, but should the Tribunal be needed, closer would be better."

"He's American," I said. "Maybe he'll be transferred to an American hospital."

Stuart said, "That's unlikely. He's tangled up in the Canadian legal system. It could be months before he's released."

This whole Carson Manse business wouldn't sit comfortably with me until I had a chance to talk to James. I needed to hear first-hand exactly what was happening.

Maria served another delicious meal. This time, it was steamed artichokes and a fresh pea and rice salad. I excused myself as soon as I could and dialled James's number, closing Jolene's door behind me. "Is it true?" I asked when he answered. "Is Carson being moved?"

"And hello to you, too," James replied.

"James!"

"Okay. Yes. Looks like tomorrow."

"You're sure?"

"As sure as I can be. According to the hospital's computer records, Dr. Abrahams ordered a transport for Manse to St. Matthew's tomorrow."

"St. Matthew's is a nursing home?"

"It's a long-term care facility for the lowest functioning patients."

"Is there any chance he'll be returned to the States?"

"Not right away. Detective Jordan is building a case against him, so he's not going anywhere soon."

I met Detective Samuel Jordan six weeks ago after he took over the investigation of the Wrights' disappearance. Charles and Gabby Wright had taken care of our west coast home for ten years and when they disappeared without a trace, Detective Jordan put me and several other of the Wrights' acquaintances under his microscope. He was a bulldog personified. Now he was also working my kidnapping case.

"Why didn't you tell me his security was removed weeks ago?"

"Em, he's in a coma that he's never coming out of. That's one step away from brain dead. Security isn't an issue."

"All the same, I wish you'd told me before I heard it from someone else."

"Are you making any progress on your other objective?"

It hadn't escaped me that he'd changed the subject. "I had my first lesson this morning, but no success. Mason said it could take a while."

"Are you sure he's not just manipulating you into staying longer?"

"I wish you wouldn't do that."

"Do what?"

"Think the worst."

"It's justified. And that's a long way from the worst."

"I'll take your word for it, but I'm sticking to my plan. Success or not, I'll be home Friday." James's loathing of the Reynoldses and the Tribunal was relentless. "I've got to go. We're going to try again this afternoon. I'll call you when I get to the hotel."

"Good luck."

If only that was all it took.

I used the bathroom then headed back downstairs to find Mason. He and Stuart stood in front of the marble fireplace with solemn faces. "What's wrong?" I asked, stopping short.

"Nothing's wrong, Emelynn," Stuart said. "In fact, it couldn't be more right." His face brightened and he reached out to pat Mason's shoulder. "I'll be with Jeannette." Stuart crossed in front of me and his footsteps faded going up the stairs.

"What was that all about?" I asked, stepping closer.

Mason opened his palm revealing a familiar necklace and silver crystal case. "Dad wants you to have this."

"Your crystal?"

"Not mine, and not just any crystal. It's my mother's."

I took a step back. "No, Mason. I couldn't." The hairs on the back of my neck bristled. I would be indebted to them if I accepted it. "I have some money—I'll find one of my own somewhere else."

"You should have this one. Mom's too weak to use it and her health is only getting worse. It's good that Dad's accepted that."

"It's too much." If James were here, he'd call it a bribe.

"Please. It was difficult for Dad to make this decision. It would be hard on him if you didn't accept it."

"I couldn't." I took another step back.

"It would mean a lot to all of us." Mason looked uncharacteristically vulnerable.

Did I need Jeannette's crystal? Mine wasn't like theirs, but it might work. Yet the fear that my crystal might be irrevocably damaged nipped at me.

After a quiet moment's consideration, I relented. "This is very generous of Jeannette and your father. Thank you, though words hardly seem adequate."

He exhaled with a smile. "Let me," he said, stepping toward me. I pulled my hair up and he reached around to secure the clasp. Up close, I could see that this case was more ornate than Mason's.

"It's beautiful." I rolled the cylinder in my fingers to get a closer look at the etching. I would return it, I decided, if they tried to use it to manipulate me.

"It's white gold." He showed me how to open the case and I slid the crystal out into my palm. It felt just like the others—warm and smooth, but without the tingle of power I got from my own. He stood back and tilted his head, gazing at the necklace with the hint of a smile on his lips. He watched me slide the crystal back into its case. "Keep it safe."

"I will," I promised.

He straightened up as if he'd just accomplished something important. "Let's go see if it works."

Once again, we headed across the manicured lawn. We entered the large outbuilding and resumed our position in the indoor corral. He reminded me that re-forming would be my biggest challenge. "The cot's in the trainers' quarters, through that door," he said, pointing down the corridor on the far side of the corral. "If you get stuck, use it and don't leave the building."

I slipped Jeannette's crystal from its case.

"Don't rush it. Slow and steady pressure," he coached, keeping his distance.

My best effort produced nothing more than half-moon indents in my palm from the pressure of my fingernails. I switched hands and tried again. The crystal was warm but held no energy. When I closed my eyes, I reached for my own crystal and the hum of power was instantaneous. What would happen if I applied pressure to my own crystal, I wondered? I let the temptation drift away. With Mason so close, I couldn't take the chance.

"Are you sure I'm doing this right?" I asked.

"Yes. There's no great technique involved. It's more a matter of tuning in to the crystal's energy. They're all different."

He paced the perimeter of the corral while I continued to press on the crystal.

"You don't need to stick around," I said.

He stopped and looked over. "I don't mind. Besides, I'd like to be here for you the first time it happens."

"Somehow, I don't think that's going to be today," I said, resigned to another failed attempt.

Mason made himself scarce, leaving me to concentrate without an audience. I appreciated the space and re-doubled my efforts. It was late afternoon when I finally called it quits. I called for Mason, having lost track of his whereabouts. He came out from the garage, where the quad was stored, wiping black grease from his hands.

"Are you ready to go?" he asked, making no reference to my lack of success. At the nod of my head, he led the way back to the house.

Stuart waved from the balcony as we approached then quickly disappeared inside. He was winded when he met us under the bougainvillea vines, his face lit up with expectation. His excitement quickly faded when Mason shook his head.

"No luck today?" he asked.

"Not yet," Mason said in a cheery voice.

"It'll come," Stuart responded, mirroring Mason's reassuring tone. "You mustn't be impatient."

"Thank you for letting me use Jeannette's crystal," I said. "I'll be very careful with it."

"I know you will. It's yours now. I hope it brings you the same joy it brought Jeannette all these years."

"I'm sure it will," I said, feeling the disappointment of my failure. "If you don't mind, I think I'll get my things and head back to the hotel."

"Why don't you stay for dinner?" Stuart suggested.

"I appreciate the offer, but I can't stay."

I thanked them both for the day, and then swiftly climbed the stairs. I heard Mason ask Ryan to bring my car around.

Jolene's bedroom was dim in the fading light of day. I reached for my bag. It rested against a bookcase I hadn't noticed in any detail before. I bent to take a look and saw a copy of Dr. Spock's *Baby and Child Care*. I tugged on its spine. The book flopped open like a much-read favourite at the library. I replaced it and scanned the shelf with renewed interest. My gaze latched onto a small photo album jammed between two hefty tomes.

I pulled it out and discovered a careless collection of photos with their edges askew and the pages loose. Shots of Jolene with Mason mesmerized me. A curly mopped Mason stood two feet shorter than his blonde sister. Another turn of the page revealed photos of Jolene with my dad. My breath caught. God, he looked young. My father posed in awkward contrast to a much more relaxed Jolene. His rugged features looked harsh next to her refined bone structure. There were a handful of photos of Stuart and a laughing and healthy Jeannette lounging beside the pool in dated bathing suits. It was a harsh reality knowing that the people in these photos, short years later, would suffer the losses they dealt with now.

Feeling like a thief in the night, I tucked the small photo album into my bag. I'd return the photos tomorrow after I'd had time to look at them more carefully.

I hurried downstairs. Ryan opened the car door for me and I tossed the bag into the passenger seat. "See you tomorrow," I said, turning the key. I stepped on the gas and stole down the driveway with the blue hue of darkness quickly replacing daylight.

A few miles down the narrow and twisty coast road, I pulled off at the beach I'd visited earlier. I drove into the deserted parking lot and shut off the engine.

Jolene's photo album had me hopelessly distracted. Like an addict, I reached for the small album and found immediate gratification in a photo of Jolene swollen with pregnancy. She grinned contentedly at the photographer, curling both hands under the arch of her baby bump. Was the photographer my father?

I flipped through the assortment of photos searching for a face I didn't know and was desperate to see. When I found it, I sighed and smiled at the fuzzy-headed baby that could only be Andrew. He looked pink and creased, like he'd been squished, though I suppose it was more likely fresh from the womb. Jolene's hand and hospital bracelet framed the photo. There were three more photos, all taken at the same time, though none as clear as the first.

I flipped through the collection one more time then slid the small album back into my bag. I couldn't take these photos from her family, but the thought of returning them caused me to sag into my seat.

The first stars of the night twinkled on the horizon. I climbed out of the car and opened the trunk. After a quick rummage through my carry-on, I found my dark clothes then dropped Jeannette's crystal-case necklace into my purse and locked up. With the bundle of clothes under my arm, I followed the sound of the pounding surf. My thoughts were a jumbled mess: Jolene's photos, Jeannette's crystal, my failed attempts to ghost, Carson Manse's pending move.

When I was out of sight of the parking lot, I tugged the hoodie over my borrowed halter top and wiggled out of the jean skirt, replacing it with my black yoga pants. I sat on the cool sand to lace up my black sneakers. The surf sounded so much louder here than at home. The waves rolled to the shore in long unbroken arcs of water, crashing hard against the sand in a predictable thunderous rhythm. At the cottage, the waves never made it to shore in one piece.

Since my release from the hospital, I'd not attempted flight. I'd tested myself by breaking free of gravity a few times—I'd even sustained a short hover, but I'd not yet had the stamina to fly. I was ready now.

I bound my unruly hair in a ponytail. The beach was abandoned. I made a mental note of where I'd left Jolene's skirt and strode north, hugging the shoreline. The salt air was refreshingly cool. I closed my eyes and inhaled then reached my mind's eye deep inside myself. I found the clear warm crystal and felt its hum of raw energy. It manifested itself in a reassuring tingling sensation just beneath my skin. I'd learned of late that there were few movements the human body could make without involving back muscles, and lifting my right arm above my head was no exception. I drew on the crystal's energy in a rush, and with a quick twist of my torso, broke free from the bonds of gravity. Exhilaration soon drowned out any lingering discomfort in my back and I slowly ascended, leaving the sand below to the crabs. I let myself drift to horizontal and rode the gentle offshore breeze.

The relief that my gift appeared to be intact was tempered by the knowledge that I wouldn't be fully free of the fear until I could test all aspects of it, including the extraordinary speed that Jolene had given me. But that could wait until I was on familiar home turf. For now, this low-velocity exploratory flight was enough.

Billowing clumps of grass and lichen-encrusted black rock separated the beach from the base of the arching hills. I flew silently in their shadow, following the curve of the shore. It was very different from the seashore at home but just as beautiful. Soft sand stretched on for miles, broken only sporadically with hulking black rock formations. A lone light on a tall pole glowed ahead. My GPS indicated it was another beach access parking area. I skirted out over the water to avoid the light's glare. Safely on the other side, I continued north. Cairabrae lay another few miles ahead. I felt good. I hadn't thought to fly as far as Cairabrae, but my stamina was better than I expected and my back wasn't causing as much discomfort as I'd anticipated.

Only a few clouds marred the night sky. I rolled onto my back and picked out the big dipper, but I never lasted long on my back; it was disorienting. Returning to a prone position, I followed the rise of the cliff. A handful of stunted coastal cypress trees clung to the top edge. I flew close enough to run my fingers over wind-sculpted green tips that had never before felt human touch.

When I thought I'd flown as far north as Cairabrae, I checked my GPS. It was just a little northeast of me. I rose above the cliff face and gained enough altitude to avoid detection over the Shoreline Highway. Car headlights swept the hills far below. The ribbon of road off the highway that led to the Reynolds estate looked like black satin. I passed high over the gates and carried on over the rise where I caught my first glimpse of the lights of Cairabrae. I admired the view of its lovely stone façade as I flew over it, up-lit now by dozens of landscape lights hidden in the shrubbery. It looked like something out of the pages of *Architectural Digest*.

I turned south. I might not have a handle on ghosting yet, but I was flying again and feeling stronger than I had in a long time. I felt safe and untouchable high above the Earth. Even James and his dire warnings about the Reynolds clan couldn't reach me up here.

In fact, I felt good enough to pour on a bit of speed. Perhaps I'd test it out tonight after all. I secured my Ryders to protect my eyes then streamlined my body and ramped up the speed. I tested it slowly at first, but when I didn't encounter any resistance, I kicked it up a notch . . . and then another. The freedom was overwhelming and I found myself flying flat out, barely able to contain the laughter that threatened to boil out of me. Soon, to my right, I saw the lights of the beach access north of where I'd parked. I slowed to a more reasonable speed, and a smug smile crept across my face. I carried on just south of the parking lot and circled back, making a secure landing where the beach met the rocky cliff face.

Feeling flushed and breathing heavily, I scooped Jolene's skirt off the sand and walked briskly up the narrow path to the car. The exhilaration I felt kept a smile on my face all the way back to Bodega Bay. I ditched the car in the parking lot of the Lodge and checked to make sure no one was watching before I walked the few blocks to Bailey's Motel. The clerk was surprised to see me again.

"I thought you'd checked out, Ms . . ." he said, searching his memory for my name.

"Dana," I reminded him. "Dana Christopher. And I did. Check out, that is. But I've decided to stay one more night."

"That's great," he said, filling out the paperwork and giving me a flirty smile. "I'm glad you came back." He took the cash I offered and I turned away, looking disinterested. The man was nice enough, but I didn't want the attention. It would be better if he didn't remember me. He dropped the key in my hand and I immediately left the office.

Tonight's room was as sadly appointed as last night's. I sat on the bed and hesitated before dialling James. The euphoria from tonight's flight and learning that my speed was intact wouldn't survive the discussion I was about to have with him. Not for the first time, I wished Carson Manse was dead. And not just die-in-his-sleep dead. I wanted him strung-up-and-beaten-to-a-pulp dead. I wanted him to pay for what he'd done to Jolene and then I wanted him to pay again for what he'd put me through. I used to be a nicer person.

The happy endorphins evaporated. I called James.

"How'd it go this afternoon?" he asked after we'd said our hellos.

"No luck yet, but Mason's not worried." I tried to sound casual about it. "He says my lack of progress isn't unusual." I didn't share the news of Jeannette's crystal.

"What's the latest on Carson's transfer?" I asked.

"It's happening tomorrow. Eight in the morning. The transport company confirmed the pick-up late this afternoon."

"Are you going to be there?"

"No. And neither are you. There won't be a Flier within miles of the place. I'll have a line on him as soon as he's entered into St. Matthew's computer system."

"You're not worried about something happening during the transfer?" I asked.

"Emelynn, what are you thinking? What could possibly happen during the transfer?"

"I don't know. Maybe the disruption will cause him to come out of his coma."

"The doctors are convinced it's irreversible. But say you're right, and he miraculously snaps out of it. What's he going to do? Run? How far could he possibly get? He's hooked up to a feeding tube, a catheter and an IV drip. He'd be weak and disoriented at best."

"I suppose."

"You're driving yourself crazy for no reason."

I took a deep breath and exhaled. "You're right. I'm sorry."

"You don't need to apologize. Just stop letting Manse do this to you. You're the one giving him control. He's harmless. You need to let go of it."

"I'll work on that." Just the thought of him made me shake as much from fear as from rage. "I'll call you tomorrow night when I get back from Cairabrae."

We hung up and I tried to keep Carson Manse out of my thoughts as I drifted off to sleep in the too-soft bed with thin sheets that smelled faintly of disinfectant.

Chapter Five

Thursday dawned clear if somewhat cool. I'd vacated Bailey's Motel in time to watch the sharp-edged orb of the sun poke over the shadowed hills that rose behind the shops of downtown Bodega Bay. I sat on a bench with a plaque that said it had been donated in memory of Mrs. Lloyd Stratus, as if the missus had no name of her own.

Once the sun broke free of the hills, I moved on. I passed the café, which hadn't opened yet, and walked to the Lodge where I'd parked my rental car. I dropped my luggage in the trunk and thought of the Reynolds anthology in my bag. Perhaps I'd return it today.

I reluctantly reclaimed Mrs. Stratus's bench on the edge of the damp sand of the public beach and waited for the café to open. The sun had turned from pink to gold. I wore a hoodie over my ugly blouse and cargo pants. I kicked off my sandals and dug my toes into the cool sand.

The café's open sign lit up moments before seven and I was the first one in the door. The coffee hadn't even finished dripping. It was only my second time here, and maybe it was the early hour, but I already felt like a regular and snagged a newspaper and a window seat. They served me a chewy toasted bagel smothered with cream cheese. I lingered over the local news until a more respectable hour and then strolled to the Lodge to collect yesterday's dry cleaning and the rental car. Jolene's black linen dress looked crisp and clean wrapped in its plastic sheath. I hung it on the hook behind the driver's seat and climbed in.

It wouldn't be catastrophic if I didn't manage to ghost today, but it would be a huge disappointment. It wasn't just the ghosting that I needed Mason's help with. Once I achieved that form, I needed to know how to control my movements. The few times it had happened before, I'd drifted without a rudder. My hands passed through objects rather than connect with them. I never lost touch with my own body, my hair or clothing, but after the first minute or two, I could no longer feel other people or material things. Simple things like dialling a phone or turning a door knob were mysteries I needed Mason's help to solve.

This time, when I pulled up to the gates of Cairabrae, I waited in my car. Within moments, the big black gates swung open. I couldn't pinpoint the camera, but clearly, they had one. Ryan greeted me in the driveway and once again took my keys, but not before I rescued the dry cleaning.

This morning it was Phillip who met me inside and escorted me to the kitchen. He relieved me of the dry cleaning. "We could have taken care of that for you," he said with a hint of admonishment in his cultured voice. "There's a hamper in your closet." I shot him a quizzical look. "Jolene's closet," he clarified, nodding his head in the direction of her room. He pushed open the kitchen door.

"Good morning, Emelynn." Stuart set his coffee cup on the kitchen table and rose to greet me. He wore a plaid shirt today, well-worn jeans and cowboy boots.

"Please, don't get up," I said, but he ignored me. He grasped my hand and leaned in to kiss my cheek. I stiffened at his too-familiar touch. He released his grip then pulled out a chair for me.

"Where's Mason?" I asked.

"Not far." I sat down and arched my eyebrows in an unspoken question. "We had an intruder last night," Stuart said. "He's been up most of the night monitoring the sensors."

I froze. "An intruder?" My heart rate escalated. "Redeemers?"

"No." He caught my gaze. "The alarms went off, but we didn't find anyone. We think it's just a malfunctioning sensor."

I took a calming breath. "Maybe you've got squirrels," I offered. "That's what set off the alarm at my cottage." It seemed funny now but it wasn't so funny at the time.

"Squirrels?" Stuart said, chuckling. He reached over to pour me a coffee. "They'd have to be flying squirrels to set off our alarms. The laser sensor at the main gate was breached at sixty feet."

"What?" I asked, confused. "Sixty feet?"

"The lasers maintain a vertical barrier, straight up." He emphasized the direction with his arm. "The beam was broken sixty feet off the ground and the heat signature was too big to be a squirrel. Naturally, at that height, we suspected a Flier, but we couldn't trace it."

Slowly, realization dawned and I blanched: I was the intruder who'd set off their sensors last night. Crap! I would have steered clear of Cairabrae had I known they had such a sophisticated system. Hopefully, Stuart wouldn't see the guilt written on my face. I would have fessed up, but that might cause Mason to re-visit his distrust of me . . . again. Best keep quiet, I reasoned.

"The system has been operating flawlessly for months—we were due for a blip."

"Yes, maybe it was a blip," I said, oozing sincerity.

"I thought I heard voices," Mason said, coming into the kitchen from the patio.

"Good morning," I said, my voice an octave too high.

"How was your night?" Mason asked, pouring himself a coffee.

I cleared my throat. "Better than yours, I hear."

"I don't think it was anything," he said, more to his father than to me.

"That's what I told you, son," Stuart said. Mason didn't hide a shake of his head. "These high-tech contraptions aren't foolproof, you know."

Mason's smile was indulgent. "I still need to check it out, but I'm sure you're right. At least nothing's turned up yet."

"Good. We're driving the cattle to the north pasture today, so I won't be here for lunch." He scraped his chair back and stood. "Dinner's at eight," he said, looking at me. "You'll join us tonight, Emelynn?" He had the grace to make it sound like a question. "I understand you're heading home tomorrow?"

"Yes, that's right," I said.

"I'll see you tonight, then," Stuart said.

Damn! How did he turn a questionable dinner invitation into a command appearance? He pivoted on his heels and walked back through the kitchen into the hallway.

"What happened last night?" I asked Mason when we were alone. Like his father, he'd dressed casually today in jeans and a dark T-shirt. I liked when he dressed casually—it usually meant he was in a better mood.

He was more forthright than I expected. Their system caught a heat-trace on the "intruder," but whatever it was disappeared so quickly that they never got a clear image. Thank god for Jolene's speed, I thought. Mason added that he had flown the property immediately after the breach but saw nothing amiss. He was prepared to let it go as a malfunction. I hid my relief.

"Regardless, I'm testing each of the sensors this morning. Are you okay going to the barn by yourself?"

"Of course." Alone was my comfort zone.

"Great. I'll come get you for lunch, all right?"

"With any luck, you won't be able to find me," I said, grinning at the thought that I might have some success this morning.

Mason smiled back in encouragement.

We parted ways on the patio. My footsteps left a path in the lingering dew as I made my way across the vast lawn to the barn. Only one horse loitered close to the white fence and he lifted his head and flared his nostrils at my approach. "Good morning, handsome," I said, admiring his sleek flanks and sneaking a peek to make sure I'd got the gender right. I carried on to the barn and pushed the heavy door across on its overhead rail then closed it behind me and made my way to the corral at the centre of the building.

I pulled off my hoodie and hung it over the rail, tugging down the hem of the unflattering blouse. As soon as I got home, the blouse was going in the rag bag. It didn't even rate recycling at the Sally Ann.

I walked the perimeter of the training circle and cleared my head of negative thoughts. Jeannette's crystal-case pendant tapped against my chest with each step. I released the curled hook-style clasp of the case and dropped the crystal into my palm. After yesterday's efforts, I had hoped I would feel something more from it today, some connection. All I felt was disappointment. Perhaps physical crystals didn't exude energy like mine.

I rolled it in my palm and held it loosely then closed my eyes and applied steady pressure. I concentrated on absorbing it like I'd seen Mason do. Nothing.

The rest of my morning was spent similarly occupied and singularly frustrated. Why was this so difficult? I reached for my own crystal and its energy sent an immediate surge of heat through me. Without a second thought, I wrapped its warmth around me like a blanket and broke free of the dirt floor. The space wasn't as large as the barn our covey used for paintball and laser tag training, but it was big enough to let off some steam.

I flew circles around the loft windows and swooped down to dip into the hallway, hovering horizontally above the floor. Did other Fliers use this space? I wondered. I flew its length and when I ran out of hallway, I completed a perfect end-of-pool style flip turn. I raced across the circle and repeated the manoeuvre at the other end of the hall then returned to the corral and perched high up on a rafter. A swirl of dust motes danced in the sunlight streaming through the loft's small windows. It took me a few moments to realize that I hadn't once thought of my back during my flight. At least something was improving, I thought.

Down below and off in the distance, the heavy barn door rolled open. "Emelynn?" Mason called.

"In here."

I heard footsteps. He walked cautiously into the space below me, looking all around. "Emelynn?" he repeated, hope evident in his tone.

"Afraid not," I said, and his head whipped up to where my feet dangling from the rafter.

"Nothing?" he asked.

"Nothing." I hopped off the rafter and floated down to land beside him. "It's very frustrating." Mason's windblown hair and T-shirt were covered in a pale film of dust.

"I'm sure it is. You hungry?"

It only took a moment to realize that I was. "Starving."

"Good. Maria packed us a picnic lunch. Want to go up to the ridge?"

"Yeah, let's get out of here," I said with a sigh.

The quad awaited us outside the barn door. It also sported a coat of dust, which explained the mess of Mason's hair and the state of his shirt. We buckled up and Mason, not yet tired of the quad, spun it around in a cloud and bolted up the road toward the upper-level trees. We stopped for a moment to admire the bird's eye view of Cairabrae and then continued up the slope farther than we'd gone yesterday.

He stopped under the perennial shade of an ancient madroña tree. At home, the crooked-trunked tree was called an arbutus. Pine trees, where they grew, stood in small clusters. The groupings were scattered as if the seeds had been tossed on the wind a hundred years ago and settled into the clefts of the hills.

"How's this?" he asked.

"It's great," I said, but his question was rhetorical; he'd already jumped out of the quad.

He retrieved a tablet from the door pocket and quickly engrossed himself with it. "I'll be right back," he said. Then without a moment's hesitation, he soared into the sky, up over the top of the gnarly old tree. I lost sight of him in the glare of the sun. He'd taken me by surprise. Perhaps flying at mid-day out here in the middle of nowhere wasn't risky, but I'd never chance a daylight flight at home. I tried to be casual about it.

Maria's basket was tied to the back of the quad with bungee cords. I loosened the cords and freed both the basket and the blanket beneath it, then spread the blanket beside the quad in the shade of the big tree. With no sign of Mason, I moved the basket to the blanket and opened it. Yum. Devilled eggs and what looked like crab-salad sandwiches. I loosened the wax paper enough to lift the slice of bread and saw big chunks of pink seafood and avocado. Ooh, and iced tea too. I uncapped a bottle and chugged a big gulp.

I was on my second devilled egg when Mason returned. A swig of iced tea washed the evidence away.

He landed beside the quad and reached in to set the instrument on the dash. "What's for lunch?" he asked eyeing me suspiciously. "You started without me!"

"Hey, I was hungry," I said, laughing at his indignant expression. "Where'd you go?"

"There's a sensor up here that I wanted to test. Seems to be working fine."

They're all working fine, I thought, with a twinge of guilt. He leaned down to take the tray of devilled eggs I offered him, then stepped back to sit sideways on the quad's seat.

I unwrapped the wax paper from my sandwich. "Can I ask you something?"

He nodded, his mouth full of egg.

"Did my father know about us? About Fliers?" I held a sweating bottle of lemonade in one hand and an iced tea in the other.

"Yes, he did." He pointed to the lemonade and bent over to take it from me, twisted the cap and took a sip. "Why would you think he didn't?"

"No reason. I just didn't know. I was curious."

"He knew. In fact, he was fascinated with our eyes. He examined mine on more than one occasion. I can only imagine how many times Jolene had to put up with that damn penlight of his." He smiled at the memory and I suppressed my own chuckle, remembering the same annoyance I'd felt when Dr. Coulter did the same thing to me in the hospital the night I fell out of the sky.

"I'm glad he knew. It means Jolene didn't really abandon me." She knew my father would recognize the gift in my eyes. She knew he'd teach me; she just didn't know that he wouldn't live long enough to get that chance.

"Jolene would never have abandoned you."

I ate my sandwich leaning against the madroña's smooth trunk. From here, it looked like we were the only people on the planet. It was a warm day with cotton-ball clouds dotting the sky. I thought about my father while I soaked in the vista, but a worrisome apprehension intruded. If my father was fascinated with the eyes of Fliers, could that be what his old research was about—the very research notes my mother planned to pass on to a colleague at the university? Surely, my father wouldn't have committed to paper anything so dangerous. Would he? The nagging thought bothered me. I couldn't ignore it. The last thing I needed was my mother caught up in Flier drama. The moment I got home, I'd look into it further.

Mason was eating the second half of his sandwich when his phone rang. "Yes," he answered, breaking the quiet spell. He listened intently, then stood and motioned for me to gather our things. "I'll be there in twenty minutes," he said, then disconnected.

"What is it?" I asked, stuffing the wax paper and unfinished bits of our picnic into the basket.

"Dad needs me back at the house." But that wasn't the whole story, and it wasn't just the bone-jarring ride back down the ridge that had me thinking that way. Mason's brow was drawn in a worried pucker and he hadn't said another word.

He dropped me at the barn. "Come back to the house when you've had enough," he said, not even waiting for me to say goodbye.

I watched him wheel the quad across the yard and sprint down the dirt road that ran parallel to the white fence. Something was wrong, that was for sure and apparently, it was something I wouldn't be privy to. I stifled my curiosity. It wasn't my business. Get in, get what I need, get out.

Returning to the training corral felt like drudgery. The space was oppressive after the break outside in the fresh air up on the ridge. I gave my efforts another hour and then some, but my heart wasn't in it.

Perhaps it wasn't meant to happen today. There was no need to rush things, I rationalized. I'd probably have better luck in the comfort of the cottage anyway, and Mason could talk me through things over the phone. It's not like he could do more than talk me through it anyway.

I walked out of the barn into the afternoon sunshine and closed the rolling door behind me. Tomorrow, I'd go home. I might never return. Maybe I should take advantage of the pool one last time before dinner. I took my time sauntering across the lawn toward the back of the house.

Jeannette wasn't out on the balcony, but I thought I could hear voices ahead. I crossed under the bougainvillea vines and spotted Stuart and Mason. They stopped mid-sentence when they saw me. "Hi," I said, noting something awkward in their demeanour. "Is everything all right?"

They looked at one another before saying that everything was fine, but it wasn't. "What is it?" I asked and my concern grew with their denials. I looked pointedly at their clothing, which they'd changed in favour of dark flying clothes.

"It's nothing," Mason volunteered. "I've been called away on Tribunal business. I'm afraid I'm going to miss dinner."

Stuart spoke. "I've asked Maria to prepare an early dinner for the two of us," he said. "They likely won't need me—they never do—but I want to be ready, just in case."

My skin prickled. I rubbed my arms and looked over their shoulders into the house. An odd feeling overwhelmed me—like we were being watched. I spun around, alarmed, because I suddenly recognized that odd feeling; a Ghost was close by. "Someone's here," I whispered, already backing up to make an escape.

"Very good, dear," a disembodied voice spoke, and goosebumps fled across my skin. It was Sebastian's voice. He materialized beside Stuart. "Didn't mean to startle you." I took another step back. "You're looking well, Emelynn. It's so nice to see you here in the fold."

"What's going on?" I asked, looking to Mason while intentionally ignoring Sebastian. I remembered all too well how readily he'd back-handed me when he took the Tribunal's lead in my interrogation. That hit was responsible for the scar over my left eye. And he hadn't stopped there either.

Mason shot Sebastian a dirty look, then looked back at me without bothering to soften his features. "I told you. Tribunal business, that's all. Nothing for you to worry about." There it was again, that phrase, *nothing to worry about.* Mason turned to Sebastian. "Let's go. Emelynn," he said, addressing me again. "Have Ryan arrange a flight home for you. The jet won't be available tomorrow."

"All right," I said, as he turned to leave, but Sebastian didn't fall into step.

"I'm looking forward to seeing you again, Emelynn. Soon. The founding families are planning a fabulous coming out party for you."

I swallowed hard. His smile chilled me. I knew from experience that one flick of those dark eyes could unleash a jolt that would inflict unbearable pain.

"Good night," Stuart said, dismissing them. He reached for my hand and tucked it into the crook of his arm then forcibly spun me around away from them. I stumbled a few steps and then caught myself. "My apologies, Emelynn."

"What was he talking about? What *coming out* party?"

Stuart guided me to a grouping of four chairs. "Have a seat," he said, patting my hand before releasing my arm. I sat, pinning him with a glare. "Sebastian Kirk's an impatient man who's used to getting his way. In your case though, I think it's his wife and some of the other women who are pushing this party idea."

"Why?"

"Probably because they knew Jolene. She grew up with some of them. They just want to meet you—get to know you."

I rolled my eyes. "That's ridiculous, Stuart. They're being nosy and I don't want any part of it." Getting any further into the Tribunal's inner circles was not on my agenda.

"We're a small community, Emelynn, but a powerful one. All that power breeds politics and volatility. I should know—I've been dealing with that lot and their bickering for a long time." Stuart snapped his fingers and Debbie's head popped up from behind the bar. "What I've learned over the years is that the easiest way to keep peace with this group and ensure their continued cooperation is to give them what they want, especially when the price is so small—in your case, a party. I don't think it's unreasonable."

Debbie approached and waited patiently for Stuart's order. "Martini?" he asked and I stifled my surprise.

"Yes, thanks," I said, marvelling that this was the first time he'd actually asked.

"Two, then," he said, and Debbie turned back to the bar.

"I am, however, prepared to deal with their wrath if you really think a party is too much to ask."

He'd set that up perfectly. How could I justify incurring the *wrath* of the mighty tribunal by saying no to a trivial cocktail party?

A smile twitched at the corner of my lip and I dipped my head in acknowledgement of his splendid manipulation. "I see just what you mean," I said, shaking my head. He smiled in response, and then broke out in laughter, throwing his head back and slapping his thigh.

He reached across and squeezed my forearm. "That's a clever girl. You learn quickly. I think you might just give them all a run for their money one day," he said with a gleam in his eye.

The afternoon was cooling off and our drinks were empty when Phillip came to collect us for dinner. "I'll go change," I said.

"Don't for my sake," Stuart replied. "It's just the two of us."

Maria had prepared another delicious meal. A fresh butter-lettuce salad was followed by pork tenderloin with a creamy caper and gin sauce, steamed potatoes and buttered carrots with rosemary and lemon.

Over dinner, Stuart told me more about Sebastian Kirk and his wife, Kimberley, who had known Jolene. They had one daughter about my age. Stuart described Kimberley as a social climber who Sebastian was constantly reining in. Their daughter, Tiffany, was almost as bad, but her target of choice was unsuspecting men of the married variety.

"It's hard for me to believe he puts up with those two, considering how little else he puts up with. Kimberley and Tiffany can't be trusted, but Sebastian's loyalty to the Tribunal is rock solid. He's absolutely lethal when he needs to be." A trait I knew first-hand, but I suspected Mason had already filled Stuart in on the night of my interrogation.

The sunlight was fading when coffee arrived. "Would you mind if I took this up to Jolene's room?" I asked. "I'd like to have one last look around before I leave."

"Speaking of which," he said, looking around for the help who were never far away. "Phillip, would you please fetch Ryan."

"Certainly," Phillip said, pulling a phone from his pocket and turning away from us.

"Ryan arranges all our travel," Stuart explained. "He'll get you a flight home tomorrow. Do you have a preferred airline?"

One with planes, I thought as I shook my head. This family really did live in a world of privilege. Were they aware of that? Were they aware that I didn't belong within a mile of the place?

Ryan promised to organize something and leave the details on my cellphone.

I refilled my cup and balanced it in its saucer all the way up the stairs and down the hall to Jolene's room, closing the door behind me. The last tendrils of daylight were turning a reddish pink. It was a glorious sunset and I watched it while sipping my cooling coffee in a hay-scented breeze out on Jolene's balcony. When the show was over, I returned to her bedroom, deposited the coffee cup on the top of the bookcase then sat cross-legged on the floor in front of it.

What other treasures lay hidden here? I ran my hands over the book spines. The biggest collection was *The Chronicles of Narnia* by C.S. Lewis, comprised as it was of seven books. On inspection, I found them to be well thumbed. Were they from Jolene's childhood, I wondered? Dr. Seuss was represented as was A.A. Milne's *Winnie the Pooh* series. Some of the books were brand new—their spines not yet cracked.

I found a journal, but it wasn't as exciting as I'd initially hoped, having only a few entries mostly devoted to morning sickness and swollen ankles. But it did contain another photo. It was one of Dad playing croquet on what looked like the manicured lawns here at Cairabrae.

Was I really part of this family? Mason and Stuart certainly thought so, but I felt no such connection. Even learning about my half-brother and seeing the photographic evidence of Jolene's life so intimately connected with my father's hadn't melded me to their world. It wasn't real. I retrieved the photos from my backpack, the ones I'd pilfered last night, and returned them to their place on the bookshelf.

My father had known about Fliers. He didn't know I would become one, but he knew about them. What would he think now, knowing how my life had turned out? I stood and kicked off my sandals then padded to Jolene's bed, crawled up to the pillows and laid back. If I could just learn to ghost, I could freely choose whether or not to become a part of the Reynolds clan. My need for their knowledge wouldn't rule the day.

My cellphone's ringtone told me a text had come in. I retrieved the phone from my purse on the floor beside the bed. Ryan had organized a 10:00 a.m. flight on Air Canada arriving in Vancouver at 12:30 p.m. He offered to drive me to the airport. I declined via return text, citing my need to turn in the rental car, and sent along my thanks. A moment later the phone blipped and the electronic boarding pass popped up. Impressive. Everyone needed a Ryan.

I lay back against the pillows and again wondered if I could use my own crystal to ghost. I'd ghosted before without the aid of someone else's crystal. Sure, those times had been flukes and unintentional, but it had to be connected to my own crystal. Ghosting didn't happen any other way. Mason had emphasized that very point just yesterday.

Jeannette's crystal wasn't working and there was no guarantee it ever would. I reached to my throat and held the crystal's intricate case in my hand. My crystal might not work either, but if I didn't at least try, how would I ever know? I'd promised Mason I'd conduct my ghosting trials in the safety of the barn with its just-in-case cot, but I was safe in the house. If I had trouble re-forming, I could pass out right here.

I closed my eyes and drew my crystal into the forefront of my mind. It thrummed with energy. I sensed its heat as if I held it in my hand, and it felt like home. Dare I? If I wanted to fly, all I'd have to do was tap into its power. I gave the crystal a gentle squeeze and felt it pulse, like a beating heart. I squeezed it again, more firmly this time, and without warning, the crystal melted away like a snowflake on my tongue. My eyes shot open. I raised my hand . . . and watched it fade.

I'd done it! I hadn't expected it to be this easy. I hadn't expected it to work at all. I looked down to my torso and saw nothing. No body, no arms, no legs. I had ghosted.

An off-balance sensation crept up on me. I'd grappled with this same sensation before when I'd accidentally ghosted. I drifted in unpredictable directions. If I were prone to motion sickness, I'd throw up. I'm not sure what I felt was any better.

Experiencing it again now, and knowing the speed and ease with which I'd ghosted, confirmed something Avery had speculated about. My crystal was embedded in my psyche. Squeezing it in response to sudden stimuli would be reflexive, like closing my eyes when I sneezed. That it hadn't happened dozens of times before, was a wonder.

The ceiling approached as I floated upward. I flinched, expecting my shoulder to make contact, but it didn't. Instead, my body flattened and rolled against the surface, like smoke. It took all my effort to tamp down the threatening panic. I took deep breaths and closed my eyes. I remembered controlling this feeling before, when I guided Sandra to safety on the night of her rescue. That memory helped me keep the panic at bay. I needed to take charge; that was all. But how did I do that when I felt so scattered?

I drifted around the ceiling, viewing the room from my new

perspective. The curtain that half-covered the window billowed with a breeze, and I felt a trickle of fear. I should have closed that window before I ghosted. If I'd been thinking, that is. The draft gently pushed me across the ceiling and no amount of effort on my part seemed to dislodge me from its grip. The breeze pressed me against the far wall then downward, only losing its hold on me when I reached the floor.

To distract myself, I took mental notes. There was no friction when any part of my body came into contact with what I knew to be a solid surface. Walls, ceiling, lamps or furniture—it made no difference. I'd float by them, conform to their shape without incident, and glide past. The lamp didn't topple over when I nudged it; my hip didn't bruise against the sharp edge of the table; the vase didn't crash to the ground when I bumped it. Nothing happened. How was that possible?

The sound of raised voices rushing down the hall in my direction made invisible hairs stand up on my invisible arms. A loud bang on the room's door heightened my alarm. Unaware of just how I'd done it, I'd flung myself as far from the door as possible, curling my ghostly form into a ball against the ceiling in the top corner of the bedroom. I cowered there, willing whoever was out in the hall to go away.

"All right, Mrs. Reynolds, you don't need to break it down. I'll open it for you," a frazzled female voice said, as the hall door swung open. "Let me do that," the voice said, and then I saw Jeannette's small form wheel into the adjoining room. Her dark-haired, middle-aged attendant pushed the chair through the French doors to the foot of the bed and stopped when Jeannette thrust out her curled right hand. "Phillip told you she'd left, Mrs. Reynolds. There's no one here."

Even from my vantage point, I could see the stubborn set to the frail woman's shoulders. She had a mass of fine white hair carefully piled on top of her head. A quilt covered her knees and her left hand lay tucked in its folds.

"What on earth has gotten into you?" the attendant asked. Jeannette mumbled something incomprehensible in response, which the attendant understood without hesitation. "The things I do to humour you," she muttered, patting Mrs. Reynolds's bony shoulder. She then marched toward the dressing room, calling over her shoulder as she disappeared around the corner, "But I can already tell you, there's no one here."

I didn't breathe and I didn't take my eyes off Jeannette's perfectly coiffed head. She slowly, deliberately lifted her chin and with pinpoint accuracy, turned her gaze directly toward me and met my eyes. My heart stopped beating. Her eyes, the exact pale blue of Mason and Jolene's, sparkled, and her face would have been beautiful were it not for the left side that sagged lifelessly. And then she smiled, or half of her mouth smiled, drawing the thin skin of her face into folds of silk. She seemed to relax into her chair.

"All clear," her attendant said in an I-told-you-so tone, as she walked with purpose back into the room. "Shall we go, then?"

I hesitantly returned Jeannette's smile. Could she really see me? She lifted her chin—just once. An acknowledgement of my smile perhaps, and then she lowered her head and let her attendant wheel her away.

It was a long time before I dared move. The adrenalin that had accompanied my earlier panic subsided, leaving me cold and shaky. Jeannette's visit puzzled me. I'd been among Ghosts on several occasions and not once had I been able to see them, but Jeannette had seen me. I'd be fooling myself to think otherwise. I hoped my presence in her daughter's room hadn't frightened her.

How long ago had I ghosted, I wondered? My sense of time was foggy. Fatigue pulled at me and I drifted down to the bed. I chuckled at the realization that when I didn't consciously think about movement, it happened with ease. I'd just done it. It only took a thought, *I'm tired, I'll just go lie down*, and here I was resting my head on the pile of pillows. Still, it was the oddest feeling. Surfaces produced no pressure; they were a benign barrier. Lying on the mattress was like lying on the bottom of a pool.

To test my theory of movement further, I thought, *wouldn't it be nice to take a stroll down the hall*. With seemingly no effort, I rose from the bed and moved with deliberation into the sitting room and toward the door to the hall as my spectral body obeyed my thoughts. I reached out to turn the knob, but felt no pressure in my palm. My hand sifted around it. There had to be some way to deal with doorknobs. The entire Tribunal had ghosted into my cottage; surely, there was a way to get through a door. I flattened my shoulder against it and pushed, but my body's response was to flatten out and conform to the door's surface. I pulled back in frustration and took a run at it. Alarmingly, I found myself flat against the wall on the other side of the hall.

"Well, what do you know?" I said with amazement, as I gathered my wispy self together, pleased to confirm that all my body parts were intact. I looked over at the closed door to Jolene's room. What if I couldn't get back in? Was whatever I'd done a fluke or for real? I steeled myself, took a run at the closed door and shot back into the room. It worked! If only Mason were here; I'd love to show him. Maybe Stuart was still here. I rushed the door again and found myself back out in the hall. "Piece of cake," I said, bloated with prideful ignorance. I felt like I'd had one too many martinis—maybe two, too many.

I tripped along the hallway and careened headfirst down the curved staircase, grazed the marble floor and ricocheted upright with no ill effects. Just then, Ryan raced through the front door and rushed down the hall, completely unaware of my presence. I was literally caught up in his wake wondering where he was going in such a hurry. He cut left and jogged silently down the hallway that ran below Jolene's room. I pulled myself together and followed. He hurried past closed doors into a part of the house I'd not ventured before. Near the end of the hall, he stopped and knocked.

"Come in." It was Stuart's voice. Ryan entered the room and closed the door in my face. Never mind, I thought, rushing at the door with my new-found skill. I picked myself up on the other side and found not only Stuart but also Ron, the man whose nose I'd broken the night of my Tribunal interrogation. I yawned and then out of habit, I started to straighten my clothes before the absurdity of it struck me.

I took note of the room, which was even bigger than the dining room. A heavily grained wooden conference table dominated the space. I couldn't identify the wood; probably something exotic if the rest of the room was any indication. There was nothing appealing to me about the dead animal heads hanging on the walls. Not to be judgemental, but I hoped the hunter hadn't wasted the meat from his gruesome trophies.

A desk, made from the same grainy wood as the conference table, sat partially obscured in an alcove at the far end of the room. This was where Stuart held court like the king of the hill, which I suppose he was—at least here. Heavy drapes shrouded the windows along the entire length of the room, concealing what should have been a panoramic view of the pool and manicured back lawns.

"What did you learn?" Stuart asked.

"It's definitely the Vosburghs' Mercedes and it's intact. The keys were in the ignition."

"That's not good," Ron said, as the phone on the desk rang.

Who were the Vosburghs, I wondered?

Stuart picked up the receiver. "Yes," he answered. "Not yet. We don't have all the details." Stuart shook his head and rolled his eyes in exasperation for Ron's benefit. "No, there's no indication the Redeemers had anything to do with this. Just take the regular precautions, Albert, and don't go off the rails. Do what you need to keep your family safe. Yes, I'll send word as soon as we know anything concrete." Stuart nodded his head and uh-huhhed a few times before he disconnected.

"They're scared," Ron commented. "If we don't get this under control, they'll take matters into their own hands."

"Mason and Sebastian will get to the bottom of it quickly," Stuart said.

So this is what Mason was dealing with. He'd said there was nothing to worry about. Nothing to worry about, my ass. I stifled a yawn and shook myself. I couldn't afford to be sleepy. Not now.

"Let's hope it's not the Redeemers," Ron said.

Redeemers were gunning for Tribunal members. The Vosburghs must be Tribunal. Had the Redeemers got their hands on them? Damn it. I needed to get out of here, to warn the covey. If Carson Manse's bastards were active again, no one was safe. The Redeemers may have been targeting Tribunal Fliers, but they weren't fussy. They'd steal anyone's gift to further their goal of usurping the Tribunal's position of power.

With renewed vigour, I turned for the door and charged it, passing through easily and didn't stop to collect myself on the other side. My head spun as I barrelled down the hall. I got as far as the front door. What now? I couldn't go to the airport like this; I couldn't contend with the wind outside. Bloody hell!

With nowhere else to go, I floated back up the curved staircase and along the hall to Jolene's room. I felt dangerously cocooned by this drunken feeling that was surely an effect of ghosting. I'd have to re-form before I could get on my way. I pushed through Jolene's door and drifted around her room, swirling wisps of me scattering everywhere.

"Concentrate!" I snarled impatiently at myself. Mason had said all I needed to do was re-form my crystal. I gathered myself and lay on Jolene's bed. Was it like forming a snowball? I make the motions with my hands. No result. Obviously not like snow. I shut my eyes and tried to re-form the crystal through visualization. Crap. This wasn't working and the fatigue that Mason warned me about, pressed on me.

Frustration and panic lurked beneath my concentration. No, it wasn't panic. This was something less. Fear or anxiety perhaps—I was too tired for panic. I had no time for anything less than re-forming.

I thought of Avery and tried to envision his calming intonations . . . breathe, relax. Breathe, relax.

I couldn't breathe; I couldn't relax. I felt hot and flushed. I pulled off my blouse and tossed it aside. Once it left my fingers, I lost track of it. No great loss, I thought. I discarded my cargo pants. That was better, I thought, lying back again. I rolled onto my side and curled around a pillow, cooler without my clothes. Calm, relax, breathe. I pictured the cottage and the rock-strewn beach that I knew so well. I could even smell the strong briny scent of low tide.

Calm, relax, breathe. Calm . . . relax . . . breathe . . .

CHAPTER SIX

I woke in a rush of adrenalin to the thudding stampede of footfalls in the hallway. Fear paralyzed me. What was happening? I darted my eyes around Jolene's bedroom, reorienting myself, remembering.

The door into the sitting room burst open. "Emelynn!"

Shit! I bolted upright and fumbled for covers that weren't there—I'd thrown them off in the night. Mason breached the bedroom's threshold in a swirl of angry black leather. I turned and dove for cover in the nest of pillows. In a flash, he rounded the end of the bed to where I huddled. He grabbed my shoulder and shook.

"Emelynn!" he growled.

I held fast to the pillow I'd snatched to my chest and resisted. "What!" I said, cowering. More heavy footfalls announced the imminent arrival of others.

Mason leaned over me, his face set in hard lines, his nostrils flaring. "What are you doing here?" His eyes flashed to my back and I twisted out of his grip. Stuart and Ryan entered the room, coming to an abrupt halt near the foot of the bed. They stilled, breathing heavily. I flushed with embarrassment, half-naked and with my scars in full view. Debbie rushed into the room like an afterthought and gasped. She approached the other side of the bed. Great, now I was surrounded. I scooted away from them, clutching the pillow to my chest.

"What the hell, Mason?" I struggled to put my back against the headboard.

Debbie pulled a twisted sheet from the floor and handed it to me. I gave her a grateful nod and dragged it over my legs.

"Answer me!" Mason straightened to his full height. This wasn't "Uncle" Mason, this was Tribunal Mason at his most menacing and it was working.

"Why are you so angry?" I asked, terrified and confused.

"What are you doing here!" he bellowed, and I flinched again.

"I *was* sleeping."

"Don't get smart with me. Why have you been lying to us?" He balled his hands into white-knuckled fists and worked the muscles along his jaw.

Lying? With so many lies to keep track of, which one were they referring to? Had they learned about me ghosting last night? Perhaps Jeannette told them. Maybe they found out I'd eavesdropped on their conversation. Oh no! What if they found their anthology in my car?

"May I get dressed?" I asked, flustered.

Stuart huffed audibly and backed away from the foot of the bed. "Please do," he said, his voice cold. "Then join us in the kitchen."

Debbie turned and made her exit. Stuart ushered Ryan ahead of him and they too left. Mason gave me one last angry look then turned on his heel and slammed the bedroom door so hard the glass rattled. A moment later, the hall door clicked closed.

I dressed quickly, brushed my teeth and grabbed my belongings, taking one last look around. Given the ferocity of Mason's anger, I wouldn't likely see Jolene's room again. I closed the door softly and descended the stairs to face whatever mess I'd made.

I gripped my bag and nudged open the kitchen door. Stuart sat at the table with his hand curled around a mug. Mason paced, his anger momentarily at bay. He ran a hand through his hair, stopping abruptly when he spotted me. "Sit," he commanded, pointing to the chair opposite Stuart. I crossed the kitchen in a hurry and did as he asked.

"Where did you go after I dropped you off at the Lodge?"

How had he learned I hadn't stayed at the Lodge? Was he having me watched?

"Where!" he shouted and slammed his fist on the table.

I jumped. What could I have done to make him this angry?

"Where have you been staying? And don't tell me it was the Lodge because I checked. Your room hasn't been used." Mason made an effort to calm his voice. "Answer me, Emelynn. Why have you been lying to us?"

I swallowed. "I didn't want anyone to know where I was."

"You didn't want *us* to know where you were," he said, adding a touch of hurt to his anger.

"I didn't want *anyone* to be able to track me. It was a precaution."

Mason shook his head. "This has Moss's fingerprints all over it."

"Carson Manse's people are still out there," I said, more strongly than I intended. "They know about me and if they know I'm here, they can find me. James is trying to protect me."

"What the hell do you think *we're* doing? We're not exactly unfamiliar with security." Mason took a deep breath. "Why do you think we wanted you to stay here?" He resumed pacing, but he was no longer frenzied. "Jesus, Emelynn. That's why your room at the Lodge was in my name." He finally stopped moving. The notion that he'd been worried about me hit like a two-by-four.

For the first time, I noticed that both Mason and Stuart still wore their dark flying clothes. Had they slept last night?

"You don't need to take on everything by yourself. We can help." Mason closed his eyes and rubbed his temples. "What happened last night?"

I shrunk in my chair, fearful my answer might re-ignite his anger. "I ghosted," and hastened to add, "I know you asked me not to attempt it outside the barn, but when I went back to Jolene's room after dinner, I thought I'd give it one last try. I really didn't expect it to work."

Stuart leaned forward, engrossed.

A hint of a smile cracked Mason's scowl. "Let me guess," he scolded. "You had trouble re-forming?"

The tension in the room flitted away. I shrugged, happy to take the admonishment in exchange for his anger. Mason leaned back against the marble work table and folded his arms.

I frowned as another thought struck me. "How did you know I wasn't staying at the Lodge?"

"That, you can blame on James Moss."

"James?" I asked and Mason pointedly raised his eyebrows.

"You were supposed to phone him last night. When you didn't, and he couldn't reach you, he called us."

Crap! It completely slipped my mind. James must have been worried sick to stoop to calling Mason. "I need to call him."

"Yes. You probably should, but before you do, there's something you need to know." Mason pinched his brows, pulled out a chair and sat down. "Two Fliers have gone missing."

"Oh?" I said, surprised with his disclosure.

"Henry and Amelia Vosburgh. They're from one of the founding coveys."

"Ghosts?" I asked, keeping my concern in check.

"Yes, unfortunately."

"Tribunal, then."

"I'm afraid so."

I stiffened in my chair. "Oh my god—Carson. They moved him yesterday."

"It wasn't him." Mason raised his voice to temper my alarm. "Manse is right where he should be. We've checked."

I settled at that, breathing again.

Mason continued. "The Vosburghs never made it to their vacation home on Lummi Island last night."

"What happened?"

Stuart answered. "We don't know yet. Their car was found abandoned just before dawn. Their daughter was expecting them. She's the one who called us. We've got people searching the area. A resident reported the abandoned car, so the local police are involved. It makes it harder for us, but we'll find them."

Maybe, I amended to myself. "Are the Redeemers responsible?"

"They're our prime suspects, but we don't know who they are." Mason's voice was laced with frustration. "Moss tells me that Samuel Jordan, the detective who worked your case, may have some leads."

"I didn't know James was still in touch with Detective Jordan."

"Well," Mason raised an eyebrow, "he might not be *in touch* in the traditional sense."

"You mean he's hacked into the detective's files." It was an educated guess given what I'd learned of James's skill set.

"Let's just say James Moss is very resourceful. In any case, none of this is your concern. I'm only telling you so you won't worry." Damn, there was that phrase again. I wish they wouldn't do that—it was an invitation for me to worry. "Your biggest threat is still neutralized in a nursing home, and we're doing all we can for the Vosburghs. In fact, I'm meeting James on Lummi later today."

That answered my question about whether James would be at the cottage when I got home.

Stuart got up to make another pot of coffee. It turned out that my flight was departing within an hour of Mason's flight to Bellingham. He agreed to come with me in the rental car. Stuart insisted on making breakfast. Kentucky fried eggs, he called it, which turned out to be fried eggs that were cooked so hot and fast that the whites turned crispy, while the yolks still ran.

The entire time he banged around the kitchen, Stuart asked questions. He insisted I tell them every detail about my ghosting adventure last night. I left out a few bits, like Jeannette's visit and eavesdropping on him, but I got a wealth of information in exchange for the bits I did reveal.

The most interesting was that hitting a door with some force, like I did, was a bona fide way to breach doors. It also worked for windows and air vents. "What actually happens," Stuart explained, "is that the molecules of the ghosted form are forced through the tiny air spaces found around most doors and all but the best windows."

Mason assured me that when I had more experience, I wouldn't be limited to that method. He explained that the process of ghosting was rather like putting your foot on a gas pedal. If you floored it, you ghosted quickly and completely, but if you applied gentler pressure, you had more control. He encouraged me to be mindful of the rate at which I applied pressure to the crystal. If I didn't absorb it completely, it was easier to re-form. It was also easier to partially re-form so that there was enough solidity to manipulate physical objects, like doorknobs, an ability that faded in the deeper ghosting forms.

When we finished eating, Mason excused himself to pack his bag. It occurred to me that if I wanted to return their family anthology, now was the time. If they were infuriated, I wouldn't have to deal with their anger for long, and if they were ecstatic, maybe they'd be more inclined to forgive my recent deception.

While Stuart cleared the table, I slipped out to my car and retrieved the brocade bag that held their heirloom. Mason was still upstairs when I returned. Back in the kitchen, Stuart was pre-occupied with his newspaper. I gently placed the package on the table in front of him. He glanced up at me before he looked at the package and then his features fell. I couldn't tell what he was thinking. He pulled it closer and smoothed his hands over the brocade.

He stole an expressionless glance at me then quickly pulled the leather-bound anthology free. He traced the Reynolds crest on the hand-crafted cover with his fingers and slowly, reverently, opened the heavy tome. "Where did you get this?"

"I found it in a box of my father's journals in the attic at my cottage. I didn't know what it was until recently." The book had been intentionally hidden. James knew what it was the moment he saw it. He told me that the Tribunal considered these old family anthologies dangerous contraband and they'd confiscate it if they knew I had it.

Stuart turned the pages, poring over each one as if seeing it for the first time. "I thought we'd lost this, years ago." I didn't say a word as his careful inspection continued. At some point in this process, Mason returned. I'd been intent on Stuart and he'd been intent on the anthology, and neither of us noticed him come into the kitchen.

I looked up as he walked behind his father and leaned over. "Is that what I think it is?" he asked. He'd changed into grey slacks and a button-down shirt, open at the collar.

"Yes. Emelynn brought it," Stuart said. Mason looked to be as mesmerized by the book as his father.

"How did you come to have this, Emelynn?"

I repeated what I'd told Stuart and waited for Mason to explode. He didn't. Instead, he laid a hand on his father's shoulder and watched as Stuart turned page after page. When Stuart reached the end, he carefully closed it. Once again, he ran his fingers over the Reynolds family crest on the cover. When he was finally able to part with it, he pushed it aside to give Mason a closer look.

Stuart's face held no expression as he rose from the table. Maybe he'd be the one to explode, I thought. Before I could retreat, he pulled me into an embrace that threatened to cut off my air supply and didn't let go. "Thank you, Emelynn. You don't know how much this means to me." The strength of his embrace gave me some indication and I sagged with relief.

"We've got to go," Mason said, and Stuart finally released me.

"Come back soon," Stuart said, clasping both my hands in his. "You're always welcome here."

I thanked Stuart for his hospitality. He escorted us to the front door where he once again hugged me then pecked my cheek. We said goodbye and I didn't argue with Mason when he insisted on driving. At least we wouldn't get lost.

During the ride to the airport, we made awkward small talk, like strangers. My mind kept drifting back to all that I'd achieved in the last three days. Lady luck had kicked ass. I stared contentedly out the window, letting the scenery distract me.

Mason was uncharacteristically quiet. Guilt poked at me. I felt like I'd used him. Get in, get what you need and get out. I'd gotten everything I came for. What had he gotten? I owed him an apology at least, or a thank you. Under all his anger, he'd been genuinely worried about me.

"I'm sorry about lying to you, Mason."

I'd interrupted his thoughts. He glanced at me and forced a smile. "You're so bloody independent."

"Well, that, I'm not going to apologize for."

"No, I suppose you've had to be. But you're not alone anymore."

"Mason—" I started, but he interrupted.

"Let me finish. I know it's going to take more than a few conversations and a couple of days at Cairabrae to convince you, but I want you to think of us as family. We're in this together. You're part of our family now and we're here for you, but I'm not going to shove it down your throat."

"What I was going to say, was—thank you."

He spared me a brief glance from the road again. "You're welcome."

I stared out the window, contemplating his outburst when he interrupted my thoughts.

"Has Avery Coulter been good to you?"

"Yes, the best," I said without hesitation. I didn't like Mason's interest in Avery. Beneath all the warm, fuzzy family talk, he was still Tribunal. "Why do you ask?"

"Sometimes I get the impression he's more than just your doctor."

"Well, he's not," I blurted out.

"No need to get defensive. I'm just trying to get to know you better."

"Oh," I said, and relaxed a bit. I had to give him credit for his efforts to be a good uncle figure. But I wouldn't give him reason to dwell on Avery. More than anyone else, Avery had been my saviour and guide. He'd taught me how to use the power of my eyes to protect myself. He'd even let me test my *sparks* and jolts on him and taught me how to put up a *block* to defend myself from those same weapons. I would protect him.

"Are you dating anyone?" he asked.

His question took me aback and I hesitated. "Not that I feel obliged to answer, but no," I said, establishing my position on his little fishing expedition. His lips curled into a smile.

"Who are *you* dating?" I asked.

He glanced at me in mock surprise. "Touché," he said, and I think he considered not answering because he took his sweet time responding. Finally, he said, "I'm not dating anyone right now, either."

He hung up his rod and reel after that and we drove on in silence. After we returned the rental car, he walked me to international departures and waited patiently while I checked in.

"Dad says you may have changed your mind about an introduction to the founding families."

"Your father can be very persuasive."

"He can," Mason said, grinning. I imagine Mason had been on the other end of Stuart's persuasion more than once. "Shall I set it up then?"

"A party?"

"Would you rather do something else, a barbecue perhaps?"

"No. Do whatever you and your father feel is appropriate. It's just one night. It won't kill me."

"All right. I'll be in touch. Oh, before I forget." Mason dug into his pocket. "I meant to give these to you yesterday." He handed me a folded pair of black leather gloves—the softest leather I'd ever felt. "Look at the palm." I examined the gloves more carefully and spotted interesting stitching in the crease of each palm. As I poked at the unusual detail Mason explained that it was a pocket for my crystal.

"Handy," I said. "Thank you."

"You're welcome." He pulled me close and brushed a kiss on top of my head. "Thanks for bringing our anthology back. You've made Dad very happy."

"I'm glad."

"Safe travels. Call me if you have more questions and please, Emelynn, think about what I said."

Chapter Seven

I dozed on the flight home, a much easier feat in first class. I made a mental note to thank Ryan for that little bonus when I could use my phone again. The aircraft broke through the clouds and my heart raced when Vancouver came into view. Home.

The moment I walked out of the airport, I felt that peculiar sensation unique to autumn, when the warmth of the sun is countered by a brisk coolness in the air. The kind of day that makes you wish you had a sweater even though the sweater would be too warm.

During the thirty-minute cab ride to Summerset, I noted signs of fall encroaching. Patches of boulevard grass had dried to a maintenance-free light brown. Snowberry bushes that grew wild in untended spaces were now loaded with white fruit. Had their leaves been yellow when I'd left? Fall had arrived in the three days I'd been gone, but September in British Columbia was changeable like that.

When we got to Deacon Street, I asked the cabbie to stop at Rumbles. I had promised Ruth Rumble that I'd pick up some paperwork before the weekend. She and her sister, Anne, hired me two weeks ago to help them sort through a mountain of bookkeeping and inventory records that they'd acquired when they bought their new venture, a second bookstore called Chrysalis.

The cabbie pulled in under the shade of cherry trees on the south side of Deacon. I told him I'd just be a minute, hopped out and crossed the street. The shops along this section of the strip had a distinctly Victorian feel. The boutique-sized stores boasted shaded entryways, some still paved with tiny white and black tiles. Most had been renovated, and exposed brick was the new interior norm with wiring and ductwork visible and displayed as proudly as Dyson vacuums.

Rumbles was an example of what these shops used to look like. A jingle of bells announced my entry. The scent of new paper with an undertone of glued bindings and ink greeted me. The door didn't close on its own. I pulled it shut and called out to Molly.

"Back here," a harried voice answered, but it wasn't Molly's.

The counter to the left of the door was stacked unusually high with new books. Molly must have been behind on re-stocking the shelves. I rounded the cookbook section and headed toward the voice, that I thought was likely Ruth's, coming from the travel section. The shelves in the store reached to the ceiling, and I found Ruth up on a ladder.

"Hi Ruth, how are you?" I said. Ruth and Anne were both in their sixties. If you didn't know they shared a last name, you'd never imagine they were related. Ruth had smartly cut dark hair that I suspected came from a bottle and big brown eyes. She was trim and always immaculately dressed in conservative clothes made of the finest fabrics. Her sister, Anne, had grey hair that cascaded down her back and she rarely wore anything other than blue jeans. Anne was a little round in the middle though I couldn't think why because she was constantly on the move.

"I'm good, thank you. When did you get back?"

"Just now. My cab's waiting outside. I came by to collect the paperwork."

"Oh, dear," Ruth said, scurrying down the ladder. "I'll have to unearth it. With the delivery just in, and Molly away, I'm not sure where it got stashed."

"Where's Molly?" I asked, following Ruth back to the front of the store. Molly hadn't mentioned that she was going away. We'd been friends growing up in Summerset, but lost touch when I moved to Toronto. By coincidence, we'd bumped into each other here in Rumbles when I moved back to Summerset in May. We'd picked up our friendship right where we'd left off ten years ago.

"She hasn't been feeling well. Poor girl needed a break. She's only taken a day or two off all summer." Ruth shuffled stacks of books, and dipped and bobbed behind the counter. She stood up with a huff and a crease between her eyebrows.

In all my years in Toronto, I'd never found another friend like Molly. I envied her the life she led. I would have travelled the same path had I never accepted Jolene's gift. And if my father hadn't died. I used to worry that my secrets would ruin our friendship, but they hadn't. Eden, who'd grown up a Flier, helped me understand that the secrets I kept protected Molly from the dangers of being exposed to our life.

Ruth's face brightened. "Oh, I know where I put it." She looked toward the battered coffee table between two old wing chairs near the front of the shop. These were the chairs where Molly and I often sat to visit over coffee or lunch.

I followed her line of sight to a pile of paper six inches thick. "I'll get it." I was still enthusiastic enough about my new job that the volume of paper didn't daunt me. I held the pile in my arms, against my hip. "If you need a hand with that, give me a call," I said, nodding toward the tower of new books threatening to tumble off the counter.

"Oh, don't worry," she said, waving her arm at the pile. "I did this for years before we found Molly."

"All right, then. I'll input this and get it back to you as soon as I can."

"See you later, dear," she said, turning back to the stacks and her ladder.

I managed to get into the cab without dropping a sheet. Ten minutes later, the cabbie turned down Cliffside Avenue. The old neighbourhood brought a smile to my lips. My Arts and Crafts–style cottage was the last residence on the street. When it was built, it stood alone. Now it looked like the poor cousin to its neighbouring mansions.

The cottage occupied a small footprint on the southern half of two acres, resulting in a respectable degree of privacy from my only neighbour to the north. Sunset Provincial Park bordered the southern and most of the eastern edge of the property. I'd shared polite hellos with my neighbours on the rare occasion I bumped into them, but that's as neighbourly as we got.

My father purchased the cottage from the elderly couple who'd built it. Back then, the grey cedar-sided structure really was a cottage, a term of endearment that I used to this day. Now, as the freshly painted white trim came into view, it evoked the warm memories I always associated with it. Memories of my mother and father when they were happy here—when we were a family—before Dad's float plane disappeared beneath the cold waves of the Pacific.

I thanked the cabbie, carried my bag to the front porch and unlocked the door. It felt good to be home. The soft ding of the home alarm immediately got my attention. I input the disarm code and walked down the hall to the kitchen to deposit my load of paper on the counter.

The interior of the cottage was laid out in a simple centre-hall design. Dad's study and the guest room were either side of the hall close to the front door; my bedroom and the living room were across the back and both opened to the full-width deck; and the dining room, kitchen and bathroom were sandwiched in between.

The sight of drapes across the living room windows was a startling reminder of my stamp on the cottage—an unwelcome blot on what used to be an unobstructed ocean view. Security concerns had become a priority, hence the drapes; it couldn't be helped. I grinned thinking I felt the same way about the drapes as Stuart felt about Mason's helipad.

Crossing the living room, I yanked open the drapes and greeted the sparkling Pacific with a contented sigh. God, I loved this place; the ever-changing ocean, the tangy scent of sea air, the recollections of a happy childhood spent building castles on the beach. I'd never once felt this way about the condo my mother and I shared in Toronto.

The cottage connected me to my father more than any photo, any letter or anyone else's memory of him could. My own memories of him in this house made it special and irreplaceable. I could picture him tickling me on the living room floor; sitting on the sofa with his feet up on the coffee table, face buried in a newspaper; or leaning back in his office chair, hands behind his head, staring up at Jolene's painting. I had so much to be grateful for and on days like this, I felt like the luckiest girl in the world.

A gust of wind swirled the leathery arbutus leaves on the deck and brought me back to the present, but a smile lingered on my face. This place balanced the crazy. It was a haven of normalcy in the midst of the wondrous and sometimes dangerous world of Fliers to which, thanks to Jolene, I now had an irrevocable, lifetime membership.

I retrieved my luggage and unpacked the small bag in minutes. An empty space on the counter reminded me that my old coffee maker was gone. There was no point in being sentimental about appliances I suppose, but I'd have to drink tea until I could replace it.

While the tea steeped, I put in a load of laundry and fired up my laptop. My mother would be anxious to hear from me and I needed to ask her about my father's research. I logged on to the website that James had set up and sent her an email. She would know it was me, not from the randomly generated sender's name, but from the subject line that would drop the message into her junk email folder. Today's subject line was *We ship same day free; Cialis, Viagra, Vicodin for $6*. She would know it meant I'd Skype her on our new untraceable phones at 6:00 tonight.

Sometimes these measures felt like overkill, but they were necessary. My mother didn't know about the gift or Fliers or the fact that being connected to me put her in danger. Therefore, convincing her of the necessity of these procedures had been tricky. Happily, Detective Jordan helped out. He had no more clue than my mother about the gift or Fliers, but he explained to her that one of the men who had been involved in my kidnapping was still at large. He confirmed that the missing man might try to use her to get to me. James reinforced that possibility and also worked behind the scenes to erase all trace of her from government birth and passport records. I'd never asked James if his methods were legit. I didn't want to know. I was just grateful for it.

The doorbell's chime startled me. I hurried down the hall and spied Avery through the peephole. He'd pushed his sunglasses up into his short blond hair. I opened the door.

"I see you made it back in one piece," he said, wearing my favourite crooked smile. He leaned over to give me a hug. "Is your cellphone dead?" he asked, his hands still on my shoulders. He was over six feet, so I had to look up.

"No, sorry—I forgot to turn it back on after we landed. Come on in," I said. We walked down the hall and I ducked into my bedroom to grab my phone and turned it on.

"I want to hear all about it," Avery said, beaming enthusiastically. He was the only one in my covey who knew I was a Ghost. It was dangerous knowledge. Part of the reason Fliers protected the secret was because the gift could be stolen. And if the gift itself was a coveted bauble, then the ability to ghost was the crown jewel. A fact aptly demonstrated by the lengths Carson Manse went in his attempt to steal it.

Avery dropped his sunglasses on the hall table and tidied his hair with his fingers. The grey in it was hardly noticeable. He joined me for a cup of tea on the deck and I told him all I had learned about ghosting. It took a while: I'd learned a lot in three short days.

"What did you find out about amber?" he asked. Being a doctor, he was particularly interested in the ill-effects amber had on Ghosts. He'd treated the burns caused by the beaded amber belt my kidnappers used to keep me from ghosting. The amber did more than burn; it weakened my crystal to the extent that it compromised every facet of my gift.

"The subject never came up," I answered apologetically.

Avery frowned. "You need to ask them, Emelynn. We talked about this. We need to know if the effect is cumulative. Further exposure might provoke anaphylactic shock. It's serious. It could prove life threatening." He shook his head in disappointment and then changed the subject. "How did they react when you returned their anthology?"

"They were shocked, but it was a good shocked."

Avery smirked. "I found something interesting in the photocopies I took of it."

"You did? What?"

"Do you remember the section in the book about coveys?" I nodded as he drew a few sheets of folded paper from his jacket pocket. "I think the anthology reveals which families comprise the Tribunal Novem. There are nine founding coveys, remember?" I wasn't about to forget that number any time soon. He flattened out the papers on the weathered table between us. "We know the Reynolds family is Tribunal and you told me another name, Sebastian. There's only one Sebastian in these records and his last name is Kirk."

"That's right. Stuart referred to him as Sebastian Kirk."

"Good, then I'm on the right track. The coveys are identified by their geographic locations. Sometimes it's a city or town, other times a feature, like a lake or a mountain. The name Reynolds shows up twice. Once here," he said, pointing to a group of names under the heading Blackwater. "And again, here." He pointed to another list of names under the San Francisco heading.

"Where's Blackwater?" I asked, interrupting.

"There are places called Blackwater all over the world, but the Reynolds crest is Scottish, so I'm thinking it's the town in the northeast of Scotland. The name Kirk also shows up twice. Once here." He pointed to the names listed under Ayr. "Ayr is also in Scotland. And again, here." He pointed once more to the San Francisco list. "I've raked through these lists time and again and only nine of the family names show up on two lists. And the second list is always San Francisco."

I examined the San Francisco list. "But there are dozens of names here."

"There are, but only nine of them are also found elsewhere. I think those nine are our Tribunal, which means their home coveys are the Tribunal Novem's founding coveys. In fact, I think they're hiding in the San Francisco covey exactly because it's so big. They're hiding in plain sight."

I ran my finger down the list and my heart lurched when I read the name, *Vosburgh*. I looked up at Avery, the shock plain on my face. "The Vosburghs are Tribunal," I said. Avery tilted his head in a questioning fashion. "They're also Ghosts," I added.

I turned back to the list, but Avery snatched the papers off the table. He flipped frantically through the pages, then flattened them out again and sat back. "What is it?" I asked. He was clearly pensive about something, and the worried look on his face said I might not want to know.

"I can't say whether other family anthologies are like this one, and maybe it's only because this one belongs to the Reynolds family, but I think the Ghosts are also identified in there."

"What!" I reached for the photocopies. "How?"

"Look carefully. See how Reynolds, Vosburg and Kirk are written? It has to be intentional; these pages were handwritten."

I scanned the sheets. All three family names were written entirely in capital letters. He was right. A quick review uncovered more names, which were easy to pick out once I knew what to look for. "You think all these families carry the ghosting gene?"

"It's one explanation."

"This must have been how Carson Manse knew that Jolene Reynolds was a Ghost." Could it also be the source behind the rumour that made Jackson suspect me of being a Ghost?

"We know Manse had access to at least one incantation and we know the incantations are found in the anthologies," Avery said. In fact, it was one of those anthologies carelessly left unattended that resulted in Avery losing his gift of flight. He and a friend were just being kids, messing around with a seemingly harmless incantation when they learned that the words, when spoken by Fliers, weren't harmless at all.

"Could this be the reason why the Tribunal is confiscating anthologies?"

"It's a compelling incentive."

I sat back and stared into my cup. If Carson Manse had figured it out and Avery had figured it out, who else would figure it out? How long before everyone knew who the Ghosts were?

A heavy silence fell over us. Mason knew about this—he had to. He hadn't suspected other Ghosts of revealing our identities because he knew the source of the information. Mason was keeping secrets, a fact I'd have to keep in mind. I shared those happy thoughts with Avery.

Our tea grew cold and so did the early evening air. Avery took his leave promising to call tomorrow.

At 6:00 p.m. my time, 9:00 p.m. in Toronto, I Skyped my mother using James's untraceable cellphone. He'd explained the whole encrypted IP address thing and something else about flipping signals around the world. I hadn't understood it, but I trusted James to keep us safe and that's all I needed to understand.

"Where are you?" I asked. The hood of her trench coat obscured her face.

"In a cab. It's raining." My mother didn't entirely trust the *untraceable* promise of James's equipment. "How was California?" She pulled her hood back and the small screen lit up her face.

Talking to my mother felt like negotiating a mine field. I stepped carefully and contorted my words to avoid anything Flier, covey or Tribunal related. It was for her own protection, but it was also because I didn't want to explain why I'd never shared this secret with her. It would hurt her to learn about my long-standing deception. We had just started to clear away the rubble of the walls we'd each built to protect ourselves after my father died. Those walls had crumbled in the wake of my kidnapping, and I was loath to interrupt our efforts to forge a new, healthier connection.

"California was hot."

"It was kind of Mason to invite you to visit," my mother said, as she fixed her hair. It fell to her shoulders and was threaded with silver, but you couldn't tell from the small image.

She had met Mason in my hospital room. I'd introduced him as James's friend. It was the best lie I could come up with on short notice.

"I'm glad I went. You should see Cairabrae. The house is palatial. They've got a swimming pool and horses and acres of land. I didn't have to lift a finger the entire time I was there."

"Did James go with you?"

"No, he had to work." She'd not asked, but I think she had the impression James and I were romantically involved, which was not the case. James was grateful for my part in his sister's rescue, and he probably felt guilty that I'd been shot because of it, but he wasn't interested in me romantically. Having read my memories, he knew far too much about me and my dismal love life to have any interest except the morbidly curious kind, like rubberneckers at the site of a gruesome car wreck.

"Did you get Dad's journals?" I asked, broaching the subject of his research. I'd mailed her the two issues of the *American Journal of Ophthalmology* that I'd found in my father's belongings. She'd thought the scribbled notes and underlined sections might be connected to his research.

"Yes, thanks. They arrived last week."

"You know, you never did tell me what his research was about."

"It involves the early development of the optic nerve, but I'm not familiar enough with ophthalmology to elaborate." My mother was a behavioural research scientist whose work involved studying anti-psychotic meds. "I'm looking forward to hearing what Dr. Stein finds when he's had a chance to review it. I'm so pleased he showed an interest in your father's work." Mother and Dr. Stein were colleagues at the University of Toronto. He was a professor in Pharmaceutical Sciences.

Maybe I was in luck. If she hadn't yet handed over Dad's research, I might be able to stall her plans. "Dr. Coulter was saying just today how interested he would be in seeing this research of Dad's. Do you think he could take a look at it before you pass it on?"

"I'm sorry, sweetheart, but Dr. Stein already has it."

Damn. I'd have to figure out something else. Mother hoped that my father's work might spark some new research and lay the foundation for further study in his name. I sincerely hoped that research didn't involve the second lens in Fliers' eyes. *Early development of the optic nerve* sounded dangerously close. I needed to get my hands on his notes to rule it out.

And had my mother's face brightened at the mention of Dr. Stein? I'd never known her to have a man in her life after Dad, but now I wondered. Were she and Edgar Stein exchanging more than my father's old research? I couldn't help but grin. "And how is Edgar?" I asked.

"*Dr.* Stein and I have a strictly professional relationship," she said, but her smile betrayed her. In any case, she didn't divulge anything more on that front and after a brief exchange of neighbourhood gossip and weather complaints, we said goodbye.

My mother and Dr. Stein... I tried to picture them together. Thinking of my mother as a woman rather than just my mother, made me see her in a different light. This new relationship we were forging was full of pleasant surprises.

My stomach growled. I rattled around the kitchen, scavenging for dinner. I'd not thought to get groceries on the way home and now it looked like I had the stellar choice of either a long-neglected frozen pasta primavera or a can of Campbell's cream of mushroom soup. I chose the primavera, which I knew wouldn't live up to the promise of the photo on the box. I nuked it and gave it a stir then bypassed the table in favour of the sofa.

A phone call interrupted my elegant meal. It was James.

"Hey. What's up?" I asked.

"I'm at the airport. I know it's late, but do you mind if I crash at your place?"

The cottage had proven convenient for James when he had to stay in town. "Not at all. I'll just go toss out the wino I picked up on Deacon Street and fluff your pillow."

"You do that," he said, chuckling. "I'll be there in thirty minutes."

I hadn't expected him to be finished with the business in Lummi for days yet. Hopefully, he'd come with good news—maybe they'd found the Vosburghs safe and sound.

Half an hour later, James used his key and called out as he opened the door. "Emelynn?"

"In the living room," I answered.

I heard a soft thud as his bag landed on the floor followed by the beeping of the alarm as he input the disarm code. The door and window sensor alarms were always on, even when I was in the house. It was another precaution that had become habit.

I rose from the sofa with my plate and caught a glimpse of James dumping his bag inside the guest room. Until I met Mason, I thought James was the most menacing person I'd ever known. Now that I knew James better, I knew he had a softer side; he just wasn't comfortable showing it. James Moss was tall and lanky, and the sharp angles of his face heightened the intimidation factor when it suited him. He'd proven himself quite adept at assuming any number of different personas when the occasion called for it. He could be charming, shy, nerdy or soft-spoken and then turn deadly in an instant. In fact, he probably had a gun on him right now. He rarely went anywhere without one.

"I didn't think I'd see you again so soon. How'd it go on Lummi?" I asked from the kitchen.

He came around the corner and tore a beer from the six-pack he carried. His dark hair was tied in its usual ponytail. "There's no sign of the Vosburghs yet, but they're still looking." He put the rest of the beer in the fridge and pulled the tab on the one in his hand.

"If they're still looking, what are you doing back here?"

"Detective Jordan's made a connection that I have to deal with."

"What connection?" Detective Samuel Jordan had been circling like a rabid dog for months. I'd hoped he'd find something else to bite and leave us all alone.

James took a swig of beer. "You remember I told you he's on the cross-border task force that's investigating a string of missing-person's cases?"

"I do. You told me four Fliers are on that list."

"Yes—and the cases stretch from California to BC." I hadn't forgotten and nodded my head. "Well, he's finally found a common thread." He pursed his lips and shook his head. "He's found Infinity. It doesn't connect everyone, but it connects the Fliers on that list." Infinity was a secure Internet message board. It was one of several that Fliers used to share news and communicate with one another.

"They're unravelling our world," James said. "Figuring it out." James was adept at controlling his features, but he didn't bother to hide the worry etched on his face.

"How did they find Infinity? It was shut down after Rupert compromised it months ago." Rupert Dowling was dead. He was the man who had carried out Carson Manse's instructions and whipped me. His name still sent a chill up my spine.

"Once something's been on the Internet, it's never really gone. The task force will be able to reconstruct it—they may have already. That's probably how Jordan got the IP addresses to link the missing Fliers. It's how the task force connected the Vosburghs to the investigation."

No wonder he looked worried. "Everyone I know has been on the Infinity site. We'll all be exposed. Can't you stop them?" I asked.

"No. The damage is already done. But I do have a plan. If it works, I'll be able to make Infinity look like an elaborate online fantasy game. It'll give us all a legitimate reason for accessing the board. I'm going to drop by the detective's office tomorrow."

"Oh crap. This probably means another visit from the detective and more of his questions."

"If he noses around, there's no point in denying that you knew about the site—especially if he finds out later that you accessed it. Tell him Avery sent you the password by email and you checked it out. I'll touch base with Avery first thing tomorrow. He'll be able to spread the word to the covey." James certainly couldn't do it—the covey hadn't forgotten his lie by omission where Jackson and Sandra were concerned.

"But won't that put Avery under their microscope?"

"Not if I can help it. Avery's computer was hacked. I'm going to make sure the task force learns that Dowling was the one who hacked it, and I'll make it look like he instigated a spam mail-out to Avery's contacts, passing along Infinity's password. That should cover everyone in our covey, and some others as well. Hopefully, it will be enough to get the detective off our scent."

"That's pretty clever, James. It might actually work."

"You doubted me?" He feigned hurt and made me smile. I liked it when he was being coy like this; he could be quite handsome when he tried. Lethal, but handsome. "You got anything to eat around here?"

James settled for the only thing left on the menu: soup. "I have crackers," I offered like an apology.

He was much more civilized than me and ate at the table. I turned on the radio. "We are Young" by Fun was playing and it was hard not to sing along.

James and I had grown comfortable sharing space. We didn't need to fill the quiet with talk. I did a bit of catch-up on my computer. He washed his dishes then settled into one of my mother's blue gingham chairs with his cellphone.

Just after 10:00, James stood. "I'm going to hit the sack. I've got an early start tomorrow."

"Good night," I said. "See you in the morning." James's footsteps faded down the hall. Moments later I heard the water running in the bathroom. Perhaps I'd go to bed too. I closed the computer and turned off the music.

Later that night, tucked beneath my cozy comforter, my thoughts drifted to my father's research. Damn! I'd forgotten to speak to James about it.

I looked over at the photo of my father that I kept beside the bed. I'd draped Jeannette's crystal case necklace over the frame. They were all gone now: my father, Jolene, their son. I liked to think they were together again in the afterlife. Wouldn't that be wonderful, I thought, as I drifted off to sleep.

Chapter Eight

The next morning dawned bright despite high overcast clouds. The days were getting shorter I noted, wrapping my hands around my tea mug. Cooler too—I'd had to pull on jeans this morning before venturing down to the beach. James had already left but his Dopp kit sat out on the toilet tank.

The tide looked to be about halfway out. Though the tides were only seventeen feet, the surrounding shoreline was shallow, forcing the water to travel fifty yards or more between its highest and lowest point. This wasn't a lazy, sandy shore with lapping water that most people pictured when they thought of a beach. It was littered with ankle-twisting rocks and the water was forbidding and cool. What little sand there was laid in shallow pockets between slabs of sandstone. Building castles on this beach was a challenge, one I loved when I was a child.

I wandered to a familiar beached log, faded white with salt and sun, and with a girth large enough to be old growth. Coffee on the beach was the best way to start the day. Tea was a close second.

This beach held many bittersweet memories for me: childhood games, my father, Jolene, the accident that led me to Avery . . . Jackson. Thinking of him no longer hurt. I'd finally moved on. The only thing I missed about Jackson was his *rush*, that special Flier gift that we all had to some degree though I'd not yet figured out how to use mine. If I let Jackson lock his eyes onto mine, he could use his rush to ignite my libido from the inside, raising it to heights I'd not known existed. God, that man could give me orgasms. It was the only thing I missed about him.

The memories washed over me while I finished my tea, and then I headed back to the cottage where Rumbles's paperwork awaited.

After I moved the unruly pile of documents to the dining-room table, I started sorting it. Packing slips that had never been unfolded were crammed in with bank statements and invoices from suppliers and book distributors. The pile was as disorganized as the first batch I'd gone through. I dug in, happily immersing myself in the work. The hours flew by until my gurgling stomach made me look at the clock. No wonder, I thought. It was after two and I hadn't eaten lunch.

My phone rang, putting my hunger on hold. It was Molly. "Hey Molly, how are you feeling?" I said, getting up to fill the kettle.

"Great. Where are you?"

"At home. I thought you were sick."

"Not really. Can I come over?"

"Sure. I just put the kettle on. I'll wait for you." The doorbell rang. "I've got to go. Someone's at the door."

Molly's phone was still in her hand when I opened the front door. "Aren't you the funny girl," I said. "Been waiting long?"

Molly wore her usual fifties style with a sweater set over cigarette pants. She'd skipped the matching hair band today.

"I thought you were at your parents' place." I closed the door behind her.

"I was. Came back this morning."

"Is everything all right?" She loved the Sunshine Coast and would normally have spent the whole weekend there. We headed down the hall to the kitchen.

"Never better," she said, and plastered a goofy smile on her face. She blinked, doe-eyed.

Hmm, something was up. "Do you want tea?" I asked, turning to the stove to lift the kettle and make sure it held enough water for two.

"Do you have something decaf?" Molly asked.

"Decaf?" I repeated, swivelling back to her. "You never drink decaf." Her goofy smile morphed into an expression more like that of the cat that ate the canary.

"Oh my god. You're pregnant!" I watched a beautiful smile bloom across her face. "I mean—you're pregnant?" I repeated, more calmly this time. She nodded vigorously, sending her curls bouncing. "This is good news—right?" I asked cautiously, taking her hands in mine.

"The best," she said, and I felt relief down to my toes.

"And you're okay? I mean, Ruth said you were sick."

"Just a touch of morning sickness. Nothing too bad."

"How far along are you?"

"Nine or ten weeks."

"So you went home to tell your parents?"

"Cheney and I both went."

"Oh," I said, and tensed again, crossing my mental fingers. "How'd Cheney take the news?" Please, I thought, let it be good.

"He was thrilled. He asked me to marry him."

"Oh, Molly. I'm so happy for you." I pulled her into a hug. "Happy for you both," I said, and then finally let her go. "I think I need to sit down." A lifetime ago, Cheney had asked me out on a date, and I'd foolishly turned him down. After he met Molly, he never looked back. Looks like it was meant to be.

She laughed and led me to the living room where we collapsed, side-by-side on the blue sofa.

"How'd your mom and dad react?"

"Pretty much as you'd expect. They looked shell-shocked for a few hours, but they really like Cheney and they know we love each other. I think it may take them a while to get used to the idea that they're going to be grandparents though."

"I know how they feel. I can't quite wrap my head around the fact that you're going to be a mom."

"A mom . . . I like the sound of that," Molly's said, beaming.

"And a wife."

"Yes, speaking of that," Molly said, straightening herself up.

I sat back, surprised at her sudden change in demeanour.

"I need to ask you something."

"Sounds serious."

"Gosh no, it's just important to me, that's all." I looked at her expectantly. "Emelynn, will you be my maid of honour?"

"Oh, Molly—this is just what we planned when we were kids. Absolutely, I will." I grabbed her hand and squeezed. Her beaming smile returned. "Have you and Cheney discussed wedding plans yet?"

"We want to get married in Vegas."

"Vegas?" That wasn't in our childhood plans. "You're not thinking about having an Elvis impersonator marry you," I said in a wary tone. It wasn't out of the question given her penchant for all things fifties-style and Cheney's muscle-car fetish.

"We hadn't thought of that." She touched her cheek with her forefinger and gazed to the ceiling. "But now that you mention it . . ."

"You wouldn't," I warned, laughing. "Will you wait until after the baby's born?"

"Actually, we were thinking of the first week in October."

I did the mental math. "Molly, that's in two weeks."

"I know, but I'm going to be showing soon and I don't want my wedding dress options to be limited to one of those six-man-tent-sized, I-got-knocked-up numbers from Tarts-R-Us."

Fashion was Molly's passion. "You've already got one picked out, don't you?"

She smiled a guilty smile. "Three actually."

Anxiety flared, tightening my chest. Two weeks and so much to do. "I'm going to have to organize a wedding shower. Wait, maybe I should make it a baby shower." I was thinking out loud. "No, there's lots of time for that; it should be a wedding shower. I'll need to get the contact info for your school friends and your friends from college—the ones you used to live with."

"Oh Emelynn, I don't need a bridal shower." She frowned and shook her head. "I'm not worried about the wedding. As long as my folks are there, and you're there, it will be perfect."

"Aren't you forgetting someone," I said, laughing at the obvious omission.

"Cheney, how could I forget," she said, mocking herself. "And Dean," she added hastily, watching for my reaction. "Cheney is asking Dean to be his best man. You're okay with that, right?"

"Of course. Dean's a great guy." Dean and I had gone on a date a while ago, but it never went further than that. I hadn't been ready to trust another man so soon after Jackson's betrayal. Dean and Cheney were both mechanics. They'd gone to trade school together. It would be nice to see Dean again.

"I knew you'd be okay with it." Molly slouched into the sofa, looking relieved.

The rest of the afternoon washed away on a wave of brainstorming and Internet searches for hotel and wedding venue options.

"Will you stay for dinner?" I asked. "I'll order pizza."

"I don't think I should," Molly said, checking the time. "I need to see Cheney and start making some of these decisions." She looked warily at the stack of notes and lists we'd generated.

"Invite him over. In fact, have him bring Dean too. It'll give us a chance to work out some of the details."

"All right," she said, and started dialling. She hung up moments later. "They'll be here in thirty minutes."

Cheney arrived first and the moment I saw him emerge from his '64 Mustang convertible, I knew: he was happy, truly happy. He walked taller, more confidently, and his face looked lit up from the inside. He wore a jean jacket over his standard T-shirt and jeans. The only time I'd seen him wear something else was at work where he donned coveralls.

"Congratulations, Cheney," I offered and squeezed his shoulder. He leaned over and kissed my cheek. He smelled of cologne but hadn't bathed in it. Cheney was about five nine with memorable sky-blue eyes and thick hair that he kept short.

"Thanks, Emelynn." He kissed Molly and pulled her into a protective hug, smiling down at her. "Hello mom," he teased and we made our way to the living room.

Almost as soon as they were settled, the doorbell rang again. I took the pizza and before I closed the door, I heard the roar of Dean's motorcycle coming down the street. He passed the delivery car at the foot of the driveway, pulled around Cheney's car and parked in front of the garage. I held the door open, waiting for him. He put his gloves inside his helmet and rested it on the bike's seat then straightened his hair and strode over to the porch.

"Looks like I found the right house," he said, flicking unruly hair out of his eyes with a toss of his head. Dean Mitchell looked just like I remembered: uncontrollable straight brown hair falling over his forehead into his eyes. The ragged scar that ran from his temple to his jaw did nothing to take away from a handsome face.

"It's good to see you, Dean."

"You too." He stepped onto the porch and leaned in, brushing my cheek with his lips. It was the only kiss I'd ever had from him and I hoped he noticed that I hadn't flinched. Perhaps my memory was faulty, but it seemed to me I'd spent our entire first date dancing away from his touch.

"You look good," he said. He hadn't seen me since the kidnapping, but he'd know about it; the details were all over the news.

"A little worse for wear, maybe. Come on in. You're just in time," I said, gesturing to the pizza boxes in my hand.

"Let me," he said, relieving me of the pizza.

Cheney shouted a greeting from the living room. "Did you get lost?"

"Nah, I just followed the exhaust fumes from that beast in the driveway." Dean dropped the pizza on the kitchen counter at my direction.

"Molly," Dean said, spreading his arms to greet her. She and Cheney had both risen and she stepped forward with a shy grin and accepted his hug. "So . . . he knocked you up?"

"Well, we've been practicing," she said, rolling her eyes for my benefit.

This was the first time Dean had been to the cottage and after he released Molly and shook Cheney's hand, he looked around appreciatively. "Nice digs," he said, removing his leather jacket.

"Thanks." I dropped plates and napkins on the coffee table and retrieved the pizza, snatching a furtive look at Dean's backside. My lingering smile wasn't solely in appreciation of his backside; the fact that I'd noticed at all meant that I really was past the ordeal—back in the land of the living.

Dean stepped up to the patio door and took in the view of the Pacific, which rippled calmly under a fading sky. He looked remarkable—broad shoulders tapering to narrow hips and he wore jeans like a god. I quickly looked away when he turned around.

I poured chilled apple juice into wine glasses for Molly and me. Cheney and Dean scoffed at the suggestion, opting for a beer instead. Amid toasts, laughter and pizza, we discussed plans for Las Vegas.

By nine o'clock, Molly was yawning. "I'm sorry," she apologized. "This being preggers knocks the oomph out of me."

"Let me take you home," Cheney said, standing up and offering Molly his hand.

They said goodbye to Dean, and I walked them down the hall, noticing that Dean wasn't making any moves to leave.

"Thanks for agreeing to be my maid of honour," Molly said, giving me a hug at the front door.

"Yeah, thanks, Emelynn," Cheney added.

"Hey, thanks for asking." I waved from the porch and when the Mustang's tail lights disappeared, I stepped back inside and closed the door.

Dean hovered in the hallway by the kitchen, his jacket in hand. "I should go, too."

I wasn't so sure. Half of me wanted to run and the other half wanted to see what he looked like without a shirt. The other half won. "It's still early. Would you like another beer?"

"Sure," he said, and tossed his jacket over the back of the sofa.

"Good because I'd like to upgrade; I've had enough apple juice." I handed him a beer.

"I didn't want to ask in front of Molly and Cheney, but how are you . . . really?" he asked.

I poured a glass of Malbec and inhaled the heavy scent. "I'm fine . . . really."

He smiled but probed further. "Physically, I can see you're doing great, but how are you dealing with the rest of it?"

I tasted the wine and then swallowed a large mouthful. "The rest of it?" I repeated quietly, taking a seat on the opposite end of the sofa. "That's a big question." I knew he meant the emotional part of my ordeal, but that paled in comparison to the real storm that brewed. Dean was blissfully unaware of the Tribunal and the Redeemer threat. He knew nothing about the other Fliers and Ghosts who had gone missing before me. I wished I had that luxury.

"I'm coping," I said. "It gets easier every day. My mother and my friends have been a great support." This wasn't a subject that got better with rehashing. Talking about it just made me think about it, and thinking about it only made me relive it. I didn't want to relive it.

"I'm glad to hear that."

"Yes. I'm very fortunate." I tried to push the horrible images of the mouldy mattress in that filthy trailer out of my mind. "Why don't you tell me what's new with you since I last saw you?"

I pasted a smile on my face and sipped my wine. He talked, animatedly at times, but I couldn't honestly say I heard a word of it. My head was too busy *not* thinking about Carson Manse and his accomplice Rupert Dowling, and especially *not* thinking about Rupert's whip.

"Would you take me for a ride on your bike?" I said, interrupting him mid-sentence. "I could use a distraction."

"You bet. Do you have a sturdy jacket?"

The best I could do was my jean jacket pulled over my hoodie. I locked up and Dean helped me with the strap on the helmet. It was a small skull cap he kept under the seat. He got on the bike and scooted forward to give me room to swing my leg over. I settled in behind him, relishing the excuse to wrap my arms around his waist.

"Hold on," he warned then shifted into gear and started down the driveway. Thankfully, he kept the bike quiet until we were out of earshot of my neighbours. But when we reached Deacon Street, he hit the throttle and the bike roared. The Harley's rumble ran straight through me. My heart raced and I couldn't hear a thing over the thundering motor.

He took the connector to King Street and blasted onto the highway, immediately swerving into the passing lane. I held on tight, shifting my weight with his to lean into the curves each time he swerved from one lane to another. It was exhilarating. The wind felt cool in contrast to the warmth of Dean's body, where it touched mine. I pulled my head out of the wind and laid my helmeted ear against Dean's back, and enjoyed the ride.

He took an exit to a rest stop and slowed down along the access road, coming to a stop at the far end of the parking lot. We were as far as we could possibly get from the building that housed the restrooms. He shifted forward to let me off the back and I immediately felt the absence of his heat.

"How was that? Distracting enough for you?"

"God, yes!"

"It's a little taste of heaven, isn't it? I love the freedom—the blast of the wind and just a bit of leather between you and fresh air." I followed his lead and removed my helmet. He looked as content as I'd ever seen him. "Come here," he said, offering me his hand. "There's an awesome view through there."

I took his hand and he led me over the curb and onto a weedy patch of lawn. We pushed through a thin line of trees. On the other side, mere metres from the parking lot, the ground dropped away. I stood beside him with legs still vibrating from the ride.

"You can't see much now, but in the daylight, you can see for miles from here. It's called Juniper Point." Even without light, you could still get the sensation of wide-open space especially with the scattered lights twinkling off in the distance. But I didn't need the daylight to see the stunning view of thatched farmland with white-capped mountains in the distance. If I were here by myself, I'd be tempted to fly out over the fields and roll across the crest of the feathery grass that gently rippled in the breeze.

He put his arm around my shoulder and I liked how it felt. I desperately wanted to latch onto his life and live in his reality. If only I could. But Dean and I lived in different worlds. Sometimes I wondered if I belonged in either one. His sense of freedom was a mere grain of sand on my beach. There was no comparison between his version of euphoria on a motorcycle and the unfettered wonder of flight. I could bring him into my world, share some of it with him, but it would be a half-life for both of us. And sadly, his life, his world, was safer without me in them. With a heavy sigh, I suggested he take me home.

I snuggled between his shoulders the whole way back to the cottage, holding him close, savouring the moment. I tried not to think about the "what ifs." It was pointless to dwell on something I couldn't change. I would push Dean away, just like I'd pushed Cheney away. This time, it would have nothing to do with Jackson and the trust issues he'd left behind. This time, it would be for the right reasons.

We dismounted and I reluctantly returned his helmet. He walked me to the front door and I made small talk about Vegas and our roles in the upcoming wedding.

"I'm glad you're going to be there," he said, and wrapped his arms around me. Then, without warning, he leaned down and kissed me. His lips were warm and soft and I could smell the fresh air still clinging to him. The "what ifs" drifted back. I returned his kiss and let him push his tongue into my mouth. He still tasted of beer. Maybe just once, my slutty mind suggested. I'd push him away tomorrow.

But I didn't get the chance. My phone rang. I let it go to voice mail, but the moment was gone and Dean re-organized his thoughts. "I've got to go, but it was great to see you again. I guess we'll be seeing a lot of each other in the next few weeks."

"Yes, I'm sure," I said, tucking my libido away. He gave me another peck then turned and left. My libido peeked out, admiring every step of his retreat before I slapped her back under cover. God, turning him down was going to be a challenge.

Chapter Nine

The phone call had been from James. He'd left a message saying he was on his way. Hearing his voice was all it took to drag me back into the craziness. The speed with which it happened was jarring. I stripped off my hoodie and poured another glass of wine.

I heard James's key in the lock. "It's me, Em," he called out. It sounded like he was struggling with something. A bag dropped to the floor with a thunk. "Damn," he mumbled, punching in the disarm code.

"Hi." I craned my neck to watch him come down the hall. He had a large box in his hands.

"Did I miss pizza?" he asked, eyeing the empty boxes on the counter. "Looks like you had a party." His hair was neatly tied back at the nape of his neck. I'd never seen it loose.

"There are a couple of pieces in the fridge. Help yourself. What have you got there?" I asked, curious about the big box he laid on the counter beside the fridge.

"That's your new coffee maker," he said, pulling the pizza and a beer out of the fridge. He wore a long-sleeved T-shirt over black jeans.

"You didn't have to do that, James. I would have gotten around to buying a replacement."

"Consider it my room and board." He pulled the tab on a tall can of Estrella and swallowed a big gulp. "Man, that's good." He removed the plastic wrap from the plate of pizza and popped it into the microwave. I cringed. Yuck—soggy pizza. I would have heated it in the oven.

I moved to one of the stools at the breakfast bar. "An espresso machine?" I asked, reading the box on the far counter.

"It's a Saeco," he said, taking his now horribly soggy, but steaming, pizza from the microwave and coming around to sit beside me. "Don't worry—it makes regular coffee too." I went into the kitchen and moved the box to the breakfast bar beside him. "Careful—it's heavy," he warned.

It was too. I spun the box around, reading about the Saeco while he devoured his pizza. "Any word today on the Vosburghs?" I asked. He shook his head. I sat back down beside him and told him about Avery's discovery in the Reynolds anthology.

He listened intently and washed down the last of the pizza with a mouthful of beer. "That explains how the Redeemers knew which Fliers were Tribunal and which ones were Ghosts. One of them obviously has access to an anthology."

"It also explains how Carson knew how to transfer the gift." The incantations were in those old books. Add an ash circle and a couple of candles, and you had a recipe for a horror show. "Too bad he hadn't understood that the gift could only be given once."

James pressed his lips into a straight line, managing a sympathetic smile. He jumped up and put his plate in the dishwasher. "Who ate the rest of the pizza?"

I was grateful for the change of topic. "Do you remember Molly?"

"Sure. Short, dark hair—bubbly." He pulled a penknife out of his pocket and turned the Saeco box around, sliding the sharp edge under the flaps.

"Well, Short, Dark and Bubbly is pregnant, and she and Cheney are getting married." He paused mid-slice. "She asked me to be her best woman."

"That's . . . great. Good for Molly." He resumed his chore, but his sombre tone left me wondering if the pregnant and married topics made James uncomfortable. He folded back the box flaps. "Help me out here, would you?"

"Sure." I walked around to his side of the counter and held down the box while he lifted the machine out. Moulded Styrofoam was press-fit to either side. I pulled it off then loosened the plastic bag that covered the whole thing. James set it on the counter and I plucked free a box of accessories that had been neatly jammed into the packaging.

While he examined the coffee maker, I stuffed the packaging back into the empty box. I piled the empty pizza boxes on top and started down the hall to set it by the front door.

James raced after me. "Careful!" he called out.

But he failed to mention the fact he'd left a bag of groceries on the floor in the middle of the hall. Blinded by the boxes, my foot found the bag and I lurched to avoid stepping on it. My foot tangled in the bag and I sprawled forward, tossing the boxes. If James hadn't caught my arm, I would have crashed headfirst into the front door.

He pulled me back and steadied me against the hall closet door. "Thanks, James. I've got it." But he didn't let go. He held me in his grip and his pale eyes widened. In an instant, I knew he'd taken advantage of my block being down to read my memories.

I twisted out of his grasp. "How could you?" The memory of Dean's ass as he strode back to his bike was stuck in my head. When James read my memories, it felt like icy fingers touching images in my mind, lighting them up like photos on an iPad. That memory of Dean's ass would be the one I left him with. Served him right.

"God, Em, not him again. What the hell are you thinking?"

I drew myself up in righteous indignation. "Don't you dare," I warned. "I don't want to hear it. You do *not* get to comment on that. It's none of your business." My voice was firm and steady. "I can't believe you've done this again. I thought we had an agreement."

"I'm sorry," he said, stepping back with his hands in the air. "You're right." His blue eyes bore into mine. "But it's like trying not to smell smoke in the middle of a fire." He bent down and grabbed the bag I'd tripped over and stormed into the spare room.

I sagged back against the closet door. Maybe I'd been too hard on him. He hadn't read my memories with any premeditation. My arms just happened to be bare. It was second nature to him. And he had warned me to keep my block up around him. I guess I'd grown lax in his absence. I took deep breaths and calmed myself. It was short-lived.

James propelled himself out of the bedroom like a freight train and drove the calm away. He lurched to a stop before me, glaring. "You know what, Em. I'm not sorry." Startled by his declaration, I slammed my block into place. What the hell?

"I'm glad I know where you're heading with that guy—and I *do* know where you're headed." I raised my eyebrows—he didn't know. "You want to know why I'm glad?" he continued. I shook my head. He was really angry and angry James was frightening.

"Because," he leaned close, invading my personal space. I pressed my back into the closet door. "I'm going to give him a run for his fucking money," he whispered.

And then he kissed me. I mean he *kissed* me. Full-on, no-holds-barred, blow-my-mind kissed me. I was so completely shocked by his reaction that I let him. In fact, I participated, opening up to his desperate, angry tongue. He had just enough beard stubble to irritate my skin. One of his hands slid around my back, gripping my shoulder and his other hand pressed the back of my head into the kiss. He pushed his hips into me, pinning me to the closet door. I felt the hard lines of his body and the closet let out a strained crack behind me. The noise broke his concentration and he lifted his head, examining my face. He looked calm, but I wasn't fooled: he was a volcano ready to explode. He brushed the hair off my forehead then stood back and looked at me like he was unsure of something.

And then he was gone. He just turned for the front door, swung it open and fled. Where?—I hadn't a clue. I didn't even know if he was coming back. I stared into the night for a few minutes, and then closed the door and rested my forehead against it. What the hell was James thinking? We'd known each other for months and not once had he given me any indication he was interested in me that way.

Apparently, I'd missed something pretty big. I refilled my wine glass, turned out the lights and sat on the sofa, trying to recall every encounter I'd ever had with James. My chin stung from his stubble burn. I raised my fingers to touch my bruised lips. That kiss was amazing. An unbidden image of James popped into my mind. It was the night I'd returned to the cottage unexpectedly. He thought I was an intruder and he'd tackled me wearing nothing but his underwear. Those black jersey boxers fit him incredibly well.

But I couldn't reconcile tonight's kiss in light of our history. His behaviour didn't make sense. He, more than anyone else, had reason to think the worst of me. In fact, when we met, that's precisely what he thought. He could barely stand to look at me and was downright hostile. He knew I was sleeping with Jackson, his sister's husband, and he thought I knew Jackson was married. And then he learned of my involvement with Case, a man whose last name I didn't even know. A fact made worse when he witnessed the intimate encounters in my memories. I'd given James plenty of reasons to keep me at arm's length. How could he possibly think of me as girlfriend material?

This didn't feel like James at all. James was aloof, a loner, about as far from boyfriend material as you could get. Something else was going on with him. But what?

Wait a minute: maybe it did make sense. As realization dawned, indignation set in. He wasn't thinking of me as girlfriend material at all. He was a guy; he thought I was an easy lay. And why shouldn't he? He'd had a front-row seat to my sex life. As far as he knew, *promiscuity* was a core competency on my resume. Why wouldn't he get in line and give it a shot?

I downed the wine and headed to bed. I pulled on my nightshirt and settled between the sheets. I'd have to straighten James out. Why did he have to pull that shit and kiss me? I kind of liked having him here. If he returned, he could stay the night but tomorrow, he'd have to find his own place and he could take his Saeco with him. I rolled onto my side and a tear dropped onto the pillowcase, but just one.

It wasn't yet daylight when I woke. A sense of dread washed over me. Something wasn't right. I rolled over and gasped. James stood in the bedroom doorway, staring at me. I threw up my block and clenched a pillow to my chest. My feet tangled in the sheets as I scooted up to put my back against the headboard.

"May I come in?" he asked.

"Absolutely not. What are you doing back here?"

"Not to apologize, if that's what you're expecting."

"Why'd you kiss me, James?"

"I told you. I'm not letting you fall for another guy without putting myself into the mix."

"I'm not *falling* for Dean."

"I'm happy to hear that. May I come in?" He reached his hands to the side of the door frame, bracing himself.

"No. I'm not some easy lay, James, and it pisses me off that you think so."

"You think I see you as an easy lay?"

"Why'd you kiss me, James," I asked again.

"It would never work out for you and Dean."

"Not that it's any of your business, but why the hell not? He's a decent guy with a good job and hell, you saw his ass."

"Dean Mitchell is not one of us. He'll never be one of us. You'll spend half your time lying to him and the other half fabricating stories to cover up what you are. Do you really want that? Do you really want to drag this guy into our mess?"

"Why do you care? You don't even know him."

"No, but I know you. I know you hate deception and secrets, and yet that's exactly what you're setting yourself up for with Dean. You don't need to deceive *me*; keep secrets from *me*; you can trust me. Jesus, Em—tell me I've at least earned your trust."

"I do trust you, James, just not with my heart. No one gets that again."

"Someone will. You can take that to the bank. I want you to consider *me*. Please, Em. May I come in?"

"Consider *you*? James, this is coming out of the blue."

"Maybe for you."

"Come on. You thought I was a whore for sleeping with Jackson and let's not forget your opinion of me and my relationship with Case." My voice rose as anger and confusion boiled out of me. "You wouldn't even be here if it weren't for some misplaced obligation, some leftover guilt."

"Is that what you believe? Every time I came here? What . . . you think I don't know how to find a hotel?" He was angry too; I could hear the heat of it quivering in his voice. He reached up and grabbed the top of the door frame with his fingertips. "Open your eyes, Em."

He wavered in the doorway not breaching the space, but not backing away. My mind raced. How long had he felt like this? How many signs had I missed?

I had never even considered him that way. I was attracted to the Cheney-type, the Dean-type. The clean-cut, Boy-Scout, buy-you-a-puppy type. James was as far from that as it got. He was muscle and menace and hidden weapons. And beard stubble, I thought, remembering his kiss.

"James, this," I said, pointing from him to me, "you and I. It's a bad idea." Yet even as I said it, I contemplated it and my libido stirred.

"Probably."

"Definitely: you and I are friends."

"Friends is a good place to start."

"James, friends don't *do* friends—not if they want to stay friends."

"We could be so much more than friends."

Could we? Could I cross that line and not regret it? Moving James into the lover column felt darkly ominous, like tempting the devil. How long had it been since a man had touched me intimately? Touched me in places that craved to be touched? Too long. That was the thing about sex—once you had a taste for it, your body wanted it, needed it. And mine was remembering how good it could be.

He sensed my hesitation and pounced. "Let me show you, Em.

Please let me in." Yearning contorted his features. He rolled his hips forward with a carnal promise that made my insides clench. If he could do that from ten feet away, what could he do up close? The muscles in his arms flexed and that little knot of potent nerves at the apex of my thighs quivered. "Please," he whispered, licking his teeth as he lowered his gaze to my mouth.

I didn't say yes; I didn't need to. I simply thought of his kiss and my body gave me away. I rose to my knees to meet him. In a split second, he'd crossed the bedroom's threshold, pulled the pillow from my grip and threw it aside. He cradled my face in his hands and spoke sternly. "You were never an obligation and you are most certainly *not* an easy lay. You are exquisite. You're brave and smart and sexy as hell." He kissed me then, and all thought was lost in a tangle of tongues and desperation. I ran my palms up the back of his thin shirt, feeling the taut muscles beneath.

When we finally came up for air, we were gasping like pearl divers. He stood before my kneeling form, a head taller than me. He wrapped me in his arms and held me tightly against his chest. I could feel his pounding heart. "I've wanted to do that for months," he whispered. My mind raced to find a new equilibrium—one that included James as a lover. He nuzzled my hair and then tipped his head back to look into my eyes. I searched his familiar face looking for the James I knew in his features, but his sharp angles were gone. The man before me was a stranger—focused, but softer.

He kissed me again, slowly this time, placing gentle kisses along my jaw, over to my ear. His stubble prickled, but I didn't care; not tonight. I exposed my neck in encouragement. Would I care tomorrow? The unwelcome thought seeped in but dissipated with the swirl of his tongue.

I reached between us and loosened his belt then popped the button on his jeans. Not so long ago, that wouldn't have been a smooth move, I thought, blushing. When I stroked the bulge in the front of his jeans, he moaned softly, touching his forehead to mine. He pushed the bulge into my hand. I wanted more of him, but he stymied my attempts to remove his jeans by pushing his hips back, almost out of reach.

He drew tiny circles with his tongue down my neck and undid the top button on my nightshirt. My insides clenched again in sweet anticipation. He struggled with the next button and I let a laugh escape.

"What?" he asked, looking awkwardly amused.

"I've never undone these buttons before." I'd never seen the point. His amusement turned to confusion and I curled my lips around my teeth, trying not to laugh at the look on his face. He released me and I reached down to the hem of the nightshirt and pulled it right over my head. Bold hussy is what my childhood nanny Fran would have called me, kneeling naked in front of him like that. He inhaled and took a small step back. I don't think he realized his mouth was open. His eyes took in every inch of me. I bit my lower lip and the motion drew his gaze to my lips then to my eyes.

The air crackled between us. Without taking his eyes off mine, he reached behind and removed the gun I knew he kept at the small of his back. He broke his stare to set it on the bedside table, right beside the framed photo of my father. His gaze lingered there and I watched him reach up to the frame and lift the weight of Jeannette's crystal case in his fingertips. He turned it, and then let it drop back against the photo.

"They're pulling out all the stops, aren't they?"

"What do you mean?"

"The Reynoldses," he said.

"You know what that is?" I asked cautiously, uncertain of the extent of his knowledge.

"Yes, they all have them . . . crystals. You really are one of them." He sounded heartbroken.

"James, I'm the same person I've always been."

He refocused on me, as if he'd forgotten I was kneeling on the bed. Naked. A smile curled his lips and he shook his head. "Yes, you are." James whipped off his shirt and now it was my turn to gape. James's chest and stomach were perfection. He could have modelled for Jockey. I'd seen good torsos before, but James had an honest-to-goodness six-pack. How had I not noticed that before?

He stepped up to the bed, close enough for me to feel the heat radiating off him. His hands twitched at his side but he didn't touch me. My heart beat double-time. If he was testing my willpower, I was happy to lose. I laid my right hand on his left pec and leaned in to lick his nipple. His breath hitched. Did he like that, I wondered? I stole a glance at his face. His gaze was locked on my fingers. He did like it. Encouraged, I continued. He gave away his pleasure with quick sharp breaths. James's reaction was like plugging me into an electric socket. It charged me with a warm current. This could prove to be fun. Or would it, I wondered as I felt his fingers pull my chin up.

"You don't like that?" I asked coyly.

"Oh, I like that just fine." His face with eyes half closed, lips moist and slightly parted, could be posted under *horny as hell* in the dictionary. "I'm just anxious for my turn." He kissed me then broke away, heeled off his shoes and peeled down his jeans. He tossed a condom onto the table beside the gun and the small square packet skittered into my father's photo. I had an urge to lay the frame face down, but was quickly distracted.

I grinned at the sight of his boxers. The in-the-flesh version was so much more enticing than my earlier flashback. The bulge straining the fabric in front was especially eye-catching. That rather large detail, I was certain I hadn't seen before. "Why James," I said, not hiding my stare. "You did like that."

He started to remove his boxers and I yelped, "No!" He froze, startled. "Let me," I said, crawling off the bed. He straightened and watched me approach in anticipation, like a kid at the Dairy Queen counter.

I circled behind him and ran my hand across his butt. He tightened his cheek muscles and they danced under my palm. Damn! Buns of Steel wasn't just a workout slogan; it was a proverb. I pulled the tie from his hair and thick dark waves of it fell loose to his shoulders, enticing me to run my fingers through it.

I laid my head against his back and snaked a hand around his taut stomach, dipping my fingers under the waistband of his boxers. He inhaled a ragged breath and arched his head back. His reaction to my touch gave me confidence. I reached my other hand around and gripped his erection through his boxers. That couldn't be right, I thought. The proportion was all wrong. I stroked him through the soft fabric until he grabbed my wrist. "Jesus, Emelynn—you're killing me." He held me still and took several deep breaths before releasing me. I moved around in front of him and tugged his boxers down, going to my knees in the process.

When I finally got my first glimpse of James in all his glory, his glory was mere inches from my nose. To say I was taken aback would be like saying Hurricane Katrina was a rain shower. "And you think, *I'm* killing *you*," I said, searching his face. My confidence slipped. I reached a tentative hand out to touch him. The wonder of the male anatomy amazed me. He was so hard it should have hurt. I caressed the delicate, silken skin.

He inhaled abruptly and pulled away from me. "Stand up," he said, tugging urgently at my elbow. He picked me up and tossed me onto the bed like a sack of laundry. I landed with a gasp and he crawled up the bed behind me. His shoulders rolled, looking more like a predator than a lover. His arms came to rest on either side of my head with his hair falling down around me. He bent his head and ran his tongue over my lips then crawled lower and commenced a tantalizing sensual assault.

He trailed soft fingertips across the top of one breast then below the bottom of the other, drawing a lazy infinity symbol. His fingers left a heated trail that awakened sensitive skin and served to emphasize everything he wasn't touching. On the third pass, he used his tongue. It was glorious. It felt like he was flicking a tight cord that ran from my nipples to the knot of nerves between my legs, and I squirmed. My movement seemed to escalate James's ardour. He had one nipple in his mouth and the other between his thumb and forefinger and sought out my eyes. Looking mischievous, he made a show of his teeth and nipped. I let out a squeak of protest, which amused him.

He gently kissed one breast and then the other, as if in apology, and then rolled to the side and slid his hand between my legs. "You're wet," he purred, sliding a finger inside me. I closed my eyes, inhaling at the sudden sensation. "Open your eyes," he whispered and replaced one finger with two. His arousal played out on his face. It was mirrored in mine. His thumb found that most sensitive spot on a woman's body and he pressed hard. Waves of tingling pleasure spread all the way to my fingertips and toes. His mouth found mine, swallowing my groan. He smoothed lazy circles around my clitoris, strumming his fingers inside me. I rolled my hips, unable to stay still. His tongue in my mouth mimicked his thumb, but I felt his lips curl into a smile.

"Not yet," he said, stilling his fingers.

"Don't stop," I gasped on the edge of my first orgasm in ages. I pushed my hips against his palm. He laughed and I looked up to an indulgent smile that promised he'd enjoy drawing this out. He sat up and swung his feet to the floor, reaching for the condom. I heard the tear of the plastic wrapper and watched his back flex as he rolled it on. He smiled at me over his shoulder. I must have looked like a desperate mess, lying there waiting for him.

He rose lazily, taunting me with my need for release. It was maddening. He caught my gaze and held on, trapping me. I'd felt his rush before, but this was different. This was exquisite torture. "Spread your legs," he said in a voice husky with his own need. His rush flooded me, as if his own heated desire raced through my bloodstream. I complied without hesitation.

He walked to the end of the bed, never breaking eye contact, fanning his rush inside me. He knelt on the bed. "That is a lovely sight," he said, gazing at my body wantonly displayed before him. His rush held steady, stirring the coals with his words. He stroked his erection. "Do you want *this*?" he asked. His rush quelled my fear of his size. I wasn't mute, though his rush made me feel that way. I'd never been this aroused. All thought had been reduced to a single desire.

I raised my hips up off the bed, silently begging for him. He crawled forward, one arm beside my head, the other positioning his erection between my legs. I felt the tip of him press inside me and all the air in my lungs left on a moan I couldn't control.

"That's it," he said. The intensity of his rush subsided when he closed his eyes. He pushed in and my insides protested the stretch, gripping his length rather than letting him pass. He breathed through his mouth. "Jesus, Em," he said, pulling back. He pushed again, and again my insides clutched him. James felt the barrier of my physical protest and took control. "Look at me," he said, and like an automaton, I did. He pulled me back into his rush and my arousal soared. "Relax," he cooed and my body obeyed. He thrust into me, bumping his pelvis into mine and holding it there, letting me adjust to the size of him.

"You okay?" he asked, searching my face.

"Yes," I said, stretching out the "sss" as he pulled back all the way then slowly slid back in. The vein that ran down the side of his neck throbbed. He moved tortuously slow. I pushed my hips up to speed our rhythm. "Don't tease," I said, and it was like my words were the match to his fuse.

He pulled back and slammed forward, rocking my world. "Do you feel that?" he said, driving his erection home. "That's me," he said, pulling out and slamming back in. "No one's been this deep inside you, Emelynn." He was an egomaniac, but damn, he felt good. He picked up a punishing rhythm and each time he connected with that intensity, he jerked me up another rung of a ladder to a climax I thought might kill me. I'd die happy at the end of it, that much I knew. When he finally brought me to the brink, the only thing I remembered was screaming his name as he pushed me over the precipice of the most intense orgasm I'd ever experienced.

Maybe I wasn't the buy-me-a-puppy type after all.

I awoke some time later, alone, tangled in the sheets. Had James left? Surely not, I thought, pulling free of the sheet. I walked into the living room and found him, fully dressed, beer in hand, sitting on the sofa gazing out to the Pacific.

"Hey," I said, sitting beside him. "Are you okay?" I tucked my feet under my butt and hugged my arms around my nakedness. He didn't look okay. Had he been crying? Not James, I thought and then felt the weight of the realization that he had. What the hell was going on? What had happened?

"I'm fine," he said, taking a sip of the beer. It was almost empty. "Couldn't sleep."

"I don't think you're fine," I said, wading into water I didn't realize was way over my head.

He looked at me with a depth of contempt that made me cringe. "What—you screw me once and now you're the expert?"

His callous words felt like a kick in the gut. The pain was immediate and intense. My fight or flight reaction was instant: run.

"You think you know me?" His lip curled in a snarl.

Who was this man? I didn't know him at all, did I? I was naked and he'd flayed me. I retreated, standing up then backing away until I could safely turn and run for the bedroom.

"I'm sorry, Emelynn," he shouted behind me. "Ah fuck. Emelynn, I'm sorry."

I slammed the door and fell back against it. This was a colossal mistake. Sleeping with James was possibly the worst decision I'd ever made. I didn't know James any better than I'd known Jackson or Case. How the hell had I let this happen . . . again? When was I going to learn to trust my instincts? I could now tick the *common whore* experience box on my next job application.

"Emelynn," he called through the bedroom door, banging his fists. "I'm sorry. Please. Let me explain."

My insides crawled like I'd swallowed a mouthful of cockroaches. "Go away, James." I turned the lock on the door. "Just go away."

I couldn't shake the look of cold contempt I'd seen on his face. His cruel words repeated in my mind. I was too hurt to ask why. The front door opened and banged closed. I crawled back into bed and cried myself into a stupor.

Chapter Ten

S leep pulled me under like a drug. In waking, I experienced a micro-second of blissful happiness; that tiny space of time that holds the promise of a fresh new day, before the reality set back in and the freight train hit once more.

I knew that microsecond well. I'd lived it many times before, in the mornings after my father died; the mornings after I'd fallen from the sky and woken in the hospital; the mornings after I'd been shot and learned that Jackson was never coming for me; and the mornings after the skin had been whipped off my back. The wallop to my stomach was always the same. I curled into a ball and rolled onto my side, wrapping my arms tightly around my knees.

James. Thank god, it was just the once. I turned onto my back and stared at the ceiling. Maybe years from now, I'd think that was the best sex I'd ever had. Right now it just hurt. He'd used me, and I'd let him. Damn it! I knew he'd been looking for an easy lay. What the hell was wrong with me that I'd cave in with a few lies, a bit of sweet talk? *Open your eyes*, he'd said. Well, my eyes were wide fucking open now.

I crawled out of bed and steeled myself then unlocked the bedroom door and opened it. There was no sign of James. I went to the bathroom. His Dopp kit was gone. I checked the guest room. His bag was gone, too. He'd taken what he wanted and left. Bastard!

I'd need to change the locks, I thought, heading back to the kitchen. And the security code. There were instructions somewhere around here. I'd dig them out later. Right now, I wanted coffee, though I'd be damned if I was going to use James's new machine.

I turned into the kitchen to put the kettle on—and jerked to a stop. A bouquet of flowers lay on the kitchen counter hidden by the fridge. A card on top cried out to be opened. I veered away avoiding it and put the kettle on to boil.

My anger prodded me to fling the bouquet off the deck, but my conscience wouldn't let me. The flowers were innocent. When the kettle boiled, I poured the steaming water over the tea bag in my favourite mug. While it steeped, I took a shower and debated the flowers' fate.

Afterwards, I dressed in jeans and a sweater, removed the tea bag from the mug and poured in a healthy dose of milk. I slipped on my flip-flops, opened the patio door and crept down the stairs to the beach. It was a dull day, but at least it wasn't raining.

My hair, wet in the cool air, chilled me. The tide was out, leaving several sandstone slabs exposed. I sat on the stone and stretched my legs. Crows cawed noisily overhead and the sharp smell of salt air hung heavy in the light breeze. I wrapped my hands around the warm mug of tea, comforting myself in the familiar ritual.

Malcolm was coming by tomorrow. I'd been looking forward to re-starting my fitness regimen for weeks now.

Molly was pregnant and getting married—in Vegas, no less. That was something else to look forward to.

And Mason and Stuart were planning a party. Not that I was looking forward to it, but it was a distraction and I was happy for that.

My life was all about distractions this morning. How pathetic.

Falling into bed with James was a mistake, and a big one. His reaction had hurt, but it wouldn't kill me. Maybe if I'd let him explain himself last night, then thinking about him now wouldn't feel like a knife twisting in my heart. Deep down, I knew he didn't think of me as an easy lay. I could have said no. I should have gone with my initial gut reaction. Could've, should've, would've . . . as they say. It was all moot now.

I sat up and guzzled my tea. I wouldn't wallow: I was stronger than that. Hell, he'd left me flowers. That was more than the last two guys had done. I brushed sand off my jeans and headed back to the house. Inside, I rummaged in the cupboard and found a heavy-bottomed vase. When I was done arranging them, the sunflowers, gerbera daisies, verbena, roses and lilies looked beautiful. I moved them from the kitchen counter to the bookcase and finally settled on the coffee table.

The card sat on the table, unopened. I walked around it most of the morning, changing the sheets, doing laundry, cleaning the bathroom and finally vacuuming. By noon, I'd run out of immediate distractions and sat down on the sofa contemplating the card. What could he possibly have to say after last night? I steeled my nerves and slid the card out of its envelope. On the cover, a very sorry looking English bulldog with drooping jowls and a serious underbite looked into the camera.

I'm sorry, Emelynn. I should never have taken you to bed. I knew it was wrong—more than wrong—it was unforgivably selfish. I was jealous of Dean, I suppose—as if that's an excuse. It isn't.

The truth is, I have nothing to offer. My life is not my own, nor will it ever be. I work in a dangerous job with dangerous people. I don't want kids and anyone I get close to becomes a target. I don't want to put you in that position. This is not a life I would ask anyone to share.

Last night was a slice of heaven I'd gladly repeat, if only the inevitable parting from you wouldn't hurt so much.

You won't see me again, but I'll keep an eye on you from a distance. I'm sorry. Stay safe.

Affectionately,
James

"Coward!" Last night's heartache flared.

I couldn't stay in the cottage; I needed air. Grabbing my purse, I tore down the hall, locked the door behind me and jumped into my little red MGB. I headed up to Deacon Street, past the strip and found myself sitting outside Molly's apartment. I pulled my phone out of my purse, slapped on my happy face and called her.

Today's distraction would be playing maid of honour. Molly gladly abandoned her laundry in exchange for a day of bridal dress shopping. We headed to South Granville Street to a bridal salon she'd already been in touch with that had all three of the gowns on her shortlist. They were happy to accommodate us on a slow Sunday. The irony of my best friend trying on wedding dresses the day after I'd been dumped wasn't lost on me.

Molly looked fabulous in all of them, but she was clearly drawn to the number with a bolero-style jacket. The floor-length gown was strapless and completely plain except for a line of pearl buttons down the back. But the jacket—now that was something. It was made of stiff lace with a high collar and closed with three buttons down the front. The tight sleeves ended in a point at the middle finger with a row of tiny buttons at the wrist. The train, made of the same lace, was attached to the jacket. It trailed on the floor for a few feet behind the dress. It looked stunning on her. It didn't even need alterations.

We drove back to Summerset with the giant white bag overflowing the back seat of the car. It looked like we'd captured Casper the Ghost. I dropped her off at her apartment and headed home.

By eight, it would be dark enough to fly, and that was the only distraction that could come close to restoring my serenity. The nights were getting longer, but they were also getting cooler. Happily, I'd recently discovered Mountain Equipment Co-op, or Mec as it was known locally. They carried outdoor gear and clothing perfectly suited to flying. I'd even found a wind-proof head wrap. In short order, the evidence of my credit card's workout lay strewn across my bedroom. It looked like there'd been an explosion in a garment factory.

The chime of the doorbell interrupted me. Immediately, I thought of James. But no, it wouldn't be James. Not anymore.

I got up and headed down the hall to check the peephole. Crap. It was my favourite cop, Detective Jordan. I really wasn't up for dealing with him tonight.

I exhaled and opened the door. "Detective Jordan." He stood six-two with his brush cut making up the top inch. I couldn't decide if he was going for mobster hit man, or frustrated security guard.

"Ms. Taylor. Are you avoiding me?" His deep voice resonated.

"I beg your pardon?"

He pulled a business card out from the door frame where it had been jammed and held it up in his thick fingers like a prize. "My card," he said, and handed it to me. Scrawled on the back was *Call me.*

"I didn't see it."

"You would if you'd turned on your porch light. I didn't think I'd find you home."

Too bad he hadn't taken the hint and stayed away. I reached around the corner and flipped on the switches for the porch light and the front hall. "Better?"

"Much. May I come in?"

I held the door open and closed it behind him. He was a sturdy man in his late 30's or early 40's. He wore the same tired jacket he'd worn since the first time I'd met him, the one with the bulge under his left arm that gave away his shoulder holster. He might as well have worn a neon sign with an arrow, *Gun goes here*.

"What were you doing here in the dark anyway?"

"Sleeping."

"Hmm," he said, his tone skeptical.

I turned on the kitchen light and directed him to the dining-room table, then passed behind him and turned on the lamps in the living room. He was flipping through his spiral notepad when I returned to the table.

"What do you know about a website called Infinity?"

And so it begins, I thought, barely stifling the urge to shake my head. "It's a message board."

"You've been on it?" I'd bet he knew damn well I'd been on it.

"I checked it out. Why?"

"It's a new lead."

"In the Wrights' case or mine?"

His dark, deep-set eyes darted and his reaction gave him away. He hadn't thought of that. Point for me. "Maybe both. What's the purpose of this message board?"

It was kind of fun putting him on edge. "I don't know. Looks like some kind of game to me. Why do you say 'Maybe both'?"

"Just a hunch. How'd you learn about Infinity?"

"A friend sent me an email with the password."

"Which friend?" he poised his pen, ready to scribble my answer.

"Avery Coulter," I answered with fingers crossed that James had followed through on his plans to make Infinity look like a fantasy game site.

"Have you passed the information on to anyone else?"

"No. The site wasn't that interesting."

Detective Jordan flipped his notepad closed and tucked it away. "Thank you, Ms. Taylor," he said, and stood.

"That's all?"

"For now."

I walked him to the front door. He turned back at the edge of the porch. "Tell James I said welcome to the team, would you?"

I stood there dumbfounded, but managed to squeak out, "Sure," before he got in his car and drove away. I locked the door and turned off the lights then headed back to my bedroom determined to drive James from my thoughts.

My new gear felt great: lightweight, waterproof and as flexible as a second skin. I'd never blended into the night so well. My hair and neck were covered and the gloves Mason had given me kept my fingers warm. The only white showing was the bit of my face not covered by my Ryders. I stole out of the cottage and headed south.

When I could no longer see the neighbours' lights, I stopped and caught my breath. The tide was almost in. Waves broke in a low chorus on the rocks where tiny crabs scavenged for food. They clamoured around my feet forcing me to take care not to step on them. I closed my eyes and reached for my crystal. Its warm energy pulsed through me like a live current. I let it build, enjoying the incredible feeling of strength and power that it gave me. Lingering thoughts of James and the detective melted away with the twist of my torso, which released me from my bonds with the earth. I soared up over the treetops and into Sunset Park.

It was odd not feeling the breeze through my hair, but infinitely warmer. Quieter too without the wind in my ears. I dipped up and down following the contour of the treetops. The trail to the lighthouse was below and I circled a small clearing above it with caution. The last thing I needed was to be spotted, but the path below was empty.

I took a swan dive into the clearing, levelling out a metre above the footpath and then flew headlong above it. It was a roller coaster track and a test of my agility. I conformed to the twists and curves, and boldly reached down to tap the largest of the careless roots that grew across the path. The next break in the tree canopy was my exit. I timed it perfectly, shot up and cleared the top of the trees. I poured on speed and blew past the lighthouse straight out over the Pacific.

The rush of speed, the thrill of flight, were happy addictions. I slowed and glided a leisurely circle around the lighthouse then dipped down and flew within arm's reach of the surf all the way home.

I didn't bother to change out of my flying clothes before I poured myself a glass of wine. I took my usual seat out on the deck and thought about Dean. There was no comparison between Dean's version of freedom and mine. We really did live in two different worlds. I may not have liked what James said about me and Dean, but he was right; I would hate the deception game I'd have to play if I got involved with

Dean. But if my only possibilities for romance were other Fliers, then my choices were alarmingly limited. Maybe I needed to invest in a quality vibrator. I giggled at the thought, downed the rest of my wine and went to bed.

I was up early, dressed and stretched by the time Malcolm wheeled his bicycle around to the front of the garage. He had a lean, runner's physique. It was drizzling, but the moisture would feel good in about fifteen minutes when we were warm from our run. Malcolm's tight afro sprung free from his helmet as if the tiny curls had never been restrained. He was soft-spoken, but not shy. Earnest is how I'd describe him.

I hadn't seen Malcolm since the kidnapping. He'd alerted the police when I failed to show up for our workout. Saying thank you felt grossly inadequate. I reached up and hugged him close. After what he'd done for me, he would never be just my trainer. He was way up at the top of my best-friends-in-the-world list and those friends got hugs.

"Are you sure you're ready for this," he said, returning my hug with a little less enthusiasm. Maybe my hug was a bit over the top.

"I'm ready. You can't believe how ready. Come on—let's go." I started jogging backwards away from him, and he instantly started after me with a smile so genuine it lit up his face. We headed into the park and without another word, he put me through my paces. We hit the trails at a slow jog then interspersed sprints of increasing duration throughout the run.

I'd flown over the park a number of times since my kidnapping, but I'd not run the trails. The only time I'd even ventured in was that first week I was home. That was the week the covey decided to use Sunset Park for a game of laser tag. Participating at that stage of my recovery wasn't an option, but Victoria gave up her place beside Avery so I could help him at the command station instead.

That was a fun night—probably more so because of the threat of being discovered. I'm sure the authorities wouldn't take kindly to our antics if they'd found us. In fact, we probably needed a permit to play laser tag in a public park. Hell, if they saw the life-like guns we used, they'd probably arrest us.

I remember being mesmerized by the pinprick beams of red light that flicked wildly through the air, bouncing off the tree trunks and flashing through the foliage. If I caught a glimpse of a red dot trained on someone, I immediately checked Avery's equipment for the beep that registered a hit. The trees proved an interesting challenge for the covey and that made it great training. If we ever had to do it for real, to protect one of us, we'd be ready. Given recent events, my covey's dedication to tactical training wasn't overkill.

"Five K—not bad," Malcolm announced, checking his sports watch at the end of our workout. "Next week we'll be up over six." I'd regularly run between eight and ten K before, but it would take time to rebuild my stamina. We walked our cool-down and stretched out.

"I'll see you Wednesday morning," he said, heading to his bicycle.

When he was out of the driveway I headed in for a shower. Afterwards, I phoned Avery to invite myself over. I needed to tell him about Detective Jordan's visit, but I also wanted Avery's take on James's plan for muddying Infinity's user trail.

Avery had a pot of tea ready when I arrived and poured two steaming mugs. We sat at his kitchen table and I filled him in on what I'd learned from Detective Jordan.

"James gave me the heads-up yesterday," he said, answering my question. "I've already touched base with the covey. We're ready." He nibbled a double-stuffed Oreo. "It's a good plan if he can pull it off. Of course, now that he's on their task force, it might be easier for him."

"How did he arrange that anyway?" I asked, curious.

"I have no idea. Our James is a man of mystery, but at least he's resourceful."

Our James . . . not anymore, I thought sadly. But Avery didn't need to know about me and James. Just thinking about him hurt more than I wanted to admit. James had once warned me that everyone had secrets. Perhaps he was talking about himself. What secrets did James hide? Was it a secret that made him run? Then again, maybe I didn't want to know. I would miss him but, right now, I couldn't stand to have him near me.

"Speaking of resources," Avery smirked, pleased with his segue. "I've finished deciphering the Reynolds anthology."

"All of it?"

"Every last page."

"Did you learn anything new?"

"Nothing striking, though I suppose it was a surprise to learn that Fliers can relinquish bits and pieces of their gift. That's probably how that Dowling character picked up his kinetic touch."

"I hope whoever gifted it to him did it voluntarily. Some days I think the Tribunal wasn't entirely misguided in rounding up those anthologies."

"They certainly have proven dangerous in the wrong hands, haven't they? But that's always been the curse of knowledge. In the wrong hands, it's a weapon. But I'm not convinced that keeping people in the dark is an improvement, no matter what the cost."

"Maybe," I said, pondering his words.

A deep rumble shook the glass in the French door that separated us from his back garden. Avery and I looked at one another in wonder. Thunderstorms were a relative rarity in this part of BC. I glanced outside, hopeful for a glimpse of lightning. Fat drops of rain began hitting the deck outside the door and quickly became a pattering torrent. A bright flash lit up the southern sky followed by another crack of thunder, louder this time.

We pulled our chairs around to get a better view of the garden and watched the storm while we finished the plate of Oreos. The worst of the thunder had passed by the time I left. The smell of ozone was thick in the air when I got in my car and pulled away from the curb. Brown and yellow leaves floated on the small stream of runoff that ran down the street's gutter.

The steady rainfall put me off flying. Instead, I worked on Rumbles's paperwork puzzle until I grew too tired to make sense of it. The rain had settled into a light drizzle by the time I slid between the sheets. I kissed my fingertip and pressed it to the glass over my father's face in the frame beside my bed. "Good night, Dad." Jeannette's necklace was still draped across the frame. I straightened the crystal case that hung from the white-gold chain, then rolled over and went to sleep.

Chapter Eleven

The storm returned in the dead of night. My sleepy subconscious registered a thundering boom. Shattering glass jolted me awake. An angry crash froze me in place. That wasn't a storm. The smoke detector shrieked to life, jarring me. I jumped out of bed and crossed to the open door. My mind couldn't make sense of the flames that ran along the floorboards chasing a stream of liquid. Another explosion of glass preceded a missile that scudded off the living room wall.

I slammed my bedroom door closed and watched the bedroom's patio door dissolve into a crackled wave of glass. An arc of blue flame streaked across the bed where moments ago, I'd been sleeping. The curtains billowed then flapped madly against the broken glass. I watched in stunned silence as the dancing fabric roared up in flames. Dense, acrid smoke rolled across the ceiling. Flames licked at the top of the nightstand and comprehension finally broke through my daze. I lunged for my father's photograph, squeezed my crystal and rushed the broken glass, ghosting out of there to escape the flames that whooshed behind me.

But I wasn't prepared for the stiff onshore breeze that swirled me around, pushing me over the top of the cottage and into the branches of the fir tree at the edge of the property. The wind tugged at bits of my ghosted form while I helplessly watched the horror unfold before me. Bright orange and yellow flames, some tinged with blue and green, licked out of the cottage windows. The smell of smoke was thick on the air. Bursts of breaking glass punctuated the growing roar of the fire.

Sirens cut through the air, still blocks away. A gust of wind caught me and pushed me straight through the big fir tree. I tumbled across the road and became lodged in the foot of the berm of thick vegetation that grew alongside the park. The view from this vantage point was no less horrific. A large fire truck screamed into my driveway and firemen crawled out of it like ants. They dragged thick udon noodle hoses across the lawn. A second truck parked in front of me, blocking my line of sight. Fortunately, it also blocked the wind and I was able to gather myself together.

I drifted up over the top of the truck, where the wind caught me again and blew me through the trees, deeper into the park. I felt power-less. I couldn't help and now I couldn't even see what was happening. But I could hear. The sirens multiplied but as loud as they were, they didn't drown out the roar and the unsettling crackle of the fire. I screamed my frustration to the wind.

Desperation worked against me. I needed to re-form and was com-pletely incapable of forcing it. The one thing abundantly clear was that I needed to stay out of the wind. The forest was safest. I settled at the foot of a big cedar and waited for sanity to return. The bellowing sirens were too much. I tucked my head down and tightly covered my ears with my forearms. It didn't help. Maybe this was just a horrible nightmare. Maybe if I went back to sleep it would be gone when I woke up. I curled into a ball clutching my father's photo and let exhaustion take me away.

The sky was black when I woke, the smell of smoke hung thick in the air. I knew without opening my eyes that the nightmare was real. At least I had re-formed. I sat up and looked down at my ivory nightshirt, now streaked black and grey. Thank god my father's photograph was still intact. I brushed the debris from the frame.

Muted voices drifted through the trees. I didn't want to go out there, but I had to. My eyes needed to confirm what I knew in my heart. I stood and straightened my nightshirt then smoothed my hair. The pungent stench of singed hair reached up to my nostrils. I squared my shoulders and compelled myself to place one foot in front of the other. Pale, pre-dawn light filtered through the trees at the edge of the forest.

I scanned the property from the cover of the park. An odd calm enveloped me. Ringing in my ears dampened ambient sound. I walked out of the forest and into a waking dream.

Police cars were parked askew. An ambulance had veered off the driveway leaving deep ruts in the lawn. Those would have to be patched, I thought. One fire truck remained, its hose snaked along the ground underneath the magnolia tree. Strangers milled about the lawn.

I skirted the cars in the driveway and walked up the side lawn to the left, where the garage stood. I stepped onto the apron in front and panned right. The scene before me made no sense. A cloudy sky loomed where the cottage should be. A yellow-clad firefighter stood between me and a smouldering mound of blackened rubble, watering it like a garden. On some level of consciousness, I knew that the rubble was what was left of the cottage, but I felt compelled to keep going, to find the familiar front door and through it, my home, my sanctuary.

The firefighter in the yellow slicker turned toward me, gesturing wildly. Was he pointing at my feet? They were dirty, I knew that, but I'd scrub them before I went to bed.

A tall man stepped in front of me. I looked up. His lips moved, but no sound came out. He let me push him aside and I continued to the front door. Where was it?

The tall man came back and draped a blanket around my shoulders. I stared down at the dark grey fabric then loosened a corner and cleaned my father's picture. I smiled my thanks to the man and stepped around him. I was searching for something—what was it? I paused and the tall man stepped into my path and scooped me up in his arms. That felt nice. I rolled my head against his chest and had a flash of recognition of his worn jacket. I reached my hand to the lapel. It was soft. I closed my eyes and melted away.

I came to in the ambulance. It was either the wail of its siren or the fact that I was freezing cold that brought me around. The oxygen mask was suffocating, but I couldn't move to dislodge it. The woman who sat beside me saw my panic and lifted the mask away. I inhaled deeply and glanced down at my mummified body. "It's all right, Emelynn. You're going to be fine. We're taking you to the hospital. You just rest."

Despite the blankets they'd piled on top of me, I couldn't stop shivering. The siren cut off and moments later the back doors opened wide, letting in blinding light and a wall of noise. The gurney I lay on was quickly extracted and wheeled indoors.

"Female, 22, BP's improving—eighty-eight over fifty, name's Emelynn Taylor," said the young woman from the ambulance, to someone I couldn't see.

"Bay three," another voice sang out and my gurney was on the roll again. The smooth ride came to an abrupt stop and a dozen hands started unravelling the mountain of blankets. After the last layer was removed, I understood why I couldn't move; I'd been strapped to the gurney. The straps came off and the grey blanket was peeled away. I was left in my nightshirt, shaking uncontrollably, and then heaven descended in the form of a heated flannel blanket. Another one was piled on top of that and some angel tucked it in all around me. Ever so briefly, I closed my eyes.

"Emelynn, we're going to transfer you now." Had I fallen asleep? The oxygen mask was back in place and an oxygen sensor dangled from my index finger. Hands reached beneath me and on the count of three, I landed on another heaven-sent warm blanket.

Hurried footsteps approached and I heard Avery's voice. "Emelynn?" He rushed around into my line of sight. A nurse called out what I knew were my vitals, but all I saw was Avery's smiling face looking more relieved by the second. "I am so happy to see you." He stroked my head. "You're going to be all right, Emelynn, just fine."

He pulled the mask away when I started to speak. "It's gone, Avery. The cottage is gone."

"I know, sweetie. I'm so sorry. It's been a terrible shock." His hand was soothing, comforting. "But you made it out and that's all that's important."

"I had to ghost, Avery. The fire was everywhere. I had no choice . . ."

"Shh," Avery said, cutting me off, shaking his head. "Let's not talk about that right now. We're going to put you on an IV for a few hours to help get your blood pressure back up. You okay with that?" I nodded. He pressed his forefinger to his lips then leaned in and whispered, "Shh."

Yes, that was right. I nodded, remembering now. We mustn't talk about that.

He straightened up. "Go ahead," he said to the nurse. "I've got to make some calls but I'll be right back."

The nurse pricked the back of my hand, taped the needle in place and started the IV bag of clear fluids flowing.

Avery came back and pulled up a chair beside me. "You already look better. How are you feeling?"

"Numb," I said, unable to process the enormity of what had happened.

"I'm so sorry about the cottage, Emelynn." A tear rolled down my cheek and Avery rubbed it away. He smiled my favourite crooked smile. "You really can't be doing that when we're trying to rehydrate you."

I bit my upper lip and laughed, despite the weight on my chest.

"I told them you'd made it out, but they wouldn't take my word for it. They combed through the place for hours expecting to find you on the well-done side."

"Stop trying to make me laugh," I said, and another tear escaped.

"You saved a photo of your dad."

"Yeah. It's all that's left. The cottage is gone."

"I know. I'm sorry. And I won't tell you that it's only a house, because I know it was more than that to you. But I am glad you're not hurt. We could have lost you along with it."

"Dr. Coulter," a nurse called, pulling the curtain aside. "There's a Mr. Aucoin here to see you."

"Thanks, Joan." Avery jumped up and returned a minute later with Gabe in tow.

Gabe Aucoin stood shorter than Avery, but was in the same fifty-plus age bracket. He was a lawyer and a member of our covey. Gabe came around to the head of the bed and squeezed my shoulder. "How are you holding up, Emelynn?"

I replied automatically. "I'm fine," I said, which I was anything but. I was, however, thinking clearly enough to wonder why he was here. Did I need a lawyer?

"She'll be okay in a few hours," Avery clarified. "It's nothing serious."

"Avery, what's going on? Am I in trouble?" I asked.

"Not at all. Do you know what happened last night?" Avery pulled up a chair beside me and motioning for Gabe to take the one on the other side of the bed. Gabe pulled off his black cap and smoothed his grey hair.

I thought back to last night and remembered the flames running along the wood planking, as if it were happening before my eyes. I saw the bedroom curtains blow out the window in a whoosh of orange fire, and broken glass all around me.

"I think someone set fire to my house."

"Did you see anyone?" Gabe asked.

"No." Last night was still a bit of a blur. "Something woke me up. I thought it was thunder, but then the alarm went off. I saw something heavy hit the living room wall. Another missile came in through the bedroom window."

Gabe exchanged concerned glances with Avery. "Maybe it's the best place for her, Avery."

"What are you talking about?" Their expressions alarmed me. "What's the best place for me?"

"The police want you to go with them," Avery said.

"Why? I didn't do anything wrong."

Avery rested his hand on my shoulder. "Emelynn, I don't want to frighten you, but someone tried to kill you last night. They nearly succeeded. The police want you under their protection."

My eyes darted from Avery to Gabe then back to Avery. They couldn't be serious. "Let me go home with you, Avery." I'd lost everything. I couldn't lose him too.

"Avery can't keep you as safe as the police can, Emelynn." Gabe looked apologetic saying it.

"Avery, please. Not tonight . . . or today," I pleaded. "I couldn't stand it."

Avery looked to Gabe.

"It's up to you," Gabe said. "For now at least." He turned to me. "Give it some thought, Emelynn. The police can protect you."

"Thanks, Gabe, I'll think about it tomorrow, okay? Just not right now." I turned to Avery. "Please?" He nodded and I heaved a sigh of relief. "When can we leave?"

"As soon as your blood pressure is back within normal range. A few hours."

The hour hand on Avery's wall clock crawled past noon. Avery placed a bowl of chunky tomato soup on the kitchen table in front of me. The hospital had let me wear a set of scrubs home. *Home*—the thought was out of my head before the word resonated. Home was gone. The smell of smoke, a bitter reminder, clung to me like I'd bathed in it.

"This is good, Avery, thanks."

"It's one of my better efforts," he said, swallowing his own spoonful. "Victoria's coming by with some clothes for you."

The enormous extent of my loss hadn't yet sunk in. There was nothing left. No clothes, no toiletries, no shoes. "Ah, damn it," I said, thinking of yet another thing.

"What?"

"My GPS! Again. I've already replaced two of them. And my computer. Oh hell, I haven't even got a phone anymore. I have no credit cards, no passport . . . no ID of any kind, so no way to get cash any time

                                                    JP McLean

soon, either." A bureaucratic nightmare of epic proportions loomed on my immediate horizon. It felt overwhelming.

I'd been on the phone with my mother for a half-hour while Avery warmed the soup. Avery had called her from the hospital so she'd known I was okay even before she'd heard about the fire. I hadn't told her it was arson. That fact was an unnecessary long-distance worry and it hadn't been officially confirmed yet. We had house insurance, but Gabe had warned me that arson complicated things. The insurer would likely hold any potential payout pending their own and the official investigation.

"Your car's still there," Avery said, offering me something positive to latch onto.

"It is. You're right—the garage wasn't touched, was it?" My eyes welled up at the thought of my father's little red MGB tucked safely inside the garage. "But the keys are gone," I said, deflating again.

"I'll bet Cheney can look after that small detail for you."

"You're right. I'm sure he can." I settled back down.

"Emelynn, your emotions are going to be all over the map for a few days. Don't let it throw you. It takes time to adjust to a loss as big as this."

"I do feel a bit like a yo-yo. Would you mind if I went to lie down?"

"Go ahead. You need the rest," he said, clearing our bowls.

I took the stairs to the second floor and flopped onto the queen bed in the room with the soft butter-yellow walls, the same room I'd recovered in after the shooting. The heavy damask drapes were already closed, giving the room a twilight feel. I should have showered but I was too tired. I crawled between the sheets cried some more then fell fast asleep.

I knew it had been more than a nap by how groggy I felt waking up. My night vision had kicked in; the blue hue gave it away without even opening the drapes. I slid my toes into the hospital flip-flops and used the bathroom before seeking out Avery downstairs.

Hushed conversation wafted down the hall from the kitchen. I pushed open the door and the conversation came to a halt. I'd never seen so many people in Avery's kitchen. At a glance, I knew most of the covey was here. Unexpected relief swamped me. One by one, they turned their solemn faces in my direction. Avery stood at the island sink. Sydney leaned against the counter behind him and the others sat around the table, which was covered with a motley collection of teacups and beer bottles. My smile cracked as emotions overwhelmed me.

Eden jumped from her chair and rushed at me, clinging like a burr. She was pixie-sized at barely five foot two, with a shock of short red hair spiked to perfection. Alex was right behind her, folding us both into his embrace. His strong arms were a comfort as he held us tight. Eden Effrome was the sister I never had. She flew with the grace of a prima ballerina. Her live-in love, Alex Klause, was an equally impressive Flier with his agility and strength. Eden and I immediately started crying and no amount of shushing from Alex stopped the waterworks.

Eventually, Eden let go, and Victoria and Danny pulled me to the table and sat me down. Danny Thornton's springy dreads bounced when he plunked a Kleenex box in front of me with a roll of his eyes. It made me laugh and cry at the same time. Danny moved behind me, standing with his back to the French doors. He was a skilled fighter with martial arts training. I felt safe with him at my back.

"Deidra and Kate came by to see you too, but they had to get home to their kids," Sydney said, offering an apology that wasn't necessary. Deidra Lewis and Kate Dennison were elementary school teachers. Sydney Davenport's shiny jet-black hair flowed like silk, in a precision razor cut. Her mixed Asian heritage gave her an exotic edge. She was as beautiful as Victoria Lang, who now stood in Avery's arms. Victoria's long blonde hair was loose today, but she would look elegant without a hair on her head.

"You all came," I said. Tears welled once again.

"Jesus, Em. Of course we came," Alex said, sounding a bit offended.

"I'm sorry, Alex, it's just . . . god, it's good to see you guys." I looked around the room. This covey really was my family. I'd never felt it as acutely as I did right then. Not a bad collection of stalwart siblings for an only child, I thought, grateful and happy and feeling truly blessed.

They wanted to know what had happened. I filled them in as best I could. Avery filled in some other details, such as the fact that it was Detective Jordan who'd called him, which led to Avery putting the covey on alert.

Eventually, Danny tackled the elephant in the room. "Who could have done this?" he asked. I was thankful that he hadn't directed the question at me. It became our problem, not mine alone.

"Carson Manse," Eden offered immediately. It was the same answer I would have given. Carson and Rupert had threatened Eden when I was kidnapped. She had a fierce hate-on for him. I happily jumped all over that bandwagon.

"It wasn't him," Avery said. "His was the very first name I suggested, but Detective Jordan says Manse is still tucked into his bed at St. Matthew's. He hasn't moved."

"It must be one of the other Redeemers, then," Sydney said. "Maybe that guy who got away?"

"If the Redeemers know that Emelynn learned of their plan, any one of them could be responsible." As soon as the words were out of Victoria's mouth, she looked at me with apology. "I'm sorry, Emelynn, it's just a thought."

I shook my head dismissing her guilt. "I know." It wasn't as if all of these thoughts hadn't spent quality time in my own head over the past few hours.

Avery piped up again. "Detective Jordan thinks this was personal. He thinks it's someone who has a particular grievance with her."

"You're absolutely certain that Rupert is dead?" I asked.

"Yes," Avery said without hesitation. I'd asked that particular question before, in fact, on more than one occasion.

While we mulled over the possibilities, I saw a red dot flash across Victoria's sweater and smiled. It was perfect timing for comic relief. Who wasn't in the room, I wondered? The red dot disappeared then rested momentarily behind Victoria on Avery's shirt before disappearing again. Someone was having fun with one of our laser guns. "Where's Steve?" I asked, quickly scanning the room. Steve Elliott had features so ordinary he could hide in a crowd. "Or is that Gabe outside with the laser?" I asked, twisting around in my seat. I poked my head around Danny's torso to look outside. A pane of glass in the French door tinkled to the floor and a loud crack drew our attention to the far wall where a hole appeared in one of the kitchen cupboards.

There was a second of silence before the room erupted into madness. Danny tackled me from behind, shoving me roughly to the floor. I landed hard in a tangle with the chair and saw the heavy oak table tip up, its load of bottles and china sliding to the floor in an avalanche of crashing glass. A series of soft thwacks accompanied the noise of more broken window panes, and splinters of wood spewed from the table top and cupboards across the room. I struggled free of the chair and slithered on my back, away from the door. Danny clenched a hand firmly over my mouth. "Shh," he whispered in my ear. I hadn't realized I'd been screaming. He covered me with his body and shuffled us back farther behind cover of the wall.

A gunshot rang out and I flinched. This shot was different from the others. Danny shifted to look out the bottom corner of the French door. I looked around for Eden and Avery. The floor was littered with broken bits of chair and china. The smell of dust hung heavily in the air. Eden and Alex were crouched down against the wall on the other side of the French doors. I couldn't see Avery or Victoria. Hopefully, they and Sydney were safe behind the kitchen island.

Outside, another gunshot echoed and that was followed by a series of cracks and rustling that sounded like tree limbs breaking. The last sounds I heard were a muffled thud, followed by a rush of heavy boots.

As if by some silent mutual agreement, no one said a word. We hunkered down, still as the dead.

"Police," a male voice shouted. "Don't move, we're coming in," he warned loudly before turning the knob on the French door and pushing it into Danny's shoulder. Danny shifted out of the way, pulling me along with him. How had the police gotten here so fast? Bright lights flooded the back garden accompanied by shouting and rushing footfalls.

"Does anyone need medical assistance?" the constable asked, scanning the wreckage that used to be Avery's kitchen. There was a general straightening up and brushing off but, thankfully, no one was hurt.

At the officer's urging, Avery shuffled us all into his study. As soon as the constable retreated, Avery opened the drapes so we could see into the back garden. A figure, male from the look and bulk of his clothing, laid face down on the grass. Half a dozen people, some in uniform, some with thick body armour stencilled on the back with "Police," searched the garden. Waves of them seemed to come and go. I recognized Detective Jordan the moment he strode into the yard. He spoke at length with another man who wore a shoulder holster over a rugby shirt, probably another detective. The two of them crouched over the prone figure.

Flashing red and white lights beamed through from the front of the house and reflected off the study's walls. We waited like the condemned at the gallows. Outside, the scream of a siren silenced abruptly. We watched paramedics swarm the body on the lawn. We could see them turn him over, but their efforts ended without success a few minutes later and a sheet was pulled over the man's face.

Detective Jordan crunched through the glass on the kitchen floor and appeared at the door of Avery's study. His eyes scanned the room and stopped when they landed on me. "Ms. Taylor, will you please come with me?" I sighed and stood up. This was all on me, wasn't it?

"Emelynn, you're bleeding," Danny said, stopping me with a hand on my shoulder. I checked my arms and looked down my torso but couldn't see anything amiss. "Your back," he said. I hadn't felt the injury.

"Just a minute, Detective," Avery called, bolting into action. Avery pulled me into the ground-floor bathroom and lifted the back of the scrub to get a better look. "It's glass," he said, poking at some spots below my shoulder blades near my spine. "Victoria," he called out the door. "Will you get my bag?"

A moment later, a black bag was thrust through the door. Avery removed the offending shards with tweezers, irrigated the small wounds with saline and sprayed me with enough antibacterial wash to sterilize a small country. "You don't need stitches," he said, applying gauze and tape. He repositioned my now torn and bloodied scrubs and forcefully turned me around to face him.

"You need to take the police protection, Emelynn." His eyes radiated concern. "Whoever has you in their sights is off-the-charts crazy. I can't protect you or anyone else from this madness."

"You're right, Avery. I'm so sorry. I should never have come here." I'd put them all in danger for the sake of a few hours of comfort. If something had happened to one of them . . . the morbid thought trailed off in a wash of self-loathing.

He gave me a hard shake and pegged me with a stern glare. "This is not your fault. None of this is. Blame Carson Manse or the Redeemers or the goddamn Tribunal if it suits you, but you are not to blame."

I stiffened my spine. I knew that—on some level—but seeing the terrified look on his face and the horrible mess in his kitchen would not be easy to reconcile with this not being my fault.

Avery surrendered me to Detective Jordan who walked me into the back garden. I avoided eye contact with everyone else. I couldn't bear to see the fear in their faces.

"Are you okay?" the detective asked, positioning me at the head of the sheet-clad body. I nodded. "I'm going to show you this moron's face. You tell me if you recognize him. Okay?"

He stepped between me and the body. "Okay?" he repeated.

The detective was half a foot taller than me. I tilted my head. That jacket, I thought and reached out to touch the soft fabric. He was the one—the tall man at the fire—who carried me to the ambulance. I looked into his face. "Okay," I said.

He nodded and bent to pull the sheet away from the man's face.

"I don't know him," I said, taking in a middle-aged face with a thick nose.

"Look closely, Emelynn." I leaned over the body, taking in the greying stubble, the slack jowls. He'd be snoring, I thought, if he was breathing.

"I'm sorry, Detective. I don't know him."

"Okay," he said. He jerked the sheet back over the man's face and straightened up. "I know you'd prefer to stay here with your friends," he said, starting into a very un-Jordan-like pitch. "I understand that, but—"

"Save your breath, Detective," I said, cutting him off. "I'll come with you."

He cleared his throat. "Good. That's good." He frowned, momentarily confused. It wouldn't last. "Stay here. I'll be back in a minute." He went back inside. I lost track of time, but I was sure it was more than a minute later when he reappeared with a Burberry suitcase in hand.

"What's that?" I asked.

"Your friends collected some clothes for you."

"That was nice," I mumbled, not daring to look at them through the window. If I started crying now, I'd never stop. "Let's go," I said, walking briskly toward the side garden gate. Detective Jordan ran to catch up and unlatched the gate before I got to it.

He tucked me into the back seat of his brown, unmarked cruiser and pushed the suitcase in beside me. "Buckle up," he said, sliding into the driver's seat. I didn't bother.

When my father died, I got very good at deflecting sympathy. Most of it was contrived anyway, disingenuous. I developed a buffer. It was like a jacket that I pulled on to protect myself. Without it, the pain and tears would have devoured me. I hadn't used it in a very long time, but it was still there. I pulled it on, checked the fit and settled calmly into the back seat. Then I set my block firmly in place. Detective Jordan anxiously checked my face in the rear-view mirror. I turned my gaze to the side window.

He spoke briefly over his radio, but I wasn't listening. He drove into Vancouver, exited off the Cambie Street Bridge and pulled into an unmarked underground parking garage. Two security checks later, he stopped the car and got out. He opened the back door and offered me his hand. I shoved the suitcase toward him. He grabbed it by the handle then stood waiting for me. I emerged without his assistance and straightened my now filthy scrubs like they were a pantsuit befitting the Burberry bag.

We were buzzed through a door into an underground corridor and walked down the hall to an elevator. He hit the call button and shifted anxiously from one foot to the other. I stared at his feet, my calm re-enforced by my protective jacket. He saw me watching him and stopped the fidgeting. "Thank you," I said, as the elevator doors opened and I stepped inside. He followed and punched the number seven, then waved a security card by a reader that beeped its approval.

The woman who greeted us at the elevator wore a badge on the waistband of her slacks. "Emelynn," she said, catching my eye. "I'm glad you decided to come in. My name's Roberta." I gave her my standard smile. "Can I get you something to eat? A coffee, perhaps?" She was shorter than me and older, perhaps in her mid-thirties. Her hair was cut close to her head and neat.

"No, thank you. I'm fine," I said.

Her gaze darted to Detective Jordan, who shrugged. "All right then," she said. "Let's get you into some decent clothes." She took the suitcase from the detective and hustled me down a long corridor. "In here," she said, swiping her security card through a reader that beeped. The door clicked open. "No one can get in here without one of these." She held up her little white card like it was a magic pass to an exclusive club.

We stood in a large, rectangular room. On the far side, a bank of windows overlooked False Creek. They were darkened in the way that suggested they were probably mirrored on the outside. I could see the lights of boats twinkling in the distance.

An oval conference table and six chairs dominated the right-hand side of the room. The furniture was bare bones, steel and black vinyl. A scuffed-up whiteboard hung on the wall behind the table with a handful of markers and a dirty felt eraser lying in its aluminum chalk rail. To the left of the door was a sitting area. A black vinyl three-seater sofa sat against the wall. Separating it and two club chairs was a glass and steel coffee table.

"There's a bathroom with a shower through there," Roberta said, pointing to a door to the left of the sofa. She swung the Burberry suitcase onto the conference table. "Why don't you have a shower and get cleaned up. I'll come back in an hour or so. Okay?"

"Thank you," I said, and gave her another deflecting smile.

She backed out of the room and the heavy door clanged shut behind her. Had she locked me in here? I walked to the door and pushed down hard on the lever, shoving my shoulder into it. Damn it! She had. I reached for the light switch on the wall beside the door and flipped it off. The dark felt comforting; I had the advantage in the dark. I searched the room and quickly spotted a red blinking light from the surveillance camera in the corner. They hadn't even bothered to hide it. I pulled the bathroom door open and the blink of another camera flashed from behind the mirror. Jesus, a camera in the bathroom? Was that even legal?

Have a shower, she'd said—yeah, sure. I walked to the windows and watched the boats for a while, then lay down on the sofa and closed my eyes. They couldn't keep me here against my will. In fact, there was no restraint—no handcuff, no cage—nothing, that they or anyone else could use on me that would ever hold me against my will again. That fact calmed me. I didn't sleep, but I rested. It was still dark out when the knock came.

"Come in," I called, unamused by the charade.

The click of the lock gave away the card-carrying status of the entrant. I didn't bother to get up.

It was Detective Jordan. "Emelynn?" Light from the hall flooded the room.

I sat up. "Detective."

He flipped on the light. "You haven't changed." He said it like it was an accusation.

"Are you aware there's a security camera in the bathroom? I don't know about you, but I'd rather not have my naked ass all over the Internet."

He smiled despite himself. "Give me ten minutes. I'll have it turned off and then you'll have thirty minutes before they're turned on again. The task force is assembling and we need to debrief you."

"Me?" I asked.

"Thirty minutes," he said. "Max." Then he stepped out the door.

He could be thirty days for all I cared; I wasn't showering any place with a hidden camera. I flipped the light switch off again and went to the window to watch the boats bob in the distance.

CHAPTER TWELVE

I t hadn't been thirty minutes, but I heard the swipe of a security card and the heavy door's lock clicked open. I didn't bother to turn around—only the card-carrying elite were permitted in here.

I saw his reflection in the window in front of me as he approached. I wasn't thrown. I knew he'd be here.

"You're hurt," James said from inches behind me.

"Avery fixed me up," I said.

"Good. I'm glad." I could feel his breath on my neck. "I'm sorry about your cottage."

"Yeah, me too," I said, hearing a waver in my voice I didn't like.

He stepped close enough that I could feel the heat of his body through the thin scrubs. My block was rock solid. I watched with detachment as he raised his hands and caressed my upper arms. His strong hands soothed me, and I wanted nothing more than to lean back into him and let him help me through this, but that would spell my undoing on so many levels.

"Don't, please," I said, twisting out of his grasp. "I can't afford that right now." Our relationship was fractured—our friendship in pieces.

"What? A little comfort?" He looked hurt.

"No. You. I can't afford *you* right now."

"I'm right here, Em. Let me help."

"You said you'd keep your distance."

"Well, you're not doing a very good job of staying safe."

I rounded on him, anger welling up in me. "You bailed on me, James. You didn't even wait for the going to get tough. Hell, the sheets weren't even cold. You just ran for the door throwing excuses over your shoulder like bombs."

"Whoa!" he said, stepping back from me with his hands up like I was a grenade with the pin out. After a moment, he bowed his head, shaking it back and forth. "You're right," he said. "I should never have let you get under my skin. I knew it was wrong." He made eye contact and added, "I'm sorry—do you hear me? I'm sorry."

"What you are, is a coward." He flinched and it felt good to say that to his face.

"A coward!" Angry-James was back and it might have been small of me, but I found some satisfaction in it. I'd been angry since I'd read his note and a garbage heap of additional crap had been piled on since then. "You think I like having those Tribunal sons-of-bitches dictating my life? Putting me and my family in danger?"

I glared at him. "And you think my life's a picnic right now? Did you ever stop to consider that every one of us is in danger? You don't own that bailiwick, James."

"I have nothing to offer, Em. Nothing!"

"I wasn't asking for anything!" I ratcheted up my anger to meet his. "You're the one who threw out kids and expectations of . . . god knows what. That's your baggage, not mine."

The door banged open and we both jerked around, caught off guard. "What the hell's going on in here?" Detective Jordan bellowed. "We can hear you all the way down the hall."

"I'm out of here." James barrelled past the detective and out the door.

"You got a problem with lighting?" the detective said, flipping on the lights. "We're meeting in here in fifteen. Will you be ready?"

"Yeah, I'm great," I said, straightening my invisible flak jacket. I sat on the far side of the sofa away from the door and pulled my legs up, wrapping my arms around my knees to wait.

Fifteen minutes later, Detective Jordan knocked then held the door open and four more people marched in. They looked like they were being shown into the principal's office and this was the last place they wanted to be. Detective Jordan had ditched his jacket, but not his shoulder holster or gun. He made the introductions. "Emelynn Taylor, this is Matt Johnson, Dino Martinez and Carl Schaefer. Roberta Montgomery, you've already met." They each nodded in turn. All of them wore badges on their belts except for Dino who had no choice but to hang his on a chain around his neck; his belt was hidden by his overhanging gut. The door clanged shut. James was conspicuously absent.

I'd expected them to sit at the conference table; instead, they took seats beside me and in the club chairs opposite. Matt wheeled a chair over from the table.

Detective Jordan, who'd taken the club chair closest to me, leaned forward with his elbows on his knees. "The fire at your house was not an accident, Emelynn. It was arson. The accelerant used was gasoline. By the time the first fire truck arrived on the scene, the place was fully engulfed. The fire crews had no hope of saving the structure. They could only contain the fire."

"You were very lucky to get out of there alive," Roberta added with a reassuring smile from her seat beside me.

"Can you tell us what you remember from last night?" Matt asked.

I repeated the story I'd told Avery and Gabe.

"How did you get out of there?" Carl asked, looking perplexed.

I took a moment to look thoughtful. I found it helped with this particular lie. "I don't remember." Carl blinked owl eyes, as if he found that difficult to believe.

"Do you have any idea who could have done this, Emelynn?" Detective Jordan asked.

"You mean do I know who would want to kill me?" I asked, thinking it was important to be clear.

"There's little doubt that you were the target, so yes." Detective Jordan almost seemed sorry to confirm that.

"Carson Manse," I said definitively.

Matt flipped rapidly through his portfolio of notes. "No. It wasn't him. His alibi is solid."

"It was Carson Manse," I said again, not moved by the certainty of their words.

Detective Jordan rubbed a hand through his brush cut. "Look, I know Manse did unspeakable things to you, but he's out of commission. Is there anyone else you can think of who might have a serious bone to pick with you, a grudge, maybe someone you know who seems a little—I don't know—*off*?"

"It could have been the kidnapper who got away, but no one knows who that is." The detective sighed heavily. "There's no one else," I said. "I don't know that many people here."

I thought Detective Jordan's bowed head would fall off the way it wobbled back and forth. Before he could speak, Carl piped up. "The notes I read from your interview in the hospital said you thought that Manse might have belonged to some kind of cult." Carl either had a good memory or he'd read that just before coming in here. "What made you think it might have been a cult?"

"I suppose I was trying to make sense of why they'd kidnapped me. They kept going on about some crystal they thought I had." As I said the words, my stomach flipped. Where was Jeannette's crystal? Her necklace with the intricate white-gold case had been draped over my father's photo. Its loss felt like another violation.

"What is it?" Carl asked. "Did you remember something else?"

"No," I said, feeling my chest tighten. "I just thought of something else I lost in the fire, that's all."

Carl redirected me. "Do you think it was a crystal skull they were looking for? We know there's occult activity around those artifacts."

"I don't think so." This discussion was going nowhere. I didn't know who the other Redeemers were and no one else knew the identity of the one man who'd gotten away. There was no one else. "I want to see Carson Manse."

"How many times do you have to hear it?" Detective Jordan said. "It. Wasn't. Manse."

"Then indulge me. I want to see him with my own eyes."

Detective Jordan exhaled in exasperation. "Tell you what, I'll take you to see Manse, if you tell me everything you know about this Infinity message board."

"I already told you."

"What's the purpose of the board, Emelynn?" Detective Jordan was back to his bulldog routine.

"Again, I already told you: I thought it was some kind of game."

"I think you called it a fantasy game?"

"Not a very good one," I said. The other detectives had yielded the floor to Detective Jordan and I didn't like being his focus.

"You know what's interesting? It was only after you made that suggestion, that our IT guys found the hidden gaming icons." Something about the way Detective Jordan framed his questions, or maybe it was his insinuating tone, put me on edge. It felt like he was pointing his thick forefinger right at me.

"You know what else is interesting? Every single person whose disappearance we're investigating had either been on the Infinity site or knew someone who was. Including you. That board is a fault-line that runs from San Diego to Vancouver, and you're on it."

That was a surprise. He'd connected everyone? "Are you accusing me of something?"

"No. I'm saying there are too many coincidences where you're concerned and I don't believe in coincidences. You're in the middle of this. I think whoever is trying to get to you wants to shut you up. Why would someone want to shut you up, Emelynn? What is it you have on them?"

"Damn it, Detective, I don't know. Do you not think I would tell you if I knew?"

Roberta interrupted. "We're not accusing you of anything," she said, offering a soothing smile.

"That's not what it sounds like." Did I need a lawyer, I wondered? Maybe it was time for me to call Gabe.

"I'm sorry, Emelynn," Detective Jordan said, visibly softening. "You are not a suspect here, but you *are* a lead. The best one we have right now."

"You wouldn't be the first victim who didn't know why they'd been targeted." This reassuring tidbit came from Matt. "Having said that, the victim usually knows the perpetrator."

"You're the divining rod in this case right now," Carl said. "We think the people who are after you are connected to the disappearances."

"You want to use me to get to them?" I asked.

"No, but if they try again, we want to be there to intercept them. We can't do that without your cooperation."

"I'm not prepared to put anyone else in jeopardy."

"Neither are we."

"Good. Then I'll be happy to cooperate. As soon as I see Carson Manse with my own eyes."

"Emelynn—" Detective Jordan started.

"It's not negotiable," I said. "And I need my driver's licence. That's also not negotiable."

The detective slowly exhaled a resigned breath. "All right. I'll take you to see Manse myself—first thing in the morning."

He turned to the others. "We're done here." They each said their goodbyes and filed out the door. Detective Jordan stood last and walked over to grab my suitcase off the conference table. "You ready to go?"

"Go where?"

"We have a hotel room secured for you. And before you ask—there are no security cameras inside the room. There are plenty of others in the garage, the elevators and the hallways. You'll be safe." I liked the detective a lot better with his tough exterior cracked.

"I'm a little surprised you don't have safe accommodation right here. The place is big enough." The building was the size of an entire city block and had to be nine storeys high.

"We do. They're called holding cells. Would you prefer to spend the night here?"

That remark earned him a smirk.

"I'll see you at 9:00 a.m.," Detective Jordan said, closing the SUV's rear passenger door. Carl was in the driver's seat. Roberta and I had climbed into the back. The back windows were blacked out. Carl took us over the Cambie Street Bridge onto Smithe then turned up Hornby. I'd lost track of where we were by the time Carl turned into a back alley and made a sharp turn into an underground parking garage. The security arm lifted at our approach and we continued into the bowels of a large building. He pulled to a stop beside a dented door that opened almost immediately. Carl nodded to the man, who had opened it from the inside.

"I've got it from here," Roberta said, and Carl unlocked the SUV's doors. She came around to my side, took my suitcase then ushered me in through the pocked door. This did not look promising. We walked through a utilitarian hallway lined with a brigade of rolling pails, vacuums and floor polishers. A tired service elevator took us up to the twelfth floor.

Visions of the grungy Bailey Motel in Bodega Bay flitted through my mind. We got off the elevator, passed a row of cleaning carts and spilled into the corridor. We'd finally reached the public area of the hotel. I took in the carpet that muffled our footsteps and the subdued lighting that made me want to whisper. My accommodation was looking up. Roberta had the room's pass card in her hand before we got to the door and swiped it without missing a beat.

She entered the room ahead of me and disappeared. Was I supposed to stay here and wait for her? The notice on the back of the door told me we were in the Wedgewood Hotel. A red dot showed the room's location in relation to the nearest fire exit. The small bathroom to my left had no shower. My hopes nose-dived. A closet hid behind the door on the right. I stepped into what I expected to be the bedroom and gazed around a well-appointed sitting room. My hopes were restored at the sight of a fireplace. Heavy drapes covered a window on the far side of the room

"I think you'll be comfortable here," Roberta said, coming out of the adjoining room. "The bedroom and bath are through there." She pointed in the direction from which she'd come. "We have an officer stationed in the security room monitoring the cameras and I'll be patrolling."

"Thank you."

"Don't talk to anyone and don't leave the room." She handed me a business card. "If you need anything, phone this number. I'll arrange for whatever you need. Do you have any questions?"

"No. Thanks for all this."

"You're welcome. We want to get these guys off the street, Emelynn, and you're our best bet. Have a good night. We'll wake you at eight."

After she left, I pulled back the drapes in the sitting room. Hornby Street's one-way traffic rolled by below. In the bedroom, I found a king-sized bed, an upholstered foot bench and two wingback chairs. Its window had the same Hornby-Street view. The bathroom, almost as big as Jolene's, came with a shower and a separate, contoured tub. I reached over and turned on the water and emptied a mini-bottle of bubble bath. Vanilla and coconut scents mingled and wafted up on the first tendrils of steam.

I brushed my teeth with the complimentary toothbrush and examined my face in the mirror. A weary reflection stared back. My life had once again taken an irrevocable turn without warning. By now, I should have been better at dealing with these life-altering events, but no. Each blow knocked the wind out of me anew.

I couldn't reach the bits of taped gauze on my back so I left them and sunk beneath the suds. The little cuts stung but only for a second. The warm water relaxed me and I was finally able to wash away the smell of smoke that still clung to my skin like wax. I scrubbed my feet and washed my hair, feeling nubby singed ends that I'd have to trim.

Afterwards, I crawled into bed. Being clean and safe was a luxury I wouldn't take for granted any time soon. Thankfully, sleep stole me away before I could wallow in my loss.

The wake-up call came precisely at eight. I'd been sound asleep. "Good morning, Emelynn, it's Carl. Can I bring you some breakfast?"

I rubbed my eyes and yawned. I *was* hungry. "Yes, thanks, Carl." He took my order and warned me he'd be up in fifteen minutes.

My body felt stiff and sore. I got out of bed and pulled on the thick white Wedgewood robe. I walked into the bathroom and gagged when I caught a whiff of the smoky scrubs I'd stuffed into the garbage can last night. I tied the plastic bag to contain the smell. By the time I'd used the bathroom and brushed my teeth, Carl had arrived with my scrambled egg wrap and a family-sized pail of coffee.

"How was your night?" he asked.

"Better than the one before," I remarked, removing the lid from the coffee and inhaling the heavenly aroma.

"Detective Jordan will collect you at nine."

"Thanks, Carl. And thanks for breakfast."

I sat in one of the wingback chairs and savoured every mouthful of the breakfast wrap. I could have eaten three of them.

The suitcase provided an adventure in dressing. I saw Victoria's influence in the silk nightie that I wish I'd known about last night. She was also likely responsible for the ankle boots and the short Burberry trench coat, which meant the suitcase was hers too. The yoga pants and designer blue jeans came from Sydney, if the thirty-four-inch inseam was any indication. It was either Eden or Alex who contributed the WSU sweatshirt, and inside its folds was a new pair of black ballet slippers in a zippered pouch. They'd even thought of underthings, I smiled, looking over the brand new panties and a soft cotton sports bra.

I pulled on the jeans, the ankle boots and the black turtleneck sweater, and laid the trench coat on the bed ready for a quick departure. Then I repacked the suitcase, tossing in every mini-bottle the hotel offered.

Detective Jordan arrived just before nine. "Manse's doctor has agreed to meet us at St. Matthew's at nine thirty." He took my suitcase and held the door open. We headed back down the hall to the service elevator. We stepped out of the elevator at the garage level, and he stopped, barring my way. "Emelynn, I don't know what's going on with you and James, and I don't care, but you're going to have to deal with him. His skill set and contacts are critical to this investigation."

Unbelievable. James had gone from new man on the team to critical in record time. "I can deal with James," I said. Whether James could deal with me was the real issue. I hadn't held anything back when I'd confronted him yesterday. I'd spoken my mind and cleared the air. The weight of that anger no longer pulled me down, but I'd bet James had a few extra pounds of crap pressing down on his shoulders today.

"That's good because he's coming with us. He insisted."

My confident "Sure," must have appeased him, because we started walking toward the exit again.

James held the rear passenger door of the SUV open. "Emelynn," he said.

"James." He closed the door behind me and jumped into the front passenger seat. Carl was driving again. Detective Jordan came around and got in beside me.

"Let's get this over with," Detective Jordan said. The tires squeaked on the smooth concrete as Carl pulled away. "I believe you wanted this," he said, handing me a new driver's licence.

"Wow, you must know the right people."

The detective smirked. "You said it was non-negotiable."

I tucked it in my pocket. "Thank you. If I'd known it was going to be that easy, I'd have asked for my passport, too."

St. Matthew's Long Term Care Facility was located in a neglected area of Vancouver's east end. The hundred-year-old building had once been a hospital. The red-brick three-storey structure was probably state of the art in about 1920. Now it looked tired and worn-out, but it still held a certain art deco charm.

Carl pulled up in front and let us out. Three scrub-clad employees smoked cigarettes under the edge of what was probably once a lovely porte cochère. The overhang on it had been shortened at some point and what remained was a stubby roof that barely covered the entrance and a row of newspaper vending boxes.

Once inside the front doors, we immediately turned right and walked down a hall of offices. Dr. Bhin Tran looked up with kind, brown eyes when the detective knocked on the open door frame. The office was neat and the doctor's desk was small. Bookshelves took up one entire wall of the office and each shelf sagged under a heavy load of journals and books.

"You must be Detective Jordan," he said, standing. Detective Jordan walked forward and shook his hand. The detective's bulk made the room seem smaller than it already was, especially in contrast to the doctor's small stature.

"This is my colleague, James Moss, and our witness, Emelynn Taylor."

"Hello," I said. James and I didn't shake his hand.

"Pleased to meet you. Will you have a seat?" the doctor said, indicating the thinly padded chairs against the wall. James and I obediently took the seats, which left the one in front of the doctor's desk for Detective Jordan.

The doctor addressed the detective. "I understand you are here to see my patient, Carson Manse."

"Yes. We would like Ms. Taylor to visually confirm his identity."

The doctor's voice was soft, gentle. "You understand you will not be permitted to physically touch the patient."

Detective Jordan was quick to reassure him. "Touching won't be necessary as long as his face is visible."

"It is and we've temporarily removed his feeding tube, but that brings me to another detail you need to understand. It involves the nature of Mr. Manse's condition. He has been comatose for a month. Even in that relatively short period of time, the body's skin slackens and muscle tone deteriorates. That deterioration may result in a change in his appearance."

"Are you saying she won't recognize him?" Detective Jordan asked. The thought alarmed me.

"Only she can determine that, Detective. What I can tell you is that the man, who arrived here at St. Matthew's, is the same man who occupies the bed today. Short of a miracle, he'll never regain consciousness."

"Could he be communicating with someone?" I asked, in a rush. "Like blinking his eyes or squeezing someone's hand?"

If the doctor was surprised at my outburst, he didn't react. "No. That's not possible. He experiences sporadic muscle movement that you might recognize as a twitch or grimace, but those movements are entirely involuntary."

"Thank you, Doctor," Detective Jordan said. "I appreciate the information. May we see him now?"

"Certainly." We all stood and filed out of the room so that the doctor could get out from behind his desk. "This way," he said, and we trailed down the hall behind him.

"Where are all the patients?" I asked, curious that I hadn't seen any yet.

"None of our patients are ambulatory. Those who are confined to beds are on the third floor and those patients in wheelchairs are on the second floor. This floor is strictly administration. Laundry and food services are in the basement."

We followed Dr. Tran into a large, ancient elevator that screeched in protest as it lifted us to the third floor. I'd had some time to think about seeing Carson again. I didn't know how I would react. I suppose one part of me would be reassured to see him in the condition the doctor described, but would it be enough?

When the elevator doors groaned open, the doctor led us past an empty nurses' station on the left. He stopped two doors from the end of the hall. "Mr. Manse shares a ward with five other patients, two of whom are easily excited. Kindly keep your voices quiet." The doctor waited until we'd all acknowledged him. "This way," he said, leading us into the room.

Curtains on tracks suspended from the ceiling, divided the large ward, much like the emergency room I'd just been in. The beds were arranged three on each side. The patients in the first two beds were grey-haired, their skin ashen and translucent. The head of one of the beds was propped up. Both patients snored. The woman in the second bed on the left let out a stroke-inducing shriek.

"My apologies, Mrs. White, we'll just be a minute." Dr. Tran quickly pulled the curtain, giving her some privacy and she quietened. Dr. Tran continued to the third bed on the right and stopped. Detective Jordan was right beside him. "This is Mr. Manse."

I'd stopped at the first row of beds, reluctant to move forward. My feet felt rooted to the floor. The detective turned, looking for me. "Go ahead, take a look." He cocked his head with an impatient tug, urging me forward.

James quickly fell back beside me. "Come on. I'll go with you." He smiled a very un-James-like reassuring smile, suspending whatever crap there was between us in that moment. I took the hand he offered and walked with him to the foot of the bed. The only part of Carson's face I could see from here was the underside of his chin.

Dr. Tran had been watching me carefully and proved astute at reading the situation. "Come," he said, holding out his hand. "He's quite harmless, I assure you." He then moved to the head of the bed, beckoning me to follow.

"I'm right behind you," James said.

I swallowed hard, pulled on my big-girl panties and followed the doctor, keeping my eyes on his face rather than Carson's. I took several deep breaths to steady myself and then moved my gaze to Carson. His skin was pasty white with blue and grey undertones. The hair was as I expected, bald on top, though it had grown out from the shaved stubble I last saw. The scar was still an angry red welt that jagged across his forehead. The black stitches were gone. Dr. Tran was right; his face had changed. This didn't look like the Carson I remembered. I moved in closer to see if I could discern exactly why, but I couldn't.

"Do you still have the photo of Carson that was taken in the hospital?" I asked Detective Jordan. He was the one who had shown it to me. Maybe if I could compare that photo with Carson's face, I'd see more similarity.

"I do," James said, pulling out his cellphone. He quickly swiped through photographs until he found it then held it out to me. The man in the bed looked similar to the photo, but more like a distant relative.

"What do you think?" I asked James.

He compared the photo to the man in the bed. "I don't know, Em. It's hard to tell, especially with what Dr. Tran told us."

"Is it him?" Detective Jordan asked me.

"I wish I could say with absolute certainty, but I can't," I confessed. "I recognize the man in that photo as Carson, even though he was unconscious when the picture was taken. But this man," I said, regarding the comatose man in the bed, "I don't know. I just don't recognize the Carson Manse I knew, in this face."

Something else occurred to me. I turned to address the doctor. "What colour are his eyes?"

"I do not know. Do you?" His question was sincere.

"Yes. They're black as coal," I said without hesitation. "I looked into them at length, Dr. Tran."

"All right then." Dr. Tran pulled a penlight out of his pocket in a move so smooth it would do Avery proud. "Please stand back," he asked, and I realized that I was encroaching on his personal space, practically leaning on his shoulder.

James put his arm around my waist and pulled me back. I tried to ignore the comforting warmth of him.

The doctor leaned in and gently pushed Carson's eyelid up. I leaned in behind him as if the doctor and I were connected by a very short cord. The flashlight reflected off the man's pale blue iris.

James tightened his hold on me. He'd seen it too. The air squeezed out of my lungs. "That's not Carson," I whispered, twisting against James's grip.

"Is there any possibility that eye colour would change with his condition?" Detective Jordan asked, having seen the same pale blue iris that James and I had.

"No. Eye colour does not change."

"Thank you, Dr. Tran. We'll be in touch." Detective Jordan turned to the door and pulled out his cellphone, lengthening his strides.

"We're coming out. Plan B," he said, his stride stretched to a jog. Dr. Tran stood anchored to the floor looking like he'd dropped his ice cream cone, and then Mrs. White's shrieks re-ignited.

"I can't breathe," I whispered, shaking James off. I darted after the detective and stumbled. James caught my arm and pulled me along with him, racing for the exit.

Chapter Thirteen

We crashed through the door to the right of the elevator and pounded down the stairwell. We passed the ground floor door and ran down a beat-up hall toward a door marked "Deliveries." I heard the squealing tires before we burst through the last door. The SUV was still rolling when James yanked the rear door open and boosted me in. He and Detective Jordan jumped in and Carl sped off, barely missing the loading ramp. The SUV hadn't stopped moving.

"Where are we going?" I shouted above the revving engine.

"Back to the station," Detective Jordan said. He held his phone to his ear and spoke, holding his hand up to silence me. "Yeah, Matt. Get someone over to St. Matthew's and print Carson Manse. No, right now."

"That wasn't Carson Manse," I repeated, shaking my head.

He ended his call. "Are you absolutely certain?" he asked. "You were under a lot of stress during that ordeal."

"I won't ever forget that man's eyes, Detective, and they weren't blue."

Detective Jordan studied my face, but he wasn't really looking at me. He was thinking. "We'll know for sure within the hour."

"You don't believe me?" I looked to James for support, but he had his head down, texting furiously.

"I don't want to. Believing you means that bastard is out there somewhere." Detective Jordan tossed his hand toward the street in frustration. He turned his head away from me and stared out the window. "Either way, we still need proof."

My head spun with unanswered questions: where was Carson; how had he fooled everyone; and who was the man in the bed at St. Matthew's?

We passed through the security checks in the underground garage at the station and Carl dropped us off. The door buzzed open just as Detective Jordan grabbed the handle and James pulled it closed behind us. The air was tense in the elevator ride to the seventh floor. Detective Jordan looked ready to explode and James was too quiet.

Matt was waiting for us at the elevator. "Benny's on his way over to St. Matthew's right now. I've been on the phone with Dr. Tran. Benny's going in as a lab tech for cover, in case someone's watching the building."

"That's great, Matt. Let me know the minute the results are in. We'll be in the Delta SCR."

What the hell was the Delta SCR? I followed Detective Jordan's long strides to the same room we'd occupied yesterday.

As soon as the door clanked shut behind us, James blew his top. "How the hell did that bastard pull this off? He was supposed to be in *your* custody, Jordan!"

"Don't give me that shit, Moss. I didn't see you throwing down any red flags. You saw the man; you read the doctor's reports. As far as any of us knew, Manse has been in the vegetable patch for weeks."

They retreated to neutral corners, both having blown off some steam.

James said, "The medical transport had to have been involved."

Detective Jordan nodded in agreement. "We'll need to track down everyone who had access to him in the hospital. He had to have been communicating with someone. He sure as shit didn't do this alone."

They were both dwelling on the past. I didn't see the point. "Where do we go from here?" My voice jarred them from their brooding. "I know you have to figure out how he pulled this off, but what do we do now? Right now." I heard the impatience in my voice, but I didn't care.

"We'll work out a plan when the task force gets here," Jordan said.

"We have to find him," I said. "Stop him."

"That's why we need to figure out how he did this. That's how we'll find him."

"That could take months!" I shouted, taking my turn in the anger ring. "We need to find him *now*. I won't have a moment's peace until he's dead or locked up." I paced to the window, shaking out my arms.

"Use me," I said, striding back to the detective. "I'll be the bait; I'll lure him out into the open. Hell, I'd shoot him myself if I could."

James turned on me with a look questioning my sanity. "Em, the man's already tried to kill you three times! We are *not* going to use you for bait."

"Why not! I'm your best bet and I have the most to gain. He kidnapped me, he torched my house and last night he had someone fire a gun at me and my friends. I have nowhere to go, James."

"It's out of the question, Emelynn." Detective Jordan crossed his arms. "This man is far too unpredictable, too dangerous."

The room quite suddenly felt too small. I threw my arms up. "I need to get out of here."

"Why?" Jordan asked. "You said yourself you have nowhere to go."

"You're right. I don't. But I will. So if you won't let me help you, then I've got things to do."

The detective stood his ground. "There's a reason you're under police protection, Emelynn. You need it. You can't run around putting yourself and everyone around you at risk."

"This is protection? Locked up in your *Delta CRS* with cameras spying on my every move? Am I the criminal here?" I spit the words out in frustration.

"SCR," Detective Jordan corrected. "Secure Conference Room."

"I don't care what you call it. Who the hell hides a camera in the bathroom?"

"It's for your own protection. The protection of everyone in this room."

"There are limits, Detective. This is not going to work for me."

"Fine. I'll arrange for you to return to the hotel."

"I need to go to the bank first. Then I'll need to pick up a phone and a laptop."

"We can supply those."

"I'd like ones that aren't monitored, if you don't mind."

James produced his cellphone. "Here, take mine. As soon as we're done here, I'll come by the hotel and drop off some new equipment."

I took a deep breath, but didn't take James's phone. "No, you need that." I addressed Detective Jordan. "Will you at least arrange for me to go to the bank before the hotel?"

"Emelynn, whoever tossed those Molotov cocktails into your house knows that you weren't killed in the fire: it was reported in the paper.

They knew enough to stake out Avery Coulter's house. Hell, even we knew enough to watch Dr. Coulter's house. Do you not think they might also be clever enough to keep an eye on your bank, the Y and that bookstore you're so fond of?"

The detective's words deflated me. That explained how the police arrived at Avery's so quickly: they were already there. Everywhere I went, I brought the threat of Carson Manse with me. I was Typhoid Mary. My earlier bravado fled, taking my defiance and my brief glimpse of freedom with it.

We waited another half-hour before the door lock clicked and the grim-faced task force filed in.

"They didn't match, did they, Benny?" Detective Jordan said, addressing a young academic dressed in black slacks with a lab coat and glasses. He didn't look much older than me.

Benny cleared his throat. "The man in St. Matthew's is not the man who Dr. Abrahams stitched up in the hospital."

The room went quiet. Detective Jordan started to thank Benny, but Benny wasn't finished.

"We do know who he is though. His name is Craig Hendricks. He went missing from Chilliwack General Hospital three weeks ago. Mr. Hendricks didn't have a scar when he went missing," Benny added.

"Thank you, Benny. We appreciate you dropping everything to do that for us. Send me the report. And Benny, on your way out, send Leslie in with some coffee."

"Sure," he said, swiping his security card at the door. Even Benny had a magic pass to the exclusive club.

When the door clicked closed, Dino and Matt chewed on Benny's news for a few moments and then the task force swung into action. Dino scrawled on the whiteboard, Matt tapped on a cellphone and Detective Jordan assigned tasks.

When the coffee arrived, James brought me a cup. "How are you holding up?" he asked, sitting beside me. I'd been watching the action from the far corner of the sofa, away from the bustle of conversation.

I shrugged. "This feels like someone else's life."

"It'll get better. These guys are good investigators. They'll find a way to get to Carson."

Detective Jordan approached. "We're going to break, do some leg-work and reconvene later this afternoon. I'll take you to the hotel now, if you'd like."

"Thank you."

"I'll drop by the hotel when we're done here, okay?" James said.

I nodded. "Thanks, James."

He smiled. Maybe we could be friends again after all.

Detective Jordan accompanied me through the Wedgewood Hotel's hidden service maze and up to the same twelfth-floor room I stayed in last night. He carried the Burberry suitcase that had been riding in the SUV all day.

"It's clear," he said, coming out of the bedroom after performing the same check that Roberta had done the night before.

"Detective, may I ask you something?"

"We're going to be spending a lot of time together, Emelynn, why don't you call me Sam."

It was the friendliest gesture he'd ever made. "All right then, Sam. Was there ever a plan B?"

"There's always a plan B in the protection game—an alternate way to get out of a building. So yes, there was a plan B for St. Matthew's."

"Did you ever consider that Carson could be responsible for setting fire to my cottage?"

He looked down and shifted his weight. "No, he wasn't a viable suspect. Obviously, we underestimated him. He played us; he waited for us to write him off, and we did." The detective looked back up and squared his shoulders. "Now we have to rectify that situation and get him back into custody." Whatever discomfort the detective had felt with that admission passed, but the fact that I'd heard it appeased me.

My questions didn't end there though. "Earlier today you mentioned that you knew enough to watch Avery's place. Are you also watching the Y and Rumbles?"

"They're under surveillance." It was a small, but reassuring comfort.

"Do you still have the card Roberta gave you?" he asked. I pulled it from my jeans' pocket. "Good. Call that number if you need anything. If you're going to use the hotel phone, input the code on the back of that card first to scramble the caller ID. And whatever you do, don't tell anyone—and I mean anyone—where you're staying."

I locked the door behind him and flopped on the sofa. There were so many things I needed to do: replace my credit cards, buy clothes, find a place to stay. Nice as it was, I could do none of it from inside the Wedgewood Hotel. There were, however, some phone calls I needed to make.

Avery was relieved to hear from me. "James told me about Carson Manse, Em. I'm so sorry."

"I can't believe he got away, Avery."

"Neither can I. Are they making any progress locating him?"

"I don't know. They won't let me help."

"Help? Help how?"

"I'm the one he's after, Avery. I want them to use me to get to him, but they won't."

"I should hope not. Em, what are you thinking? Jesus Christ! Hasn't Manse done enough damage? Get out of the way and let the police do their jobs."

"Avery!" his words stung, but his tone hurt more. He'd never spoken to me so harshly.

"Do you have any idea how terrifying it is for me to get that phone call, Em? For your friends—for me—to see you lying in a hospital bed? You are not invincible. Detective Jordan may irritate the hell out of you, but he knows what he's doing. Let him protect you . . . please, Em."

Hearing Avery wound up and worried about me, stabbed me in the heart. I had been too self-absorbed to see this from his perspective. "I'm sorry, Avery. I didn't think . . . I had no idea how hard this has been for you."

"Well, now you do. You're like a daughter to me, Em. I couldn't bear to lose you."

"You won't lose me, Avery. I'll keep out of the way. I promise. I'll stay safe."

"Good. I'm going to hold you to that."

It felt like a storm had passed. I took a deep breath and lighted on a neutral topic. "How's your kitchen? It was a mess when I left."

"It's just a kitchen. There's nothing that can't be repaired or replaced. How's that annoying detective treating you?"

"Good. He told me I could call him Sam."

"That's an improvement. Maybe he's softening up."

"I wouldn't go that far, but I think he's trying. He feels pretty bad about losing custody of a comatose man. That's got to sting."

Avery's laughter patched the tear in my heart. He sounded like his old self again. I'd do everything in my power to keep it that way. I told him that James was bringing me a new phone and I'd get him the number as soon as I could. We hung up after I promised to call Eden; she'd been hounding him for news.

I dialled Eden. "It's me, Emelynn," I said, when she answered.

"Emelynn, thank god you called. You almost missed me."

"Missed you?"

"We heard about Carson, Em. Alex and I have decided to lay low until the dust settles."

"What do you mean, 'lay low'?"

"Alex has been working with an apprentice he trusts. He's asked him to run the shop for a while. I've taken an emergency leave from work. We're taking the red-eye to Seattle tonight. I'm not abandoning you, Em, but news of Carson and the Redeemers is burning up the message boards. Our families are worried."

If anyone had cause to be concerned, it was Eden. Carson had used an Eden look-alike dummy to get to me. If there was a next time, he might just try to use the real thing.

"I'm glad you're getting out of here, Eden. You're not safe with Carson on the loose. Until he's dead, we're all in danger." It was the second time I'd referred to Carson and his need to be dead. The thought no longer shocked me. Carson had done that—forced me to think in terms of death as a preferred solution.

"Don't worry about us. We can fend for ourselves. How are you doing?"

"Detective Jordan is treating me well. He'll update me on the task force's progress later this afternoon."

"They'll catch him, Em. Have you talked to Molly?"

"Damn! No. I am such a crappy friend. She completely slipped my mind. Did I tell you she's pregnant?"

"No! You *are* a crappy friend. Spill it, girl. I want all the details."

When I'd finished telling her, she reminded me that the bar-trolling psychic, Cassandra, had predicted as much. Cassandra had been our entertainment on a girls' night out back in August. She couldn't read Eden, but she'd foretold that Molly would marry and I was in danger. Cassandra was two for two.

"You understand, don't you?" Eden asked.

"Absolutely. You're doing the right thing. Give Alex a hug for me."

I disconnected and picked up the remote for the fireplace. With the push of a button, warm flames danced to life behind the glass. Better still, the flames were safely contained.

How was I going to explain this to Molly? What was I supposed to tell her? The most important event in her life was less than two weeks away and I'd promised to be there—to stand up for her. Now, I didn't know if I could. What were the chances that Carson would be neutralized in time for the *I dos*?

I picked up the phone again, input the scramble code and dialled Molly. Her answering machine kicked on and I wasn't ready for it. It was bad enough I might have to renege on being her best woman, I wouldn't do it in a voice message. "It's Em. Sorry if I've worried you. Our detective friend is taking good care of me. I'll call again as soon as I can." That sounded cryptic, I thought, hanging up. She'd likely know about the fire if the detective was right about it being in the newspapers. At least she'd know I was okay. She'd certainly know who I meant by *our* detective.

It would be hours before Detective . . . Sam, returned. I turned on the flat screen and tried to get interested in a program, any program, but images of the charred heap that used to be my cottage kept flashing to the forefront of my mind. The unwelcome reminders hurt. Memories of my father lived in that house, and now it was gone. Everything was gone.

I got up and watched the traffic on Hornby Street for a time then called the number on the card. If I didn't find a distraction, I'd drive myself insane dwelling on the cottage. Carl answered. "If it's not too much trouble, Carl, could I get a large cup of tea and a newspaper?"

"No trouble at all. I'll be there in ten minutes."

I paced the room spilling nervous energy until Carl knocked. "I brought you a sandwich too," he said, handing me the bag. "You haven't eaten. I hope you like roast beef."

"Thanks, Carl. That's very thoughtful." My mouth watered. No wonder, I thought, checking the time. It was almost three o'clock.

Carl had brought me the Province and the Globe. I read both from cover to cover. There wasn't a word in either paper about the fire. I guess the cottage's fifteen minutes of fame were yesterday. The shooting at Avery's was reported as a botched break and enter in the St. George's neighbourhood that resulted in a fatality. No names were given. I wondered if the police knew the identity of the shooter yet.

Just after four, Carl phoned to tell me that James was on his way up. I tidied the papers and moved my suitcase to the bedroom.

"Sorry it took so long," he said, when I'd let him in. We sat side-by-side on the sofa with a large shopping bag between us. He pulled out a number of boxes and laid them on the coffee table. The final extraction from his bag was a bottle of red wine. J. Lohr's Cabernet Sauvignon. "Thought you could use this," he said with a wry smile.

I laughed. "I could have used that at ten this morning," I said, getting up in search of a corkscrew and glasses. They were tucked inside a tall cabinet. I handed James the corkscrew and he did the honours then poured us each a glass.

"To better days," he toasted.

"Yes, to better days. And Carson Manse, with a bullet hole in his head." James grimaced as he touched his glass to mine. The wine went down smoothly and left a delicious hint of cherry and vanilla behind. It was enough to wash away thoughts of Carson, at least for the moment.

James set his glass aside and started unpacking the equipment. He'd brought me a MacBook Pro and an iPhone. "This will take me a while to set up," he warned.

I had all night, I thought, and pulled my feet up onto the sofa, making myself comfortable against the armrest. He started with the computer, flipping in and out of screens I'd never seen before. His face was a study in concentration. Did he know he clenched his jaw when he did that? I wanted to reach over, untie his hair and run my fingers through it. A smile he couldn't see flitted across my face. I guess I'd forgiven him.

Every once in a while James would stop, puzzle out some detail, then get busy again. He made whatever he was doing look easy. "That battery won't be fully charged yet," he said. "Leave it plugged in."

He then started work on the iPhone. "This will be untraceable when I'm done. You can use it to Skype your mom." When he was finished, he phoned himself to test it. He then tested it using a program on the new computer.

"There, done," he said, handing the phone over. It had taken him just over an hour.

"Thank you. I can't pay you right now, but I will as soon as I get to a bank."

"No need. Mason paid for it."

"Mason—damn! I should have thought to call him. Did you tell him what happened?"

"Of course. The Tribunal's getting updates every few hours. This group that call themselves Redeemers poses the biggest threat they've ever faced. They're not just turning over stones to find these people, they're detonating them."

"Have they made any headway?"

"There were a few productive leads after you unearthed Carson Manse and Rupert Dowling, but they've dried up. They're now working their way through known associates, friends and family. The Tribunal has always been brutal, but they're setting new standards with these interrogations. It's not pretty."

"Are they involving you?"

James nodded. "I'm not fighting them on this one."

"I thought you hated them using you like that."

"I do, but it's the devil you know, Em. The Redeemers' methods are beyond abhorrent. They're murdering Fliers—their own kind, stealing their gifts for the questionable purpose of seizing the Tribunal. If they succeed, what then? When they're stronger than any of us, do you think they'll suddenly become benevolent? I don't."

"I don't either. I am sorry they're using you though."

"I just hope I can help stop them. Oh," he said, suddenly remembering something else, "Mason asked me to give you this." He reached into his back pocket and pulled out an envelope.

"What's that?"

"Cash. He thought you might need some before you get your bank sorted out."

I flipped through the hundreds and fifties. "It's too much, James. There has to be a couple thousand dollars here."

"Five grand. You can work out the details with Mason."

"Mason will be upset about his mother's crystal. I managed to save the photo of my dad, but the necklace must have fallen off somewhere along my escape route. It was a family heirloom."

"I think Mason will understand."

"I should go back to the cottage and look for it. It might have survived."

"I'll go look for it."

I tipped my head. "James, you wouldn't know where to start."

He pinched his brow. "We'll have to organize a police escort."

"I'm okay with that. When can we go?"

"Let's talk to Jordan when he gets here."

I pressed my lips together and nodded. James refilled our glasses.

"The police can't protect me, James. You know that. They have no idea what they're up against."

"They can hide you, Emelynn. They're good at that. And they're far from helpless. Manse's group has already proven they're comfortable with kidnapping and assassination. The police know that. They'll use lethal force to deal with them."

"I hope so."

The phone rang. Roberta was back on babysitting duty and warned me that Detective Jordan was on his way up. James answered the door.

"Emelynn," he said, greeting me.

"Sam," I replied, and James looked at me like I'd called the detective "sweetheart."

Sam removed his jacket and dropped a battered McDonald's bag on the coffee table. "What's all this?" he said, referring to the packaging strewn about.

"I brought her a new phone and computer. Just finished setting it up," James replied.

"Untraceable?"

"It's taken care of."

"Good. You hungry?" Sam said, opening the bag. The mouth-watering scent of french fries escaped.

I cleared space on the table then took the offered fries.

In between bites, James described what he'd done with the equipment.

"That's impressive, Moss, though I'm not sure it's legal. I'm glad you're on our side." He polished off his fries and opened the wrapper on a burger. "How are you doing?" he said, addressing me.

"I don't know. I'm still numb. There is something I need, though; I have to go back to the cottage."

"Why?"

"I need to see it again. There may be something I can salvage. And even if there isn't, I dropped a pendant necklace when I fled. It may still be there."

"It's unlikely, Emelynn. There's nothing left but charcoal and ash." Sympathy softened his voice. "There were a lot of people and heavy equipment in there. Something that small and delicate . . . it's probably buried in the mud."

"It means a lot to me, Sam. That necklace is irreplaceable. It may be futile, but I need to at least try to find it."

"It's a crime scene."

"I know."

Sam exhaled. His shoulders dropped. "I'll have to go with you. How about I take you first thing tomorrow?"

"Thanks." When there was nothing left of our dinner but wrappers, I asked what the task force had learned.

"Not a lot," Sam answered, "but we'll catch a break soon. The hospital handed over hundreds of hours of security-camera footage. Unfortunately, it'll take days to sift through but Benny's already working on it. The medical transport was a private firm. We've made an official request for names. They're checking with their lawyers, but I'm confident they'll comply. Matt's set up a team to bring in the new witnesses for questioning. He's pulling in the first wave tonight."

"And what do we do in the meantime?" I envisioned endless angst-ridden days ahead of me and fast-food wrappers piling up around my ankles.

The detective straightened. "We've got a plan." His confident tone buoyed me. "We're going to use a decoy to lure Manse to a location where we can safely take him down."

"A decoy?" I said.

"We're flying in a detective from San Diego. Grace Shipley's her name. She'll be here in the morning. She's got somewhat of a reputation for impersonation."

"I know her," James said. "She can handle herself. She's worked cases like this before."

"She's also the same height and build as you," Sam said, looking to me. "Which is critical because it won't be easy to fool Manse. The fire commissioner is releasing his findings of arson tomorrow. The media release will include the fact that Emelynn Taylor is under police protection. That should point Manse in the right direction."

"What then?" I asked.

"Then we go fishing," Sam said. An evil smile tugged at the corners of his mouth. He stood up, preparing to leave. "Can you be ready by eight tomorrow morning?"

"I'll be ready."

"Good. James, you'll tag along?" James nodded his agreement.

Sam picked up his jacket and draped it over his shoulder. A piece of paper fluttered to the floor and he stooped to collect it. "Almost forgot— this it for you." He handed me the piece of paper. "Molly Connolly is under the mistaken impression that I'm your answering service." His expression was only mildly annoyed. "Please correct that impression and let her know you'll be unreachable for the foreseeable future."

I sighed and flopped back against the sofa. "She's getting married in two weeks. I said I'd stand up for her. Do you know how hard it is to renege on something as important as that?"

"I'm sorry, Emelynn." The detective took a moment to look apologetic then turned his attention to James. "We need to talk logistics. Do you have a few minutes?"

"You can talk here," I said, getting up. "I'll call Molly from the bedroom. Can I use the new phone?" I asked James.

"Yes, it's yours. It's ready to go."

I left them and closed the bedroom door behind me. Molly would understand, I knew that, but I hated to let her down. She answered on the first ring. She'd been worried sick about me, which made me worry about her and the pregnancy despite her reassurances. I told her about Eden and Alex heading to Seattle. She agreed it was for the best. She promised to take lots of wedding photos before we said goodbye. It felt horribly final. Our tear-filled conversation left me feeling wretched.

In the bathroom, I blew my nose and splashed water on my face. My eyes were red-rimmed and glassy. I didn't want to go back out to the living room looking teary eyed. Maybe the detective and James had left. I tiptoed to the closed bedroom door and listened. They were still talking. I paused and dabbed at my eyes with a wadded Kleenex.

I hadn't intended to eavesdrop. I'd only hoped to stall long enough for one or both of them to leave, but instead, I overheard something that almost stopped my heart.

"She's like you, isn't she?" Detective Jordan asked.

"No," James replied. "She's nothing like me."

My feet froze to the carpet. *She's like you.* What did he mean by that? Like James how? What did the detective know about James? It was inconceivable that he knew about Fliers. Wasn't it? I turned the handle and opened the door.

Chapter Fourteen

James emerged from the entryway. "Jordan left," he said, before he noticed the shocked confusion on my face. "What's wrong?" he asked.

"What are you hiding from me, James?" I cocked my head and felt the pinch of my eyebrows. "Why did Sam ask if I was like you? What does he know?"

James opened his mouth and closed it again. His expression morphed from surprised to angry to resigned in the span of seconds. Was he trying to make up a suitable lie, I wondered? Would he deny what I'd overheard? Instead, he sat down and hung his head.

"They don't know what I am. No one knows what I am—what we are. But they do know that I can do certain things; things that are very useful to them from time to time."

"Reading memories?"

He searched my face before answering. "Yes."

"James! How? Why?" I sat down opposite him, perched on the edge of the seat.

"It doesn't matter, Emelynn. I've not compromised a thing and it's a long story."

I sat back and crossed my arms. "I've got all night, James."

He broke our gaze and leaned forward, resting his elbows on his knees. He inspected his fingernails, his face intense, and finally opened up. "Eight years ago, a buddy's daughter went missing. Cicely was four at the time—a real cutie. Friends and neighbours, hell, lots of people who didn't even know them, threw themselves into finding her. After the second day, the police took in a man for questioning, but all they had on him was a hunch. He denied any knowledge of Cicely. They were holding him on parking tickets and time was running out. I knew some of the cops because of my PI work so I went down and sniffed around. Eventually, I convinced them to put me in the cell with the guy."

James grew quiet. His shoulders tensed and his fingers stilled. I gently prodded him. "You found her?"

"Yes." He looked up at me, his eyes hard, his jaw clenched. I wasn't sure I wanted to hear any more. "He'd raped her. She was four years old and that sick bastard raped her."

"No!" The act was too heinous to process. Then another thought crept into my mind so ominous and dark that I shivered. James would have seen the man's memories of that depravity.

"I nearly killed him," he said, his voice dangerously calm. "I would have if they hadn't pulled me off him." The muscles in his forearms were taut and trembled, ready to strike.

"Did she survive?" I asked.

"Yes, thank god." James drew a deep breath. His eyebrows smoothed and he unclenched his jaw. I breathed a sigh of relief along with him.

"Was she all right?" As soon as the words rushed out of my mouth, I shook my head at the stupidity of my question. No one would be *all right* after that.

"Some days, I think she handled it better than me. She needed surgery to repair the damage he'd done and years of counselling, but she's okay. She's one tough little girl and resilient as hell. She's still a sweet kid."

"And what about him?"

James's blue eyes turned glacial, and I was immediately sorry I'd asked the question. "He had an unfortunate and very painful accident." A menacing scowl crawled across his face, eliminating any trace of handsomeness. Had the incident with Cicely been the impetus for that look, which he pulled off so well?

"Did the police ever figure out how you got the information?"

My question pulled his thoughts out of that dark place. He straightened up and leaned back against the sofa. "No. But a few months later, they asked me to help them again. It was another hopeless case. A woman had been brutally murdered and their only suspect was the husband who had an airtight alibi. This time they couldn't even get the guy into custody. I finally got close to him in a crowded elevator and was able to help them close the case. I've been helping them ever since."

"Aren't you worried, James? What if the police find out how you get the information?"

"Worried? No. They assume I'm some kind of psychic, so it suits them not to acknowledge my involvement. I won't testify and I won't let them identify me. It's a *don't ask, don't tell* policy that actually works. For both of us."

"What if the Tribunal learns what you're doing? You're taking a huge risk."

"It's worth it, Em. I save lives. I *choose* to do this; no one forces me. No one threatens my family if I don't. Sometimes, it's the only thing good enough to balance out the horrors of the Tribunal."

"I had no idea, James." What else didn't I know about this man?

"We all have secrets, Emelynn." It was an echo of something he'd said to me before.

"That one will get you killed if the Tribunal learns of it." Fliers were strongly discouraged from sharing knowledge of their gift with the non-Gifted. And by discouraged, I mean it wasn't tolerated. Even the youngest Fliers knew that rule. If our existence was discovered, life as we knew it would be over. The gift posed too big a threat to those in power. They'd never tolerate our continued freedom. We'd be locked up, prodded and probed. James was playing with fire.

"They won't … unless you plan on telling them." He actually looked serious, which hurt.

"Don't be ridiculous, James." I slowly shook my head.

He paused. "Just checking," he said, but he didn't smile. Had he been worried? He stood to leave. "I've got to go."

I sighed, hesitant to see him leave. Despite what had happened between us, there was something about having him here that felt comforting. His presence kept the worst of my thoughts and fears away. The sensible part of my brain knew that using James as a crutch wasn't the solution. It wouldn't help me deal with the loss of the cottage, just delay the inevitable pain.

Reluctantly, I stood and followed him to the door. "Thank you for bringing the phone and computer. The money too. I appreciate it."

"Sure," James said. He paused, struggling for words. "I'm sorry about the other night, Em. I didn't mean to hurt you."

The not-so-sensible part of me lapped up his words and wanted to fall into his arms and convince him to stay. Instead, I put on a brave face and faked it. "Thanks for that, but I'm a big girl, James," I said, feeling anything but. "Good night."

"Good night," he said, and I closed the door quietly behind him.

It wasn't until I turned the latch that the weight of his revelation hit me. After all our harsh words, James still trusted me. So much so, I now held his life in my hands. By telling me about his work with the police, he'd handed me a loaded gun and he'd forever have to trust that I wouldn't point it at him and pull the trigger. I wasn't sure how I felt about that.

I walked straight to the bathroom and ran a bath. A fresh mini-bottle of bath oil awaited. I dumped it into the gushing stream of hot water then stripped off. While the tub filled, I used the scissors from the complimentary sewing kit to snip the singed ends of my hair.

Bits of Avery's taped gauze still clung to my back like tissue paper from a shaving nick. I stepped into the warm water and sank into the duvet of suds that blanketed the tub and threatened to overflow the rim. If only I had a good book, something to divert my thoughts. My self-discipline wasn't up to the task tonight. Absently, I ran the washcloth across my arms and shoulders.

I took comfort in the fact that Eden would soon be surrounded by her family. They'd keep her safe. My mother was hidden. The other Fliers in the covey would protect one another. The police were watching Rumbles and the Y. Everyone I loved was as safe as they could be.

I dried off, donned the thick, white hotel robe and retrieved my phone from the bedside table. When Avery answered, I gave him my new phone number and repeated what James had told me about the phone being untraceable. He assured me that he, Victoria and the rest of the covey were on high alert, and managing. "They're worried about you," he said, and I wanted to cry. They'd been so kind and thoughtful, and I'd brought the plague. It wasn't right. I thanked Avery for his concern and hung up before I sobbed.

I pulled on Victoria's silk nightie and climbed into bed, pulling the covers up to my chin. Every time I closed my eyes, I saw the cottage as it once was. It felt like a living inventory of what I no longer had: the bedroom of my childhood, Dad's study, Jolene's seascape, the tiny bathroom and the narrow kitchen. I'd never again walk the stairs to the beach. I'd never hear the doorbell and be reminded of playing nicky

nicky nine doors on my mother. Jolene's letter to my father was ashes; the brand new flying clothes I hadn't even had a chance to wear were gone; James's new espresso machine was a melted lump. The tears I'd been fighting finally flowed with heaving sobs. When I could no longer breathe, I rolled over, pulled a handful of tissues from the box and blew my nose. The sob and blow continued on a relentless loop.

I hadn't lost a parent, not even a close friend, so why did it hurt so much? The grief felt out of place, frivolous, yet there it was, caving in my chest, tugging at my emotions. Tears welled up and I angrily rubbed them away. Mourning physical possessions left me raw with guilt and shame, as if mourning the cottage somehow diminished the mourning for my father.

It was crazy-making. I got out of bed and padded to the living room in search of my new iPhone. There were better ways to make myself crazy. I crawled back into the sheets I'd warmed and dialled.

"Emelynn? Are you all right?" James said, sounding alarmed.

"No, I'm not." *All right* was no longer in my lexicon. Neither, apparently was sleep. "Did I wake you?"

"No. I was up. You've been crying." The concern in his voice caressed me, soothed me.

There was no way to keep the nasal by-product of my tears out of my voice. "I was thinking about the cottage. It's like a nightmare I can't wake up from."

"I'm sorry. I know what that place meant to you."

"I feel like I've lost my father all over again. All of my memories of him are connected to that house, and now it's gone."

"The cottage is gone, but your memories aren't. Carson Manse can't take your memories away, Emelynn. Don't give him that power."

"Without the cottage, without the physical reminders, I'm afraid my father's memory will fade. I'm terrified that I'll forget."

"You won't. Would it help to talk to your mother?"

"I don't want to upset her more than she already is."

"I'm sure she's worried. What can I do to help?"

I laughed, and even to me the ring of it sounded evil. "Kill the bastard."

"We will find him," he said, his voice confident. I pictured James standing tall and lean in his black clothing with the gun at the small of his back. I imagined his muscles tensed, his eyes cold and steely and didn't doubt him for a second.

Carson was no longer interested in capturing me; he wanted to kill me. The thought chilled me to the bone. He'd obviously figured out that I couldn't gift him. He probably knew that I'd already passed on his plans to usurp the Tribunal. "Carson wants revenge, James. He's hunting me. He won't stop until he kills me."

"We won't let that happen. Things will look better in the morning," James said. "They always do."

"Sleep is elusive tonight. My head's spinning. I don't seem to be able to shut off my thoughts."

"Having someone try to kill you will do that."

"It's not just that. I saw Avery's face the night that sniper took his potshots. He was frightened: for me, for Victoria, for the rest of the covey. It's hearing the fear in Eden's voice and knowing I've forced her and Alex into hiding. And I've let Molly down—big time. I feel like a pariah."

"You know that's ludicrous, right?"

"This whole thing with Carson feels like my fault ... and I know it's not. You don't have to tell me that. But knowing it and keeping the guilt from eating away at me are two very different things."

"We'll find Manse. He's clever, but he's got an Achilles heel, Emelynn, and you're it. If he was thinking clearly, he'd know that getting revenge on you isn't worth the risk. The fact that he's tried and failed more than once, tells me he's not as clever as he thinks he is. It will be his undoing: you'll see. And the Tribunal won't wait to dispose of him next time."

"I'll do everything I can to make that happen, James. If I have to do it myself, I will. The sooner he's dead, the better."

"I hope you never get that close to him, Emelynn."

So much for shutting off my negative thoughts. Perhaps I needed a better distraction. "Where are you staying?"

"Close by."

"Are you ever not cryptic, James?"

"Sorry, it's an ingrained habit. I'm downstairs in room 207. It's not nearly as nice as yours."

"Come stay with me, James."

His silence spoke volumes. "I can't be just friends with you, Emelynn, and you're hardly a fuck buddy. Besides, your room's being monitored. The whole task force knows who's coming and going."

"You're right. I am sorry though. Sorry I didn't give you a chance to explain yourself the other night."

"I'm not sure my explanation would have helped."

Maybe. I guess I'd never know. "Good night, James. Thanks for picking up."

"Any time. Good night."

I hung up and stared at the ceiling. Fuck buddy? Did he really just say that? It would never have occurred to me. James had thought about it though. I punched my pillow and rolled over, but it was no use. Sleep was no closer now than before I'd called James, except now my thoughts were all about him. The sex with James had been spectacular; I sighed just thinking about the way all that muscle on his torso flexed with the roll of his hips . . . and his ass. God, he had a nice ass. Way down low, my insides clenched in that delicious way that anticipates sex: really good sex.

I got out of bed and paced the floor. Thinking about James was better than thinking about Carson, but sleeping and thinking about James were just as incompatible.

James hadn't actually said no. He'd said he couldn't be friends—as in platonic friends. That's not what I wanted either—at least not now, not tonight. The stakes in the battle with Carson were unfathomably high and despite James's confidence, there were no guarantees. Carson might succeed tomorrow or the next day and I'd be just a memory. James felt he had nothing to offer and now, neither did I.

In the face of all that had happened—all that could still happen—the torment that James felt about our one night together and my angry reaction to him running away seemed insignificant. We'd already compromised our friendship. What was the harm of one more night? The thought of him rattled my hormones: he'd used his rush like an orgasmic turbocharger. Now *that* was a distraction that would get me through the night.

I stopped in my tracks and shook my head. What the hell was I doing? I was actually trying to justify my desire to have James in my bed. Again.

I paced around the room another time. It didn't help. I was losing the battle. James couldn't come to me, but I could go to him. Would he throw me out? He could always say no. Maybe he'd be better at "no" than I was.

In a flash of frustration-fuelled impulsiveness, I reached down to my crystal and squeezed tight. A blast of power shot through me as I blinked out of sight. I prayed Sam hadn't lied to me about there not being any cameras in my room. I rushed the door and spilled through the cracks into the hallway then concentrated on where I needed to go. The hall cameras Sam warned me about were obvious deterrents hanging from the ceiling in the corners. I melted through the door to the stairwell and drifted down to the second floor. There wasn't a soul in sight. Room 207 was to the left of the stairs. I pushed through James's door and collected myself on the other side. The lights were off. A bathroom sat to the right, a closet to the left and the end of a bed was straight ahead. James hadn't exaggerated about the room; mine was palatial compared to his.

I floated into his room. James stood silhouetted against the window with a drink in his hand. He wasn't wearing a shirt. His back was a perfect V with well-defined muscles slipping under the edge of jeans that clung enticingly just below his hips. His chest was visible in the window's reflection. Soft skin smoothed over tight pecs and magazine-ready abs.

All that perfection begged to be touched, but I couldn't move. I never imagined what this would feel like and I didn't like it. It felt wrong, dirty, like I was a voyeur or a peeping tom. How would James feel if he knew I was here? I could speak to him—I still had a voice, but suddenly I feared his reaction.

Ice clinked in his glass as he swirled amber liquid. He upended his glass and turned for the bathroom, scattering me in his wake.

Mason had explained the different levels of ghosting, but I'd only explored this level—full-on ghost, the level at which re-forming had proven time-consuming. I closed my eyes and fought the lethargy that ghosting brought on. I couldn't stay like this. It felt too invasive. I needed to show myself—to re-form. If I couldn't, I'd return to my own room and let the exhaustion of ghosting put me to sleep.

I closed my eyes and concentrated on my crystal. If Mason was right, all I needed to do was re-form it. But my crystal was different. Maybe the way back was different too.

I lost my concentration when James returned from the bathroom. He stripped in the darkened room and folded his clothes neatly on top of his leather bag. He slipped between the sheets and folded his arms behind his head. He looked deep in thought, staring at the ceiling. The top edge of the sheet rested just below his pecs. I could see where the sheet dipped between the bottom of his ribs and his pelvis.

I'd already learned how to move around in ghosted form—all it took was conscious thought. I applied that knowledge now, imagining the feel of the floor solid beneath my feet. Reaching out to the wall, I did the same, willing the vertical barrier into existence.

You can do this. I rallied, gathering my courage. I felt drawn to him like a river to the sea and took a step toward the bed. My foot tingled. I took another step. The sensation intensified. My ankle felt strange and then my knee. Almost there, I thought as I drew closer. Conscious thought. I smiled with relief. And clear intention. I welcomed my crystal home to its place near my heart and materialized beside the bed.

My self-satisfied smile disappeared in a gasp. The sheet had barely moved, but James had his gun levelled at my chest before his eyes even focused. I squeaked and jumped back, holding my hands out as if they'd stop a bullet.

"Don't ever do that!" he bellowed, then tightly closed his eyes. He took deep, steadying breaths before he set his gun down, and didn't say another word. He pushed himself up in the bed so his back was against the headboard.

I watched his face carefully and when I thought he'd regained his composure, I apologized. He lifted his chin in mute acknowledgement. "I should have known better," I added. James sat motionlessly, his eyebrows drawn as if he were trying to figure me out. I crawled up on the bed until the side of my knee touched his thigh and sat back on my heels. I reached out and stroked the warm skin over his heart.

He stilled my hand under his. "What do you want, Emelynn?"

I looked him in the eyes. "You, James. Tonight, I want you. I want you to make me forget why I can't sleep. Help me stop thinking about the cottage and Carson Manse. Just for tonight. Please."

He squeezed my hand and searched my face. "Even knowing I have nothing to offer?"

"You have everything I need tonight."

"It's not enough, Emelynn. You're scared and vulnerable, and you'll regret this tomorrow."

I leaned forward and kissed him, pressing my silk nightie into his chest, teasing his lips open. He responded without enthusiasm. I retreated a few inches and spoke. "I won't regret this tomorrow, James. And if I do, you can say 'I told you so.'"

He reached up and brushed his fingers across my cheek. "The last time we did this, I felt like a heel afterwards."

"Are you saying no?" I asked, searching his face for clues. He ran his fingers from my temple to my jaw, deep in thought. "Do you think you're the only one in this room with nothing to offer?" He frowned. "Of the two of us, I'm the one closest to being dead tomorrow, so please, James. Don't ask me to leave."

He didn't close his eyes when I leaned in again. I watched him watch me kiss him while his body warred with his brain. When his breathing deepened I knew his body had won and he finally closed his eyes and kissed me back. "Thank you," I whispered into his mouth and then he reached his hand behind my head and twined his tongue with mine, pulling me into his lap and holding me close.

I felt safe in James's arms and relaxed for the first time in hours. I melted into him. If this was all he had to offer tonight, it would be enough.

Lucky for me, he was just warming up. When he broke our kiss, he looked at me like I was a mirage in the desert and he was thirsty. He reached his left hand out and ran his fingers under the spaghetti strap of the nightie, tugging it down so the strap fell loosely around my elbow, leaving the silk clinging to my breast. He swiped his thumb across the thin fabric and I arched into him. That was all the invitation he needed. With a quick shift, he laid me back against the pillows and moved to straddle my hips. He reached forward and flipped the silk free from my other breast and trailed his fingers lightly around the edge. "You are quite a sight," he said, and ran his tongue along his bottom lip. "Are you sure about this?" I flinched when he pinched my nipple, which drew a slow seductive smile across his face.

"I'm sure," I breathed. He leaned forward and twirled his tongue first around one nipple and then the other. The warm wet sensation was exquisite. I felt the tingle of promised release and writhed underneath him.

"You like this?" he asked. I murmured my appreciation. He rubbed his nose up my neck and nipped my earlobe. "Tell me," he whispered.

I turned to face him. "Yes, I like this," I said, and then, so there could be no doubt, I pulled him to my lips and plunged my tongue into his mouth. The tie in his hair came out easily and I pushed my fingers through to his scalp shaking the strands to fall loosely around his shoulders. I'd be a fool to regret this, I thought, running the silken hair through my fingers.

The bottom of my nightie had floated up to my waist. He reached down to press the heel of his hand against my pubic bone then fluttered his fingers between my legs until I moaned. "I'm going to make you come like this," he breathed and I shamelessly eased my legs apart, pushing my hips against his hand.

"Promise?" I said. He laughed and then slid his fingers inside, stealing my breath away. He worked me to the precipice with his talented fingers all the while kissing his way down my body.

"James," I groaned when he nipped the tender skin at the top of my inner thigh. He nuzzled between my legs and darted his tongue to that most tender spot on a woman's body: the place where all the nerve endings came together to rejoice. He twirled his clever tongue and delved and suckled until he owned me, body and soul. I tumbled off the edge of an orgasm that bowed my spine and forced a torrent of incomprehensible babble from my throat. He hadn't searched out my gaze for his rush. His tongue had more than done the job.

I lay back, spent and quivering, sweet aftershocks rolling through me. James kissed me just below my belly button and then the bed moved and stilled. He'd stepped away. I reluctantly opened my eyes. I'd already had an earth-shattering orgasm and I'd barely laid my hands on him. Was that dreadfully selfish of me? James's delectable backside was bent over his leather satchel. I leaned up on my elbows to take in the view. When he turned back around, he held up a condom like he'd found the last match on a cold, dark night.

"Let me," I said, holding out my hand. The smile that curled my lips was more than appreciation—it was a promise of my own.

He swung his hips in my direction and handed me the condom. I sat up and used my teeth to open the package while he ran his hand through my hair and positioned his considerable self front and centre. His eyes were hooded, his shoulders hunched forward. I was tempted to make him beg, like he'd done to me. Instead, I leaned forward and licked the tip of him, tasting the drop of salty sweetness that threatened to fall. James's face splintered in ecstasy. I took him into my mouth and took great pleasure feeling his knees falter as I swirled my tongue in circles. I rolled my lips over my teeth and dragged the pressure along the length of him. He growled deep in his throat and tightened his hands in my hair. James had an edge to him I didn't quite understand, but I was willing to play in his sandbox.

I released him with a final lollipop lick up the underside of his erection then carefully pinched the tip of the condom before rolling it over his length. He leaned down to kiss me, wrapping an arm around my back. We inched up the bed, connected by a kiss until my head reached the pillows. I settled back.

"Not like this," he said. "Turn over." In a bubble of aroused distraction, I obliged. He straddled my backside and stilled. His stillness alerted me to the fact that he'd stopped breathing. James hadn't seen my scars before. We'd spent a few naked hours together during our previous encounter and he'd not seen my back. What a massive turnoff, I thought and struggled against him to flip back over, but he wouldn't let me. "Shh," he whispered, folding his torso over my back. He pressed a soft kiss on my shoulder blade. I felt his fingers trace a line. He trailed kisses in his fingers' warm wake. I stopped struggling.

"I'm sorry, I forgot," I said, burying my face in the pillow.

His fingers picked up another line going in the other direction. That one curled around to the side of my breast. He followed each line with tender kisses, releasing my anxiety. He gently eased off the remaining bits of Avery's gauze, kissing each one. His warm hands were gentle, reverent. Soon I was able to enjoy his caress without thinking about the scars. James had masterfully recovered my arousal. The bed shifted as he moved to kneel behind me. The feel of his knee nudging my legs apart made me purr.

"Lift your hips," he said, tugging me gently to my knees. He dragged a mewling murmur out of me as he positioned his erection against the moistness between my legs. He pushed the tip of himself inside me, inhaling with a sharp hiss. Strong hands gripped my hips and he thrust forward, pulling me against him. My body accepted him without hesitation. I would have collapsed had he not been holding me up. Slowly, he pulled out of me then drove back in, driving the air out of my lungs in an unladylike grunt. He held his position inside me until I bucked against him. James took that as "go" and he commenced a hard rhythm.

He connected deeper inside me than I'd ever felt before. The bump and pressure was sensational, suggesting an orgasm that could easily eclipse all previous contenders. I missed seeing his face in a state of ecstasy, but it was evident in the lusty groans that accompanied his heavy breathing. He slowed our rhythm, prolonging the experience, and leaned forward, moving his hands up my sides and under my shoulders. I let him pull me upright until I was sitting backwards, impaled on him. I'd never felt so exposed, so vulnerable.

He stilled under me but I could feel him pulsing inside as he massaged my breasts, holding me tightly. "James," I moaned in protest.

"What," he breathed into my ear, teasing.

"Don't stop."

"What do you want, Emelynn," he asked, moving one hand to my throat and pulling my ear lobe into his mouth. His other hand pulled at my nipple and I felt his erection twitch deep inside of me.

"You, James."

He punched his hips. "This," he asked and I could feel the smirk on his lips.

"God, yes!" I hissed and he groaned then flexed sharply again.

He pushed me forward onto my hands and transferred his weight to his arms on either side of me. He swung his hips in a rhythm that caused my breath to hitch. The acute sensations quickly built to an intense explosion. All sense of decorum abandoned me in the unruly business of orgasm. My insides gripped James and the sounds coming from him echoed my own. Waves of ecstasy flowed from me to him and back again until we folded onto our sides, still connected, breathing heavily and sweating.

We lay like that, wrapped in each other, for what seemed like hours. He pulled my back close to his chest and reached to pull the blankets over us. I fell fast asleep with him still inside me.

I woke to James pressing kisses down my neck. It was still dark out. "What time is it?" I mumbled.

"Six."

"Hmm," I sighed contentedly, rubbing back against him like a cat. "You didn't run."

He ignored my comment and pulled me closer. "How are you feeling?"

"Heavenly," I smiled. "How about you?"

He pressed a kiss to the back of my head. "Happy," he said. "I'm glad you came to me last night." He smoothed my hair with his hand. "Unfortunately, you can't stay. You have to be in your own room when Jordan shows up."

I turned in his arms. "I don't even remember when he said he was coming by."

James's hair was still loose. He looked delectable in sleepy, well-fucked hair. "He said eight."

"Crap!" I struggled to sit up. I had to ghost, get to my room, and then re-form. I wasn't sure I could manage all that by eight without last night's incentive.

The sheets had me tangled in their grip. I looked down and a laugh bubbled out. My silk nightie was twisted around my waist like a scarf. James reached over and caressed my naked breast, brushing a thumb across my nipple. Even in my morning fog, I bit my lip and sighed remembering how his mouth felt in place of his thumb. I pulled his hand to my mouth and kissed his fingers then disentangled myself and got out of the warm bed. The nightie's straps were wound in the wrinkled mess and it took me a moment to find them and re-dress. I smoothed the silk down my thighs.

"I'd better go," I said apologetically.

James crawled out of bed behind me and brushed my hair aside, planting a tender kiss on my shoulder. He reached around and cupped my breasts in his hands, sighing into my hair. "I'll meet you upstairs after Jordan arrives. He wants to talk strategy before we head to your place."

I turned around in his arms and, conscious that I hadn't brushed my teeth, gave him a closed-mouth kiss. "All right. I'll see you upstairs." I reached deep inside to my crystal and wrapped my fingers around it. It was warm and smooth, purring with vitality. I gave it a gentle squeeze and felt the surge of energy that heralded my ghost. James's eyes opened wide and I knew I'd disappeared.

"Emelynn?"

"I'm right here," I said, and pressed a hand to his chest. He looked to the spot where I'd touched him. My mouth dropped open. He'd felt it. I hadn't ghosted as deeply this time. "I'll see you soon," I said, and breezed through the circle of his arms.

Even my footsteps felt like they connected more solidly with the floor as I walked to his door. It felt so different from the other times that I had to check to make sure I was really gone. I reached for the door latch and felt it give under my fingertip. I flipped it open then turned the door lock. Even to me, it looked like something from an old sci-fi movie. I pressed down on the door lever, opened the door then closed it behind me.

Getting around wasn't like the previous times when I'd ghosted and had to float. At this level, I actually needed to take steps and walk. It felt clunky and somewhat uncoordinated. Perhaps getting back to my room like this wasn't a good idea. Whoever was watching my room would send in reinforcements if they saw my door open and close without the benefit of a body. Once again, I reached inside to find my crystal humming quietly, waiting. I squeezed it gently and a flush of energy pushed me deeper into my ghosted form, lifting me from my feet like a current in the ocean.

Yes, this was more familiar. I drifted to the stairwell door and rushed it then floated up to the twelfth floor. I blew through that door and down the hall to my own room, forced myself through the cracks and gathered myself inside. I drifted through the living room and into the bedroom and settled on top of the covers.

Someone would wake me before Jordan arrived, I wasn't worried about that, but I wanted to re-form again without passing out. Controlling my ghost was just as important as learning how to fly. Conscious, deliberate thought was what it took to materialize. I rolled on my side and splayed my hand on the pillow then kept my eyes on it. I thought about James and the feel of his hair in my hand. I pictured his chest under my hand and the feel of his soft warm skin. Metaphysically, I groped around for my crystal like a blind woman with her hand in a sack. Finally, I felt the pointed tip of it. I worked my mind's eye around the crystal and felt it slowly come back to me. As it solidified, so did my hand. I watched in amazement as my body returned, along with gravity, pressing me into the mattress. I pulled the comforter around my shoulders and contentedly drifted off to sleep.

Chapter Fifteen

After the second ring, I reluctantly opened my eyes. The bedside clock read 7:30. "Hello," I answered, not bothering to disguise my sleep-infused voice.

"Sleeping in, this morning?"

The detective's social skills were as sharp as ever. I yawned. "Rough night," I said, unable to keep the smile off my face as memories of last night flitted through my thoughts.

"Can you be ready by eight?"

"Sure."

"Coffee?"

"Yes, please. With milk."

"I'll see you in thirty minutes."

I rolled over and hung up the phone, then traipsed to the bathroom. Fifteen minutes later, I was squeaky clean with a towel wrapped around my head. I chose a selection from the Burberry suitcase, thankful once more for my friends.

By the time the detective arrived, I'd dressed and applied some makeup. My hair was still damp. Blow-drying hair like mine only served to frizz it up to embarrassing volumes.

"Sam," I said, smiling a welcome. The sight of his familiar jacket reminded me to be nice to the man.

"Emelynn."

"Thank you," I said, accepting a cardboard tray of coffees he'd been juggling. He had a Tim Horton's bag in one hand and a large Hudson's Bay bag in the other.

"Moss is on his way."

Sam sat on the sofa and accepted the coffee I'd squeaked out of the tray. "Doughnuts?" I asked referring to the Timmy's bag.

He mistook my enthusiasm at the prospect, for sarcasm. "Scones," he said, with a roll of his eyes. "Help yourself."

I pulled the bag close and peered inside. Sam stood to answer the knock at the door and admitted James.

"Emelynn," James said, and with that blasé greeting, I knew how good an actor he was. There was no hint of familiarity beyond casual acquaintance. He shoved the newspaper he brought at Detective Jordan.

"James," I said, and quickly looked away. I wanted to jump him, feel his hands on me. God, I hoped that wasn't written all over my face. Luckily the detective was preoccupied with the paper.

"Page five," James said, and the detective flipped to the page. James sat down across from me, avoiding eye contact.

Sam studied the article and nodded. "Good. Should do the trick."

"Is that about the fire?" I asked. Sam took a seat and handed me the paper. They'd run a horrible photo of my ruined Arts and Crafts cottage. It hurt to look at what was left of it. The article hit all the highlights: arson, my name, and the fact that I was under police protection. "What if he doesn't see this?"

"He'll see it," Sam said, brokering no doubt. "After the lengths he's gone to, he's not going to give up. He's looking for you and we're going to help him find you … not you, of course—Grace Shipley. She'll be here in an hour or two." He pointed to the Timmy's bag and offered me a scone. I took the one on top. It was still warm and looked like it had cheddar and bits of ham.

"That bag's for you," Sam said, referring to the Hudson's Bay bag he'd arrived with. "Clothes. Two identical sets. When you're done eating, change and we'll head out."

The scone stuck in my throat like sawdust. I had to wash it down with coffee. I knew it wasn't the scone. It was the prospect of seeing the cottage again and reliving the fire. The small hope I clung to, the one thing that would justify the pain, would be finding Jeannette's crystal-case necklace.

While James and Sam talked about Grace and discussed strategy, I excused myself and took the bag of clothes into the bedroom. On top were two pairs of drugstore sunglasses, which would cover half my face, and two baseballs caps. Underneath, I found two pairs of tan-coloured slacks, two UBC sweatshirts and two light-weight grey bomber-style jackets. At the bottom of the bag were two pairs of blindingly white Ked sneakers.

I dressed quickly and returned to the living room.

"Put your hair in a ponytail and through the back of the hat," Sam said. There was a knock at the door. "I'll let him in."

"Who's that?" I asked James as the detective headed to the door. I dutifully bound my hair back into a ponytail.

"Matt. He's bringing body armour."

The Kevlar vest was heavier than it looked and I needed help putting it on. I pulled the grey jacket over top. "It's too big."

"Grace needs room for her guns," James said. I heard the plural and raised my eyebrows.

I put on the hat and threaded my ponytail through the back, catching a glimpse of myself reflected in the window. The getup looked contrived. "I look like I'm trying to disguise myself."

"That's the point," James said. "We want him to think we're doing our job." James stood in front of me and tugged the hat down low. "Grace will need to have her hair out of her face and the hat can't be flopping around impairing her vision. Try these on," he said, handing me the sunglasses. "Shake your head." I did as he said, and everything stayed in place. "You're good to go." With his back to Sam and Matt, only I saw his smile. It was one of those I-know-what-you-taste-like smiles that lovers share and it was all I could do to not react. My heart skipped a happy beat.

"Matt will stay here and brief Grace when she arrives," Sam said. Then he turned to me. "Are you ready?"

I nodded. "Let's go."

We wended our way back through the utilitarian employee corridors to the service elevator, Sam in front and James behind. Sam and I waited inside the door of the underground garage while James retrieved the SUV. James knocked once on the door. We entered the garage and piled into the vehicle. The smell of exhaust was nauseating.

"Do you think Carson will see us?" I asked when we cleared the garage. I opened the window a crack to let in some fresh air. It was too warm for a sweatshirt and I pulled the neck of it away from my throat.

"Not yet, hopefully. At least not until Grace is in place. There's a good possibility he's watching the cottage though. People often come back to search for things after a fire."

　　　　　　　　　　　　　　　　　　　　　　　JP McLean

We drove in silence until James turned on the radio. At nine, I had the memorable experience of hearing my name mentioned on the morning news. Oh no! I hadn't called Malcolm. I hung my head in my hands. He would have expected me yesterday. Damn. I hoped he hadn't ridden his bicycle over to check on me.

Sam misunderstood my angst. "Don't let it get to you, Emelynn. It'll probably hit the evening news, as well."

I sighed heavily. "It's not that," I said. "It's Malcolm. We had an appointment yesterday and I didn't even think to call him. Now he's going to hear this or read it in the paper."

"The trainer from the Y?" Sam asked.

"Yes," I said, nodding my head.

"He knows. I spoke with him yesterday. You don't need to worry about Malcolm. You have enough on your plate."

"He's been a very good friend to me."

"I remember. You can make it up to him when this blows over."

Assuming it did blow over. "I hope so."

It took thirty minutes to get to Cliffside Avenue. A black and white cruiser lurked in the cul-de-sac at the end of the street just outside Sunset Park. Two constables emerged from the car when we pulled into the driveway.

Immediately, I lurched forward and put a halting hand on James's shoulder. "Do you recognize them?" I asked, ducking my head. They were still too far away for me to see clearly. I squinted in search of beady black eyes.

Sam said, "They're ours, Emelynn. Relax."

I took a breath and sat back. Yellow tape encircled the burnt remains at the other end of the driveway. Even from inside the car, I could smell charred wood like a rain-dampened campfire, though "campfire" seemed far too cheery a word.

James released the door locks, and he and Sam got out to greet the uniformed officers. As soon as their doors closed, I felt tears well up. Looking at the blackened ruins of the cottage felt like gazing at a grave. I knew I'd remember this moment for a long time. This is what hatred felt like. It burned cold, like dry ice. Carson Manse had done this. For this alone, I could kill him. When I considered everything else he'd done to me, I could kill him with a smile on my face while doing the Macarena. Bastard! I angrily wiped my tears then opened the door and got out.

"You okay?" Sam asked, coming to my side.

It was one of those questions you ask when you can't pretend you haven't seen the tears, but you don't want to deal with the emotional fallout. "Fine," I said, appreciating his effort. Kevlar had nothing on the sympathy deflecting protection of the flak jacket I pulled on.

Sam accompanied me on my walkabout. I tried not to look too carefully at the cottage's remains, concentrating instead on the ground where I might find the necklace with Jeannette's crystal. As best I could remember, I backtracked along the path I'd walked barefoot in the early morning hours that day.

"Is the car still in there?" I asked when we got close to the garage. The lock looked intact. I didn't have a key.

"As far as I know," Sam said.

James and the two constables spread out around me, keeping a respectful distance. I kept my head down and scanned the muddy grass. My route was just a guess. I'd skirted some emergency vehicles that night, but I couldn't remember where they'd been parked. I'd reached the edge of the property by the cul-de-sac when the futility of my search hit like a dousing of cold water.

It must have shown on my face because Sam offered a lifeline. "You came out of the park right there," he said, pointing ahead. "Do you remember where you were before that?"

I grabbed his lifeline like a drowning woman, buoyed with another thread of hope. I'd been blown into the scrub brush behind the fire truck. The cruiser now sat in roughly the same spot. He followed me to the far side of the vehicle where the ground was not trampled to mud and ashes. Sam stood back and let me tiptoe around the undisturbed ground, crouching down every few feet to poke at the undergrowth. The effort proved fruitless.

I looked up to get my bearings. The wind had blown me up over the top of the bushes when I'd crested the fire truck on that awful night. If the necklace was tangled up in those bushes, I wouldn't find it from the ground. But I could search around the old cedar behind which I'd taken cover. Sam accompanied me along the path and into the park. Fifty yards on, I found the tree and circled around it, bending down to sift through the dried leaves and needles.

Sam bent down beside me. "Is this what you're looking for?" he said, plucking forest debris out of his fist with stubby fingers. The white-gold crystal case dangled from its chain.

"You found it!" I exclaimed, reaching out to him.

"It's a very unusual piece," he said, squinting at the crystal's chamber. "What's the story behind it?" he asked, surrendering it to me.

I arranged my features into a grateful smile while alarm bells sounded in my head. Some critical piece of information floated just beyond reach of my memory. What was it?

"It belonged to someone important to my father," I said. "Thank you for finding it."

"What's inside there?" he asked, pointing to the intricate crystal case.

The crystal! I thought, and the memory flooded back. I'd mentioned Carson's quest for a crystal to the task force. I'd claimed ignorance. If Sam connected the dots, he'd have questions I couldn't answer.

Blood rushed to my face. I snapped my head to the right as if I'd been spooked. I'd hoped to redirect the detective and it worked. He reached for the gun in his shoulder holster and followed my gaze. I quickly tucked the necklace into my coat pocket and moved to stand up. Sam stopped me with a firm hand on my forearm, pausing to listen.

When he was convinced it was safe, he whispered, "Let's go," and escorted me out of the park, his hand in a death grip on my shoulder. He made eye contact with James and flicked his head toward the SUV. James took the cue and moved toward the vehicle.

"We're done," he said to the closest constable, as he ushered me to the rear door. James started the SUV and backed out of the driveway rather than driving around the loop.

"What is it?" James asked into the rear-view mirror when we were pointed back down Cliffside.

"Maybe nothing, but Emelynn heard something. No need to take unnecessary risks. She found what she was looking for. Let's get back to the hotel." Sam ducked his head to look out the side window. James met my gaze in the mirror then looked away, his expression unreadable.

My hotel room was hopping with activity when we returned. I stepped into the hall and bumped into Dino who was hiking his pants. The toilet gurgled in the small bathroom behind him. We walked through the hall to the living room, where Benny was hunched over an open laptop that lay on the coffee table. Matt stood talking to a blonde-haired woman who wore the same beige slacks and white Keds as me.

James stepped around me. "Grace. Good to see you again," he said, extending his hand then kissing her cheek.

"James," she cooed in a sultry voice. "You're looking good."

Grace looked to be about thirty and she may have had my build, but she was far more striking. Her hair was cut in a sharp bob and high bangs emphasized smoky grey eyes. She wore a tight, white muscle shirt and I couldn't take my eyes off her perfectly toned arms.

"You must be Emelynn," she said, startling me out of my stare. "I'm Grace Shipley." She held out her hand. "Pleased to meet you."

"You too," I said.

She turned back to James. "Matt's filled me in." Sam had come up behind James and made Grace's acquaintance with a handshake. While they exchanged mutual compliments, I moved Jeannette's necklace to my pants pocket. I took off my baseball cap and jacket, and then pulled the Velcro tabs to release myself from the weight of the Kevlar vest.

Grace rummaged in a black duffle bag and came up with a sheathed knife about eight inches long. "I understand our first stop is the bank," she said, putting her left foot on the edge of the coffee table. She lifted her pant leg and strapped the knife to her leg. "Have we got anyone inside yet?" She dipped into her bag again and produced another knife, which she strapped to her left forearm.

"We've got an undercover behind the counter and access to the video feed," Dino said.

Grace strapped on her Kevlar vest without assistance then pulled the sweatshirt overtop. Next came not one gun, but two. A quick look around the room confirmed that I wasn't the only one mesmerized by Grace Shipley.

"What about backup?" she asked.

"There's a shooter in place on the roof and a van in the alley. Emelynn will go in the front with Jordan to cover but as I said earlier, we don't expect trouble. We've taken every precaution to ensure everyone's safety."

"Sounds good," she said. "Does he know you're here?" she asked Sam as she swirled her finger in the air, indicating the hotel.

"The suspect knows I'm involved," Detective Jordan said. "And I made no attempt to conceal myself on the way over from the station this morning. Carson Manse is clever and seems to have no end of resources. He'll find us."

Dino spoke up. "We parked a cruiser in the underground garage in case he needed more convincing, and Matt here wasn't very discreet about bringing her vest up to the suite. It should have been enough."

"And if it's not, there's a very good chance he'll have eyes on the bank. He'll trail us from there," Detective Jordan said. "I'm sure of it."

"Where do we go to after the bank?" I asked, finally venturing into the conversation.

Detective Jordan spoke like he was looking sternly over a pair of non-existent glasses. "You don't go anywhere from there. Grace will take over once we get to the bank and then we'll lead him away from the public."

"How are we going to switch places?" I asked.

"The bank's getting a water cooler delivered this morning. Grace will be inside the box. The same box you're going out in, after we're long gone," Detective Jordan said.

"And then what?" I asked. The room grew quiet.

"Then we wait," Detective Jordan said. I looked around the room and understood the tension. It was the dread of waiting that had everyone on edge. During that wait, they'd all be in danger. A danger precipitated by me and my gift, and a crystal that didn't even exist.

Had James considered the unique risk that someone like Carson Manse posed to his law enforcement colleagues? The Redeemers had more than guns at their disposal; they all had the power to jolt and who knew what other gifts they'd stolen? My eyes flicked to James, who quickly looked away.

"I need to see some footage of Emelynn in motion," Grace said, breaking the silence that had us in its grip.

"Over here," Benny said from the sofa. Grace sat beside him. He worked the keyboard then turned the laptop so Grace could see. My curiosity got the best of me and I walked behind the sofa to get a look. Playing across the screen was video of us this morning leaving the hotel and then returning. She played it twice before excusing herself to disappear into the bedroom.

"Do you have something you can wear under those clothes? Something you haven't been seen in yet?" Detective Jordan asked. "You have to leave what you're wearing at the bank."

"I think so."

"Good. Go change."

I quickly rifled through the suitcase and pulled out the yoga pants, a shirt and the ballet slippers. Grace was behind the ensuite bathroom's closed door. I quickly stripped and re-dressed with the extra layer. Jeannette's necklace felt like a heavy weight on my conscience. I pulled it out of my pocket and furtively checked the crystal. Thankfully, it was intact.

I returned to the living room and tucked the ballet slippers into the pocket of the bomber jacket.

Detective Jordan approached. "You'll need this," he said, handing me an envelope.

"My passport?" I said, seeing the familiar blue cover inside. "Why?"

"After you leave the bank, you'll head to the airport. James will escort you. We've arranged for you to be flown to San Francisco."

"San Francisco?"

"The Reynoldses have offered their home as a safe house until we have the situation up here under control," Sam explained.

"But—" I started to protest, and James cut me off.

"They can protect you." With the tilt of his head, he pleaded with me not to argue.

My thoughts ran to Avery. He would want me to go. "All right," I said. The Reynoldses were probably the only ones who could keep me safe. Did they know who Typhoid Mary was? I wondered.

Grace walked back into the room. "How's the hair?" she asked no one in particular. She wore the baseball cap, and a ponytail just like mine poked out the back.

James and Sam looked her over and both agreed that the ponytail was too long. I retrieved the scissors from the bathroom then pulled on my baseball cap, so James could trim Grace's wig to match perfectly.

After Grace donned the grey bomber jacket and sunglasses, she walked around the room to practice my walk. She stopped in front of me. We looked like twins. "I'm ready," she announced.

"Please be careful," I said.

She smiled back at me. "You too."

Dino made a phone call and moments later a housekeeping cart arrived. Dino opened the door and Grace slipped into the cart unnoticed. "Can you come back later?" he said.

"Certainly, sir," the housekeeper replied, and rolled her cart away with Grace safely tucked underneath.

Dino closed the door. "Grace will call when she's in position."

"Let's pack up," Detective Jordan said. "You too," he indicated to me. "Use Grace's bag. She'll need yours."

"I'll help," James said, emptying the remaining items from Grace's bag while I picked up my things. "Leave the clothes you wore yesterday for Grace. If Manse was watching us, he'll recognize them."

We were ready when Grace's call came. Benny and Dino left first.

James took the black duffle bag. "I'll see you in an hour," he said, giving my arm a reassuring pat. Matt and Detective Jordan held back for a few minutes. Then, with me and the Burberry suitcase sandwiched between them, we headed to the underground garage.

Matt drove. Sam sat in the back with me. While we waited at the mouth of the alley to merge into the busy one-way traffic on Smithe, Matt and Sam remained tense, scanning pedestrians and passing cars. The SUV's blinker sounded like a church bell. I pretended I wasn't terrified and searched for beady black eyes.

Matt pulled into traffic and moments later said, "Dino's in place." I followed his nod to a marked cruiser a few cars ahead. He pulled a mic from under the dash. "Unit 1080, are you in place?"

Sam swivelled his head to check behind. The radio crackled to life and a scratchy voice said, "Unit 1080, affirmative."

"Carl's behind," Sam said, finally relaxing. I looked but couldn't pick out his unmarked car. "When we get to the bank, you stay in the car until I come around and open your door." The cruiser in front of us turned up Burrard Street. Sam continued, "When we get inside, we'll go directly to the information counter." Matt signalled our turn and headed into the intersection.

The screech of tires reached our ears moments before a thunderous, metal-crunching bang rocked the SUV. White air bags exploded everywhere in a spray of powder. I hadn't felt myself being thrown forward against my shoulder-strap, but I felt it when my head bounced back and the vehicle settled with a groan. Car alarms screamed in pulses.

Sam snapped into action. In one fluid motion, he released my seat belt and pulled me forward then pushed me down behind the front seats. "Keep down," he warned with a firm hand on the back of my head. He pulled his gun from its holster.

After an eternity, the car alarm fell silent and radio static filled the air. I couldn't make out a word with the ringing in my ears. Shouts outside the vehicle had Sam on full alert.

"What's happening?" I asked in a whisper.

"Looks like a car ran the light. Dino and Carl are securing the area."

This was Carson's doing, I thought, and felt myself tremble. I closed my eyes and dragged in deep calming breaths. I could still ghost. It would create a huge problem, but I'd be alive. I reached inside for my crystal and pulled on its power, holding it steady.

Close by, a fire engine blasted its air horn. Matt pushed his door open and I heard Carl speak. "They didn't even hit the brakes. You'll need to get her out Jordan's side. We're bringing another car around."

I started to rise, but Sam held my head down. "Not yet," he said.

A siren approached, cutting out right beside our SUV. Car doors slammed. "Get ready to move," Sam said, shifting in his seat. His door opened and he made a swift exit, motioning me to follow. "Keep low," he said, directing me to the back of a marked cruiser just a few feet away. Sam slid in behind me and the door thumped shut behind him.

"Jordan, Emelynn," Roberta said from behind the wheel. "Let's get out of here." She hit the gas and sped up Burrard, away from the ambulance and fire trucks that plugged the street. "Are you two all right?" Roberta asked when we were clear of the area.

"I think so," Sam said, looking at me for an answer. I nodded. He turned to Roberta. "What's the word?"

"Female driver. Young. She hit pretty hard. Looks like she ran the light. Probably texting."

"Something Carson Manse arranged?" I asked Sam.

"If it was, he missed his opportunity. Roberta, do we still have cover?"

"Carl's right behind us and we've alerted the unit at the bank. They know we're coming."

We drove on in tense silence and Sam swivelled his head like an owl looking for prey.

"Here we are," Roberta said, pulling to the curb in front of the bank. She turned around. "Take care, Emelynn. I'll see you again after we've nailed this scumbag." She smiled warmly then got out of the car and walked around to open Sam's door. I followed Sam out of the car and we quickly crossed the sidewalk. Sam held the bank's door for me and kept his hand on my back as we walked straight to the reception desk.

"He's expecting you," the receptionist said in response to Sam's introduction. She offered a professional smile and phoned her manager. I felt nervous and found myself looking for beady black eyes in every face. A handful of people stood in the teller queue: two seniors who looked like a couple, a young mother with a stroller and a middle-aged man in a suit. God forbid anything should happen to them, I thought, trying to shake off my nervous energy. Sam's touch felt reassuring.

The manager walked toward us with his arm extended as if I were his best customer. "Hello, Ms. Taylor," he said. I shook his hand. I'd never met the man before. I'd only ever been to the ATM and all of my other dealings had been online. This show was not for me. "Come in."

I followed him to his office and only checked back behind me once. In that brief glimpse, I recognized the woman with the stroller. It was Carrie—Tribunal Carrie—the same Carrie who had helped Mason rescue me from Carson and that nightmare of a trailer. I breathed a sigh of relief. If she was here, then other Tribunal would be too. James hadn't left his colleagues without protection after all. I said a little prayer of thanks and returned my attention to the detective.

The manager closed the door behind us and briskly walked to an interior door. When he opened it, Grace Shipley emerged.

"Follow her instructions . . . and don't argue with Moss," Detective Jordan said. "We'll be in touch." He dropped his hand from my back and walked toward the two chairs in front of the desk, striking up a casual conversation with the manager.

Grace motioned me to her and whispered that I was to leave my disguise in the file box she pointed to, and hide in the water-cooler box against the wall. "Keep your vest on," she said. I arched an eyebrow at the insufferably small box. She saw my expression and grinned. "You'll fit; crouch down and rest your elbows on your knees. Don't speak and don't show yourself. Someone will come and collect the box in thirty minutes. They'll take you to James." She smiled a reassuring smile and motioned me backwards into the darkened room then quietly closed the door behind her.

I felt very alone as I heard Grace's voice join the men's conversation.

CHAPTER SIXTEEN

It took only moments to strip out of my disguise and stow it in the file box. I slipped Jeannette's crystal-case necklace around my neck and tucked it inside the vest, and then I braided my hair and stepped into the ballet flats.

On closer inspection, I realized the water-cooler box wasn't cardboard at all—it was plywood with a cardboard exterior. The front panel had been left loose. I opened it and contorted myself to fit inside. Had Grace said thirty minutes? This was going to be a test worthy of a circus performer, and I wasn't that. I pulled the front panel closed.

The murmured conversation in the adjoining room faded. A door opened and closed. In a few moments, Grace and the detective would make their exit. If chaos didn't follow, I would trust they'd gotten away safely. Minutes ticked away and still, all was quiet. With nothing to distract me, the strain on my knees and ankles held my attention. I wriggled around and counted off the minutes to ease the sensory deprivation.

After what seemed an eternity, the door to the room opened. "It's in here." I recognized the receptionist's voice. The lights flicked on. "It should have been delivered to the Seaside Branch on Blanchford," she said.

"Yeah, sorry about that," a male voice responded. A shadow fell across the small crack in the seam of the box. A loud smack on the side of it covered my gasp as the sliver of light disappeared under the man's fist. He banged up and down the edge of the front panel, closing it tightly. I held my hand against my mouth when the box unexpectedly tilted forward, and swallowed another yelp. Something metallic scraped underneath and the box was righted again. I heard the slap of a strap against the outside and then ratcheting clicks. He was securing the box to a dolly. The box tilted backwards and a squeaking wheel told me we were rolling.

If I were ten years old, this would have been fun. But right now, I was scared out of my wits, barely breathing and hoping like hell the person rolling me away was one of the good guys. The box bumped and swayed and I kept my fist pressed to my mouth.

The ambient sound changed, signalling that we'd made it outside. I heard the whiz of car tires on asphalt, then the mechanical drone and jerk of a lift. "Just a few more stops," the man's voice said quietly, as he wheeled me inside what I imagined was a delivery truck. Straps slapped the side of the box again, and then I heard the rattle of a rolling door and the clank of its closing, locking me in. Moments later, the vehicle lurched forward. We made two more stops accompanied by the rattle of the rolling door each time.

Finally, the truck came to a stop and the engine quieted. This time when the rolling doors rattled open, I heard James's voice barking instructions. A wave of relief washed over me. "Emelynn?" he called.

"James. Get me out of here."

The box shifted. "Keep your hands away from the front panel," he said. I heard the thump of metal on wood and then the front of the box dropped away. I squinted against the bright daylight. It felt like coming out of a matinee.

James reached in to help me out. My body unfolded with aching protest. "Thanks," I said, slowly straightening. I could now cross contortionist off my list of potential career choices. "How did it go?"

"They were followed, but not by Manse. Whoever it was will report back to him. Now they sit tight and wait for Manse to show himself."

"I saw Carrie at the bank."

"Ron's there too. Manse won't get away this time, Em." Carrie and Ron had terrorized me the night of the Tribunal's interrogation. Now, they were here to help me. I hadn't seen that twist coming.

And thinking of twists, I asked James, "Did you hear about the accident?"

"I did. You're okay?" he asked.

"Yeah. Was Carson behind it?"

"Don't know, but we've got to go."

He took my hand and led me out of the truck, down the length of the loading bays and into a warehouse. A motorcycle leaned on its kickstand at the far end of the barren space. James's satchel and Grace's black duffle bag were already secured on the back. "Put these on," he said, and I donned the dark windbreaker and strapped on the helmet he handed me. He climbed on the bike and kicked it to life then scooted forward motioning me to get on behind him. "Hold on," he shouted as he hit the gas and we rocketed forward and down a ramp out into the street. He wove comfortably in and out of traffic like he'd been riding all his life. It felt good to hold him.

We pulled into a hangar at Vancouver airport's south terminal and parked out of sight. When we had our helmets off, I asked if we were taking the Tribunal jet. "No," James said. "They hired one under another company name." He helped me out of the Kevlar vest and left it with the helmets on the bike.

We cleared the security check after an agent searched my bag. He then ushered us to a waiting room. Ten minutes later, we were striding across the tarmac to a small private jet. The inside looked like a cross between a board room and a living room. The pilots were already in the cockpit, and one of them came out to greet us. "Mr. Moss," he said, extending his hand.

"Dave, good to see you." Dave wore a white short-sleeved shirt with black and gold striped epaulettes and a black tie. "This is Dana Christopher," James said, nodding to me. He'd used the fake name he'd set up for me before my first visit to San Francisco. I swallowed my surprise and extended my hand.

"Dave Ouellette," he said. "I'll be your co-pilot today. Are you ready to get under way?"

"Absolutely," I said.

"Take a seat," Dave said, sweeping his arm toward the empty cabin. James sat beside me and we buckled up as Dave recited a safety briefing he'd obviously done countless times. He then disappeared into the cockpit advising us he'd radio for clearance.

When he'd left, I pulled out my new passport and shook my head. "Dana?" I quizzed. "You should have warned me, James."

"It slipped my mind. I'm sorry."

I suppose I could forgive him that. We'd certainly had enough details to manage in the past seventy-two hours. From the window, I saw a train of luggage carts roll by as the jet moved away from the hangar and taxied out to the runway.

The seats were cream-coloured leather. I counted twelve others in addition to ours. The carbon footprint people would not be impressed.

After we took off, the jet levelled out and the seat belt sign went out. Dave ducked through the cockpit door. "Would you like something to drink?" He made a pot of coffee and set a cheese and fruit plate in front of us before returning to his co-pilot duties.

"How long will we be staying at Cairabrae?" I asked.

"Not *we*, Emelynn—you. I won't be staying there." James released his seat belt and stood.

"Why not?" I asked, though I had my suspicions.

He sighed heavily and moved to the seat facing me, resting his fore-arms on his knees. "I could tell you that having me off-site adds another layer of security—which is true, but it's only part of the reason."

He hung his head. "My relationship with the Reynoldses is not like yours. I'm an employee—someone they order around. You—well, you're family. I don't want to be around you in that setting and I don't want to spend any more time with them than I have to."

It was a perspective I hadn't considered. The James I knew was competent and capable, both mentally and physically. The past few days I'd spent with him, watching him in his own element, only confirmed that. Being treated like a lowly minion had to be tough on his ego.

"I'm sorry they treat you like that. I'll talk to them."

"Please don't do that. It wouldn't change anything. There's too much history between my family and the Tribunal."

"It's not right."

"It hasn't been right for a very long time." He stood up and walked to the back of the cabin.

I gazed out the window at the clouds below. Despite the need for a presence such as the Tribunal, their methods were barbaric. The Tribu-nal inspired fear, not respect, and the Redeemers inspired worse. But I couldn't help thinking that the Redeemers very existence was a direct result of the methods the Tribunal used to maintain control. There had to be a better way.

When James returned, he sat opposite me again. If his clenched jaw was any indication, his mood hadn't lightened. I understood better now why he projected menace like he did; it was deep-seated anger and he wore it like a mask. It was also evident in the set of his shoulders and his gait. The fine lines between his eyebrows and around his mouth told me he'd been angry for a long time.

Such a shame, I thought, glancing at him. He could be handsome. I'd seen his expression soften in unguarded moments and when he was projecting a different persona. His pale blue eyes were striking. He had a perfectly proportioned, straight nose, and strong jaw. Even his lips were nicely shaped when they weren't pinched.

We passed the time making small talk, both of us careful to avoid conversational bombs like the Tribunal or the fact that we'd slept together—again. Instead, he told me more about his family and his sister, Sandra, and what she was like when she was younger. Theirs was a privileged childhood growing up in New Orleans where his parents indulged both of their children. He refused to expand on his stint in the military, except to give them credit for his wide-ranging skill-set. He'd returned home after Hurricane Katrina to help rebuild New Orleans, using the considerable resources of his family and the political connections of his father's law firm.

"Enough about me," he said. He'd told me more about himself today than in all the time I'd known him. It was a welcome change. "How's your mom doing with this mess?"

"She's worried about me and sick about the cottage. Avery and Sam are keeping her in the loop as much as they're able, but I know she feels helpless. I wish I could protect her from all this." Thinking about my mother reminded me of that other potential problem lurking outside my control: my father's research. It had slipped between the craters.

"James, do you think you could get access to one of the labs where my mother works?"

"That depends on the security. Why do you ask?"

I told him what I knew of my father's research, which was next to nothing, and about the annotated journals I'd found. "My mother passed his research and those journals on to Dr. Edgar Stein. His specialty is pediatric pharmacology. It wouldn't worry me except for something Mason said about my dad's interest in our eyes—our second lens. It might be nothing, but I'm afraid he might have written down something that he never imagined would see the light of day."

"When did your mother give Dr. Stein this research?"

"I'm not sure. Maybe a few weeks ago."

James rubbed his temples. "It'll be too late, Em. Why didn't you tell me sooner? I can't undo this."

"Maybe not, but you can destroy the research. Dr. Stein will never be able to replicate it."

He exhaled heavily. "I'll look into his lab's security. I've got contacts in Toronto. We'll try to get a look at it, okay?"

"Thanks, James." If anyone could get around security, James could.

By the time Dave told us to refasten our seat belts, we'd picked the cheese tray over and emptied the small-talk bank. We flew into the Sonoma County airport, which was closer to Cairabrae than the airport in San Francisco.

After we cleared customs, we picked up the rental car that Ryan had organized. James drove; he knew the way.

We were out of the small airport town immediately and on a quaint two-lane road in the middle of cow-country. "Where are you staying?" I asked inhaling the fresh scent of clean country air.

"I don't know yet."

"Will you let me know when you do?"

He turned to look at me like I'd asked a ridiculous question. "Of course."

"Don't look at me like that," I said with a laugh. "You're not exactly forthcoming with information, James."

His face lit up with a smile and he chuckled. "I do believe you've mentioned that before." This was the James I wished I saw more often. He reached over and took my hand. It was so unexpected that I looked at our hands as if they belonged to other people. "That's probably not going to change," he said. He squeezed my hand, keeping his eyes on the road.

He slowed to pass a cyclist and I glanced at James's face. He worked his lips, giving me the impression he was struggling to put his thoughts into words. "You were right about me, Em." He frowned, worrying his mouth again before he spit out the rest of it. "I wouldn't go so far as to call myself a coward . . . but I have been running; from my family, from our obligation to the Tribunal, from how I feel about you." He intertwined his fingers through mine. "I've been running my whole life. I don't know if I can stop, but I'd like to try."

His words shot through me like hot sparks. Some good—some not. "I'm sorry I called you a coward," I said. He finally looked at me and rewarded me with another of his rare smiles. He squeezed my hand again then released it and turned his attention back to the road. His revelation made me uneasy. I was happy for the fact that he might stick around, but I hoped he was doing it for himself and not for me. I hadn't been fooling myself when I'd told James that I had no expectations of him. I no longer harboured illusions that my life would parallel anything close to normal. Molly's life of marriage and children was as far from my grasp as the moon and stars. I might gaze upon them and even share the night sky, but they weren't mine to have and hold. And I wasn't convinced I wanted them, either.

Sonoma County grapevines sprawled across vast acres of hillside in perfectly neat, undulating rows. The closer we got to the coast, the narrower and twistier the road became. Eventually, the grapevines and road shoulders disappeared in favour of grazing sheep, then dense dark forest. Picturesque towns dotted the road as it followed the Russian River to the coast. I knew we were getting close when I caught my first glimpse of the Pacific.

James's voice interrupted my thoughts. "They won't like the idea of you and me." It was a warning. I started to dismiss his concerns, but he cut me off. "Right now, you need their protection, Emelynn. Don't do anything to alienate them."

I didn't challenge James. He knew them better than I did. But it grated on me that our relationship might cause trouble with the Reynoldses. It felt like having my wings clipped and I didn't like it. Losing my father had forged a fierce independence in me. The steel of it had been tempered in the shock of learning about the gift, the sting of Rupert's whip, and now, the destruction of the cottage. I valued my independence far too much to let James or the Reynoldses diminish it.

I stared out the car window. Wind-sculpted pine and cypress poked up like errant curls from the bald cliffs. We reached the gates of Cairabrae just after six, and they opened to admit us. "How do they do that?"

"They're expecting us but even if they weren't, there's a trigger at the turnoff to the driveway that would have signalled our arrival. There's also a camera in that crest," he said, as we passed the metal gates. The crest artfully split in two, half on either side of the heavy gate.

Before we reached the top of the hill, I spotted a fat-tired, quad-style vehicle parked off-road. James saw it too and answered my unasked question. "They've bumped up security."

The impressive stone facade of Cairabrae came into view as we surmounted the rise in the driveway. It was as beautiful as I remembered. James drove around the fountain and parked under the porte cochère. Ryan swiftly appeared and opened my door. "Emelynn," he said, offering me his hand. He wore a black T-shirt and slacks, the only thing I'd ever seen him wear.

"Thank you, Ryan. How are you?"

"Well, thanks. James," he said, greeting James who already had my duffle bag in his hands.

"Ryan," he replied.

Mason stood in the open doorway, stone-faced and still as the fountain statues. "Mason," I said, approaching with the caution his demeanour dictated. He was dressed in jeans and a sweater. He didn't move until I was close, and then he pulled me into a tight embrace, surprising the hell out of me.

"You're all right?" He asked, finally releasing me to search my face. I smiled in reassurance and the tension eased from his brow.

"I'm fine. James took good care of me," I said, and the mention of James's name put the crease back into Mason's forehead.

Mason turned a begrudging eye to James. "James," Mason said, barely acknowledging his presence.

"Mason," James said, with his hands on his hips.

The pair of them were acting like feral dogs, curling their lips and showing their teeth. The tension was thick between them. James had told me he'd only met Mason a few times. How had the animosity built up so quickly?

A man I didn't know stood inside the door. He wore the black uniform that told me he was security. They didn't introduce him. All four of us swept into the house and followed Mason to the left of the grand staircase, toward Stuart's office. Mason rapped twice and opened the door.

We entered the room under the watchful gaze of the glass-eyed animals. Stuart stepped out from behind his desk. His cowboy boots echoed off the hard floor. He approached quickly with a look of relief on his face and, just like his son, he pulled me into an embrace. "It is good to see you, Emelynn. You had us worried." He held me at arm's length and squeezed my shoulders. His wide smile morphed under furrowed brows into sympathy. "I'm so sorry about your house."

"Thank you," I replied to his heartfelt words. Ryan stayed in the hall and closed the door softly behind us.

"Come," Stuart said, tugging at my elbow. He wore work jeans and a plaid shirt.

"Stuart, I'm not sure you've met James," I said. Stuart turned to acknowledge James. "Stuart Reynolds, this is James Moss." He offered James his hand—more than Mason had managed to do.

"Pleased to meet you, James. I've heard a lot about you." James's look was unreadable as he shook Stuart's hand and nodded once.

I let Stuart lead me to a chair at the conference table. He wasn't aware that I'd been in this room before. It was the first night I'd ghosted under the power of my own crystal. That night the curtains concealed the view, but now I stared in awe through the floor-to-ceiling glass panels. The panoramic backdrop took in the pool and gardens, and the pastures all the way to the fence and outbuildings beyond. "Please, sit." Stuart motioned, inviting everyone to take a seat.

Stuart and Mason took turns peppering me with questions about the night of the fire and the shooting at Avery's house. They mirrored one another, sitting on the edge of their seats and leaning forward with their forearms across their knees. It was clear from their questions that James had already filled them in on most of it. When they were finished, Stuart stood. "Can I offer you a drink, James?"

"No, thank you," he said.

"Emelynn?"

"Not right now," I replied.

"Well, I could use one," he said. "Mason?"

"Sure," Mason replied. Stuart excused himself and picked up the phone on his desk and placed the order. Stuart dialled another number and started a conversation with someone else.

"What's the latest from Vancouver?" Mason asked James.

"I'll find out. May I?" James asked with his phone in hand, motioning toward the door in the wall of windows to the backyard.

"Go ahead," Mason said. James closed the door behind him and dialled while he walked away. I couldn't hear him, but I could see him gesturing beyond the windows.

Mason turned his attention to me. "Debbie went shopping for some clothes and toiletries for you. She's put them in Jolene's room, but I'm sure there'll be other things you need. Just let us know."

I raised my hand, "Mason, stop. Your budget's not like mine, and I already owe you for the phone and computer. Please, no more."

"Nonsense," he said, dismissing my concerns with a flick of his wrist. "You forget whose fault it is that Carson Manse was allowed to keep breathing," he said, as Stuart returned to the table.

"It's to our shame that he fooled us and pulled this off," Stuart said. "We can't replace what you lost, but we'll make amends, Emelynn, mark my words."

"You've done enough. Thank you."

There was a rap at the door and Ryan admitted Phillip, who balanced two drinks on a tray. They looked like martinis. "Emelynn," he said, greeting me with a nod and a smile.

"Hello, Phillip," I said. He placed Mason's drink on a napkin in front of him, and stepped around me to deliver the second drink to Stuart. Phillip left without another word.

I saw James through the window tucking his phone away as he reached for the door. "Jordan and Grace Shipley are still holed up in the safe house," he said, closing the door behind him. "Manse hasn't shown his face yet, but they're monitoring the drive-by traffic."

"What's the plan?" Mason asked.

"It hasn't changed," James said, coming to stand beside the table. "If Manse doesn't show himself, they'll return to Emelynn's cottage and try to draw him out. Where are Ron and Carrie?"

"They followed the police to the safe house," Stuart said. "They're close by." That must have been what Stuart had been on the phone about.

I asked Stuart, "What are your plans for Ron and Carrie?"

"They'll fix our grievous error." Stuart said it casually, like they'd provide a refund or replace a faulty product. It sent a chill through me.

On the heels of that, he asked James if he would stay for dinner. I almost laughed. *We'll kill him, naturally, and would you like to stay for dinner?* The absurdity of my life knew no bounds.

"No, but thank you," James said. "I would, however, like to discuss Emelynn's security." He'd addressed the question to Stuart, but it was Mason who reacted. I didn't need to see him to feel his back go up. The temperature in the room seemed to drop a few degrees.

"That won't be necessary, James. Ryan will take over from here. You can report in with updates from Vancouver—"

"Mason," I said, cutting in. "I'm sure Ryan is very capable, but I'd like James to be involved, too." Mason turned storm-darkened eyes on me. I put my hand on his forearm and looked him in the eye. Mason's ability to frighten me was long gone despite the damage I knew he was capable of. "James is my friend. I trust him. He's been there for me since the night I met you." It was a gentle reminder, but Mason needed to hear it. Mason started to object, but I stopped him. "No. He's the one who's kept me safe so far. I need him."

Mason rearranged his features and sat back in his chair, studying me. "All right. If it's what you want; if it'll make you feel safer." He turned to James with cool detachment. "I'll ask Ryan to brief you. Do you need quarters?"

"No. I'll stay off-site, but thank you," James said with a detachment equal to Mason's. *God help us*, I thought.

Mason stood and addressed me. "I'll see you at dinner."

"Eight?" I asked, quoting the dinner hour I remembered.

Stuart answered. "Yes."

"James, I'll call you later," I said. James had already turned to follow Mason out of the room.

When the door closed behind them, I breathed a sigh of relief. It was premature.

"Are you involved with James?" Stuart asked, taking Mason's vacated seat in front of me. His frankness took me by surprise.

I raised my eyebrows. "He's a friend."

"Just a friend?"

"A friend," I repeated, hoping the lie wasn't written on my face.

A slow grin spread on his face. "All right." He stood. "I'm going to spend some time with Jeannette. Will you make yourself at home?"

"I will," I said, standing. "I'll head up to Jolene's room and dress for dinner."

"*Your* room," he said, looking me steadily in the eyes. "I'll walk with you." He offered his elbow and walked me down the hall and up the stairs. We parted ways at the top of the curved staircase. He headed through the double door straight ahead and I turned left to *my* room.

I opened the door and stepped inside. My duffle bag sat on the floor inside the door. I picked it up and carried it past the sitting room through the doors to the bedroom and dropped it on the bed. The room looked unchanged from a week ago and yet, in that short span of time, my life had been rewritten.

I stepped out onto the balcony. It was dusk, that magical time of night when my night vision kicked in. The evening breeze was cool and I breathed deeply of the fragrant air that carried the tang of the sea. In the distance, around the big barn and outbuildings beyond the fence, I spotted activity. Perhaps more evidence of the increased security. The day's events had drained me and I stifled a yawn. It was close to eight and I needed to change for dinner. Reluctantly, I went back inside. Jolene's closet had proved fruitful before; I was sure I could find something suitable.

At first glance, I didn't notice. But as I flipped through hangers, the flash of dangling tags caught my attention. These clothes were new, and they were my size—not Jolene's. Jolene's clothes were gone, as were her size-five shoes. In their place, I counted four pairs of shoes in size eight. I pulled the closest drawer open and found a neat row of pretty bras and panties, all with tags. Sports bras and socks filled another drawer, and a stack of brand new yoga pants and shirts were neatly folded on the shelves. Jeans, slacks, capris and all manner of shirts lined the closet. All in my size. This was Mason's idea of a few clothes? It was beyond over the top. I dressed simply in slacks and a blouse, leaving a small pile of tags behind.

I bumped into Mason at the bottom of the stairs. "Thank you. The clothes are perfect."

"I'm glad you approve," he said, taking my elbow. "Shall we?" He too had changed; he now wore a linen shirt and dark slacks. He led me down the three steps into the living room.

Stuart stood looking out the doors and turned when he heard us. "Emelynn," he said, sliding a smile into place that didn't quite hide the worry in his eyes. "Are you finding everything you need?"

"Yes, thank you. You've both been very generous."

"It's the least we could do. Would you like a glass of wine?" he asked, reaching for an open bottle on a nearby table.

"Thank you, yes," I said, but he was already pouring.

He stopped short of handing me a glass, his gaze locked on my neckline. Reflexively, I reached for Jeannette's crystal case. The sight of me wearing it had caught him off guard, but then his face lit up with a genuine smile—one that took in his eyes. "That looks good on you," he said, finally handing me my glass. "I'm glad you're here."

I sighed with relief and tapped my glass against his. Mason joined us. "Cheers," I said.

Before Phillip called us to the dining room, Mason told me about the beefed-up security. Additional guards were roaming the property's perimeter and every outbuilding. Ryan was overseeing it and reporting directly to Mason. Debbie monitored the security inside the house. And it wasn't just the Reynoldses who had increased security. All of the Tribunal families had either gone into hiding or put similar measures in place. The substantial cost of that effort exposed a level of wealth within the Tribunal that I was only beginning to understand.

Once seated in the dining room with a beet and fennel salad

in front of us, Stuart asked Mason for an update on the Vancouver situation.

"Nothing yet," Mason replied.

"Do you think Carson has figured out it's not me in that house?" I asked.

He shrugged. "Hard to say. It's not been that long."

I stabbed at my salad.

Stuart interrupted my thoughts. "Don't waste your time trying to figure out Carson Manse. He's a psychopath; he doesn't think like the rest of us."

"Psychopath? That's putting it kindly," I said behind a weak smile. He might be a psychopath, but he wasn't stupid. God help us if he figured out I wasn't there and came looking for me. I put that thought from my mind.

Stuart shook his head. "Psychopath or not, he'd need a tank to get anywhere near this house with the increased security."

I smiled at his reassurances. They'd done all they could. All we could do now was wait. Stuart's conversation about the syndicate that owned some of the horses washed over me as we ate a prime-rib dinner with roasted potatoes, pearl onions and baby carrots. I declined dessert, feeling the pull of sleep after what had been a very long day.

It was 9:30 when I finally excused myself. I headed back to Jolene's . . . *my* room and stripped off the new clothes. It took but a minute to find the pyjama cache. I chose a soft cotton nightie, used the bathroom, then crawled into bed and dialled James.

"Hey," he answered. "Are you settling in?"

"As well as I can. How about you? Did you find a place to stay?"

"I'm at a surfer motel just north of Bodega Bay. It's low key, about a twenty-minute drive away."

"How'd it go with Ryan?"

"Good. Mason briefed him on Manse. He knows what he's dealing with. He can handle himself."

"He's a Flier, right?" My lack of experience had me stymied; I still couldn't tell.

"All the security detail are. You didn't know?"

"No one said and I felt foolish asking. They hide it well."

"They're not all Fliers. The cook isn't and neither is Jeannette's nurse. Phillip is, but not the cleaning staff or the gardeners." That explained why Phillip always wore black.

"Good to know. Will I see you tomorrow?"

"I'll be there at eight to brief Mason, but I'll call you if anything important comes up."

"Speaking of Mason, why was he so opposed to your involvement in security? Does he not know what you do for a living?"

He chuckled. "No. He *does* know what I do. That's precisely why he didn't want me involved. He doesn't want me learning the ins and outs of their security protocols. He only agreed because of you, and I can guarantee that he's already planning how to alter their systems after this is over. He wouldn't want me to have the keys to their castle."

"Is that why you thought they wouldn't like the idea of you and me?"

"It's one of the reasons. The other is they won't want someone they consider family to be involved with someone they consider the help."

"You're hardly the help. But don't worry. I have no intention of ruffling any feathers unnecessarily." I said good night and turned out the lamp. Sleep claimed me swiftly.

CHAPTER SEVENTEEN

At 6:30, I stretched lazily under the covers, marvelling at how well I'd slept. The morning was awash in fresh hope. I jumped out of bed and stepped onto the balcony. A chill hung in the air. I gazed out at gauzy, pastoral scenery worthy of a painting. Fog patches drifted eerily over the hills like giant ghosts. The pool looked like a dry-ice science experiment with steam billowing off its calm surface to join forces with the fog. A horse whinnied in the distance.

A swim sounded like the perfect way to start my day. Would the pool be warm? I wondered. After I finished in the bathroom, I pulled on a bathing suit, wrapped myself in a housecoat and headed for the stairs. The marble felt cool beneath my feet.

The security guard I hadn't met yesterday was on duty by the front door. "Ms. Taylor," he said, greeting me.

He knew my name, even if I didn't know his. "Emelynn, please," I said.

He smiled. "I'm Derek Lamb."

"Good morning, Derek." I turned to the left and down the stairs into the living room. The folding glass wall wasn't yet open. I stepped through a glass door and softly closed it behind me. The chill in the air hurried me along. There were no towel bolsters on the chairs this morning. I draped my housecoat over the back of a dew-soaked lounger and approached the shallow end of the pool. The water was warmer than the air, but it still took me a few minutes to get wet the slow way. I could have cannon-balled in, but the morning was tender and it seemed sacrilegious to shatter the stillness.

I swam gentle laps, making a game of not splashing then settled into a float on my back. The sleep had done wonders for my mood. I felt stronger, more confident. I swam an underwater lap then emerged to dry off. The house was still quiet when I ascended the stairs to my room.

After breakfast, I'd go for a run, I decided, and dressed in workout gear. The pile of discarded tags in the dressing room was growing. I closed the bedroom door and set off for the kitchen. The heavenly scent of coffee greeted me as I pushed open the door.

Stuart and Mason were already seated at the table. "How was your swim?" Stuart asked, glancing over the top of the newspaper.

I was taken aback. "Good, thanks. The house was so quiet I didn't think you were up." They both chuckled as if that was the funniest thing they'd heard yet today.

Mason dropped his folded paper on the table and stood. "Would you like coffee?" he asked, heading for the pot.

"Yes," I said, and approached the table.

"Have a seat," Stuart said. "How did you sleep?"

"Well. Really well," I answered.

Mason set a cup of coffee in front of me and returned to the fridge. "You take milk, right?"

"Yes, please."

He returned with the milk and a crystal bowl of fruit salad. "James is coming by shortly with an update. Do you want to sit in?"

After his adverse reaction yesterday, I hadn't expected him to be so accommodating. "Yes," I said, swallowing my surprise. I poured some milk into my coffee. "Thanks for letting him in on the security, Mason."

"We want you to feel safe here, Emelynn."

"I appreciate that. Thanks."

Mason returned to the fridge and came back with a tub of yogourt.

"Can I help?" I asked as he started setting out bowls.

"Cutlery is over there." Mason pointed to a shallow drawer at the end of the counter. I pulled out spoons and removed the cover from the bowl of fruit.

"After James's update, I thought I'd go for a run."

"That's great," Mason said, dishing up the fruit salad. "I'll ask Debbie to show you the trails."

"Better still," Stuart said, "Have Debbie take her up to the firing range and show her how to use a gun." Stuart re-folded his newspaper with a sharp snap.

"Guns frighten me, Stuart," I said. "At least real guns."

"Good. They should. You should also know how to use one."

"He's right," Mason agreed. "You may not like it, but you'd be safer around here with a few basics under your belt."

I suppose it couldn't hurt. I'd been using laser guns for a while now and paintball guns prior to that. How different could it be? "I'm a terrible shot," I confessed, scooping yogourt onto my bowl of fruit salad.

"Even more reason to go out to the range," Stuart said, pulling a bowl close and taking the yogourt from me.

That got me thinking about Stuart's hunting trophy collection. Over breakfast, I asked him about it. He confessed that his only kill was the cougar, and that, he assured me, was in defence of his cattle. The rest were inherited from his father and grandfather.

At the stroke of eight, Ryan escorted James into the kitchen. James looked well-rested and was dressed in jeans and a T-shirt. I couldn't take my eyes off him and was rewarded with a big smile when no one else was looking.

"Coffee?" Mason offered. They both declined.

James got right to business. "Manse hasn't shown his face."

"Are his people watching the place?" Mason asked.

"They questioned a man last night, but he wasn't involved, just lost. They haven't IDd any suspicious drive-bys."

"What's next?" Stuart asked.

"They're going to try to flush him out. They're taking Grace on tour this afternoon to make sure he gets a good look at her."

I shivered involuntarily and James caught it. "Grace is trained for this," he said, trying to reassure me.

"It won't protect her from a long-range bullet," I said. The memory of the shooter in Avery's backyard was still fresh in my mind.

"Ron and Carrie are there too. She's in good hands," Mason said.

"I'm sure she is, but I don't even know the woman and she's risking her life for me. I can't bear to think about something going wrong and her getting hurt."

Mason pulled his phone out and dialled. "Debbie, how'd you like to go for a run with Emelynn this morning then give her a lesson on the shooting range?"

James tilted his head in a questioning fashion while Mason continued with Debbie.

"Stuart and Mason think I should learn the basics," I said, keeping my voice down.

"Finally," James said, donning a smug grin. He'd said as much weeks ago when I'd made the same confession to him about my fear of guns.

While we waited for Debbie, James and Ryan sorted out their schedule. They were working the perimeter today to familiarize James with the security and outbuildings. I watched Mason's expression for cracks, but he took it all in stride. Maybe James was wrong about him.

Debbie was dressed for a run when she arrived. "You ready?" she asked, pulling water bottles out of the fridge and zipping them into her pack.

"Let's go," I said, and we went out through the kitchen door into the backyard. It had warmed up since my swim, but it was still cool and the fog hadn't completely lifted. It would when the sun was fully up, Debbie assured me. Noon, she estimated.

We strode briskly across the vast lawn toward the barn. "Thanks for the clothes," I said. "I like your taste."

"You're welcome. It's fun to shop with someone else's credit card," she said, grinning.

The firing range was three miles from the house and I assured her that I was fit enough to run the distance. We accelerated to a jog along a well-worn footpath through the grass, heading east between two outbuildings, and across the steep slope toward the ridge. It was a challenging grade. When the path levelled out, we settled into a steady pace. Stands of eucalyptus erupted from the hills like cliques of very tall, rangy friends. The trees' bark peeled off in long hairy strips.

It took a few moments to get my breathing under control. "How did you come to work for the Reynoldses?" I asked when my breath allowed.

"My family has a long history of service to the Tribunal." She was only slightly winded. "When I enlisted, my end-game was to work for one of them."

"Enlisted?" I asked.

"US Military. Army. After my initial training, I did a stint in Bosnia then two tours in Afghanistan. The Reynoldses picked up my contract after I was discharged."

That explained a lot. "Are all the Tribunal's security former military?"

"No. They hire from law enforcement and the private sector too."

We'd rounded the ridge and got a clear view off to the southeast. The landscape looked contrived, like some artist's modern, realistic interpretation. The grass on the hillsides appeared meticulously groomed for miles. Trees grew alone or in neat clusters with no visible underbrush, as if they were planted for aesthetic effect.

The longer we ran, the more difficult speech became, but I was curious about Debbie. "With your background, you could work security anywhere," I wheezed. "Why work for the Tribunal?"

She glanced at me, her brow furrowed.

"What?" I asked in response.

"You can learn a lot about someone by the questions they ask." She was finally showing some signs of exertion. "You don't like them."

She was astute—no doubt about that. "We didn't have a *likeable* introduction. I'm not sure I can trust them."

"And yet, here you are."

"Yes, I am." I wondered how much she knew of my history and my current predicament. "You haven't answered my question."

"The Tribunal's elite are the only ones strong enough to stand between us and bastards like the Redeemers." Her face contorted into a hateful snarl. I waited for her to continue. "Protecting the Tribunal while they do their job seems the least I can do."

Was Debbie's allegiance blind, I wondered? Did she know that the Tribunal families absorbed the gifts of condemned Fliers? Did she know that the Tribunal sent a dead dove like a calling card to the families of those avenged?

In light of the fact she was about to arm herself, I thought it prudent to change the subject. "You've been working since the moment I arrived. When do you get time off?"

"I don't. Working security for the Reynoldses is like being in the army. I live and breathe the job for the duration of my contract. We all do."

"That's intense," I said, though I supposed, with her background, it was what she was used to. After ten more minutes, we slowed our pace. I saw a rise ahead and the path ran parallel to it. Debbie slowed to a walk with her hands on her hips. "The range is just up there," she said, pointing to the rise. When we got closer, I could make out a series of targets set up on thick tripods against the ridge. Each bore a different distance, from 10 to 250 yards.

We stopped at a hitching post and she swung her backpack off her shoulder and unzipped it. "Water?" she asked, offering me one of the bottles.

I cracked the lid and took a long drink.

"What do you know about handguns?" she asked.

I knew that being shot by one hurt like hell. "Nothing. My only experience is with laser tag and paintball guns, and I'm not a good shot with either."

"We can work on that." Debbie bent down and extracted a gun from her pack. "This is a Beretta semi-automatic. It's a beginner's handgun. It fires nine-millimetre bullets from a 15-round magazine. It's not loaded," she said, offering it to me. "Always check that for yourself. Like this," she said, showing me that you could see straight through the top of the gun and out the bottom of the grip. Then she showed me how to check the chamber, where an additional round could be hiding.

I took the weapon from her and felt its weight. "The safety's here," she said, pointing to a slide on the top of the gun near the rear. "When the safety's on, even if the gun's loaded, it won't fire." She explained the mechanics of the weapon and its safety features. Only when she was satisfied that I understood the basics, did she retrieve a slender magazine from her pack. She took the gun and showed me how to load the magazine into the bottom of the grip. It slid into place with a smooth click. "Never point the gun at something you're not willing to kill." She handed the loaded gun back to me.

"It's heavy." Something about handling a real gun put my experience with laser guns into perspective. That was child's play, my distant past; this was my new reality. I didn't like it.

"Just over two pounds with a loaded magazine," she said. "Don't ever rest your finger on the trigger." She showed me how to hold the gun safely. "The Beretta kicks, so use a two-handed grip and stand with your legs shoulder-width apart. And you'll need these," she said, handing me earplugs. I squished the dense orange foam into place.

"Let's start with the 10-yard target," she said, nodding toward it. She reviewed my stance then gave me the go ahead. I clicked the safety off, took aim and pulled the trigger. The shell casing immediately popped out the top. She was right about the kick and I hadn't expected the trigger to be so stiff. She nodded for me to go again, and again I missed the target.

"You're closing your eyes," she said. "Don't be afraid of it." Years of conditioning disagreed with her, but on the fourth shot, I nicked the edge of the target. She directed me to the 15-yard target, which I missed.

"Try taking a breath and holding it when you squeeze the trigger," she said. I hit the target with the second shot but missed the next two. Then I missed the 25-yard target twice and tried the 15 again. Missed.

"Let me see that," she said, taking the gun. She looked at it like I'd broken it, her forehead furrowed in confusion. She then took three shots in quick succession, hitting the 10, 15 and 25-yard targets, and for good measure, let off a fourth shot that hit the one at 50 yards.

"There's nothing wrong with the gun." She smirked, handing it back to me. "But we're going to need a lot more ammo," she said, chuckling at her own joke.

I went through a second magazine with mixed results. Despite the wad of foam in my ears, they were ringing when I dropped the empty magazine out of the gun. "You'll get better," she said, as she took me through the process of loading bullets into the empty magazines. "It just takes practice. Let's do a spin through the simulation course. It's around the other side of this ridge." She zipped up her pack and led the way.

We walked for ten minutes and rounded the ridge. What emerged looked like a cut-out-doll ghost town with two-dimensional plywood buildings set at odd angles. We approached a kiosk that stood strangely out of place at the entrance. Debbie took a key from her pocket and inserted it into a panel on the kiosk. "The targets are tripped randomly as you move through the course. Don't worry about speed; I'm not timing you. I'll stay out of your way. The targets are self-explanatory; just don't kill the nuns or children."

"That won't be a problem," I said, laughing as we strode down the centre of the dirt road that ran through flat town. The first target popped up out of the dirt, scaring the bejeebers out of me. It was a shadowy figure pointing a nasty-looking gun. If it had been a real bad guy, I'd have been dead by the time I gathered my wits. As it was, the flat image had fallen back into the dirt before I'd even aimed my gun. At least now I had a better idea of what to expect, I rationalized.

I kept the Beretta in both hands, pointed down, and swept my gaze from side to side. Debbie walked behind me. The next target, a do-ragged gangster type, also got away without injury. I did get a shot off that time, but I wasn't ready for the gun's recoil and I staggered backwards. I didn't shoot at the poodle that whizzed by, or the jogger, but took aim at a burglar. Didn't hit him either, but I was ready for the recoil. I had better luck with the combat-fatigued bush-master-toting villain, catching him in the shoulder.

I hadn't emptied the first magazine before we hit the end of the course. Debbie removed her earplugs and I followed her lead. "Your instincts aren't bad, but we have to work on your accuracy." I appreciated that she didn't say my accuracy sucked, which it did. I released the gun's magazine and passed the gun back to her. She stowed it away and we headed back to the start of the course where she retrieved her key from the kiosk.

We walked back the way we had come, taking sips of water and kicking stones. "Is there a reasonable chance I'll get better at this?"

"Sure. You may never be a sniper, but with practice, you'll improve."

"It can't get much worse," I said, smiling at her.

"You're not a natural, so it'll be harder for you, but not impossible."

We approached the tripod targets. "Could you hit the 250-yard one?" I asked.

"With a handgun? Not a chance, but I could with a rifle."

"How long did it take you to get that good?"

"I've been shooting for ten years and still practice regularly."

"Well, that makes me feel better." At this point, I'd have better luck throwing a jolt than shooting a gun. Come to think of it, jolting would feel better too. I could blow off a bit of steam in the face of a long morning of frustration. If I missed, neither Debbie nor anyone else would know it.

Debbie was on my left and the ten-yard target was on my right as we approached. I kept my head down and visualized my crystal. It sparkled enticingly. I wrapped my mind around it, gathering its warm oozing strength. It gave me enough power to fuel a tremendous jolt that I released with a snap of my head. I heard a loud crack as the target landed in a cloud of dust with a dull thud. I grinned with satisfaction.

My grin lasted a nanosecond before Debbie thrust into me and sent me sprawling to the dirt. "Stay down," she whispered, pulling a gun from her pack.

"Debbie," I said, trying to explain, but she cut me off.

"Shh," she hissed. She lay on her back with her upper body raised a few inches off the ground and used her feet to swing herself around, wielding her gun in a wide arc.

"Debbie," I whispered, again. "It was *me*. *I* knocked the target down." She glared at me. "I'm sorry," I said with a grimace.

"You did that with a jolt?"

I nodded.

"You KO'd a hundred-pound target from thirty feet with a jolt?"

"I shouldn't have done it. I'm sorry."

Debbie sat up but didn't put her gun away. She stood, left her pack and strode toward the target. I followed her, feeling sheepish, but curious to see the damage. Up close, I could see that the target was stapled to a sheet of plywood that had been snapped off its sandbagged base. It was bigger than it looked from a distance. The ragged edges of the rent wood were testament to the violence of the jolt. It was one of my best.

"I'll make sure it gets repaired," I offered, taking in the damage I'd done.

"Jesus, Emelynn. Does Mason know you can do this?"

"I'm sure Mason can do worse than this," I said, dusting off my clothes and examining the scrape on my elbow from the fall.

She looked at me with doubt on her face then asked, "Can you hit the 15-yard target?"

I shrugged, but followed her back to the hitching post to give it a try. Having her watch made me self-conscious. I closed my eyes to concentrate as I gathered the strength of my crystal into another powerful jolt. I let it fly with a swing of my head and watched the 15-yard target spin sharply before toppling. There was no snap this time, so I hadn't broken it.

Debbie looked from the target to me and back again, her mouth agape. We walked to the target and examined it. I reached down to set it upright, but it was heavier than it looked. Debbie helped me, and we dragged it back where it belonged then hefted the two sandbags into place.

Debbie didn't say a word until she had her gun stowed and we were on our way again. "I don't ever want to be on the receiving end of one of those," she said.

We picked up our pace and ran the rest of the way back to Cairabrae in silence. At the white fence by the big barn, we made plans to repeat the run and shooting practice the next morning, then parted ways. She ran off toward one of the outbuildings and I continued on across the back lawn to the house. I headed up to my room to shower and change.

Afterwards, I sat on the bed and made a quick call to Avery. All I could tell him was that I was safe and I would be well-protected until Carson's threat was neutralized. He promised to fill in the rest of the covey, who, he assured me, were doing well despite the threat. I thanked him for the update and we hung up. Then I opened the laptop and sent my mother an email. The subject line read *We ship same day free; Cialis, Viagra, Vicodin for $11.30*. It was short notice, but I hadn't spoken to her since the fire commissioner's finding of arson and if she'd heard, she'd be anxious. I crossed my fingers that she'd get my message before 11:30.

When she answered my Skype call at 11:30, she was hunkered down in a coffee shop. "I had to run out of the lab," she said breathlessly. "Where are you? Detective Jordan won't tell me a damn thing."

"I'm sorry, Mother. He's trying to protect me and it's safer for both of us if you don't know where I am. But I'm okay."

"Thank god. I've been so worried." It was the soundtrack of my friends and family, and it saddened me. "The insurance adjustor told me the fire was arson. Is that true?"

"That's what they say, but Detective Jordan is all over it. He's got an entire team working to find the man responsible."

"Sweetheart, just a few months ago you were kidnapped and now someone's burned down the house with you in it. It's a bit of a stretch to think the two aren't connected."

My mother was no dummy; something she proved every time she opened her mouth. I didn't have to give her all the gory details, but there was no point in lying to her. "You're right—they are—but the man responsible can't find me here. I'm using a new computer and this is a new phone. James set them up for me so they're untraceable. I'm as safe as I can be until this guy is behind bars."

I got us off the topic by telling her about Molly. She feigned interest, but I suspected she knew full well that I'd diverted the conversation and went along for my sake. Worrying about events that neither of us could do a thing about was pointless, so I was pleased that she didn't re-visit the topic before we said our goodbyes.

It was after noon when I made my way down for lunch. I found Stuart and Mason on the patio awash in sunshine. The dew had dried, but the heat hadn't yet penetrated the furniture and it was cold to sit on.

"How did the shoot go?" Mason asked, beaming expectantly.

"Debbie's shooting is impressive. Mine . . . not so much. I barely nicked the targets with the handgun, but I did manage to kill one with a jolt. Now that was fun, but I owe you a ten-yard target." Mason looked confused. "I'm sorry. I broke it. It snapped off near the bottom of the frame, but the front panel is still in one piece."

Stuart had started chuckling when I apologized, but his chuckle grew into a full-on belly laugh. "Doesn't that sound just like Jolene?" he said. "I'll go take a look after lunch and see that it gets fixed."

"Is Debbie not back yet?" I asked.

"She'll be here soon," Stuart replied. "We've reassigned her. She'll be your personal bodyguard until this Carson Manse business is cleared up."

Bodyguard? I didn't know how I felt about being dogged by someone day and night. It felt intrusive, but it was in keeping with Stuart's management style. "Thank you, I think," I said.

During lunch, a delicious avocado salad with grilled shrimp, Mason dropped another bomb. "We're going ahead with plans for your party next Saturday. It'll be a cocktail party. We've kept it small, only inviting the major players in the Tribunal and their families. Fewer than a hundred people."

"Are you crazy?" I said, not even attempting to disguise my horror. "This is the worst possible timing."

"We set this in motion before the fire, Emelynn," Mason said. "If we cancel now, it'll send the wrong message. The Tribunal doesn't run and hide from threats. We remove them."

"A party will put everyone at risk. It'll put us all in one location at the same time. That can't be a good idea. Not when we know so little about the Redeemers," I reasoned. Mason shook his head dismissively, so I offered another point. "There's a reason the president and vice-president don't travel together. It's the same reason the Queen and her heirs don't fly together. This is not a good idea."

"That's one way to look at it. But consider for a moment, who we are. If the Redeemers are foolish enough to take on the best of us, en masse, I say let them. Let them try it when we're all in one place, right here, together. There's strength in numbers, Emelynn, and truth in the old adage 'united we stand, divided we fall.'"

I was sure that adage was figurative, not literal. "You've invited the families. It's not fair to the children and spouses. Do they even know the risk?"

"Emelynn," Stuart said, "They're Tribunal families. They inherit the strongest skill sets among us and are raised with an expectation of duty. We'll warn them, certainly, but the families will sort out for themselves who will attend, and security will be tight. They'll probably be better protected here than in their own homes."

I cringed at their audacity. They were tempting fate for the sake of a frivolous party. It was ridiculous.

"The one bright spot in all of this," Stuart said, "It gets Sebastian off our backs."

I didn't have the energy to argue with them. They'd obviously made up their minds. "For the record, I think this is a mistake, but I won't fight you. I said I'd do it and I will, but I don't want to be the centre of attention, so please don't put me on the spot," I warned. "I'll mingle and meet the guests, but I'm not a debutante."

"It's just the distraction you need, Emelynn." This pearl of wisdom dropped from Mason, the party planner. "It'll get your mind off Manse and the loss of your home. And you'll have a great time." Not likely, I thought, but Mason's enthusiasm was infectious and I smiled despite my misgivings.

Stuart laughed. "Sometimes it's good to get out of your comfort zone, Emelynn." They'd been very kind to me; I could give them this. I nodded with a sigh of resignation.

I called James from my room later in the afternoon. "I'm glad you called," he said. "I had a report back from my contact in Toronto. He tells me Dr. Stein's lab security was quietly upgraded ten days ago. The timing suggests your instincts about your father's research were right."

"Was your contact able to retrieve my father's research?"

"Not yet. I'll let you know when we learn anything new. And there's no movement on the situation in Vancouver either."

"Why hasn't Carson made a move?" I pondered out loud.

"Don't try to figure it out. You'll drive yourself crazy. Ryan tells me that Debbie's been assigned to you. How's that working out?"

"I haven't seen her since this morning, so it's working out just fine."

"She moved out of her quarters. I hear she's bunking across the hall from you now."

"Is she? I hadn't heard. How are you and Ryan getting along?"

"Ryan's skilled, smart—someone you'd want watching your back. He tries to stay out of the politics, but it's hard with this lot. Tribunal loyalties tend to run to families. Ryan knows who signs his paycheques."

"Does that mean he's not cooperating?"

"He's keeping me at arm's length, but I understand that. He's not standing in my way."

"Do you want to get together later? I can borrow a car and drive out to your motel." His laughter surprised me. "Why are you laughing?"

"Em, you won't get out of there without Debbie, and I don't think you want a chaperone."

"I can ask her to make herself scarce."

He laughed again. "I don't think you understand the level of security Debbie provides."

"Oh come on. I haven't even seen her since this morning."

"Well, you can bet she's seen you. Trust me. She'll know every move you make from now until Manse is neutralized."

Crap. "When will I see you?"

"You'll see me around. I'm not going anywhere."

"I'll ask them to invite you to the cocktail party." Predictably, he exploded. At least someone agreed with me. He wouldn't have any more luck changing their agenda than I'd had, though I was sure he'd try. We hung up with promises to "see you around."

At dinner that night, Maria joined us for coffee and went over the drink and canapé selection for next weekend's soiree. Stuart and Mason deferred to me, but I had no experience in that area so I let Maria's suggestions stand. She was a marvellous cook and her choices sounded mouth-watering.

I had planned to return to my room after dinner, but Stuart asked me to join him in the library. He opened a door off the hallway that also led to his office. The library looked like it belonged on an old movie set. Dark wood shelving hugged every available wall, from the floor to the high coffered ceiling. Books of every size and shape were tucked neatly into tidy rows with their spines aligned. A tufted divan rested in front of the bank of windows, with a blanket folded neatly over the back. "Have a seat," Stuart said, indicating one of four chairs arranged around a low table near the centre of the room.

Mason joined us. Stuart proceeded to a small Queen Anne desk against one wall and retrieved a large envelope. He handed it to me without a word and I raised a questioning eyebrow. "Go ahead," he said. "Open it." Inside were a number of 8x10 glossy photos. "I thought you might find it helpful to familiarize yourself with the faces of the Tribunal people you'll be meeting at the party. They're not all there, but we found photos of the major players and some of their family."

"Sebastian," I said with distaste, staring at the dark, close-set eyes I remembered. "Is this his wife?"

"Yes. That's Kimberley and she'll attend. The next photo is their daughter, Tiffany. I expect she'll also show up."

I recognized Ron from his skull trim. There was no sign of his broken nose and I felt terrible now about having done that to him. I needed to apologize and thank him the next time I saw him. I managed to pick out the photos of the two women with kinetic skills, who'd held me immobile the night Sebastian interrogated me. Carrie and Rachael were their names. Carrie was with Ron in Vancouver.

"I don't recognize these others. I know I should—at least the ones who were at the cottage, but I don't." Mason and Stuart took turns telling me their names and passing on snippets of their history. Luckily, they'd had the foresight to jot down the details on the back of the photos because I'd never remember it all.

"Thanks," I said, departing with the envelope of photos under my arm. They'd been right about the pictures. I already felt more comfortable about meeting everyone. It felt a bit like cheating, but they were only meeting one of me; I had a lot more names and faces to remember than they did. This was important to Stuart and Mason, so I'd make the effort.

Chapter Eighteen

In a matter of days, I'd settled into Cairabrae and its rhythms. I learned the names of the staff and explored the house and grounds. Phillip proudly toured me through the endless rooms, but stopped shy of the kitchen. "That's Maria's territory," he'd said. "I don't interfere in there."

He really was as cultured as his voice suggested, never once dropping the formality he was obviously so comfortable with. He'd been with the Reynoldses for fifteen years and had taken over running the house when Jeannette had her stroke.

The normally quiet household was a beehive of activity in preparation for the fast-approaching cocktail party. A piano technician arrived to tune the red piano; deliveries of wine, linens and crystal were made daily; and extra staff was brought in to clean every inch of the house. An overly polite handyman named Manny rolled his big tool cart from room to room oiling hinges and fixing sticky locks.

My personal schedule of daily distractions kept me busy. Debbie and I took a run out to the shooting range each morning and I'd empty a half-dozen magazines from the Beretta. On the run back, I'd test my jolts. By noon, I was ready for lunch. In the afternoon, I'd practice ghosting in the privacy of my room. Dinner was at eight. And in the evening, I'd review the photos that Stuart had given me and test my memory.

On Monday, James reported a possible Carson sighting in Vancouver, which fizzled out. I wished the same could be said about his report from Toronto. After his daily morning briefing, James asked me to follow him out. Once clear of the kitchen, he pulled me aside. "We have to tell Mason about Dr. Stein," James advised. "It's going to take a Ghost to get past the lab's sensors without setting off the alarms."

"No," I blurted out. "There's got to be another way."

"We could infiltrate the staff, but that takes time. It's time we can't risk. If your father's research turns out to be nothing, then no harm done. But if it isn't . . ." I searched his face for signs of flexibility, but found none. "The sooner the better, Em."

It was a horrible choice. Keep quiet and risk a leak or speak up and risk a life. Dr. Stein had done nothing to deserve the attention of the Tribunal other than be given some research. Perhaps I could press that point with Mason—make him promise to keep the Tribunal out of it.

"All right," I said, resigned. There wasn't really a choice. "Will you come with me? They'll have questions I can't answer." James nodded and followed me back into the kitchen.

Mason and Stuart looked up, surprised at our unexpected return. "What's going on?" Mason asked.

We joined them at the table and I started from the beginning, telling them everything I knew about my father's research, the journals and then the parts I'd speculated on. James added details, like the timing and level of the lab's re-vamped security.

Mason grimaced. "You should have told us right away."

"This involves my mother, Mason. I don't want the Tribunal anywhere near her."

"Your delay in telling us may have left us no other option," Mason said, his face a cold mask. This was exactly what I'd been trying to avoid.

"We're not there yet," Stuart said, diffusing Mason's anger. "I'll call Paul and ask him to look into it."

Mason stared stone-faced at his father for a moment then relented. "You'd better go with him, James. He'll need your input."

"I'll check in with you later, Em," James said, and then he and Stuart left the kitchen.

A heavy silence hung in the air. The unease was my fault and I needed to correct it. "I'm sorry I've upset you, Mason. If James or I could have dealt with this ourselves, we would have."

"I'm not upset about you involving me, Emelynn. I'm upset that you waited so long. If you're right, and your father, for some unfathomable reason, left behind research about us, who knows how many people may be involved by now."

"I don't think that'll be the case. If Dr. Stein thinks he's stumbled across something valuable, he won't be broadcasting it. At least not until he can prove it and put his name on it. He'll have it secured somewhere, probably his lab. If Paul can't find it, James will—he's very good at what he does."

"You have a lot of faith in James. Maybe a little too much." He stood and walked to the cupboard where the coffee cups were kept. "And you have an awful lot to learn about us." When he was sure he had my attention, he reached his arm out and it vanished. Just his arm. Nothing else. I stared wide-eyed as he leaned toward the cupboard. The china cups rattled inside. I stared at the closed cupboard door. When Mason's arm re-materialized, he was holding a cup.

"There is nowhere Dr. Stein could hide research from us," he said with steel in his voice that matched his expression.

I must have been sitting there with my mouth open. "You've only scratched the surface of your gift, Emelynn. This," he said, dangling the cup from his fingers, "is why we're such a threat. There is no place we can't breach. If the wrong people learn about us and about this . . . our freedom—our lives—will be at stake. That's not something we leave to others to fix for us. Do you understand that?"

He set the cup on the counter and left the kitchen. I sat there until the shock wore off then returned to my room. As far as distractions went, Monday was well taken care of.

After our run on Tuesday, Debbie and I drove into San Francisco to shop for suitable cocktail-party clothing. I knew I was in trouble the moment we walked through the front doors of the first store she selected. The store sold gowns, not party dresses, and the garments were displayed face out, not hung on racks. That's when I learned that this cocktail party was a black tie affair.

"I thought you knew," Debbie said. "This isn't a tailgate, potluck kind of crowd."

I hadn't known. How could I? A small cocktail party, Stuart had said. Something inconsequential. If I hadn't screwed up so royally yesterday, I'd have words with him. As it was, I felt like I had to suck it up. After an inordinate amount of help from my own personal sales assistant, I selected a midnight-blue, floor-length sheath. Debbie picked a boring, satin pantsuit in chocolate brown with matching flats. "I'll be working," she reminded me when I teased her.

I enjoyed Debbie's easy company. She was funny when she let her guard down and she wasn't condescending when she needed to make a point regarding my security. I learned to follow her lead and, otherwise, pretend that she wasn't watching my every move.

Late Wednesday afternoon, Phillip came to my room. "Mr. Reynolds would like you to join him in the library," he said.

That couldn't be good. I'd never been "summoned" before and it felt ominous. "Which Mr. Reynolds?" I asked, stalling.

He blushed and fluttered his hands. "Senior . . . Stuart," he clarified, smiling kindly. Maybe it wasn't a bad summons. I followed Phillip as far as the stairs then turned toward the library. I knocked quietly.

"Come in," Stuart called. I closed the door behind me. "Have a seat," Stuart said. He had a FedEx package on his lap. I sat opposite him.

"Paul managed to retrieve your father's research from Dr. Stein's lab yesterday." I waited while he gathered his thoughts. "Your intuition is good, Emelynn, but you need to start trusting us." He handed me the FedEx package. "I'll need that back, but you can read it."

"This is my father's research?" I asked.

He nodded without smiling. "I wouldn't have expected this of Brian."

I swallowed. "What?"

"He wrote a detailed account of the anomaly and effects of a second optic lens, complete with anatomical drawings. His subject data is non-identifying, but your father wasn't known as a quack. His work could prove tempting to someone looking to make a name for themselves."

"My father couldn't have predicted this outcome. I'm glad Paul was able to retrieve it," I said, breathing a sigh of relief.

"Yes. Let's just hope Dr. Stein didn't copy it before he locked it up."

It was a worrying thought.

I returned to my room and called James. We talked every day. Some days we saw each other at the house but on those occasions, we behaved like friends, not lovers. With so many people around, there was no opportunity to connect privately, but I thought about it. A lot. I imagined ways to lure him to my room where I could run my hands across his naked chest and loosen the tie from his hair. I pictured the small hollows in the side of his butt and imagined his face contorted in ecstasy. Of course, thinking like that was as frustrating as the holding pattern we were in.

Tension in the house remained high in the wake of the discovery of my father's research. The days felt heavy with the burden of waiting:

waiting for the party; waiting for news from Vancouver; waiting for Carson Manse to make his move. It had been a week since the fire and almost as long since Grace and Detective Jordan had set up shop to trap Carson. I couldn't help but wonder if they were off base. How long was it reasonable to continue the charade?

After lunch on Thursday, I headed to my room and went straight out onto the balcony. Stuart and Mason had both been tense at lunch and I was happy to get out of there. The early afternoon air was warm and smelled of dry grass with a hint of the ocean's salty influence. I thought about my ghosting skills. I'd made good progress and could now ghost and re-form in moments rather than hours. I'd even learned how to dial a phone and open doors in my barely there ghosted form. If I was in the business of haunting, I could make a killing. I grinned to myself imagining a start-up company along the lines of the Disney movie, *Monsters, Inc.*

A stray thought crossed my mind. Ghosts could sense one another. I could sense Mason and Sebastian. I'd even sensed the Tribunal before I knew what that sensation was. But the night I'd overheard Stuart and Ron discussing the Vosburghs' disappearance, Stuart hadn't sensed me. Come to think of it, Ron hadn't either. Surely they would have said something if they knew I was there in ghosted form . . . eavesdropping no less. Wouldn't they?

Was it possible they couldn't sense me? It was an interesting theory, but one I'd need to test to be certain. It would be handy to know, either way. However, it would have to wait. Stuart visited with Jeannette after lunch, and I would never enter their private rooms uninvited, ghosted or not.

At the cottage, I would have passed the time with a vacuum or a dust mitt. In the spotless rooms of Cairabrae, cleaning would be as futile as winding an electric clock. Instead, I went for a swim and read Stuart's discarded morning paper by the pool.

I heard the squeak of the handyman's cart. It stopped outside the living room's patio doors and Manny extracted a screwdriver. When he finished with his tune-up, the squeak started again and he rolled his cart along the bank of windows to Stuart's office.

"Hello, Manny," I called, gathering my things. I hadn't meant to scare the poor man, but he hadn't seen me and nearly jumped out of his skin when I spoke. I apologized and retreated to my room. It was time to test my theory.

I changed into jeans and a light sweater, and checked that the balcony door was closed. I pictured my crystal and wrapped metaphysical fingers around it, applying just enough pressure to trigger my ghost. When my physical form disappeared, I approached the door to the hallway and succeeded in turning the handle. I was getting much better at controlling the density of my ghost. I'd also learned that opening doors the traditional way was a lot less draining than ghosting through them, probably because I didn't have to ghost as deeply. I floated down the hall and over the railing.

I heard raised voices and found Mason and Stuart in the library. The door was closed so I ghosted deeper to get through it. After I collected myself on the inside, I saw Stuart seated with a book face down on the table beside him. Mason stood nearby, brooding. They had stopped speaking, but their body postures were tense. Had they sensed me? I waited for a reaction from either of them—some acknowledgement that they sensed me in the room.

"She's not your sister, Mason."

"She may not have been born to it, but I've seen her. She's got what it takes."

"I agree, which is even more reason to be careful. We need her. We can't afford to make a mistake."

"She's scared right now, but if we approach it the right way, she'll come around."

"If you push her, we'll lose her just like we lost Jolene. She's not ready yet."

Their words hit like physical blows. My feet felt anchored to the floor. I hung motionless in the air, unable to shake the sinking feeling in my stomach. I couldn't believe it. James had been right. They'd been playing me from the start.

My first instinct was to run. Run far away from this place and never look back. But my anger crested and hurt overruled my instincts. I positioned myself in front of Stuart and willed myself back into solid form.

"What am I not ready for yet, Stuart?" It came out like venom and Mason spun around with a look of horror on his face.

Stuart didn't even flinch. He met my eyes with his own dark stare and shook his head. "I should have known. We could never sense Jolene, either. Jeannette's the only one who could."

"This is a private conversation," Mason said. His nostrils flared.

They'd been using me. "Trusting you was a mistake."

"Trust! You're the one sneaking around, eavesdropping. You have no idea what's at stake." Mason spit the words out and stepped toward me.

I didn't back down. "Well then, Mason, set me straight, would you?"

"Damn it, Emelynn. You aren't ready to hear what we have to say."

"Give it a try," I said, stepping toward him, my hands clenched.

"We want you to join forces with us on the Tribunal," Stuart said, taking my heated focus away from Mason.

I stepped back. Had I heard him correctly? "Me? On the Tribunal?" He nodded. I narrowed my eyes and searched my memory for whatever it was I'd said or done that would mislead them this badly. I came up empty: there was nothing. "If you think I'd join them, then you don't know me at all."

Mason was quick to jump all over me. "This is bigger than you . . ." he started, but Stuart shot out his arm and stopped him short.

"Don't," Stuart said. "Not like this."

I looked from Mason to Stuart and then finally absorbed something else I'd overheard and an even greater revelation unfurled. "Jolene wasn't just running from Carson Manse, was she?" I asked. "She was running from you."

"That's not what happened," Mason said.

"Sure it was. You couldn't protect her from Carson, because she wouldn't come to you. You drove her away and now you're doing the same thing to me."

"You don't understand!" Mason shouted.

I didn't wait for their excuses; I turned and headed for the door. "I understand all I need to!" I slammed the door behind me and Stuart's voice called to Mason to let me go.

I ran to Jolene's room and slammed that door too. Their lies burned like the flames that destroyed the cottage. My ID was on the bookcase. I stuffed it in one pocket and my cellphone in another. The one good thing about my predicament: it made packing really easy. I shuffled through Jolene's stack of photos and took the one of her and my father. There was a knock on the door and Debbie called out, "Everything okay in there?"

"I'm fine, Debbie. I just need some time alone." A moment later, I squeezed my crystal and ghosted deeply. I threw myself at the balcony door and over the rail. A gentle breeze wafted, but I pushed through it.

Adrenalin and determination got me out to the road. When Cairabrae's driveway was out of sight, I took cover and re-formed.

I dialled James. "You were right," I said, when he answered.

"Right about what?"

"I don't want to talk about it over the phone. Can I come by?"

"Ah . . . sure," he said.

"Do the Reynoldses know where you're staying?"

"No," he said, and gave me directions.

"I'm on my way." I disconnected and then did the unthinkable; I flew—in broad daylight. I headed to the coast and kept close to the cliff edge ready to duck out of sight. I was a windblown mess by the time I arrived on James's doorstep. The surfer motel consisted of a row of tiny huts that looked like they would blow apart in a strong wind. James occupied the shack on the end. A surfboard taller than me leaned against the outside wall. Maybe it came with the rental.

He looked puzzled when he opened the door. He wore faded jeans and a long-sleeved, crewneck T-shirt with the arms pushed up. He held the door open for me, then poked his head outside and checked left and right. After he closed the door, he asked, "Where's Debbie?"

"I ditched her."

He angled his head and raised an eyebrow, waiting for my explanation.

"Do you keep anything to drink in here?" I asked, walking the narrow path between the dresser and the end of the bed, which rested mere feet from the front door. Was that indoor/outdoor carpeting? The furnishings looked like garage-sale finds, including the ancient stainless-steel sink and hot plate combo that sat against the far wall beside a small bathroom. I heeled off my shoes and climbed on the bed.

"Bourbon or beer?"

"Bourbon." I settled my back against the headboard.

He rinsed a glass, poured a healthy shot and handed it to me. He let me take a swallow before he quizzed me. "What's going on?"

Before I could answer, his phone buzzed and he looked at the face of it before holding up his hand to silence me.

"Moss," he answered. "No. Why the hell don't you know where she is?" He shot me a reproving look. "I'll let you know if I hear from her," he said, then disconnected the call.

He went back to the counter and poured another glass then joined me on the bed. "Now would be a good time to tell me what's going on."

"You were right about them. The Reynoldses," I clarified, as if there was any doubt. "They've been lying to me." I swirled the amber liquid in my glass and took another drink, closing my eyes to feel the warm trail blaze down my throat. "I overheard Mason and Stuart talking. All their 'you're family' endearments were just empty rhetoric meant to manipulate me." I stared at my glass wondering how I'd let that happen.

"Stuart said he and Mason were responsible for driving Jolene away. They're the reason Carson got his claws into her." James didn't interrupt. He let me vent and I told him what I'd learned and how I'd gotten out of there. "They can't find me through my phone, can they?"

"No." He took my hand and absently rubbed my knuckles with his thumb. I threw my block up, remembering too late his tendency to read my memories uninvited. But James was deep in thought somewhere else, paying no attention to my memories.

We sat in silence, sipping our drinks. "We're missing something," he said, finally. "What's their motivation? What do they gain by having you on the Tribunal?"

"Does it matter? They lied to me. They used my father and Andrew's grave to reel me in. It's despicable."

James didn't agree or disagree; he looked deep in thought, trying to figure it out. In my mind, there was nothing to figure out. I didn't care about their motivation. They'd hurt me and now I would move their names back to the "don't trust" column.

"Manse is still a threat," he said.

Hearing those words snapped something inside me. I was sick to death of Carson's threat hanging over my head, and I didn't want to feel the pain of Mason and Stuart's betrayal. I wanted out—a new start—somewhere where no one knew me or could find me or threaten me. My path looked so clear now. "I've got some money and a passport. I've always wanted to go to Europe. Wanna come?" I said, biting my lower lip.

His smile lit up his face and he leaned over and kissed me. The kiss quickly deepened into something more promising, but he pulled back. "Why don't we start with dinner," he said, and rolled off the bed, jumping to his feet. He came around to my side of the bed and extended his hand. He helped me to my feet and kissed me again. When he pulled back, I noticed his gaze falling to my neck, to Jeannette's necklace. I reached behind and released the clasp. "I'm done with them," I said, and dropped it on the dresser on our way out. His satchel was by the door, ready to pick-up and go, as always. He grabbed the large beach towel from the porch that looked like it was set out to dry and led the way down a steep goat trail to the beach, dropping the towel on the rocks before we headed south.

My block was still locked on when he draped his arm around my shoulder. I snaked my arm around his waist and we strolled on like that, enjoying the last dregs of the afternoon's brilliant sunshine. It would be dark in an hour or so.

A short time later, we arrived at a taco shack on the beach. Three mismatched tables sat under three crooked palapas. "It's not much to look at, but they make a hell of a taco," he assured me. I didn't care what they served; it was enough that I was here with James and free of the Reynoldses.

He settled me at one of the tables and returned with a Corona and a margarita in a can with a straw. "Dinner's at 7:00," he said in a voice mocking Stuart's. "*Salud*!" He tapped my can with his beer bottle.

"Cheers," I said, and sipped the worst margarita I'd ever tasted.

The man from the taco shack dropped our tacos at the table. "*Buen provecho*," he said, before beating a hasty retreat. We split the two orders: one fish, the other beef. The sun set in spectacular fashion and James ordered another round of drinks. In a blatant show of lawlessness, and contrary to the posted warnings, we took the bevies with us as we strolled north along the beach.

The slim sliver of moon barely reflected a sparkle across the water. We meandered along, arm in arm. At the mouth of the trail to his hut, he stopped me. "I've got something else in mind," he said, trotting over to retrieve the large beach towel he'd dropped earlier. We walked another fifty metres then scrambled over a low black-rubble breakwater and found ourselves on another stretch of beach.

"The tide's coming in," he said. "No one will venture here in the dark at high tide." He guided me with his hand on the small of my back toward the soft sand at the foot of the cliff beside a jutting rock. The warmth of his touch radiated all the way to my toes. His hand fell away and he snapped the towel so it landed in a flutter on the soft sand.

He turned back to me, his gaze intense, his arousal plain on his face. He reached one hand around my waist and pulled me close. The other hand closed around my shoulder, pulling my hair off my neck. He pressed his lips to my collarbone and trailed a path upward, along my neck. I felt a rush when he wove his fingers through my hair and gripped the nape of my neck. He held my head in place and nipped my earlobe. My flinch amused him. He licked the hard cartilage of my ear. I gasped an uneven breath at the discovery of this unexplored erogenous zone.

"Lie down," he whispered and stepped away leaving me wanting more. James liked his control, I mused, happily following his instruction. He eased himself down beside me then rolled on top, pinning me to the towel. He kissed me like he hadn't tasted me in months, and his intensity made me feel desirable. I reached behind him and pulled his hair tie loose, releasing dark waves like a veil around my face.

After days of imagining it, I was finally able to run my hands under his shirt and caress his bare torso. His muscles felt tense beneath the soft, warm skin. His breathing deepened and he pulled back, straightened his elbows to give me better access while he slowly ground his pelvis into mine. The sexual hunger on his face was as arousing as the erection that strained behind his zipper.

Abruptly, he pushed away, knelt beside me and pulled his shirt off. I looked up in carnal appreciation, a smile curving my lips. "Sit up," he said, and when I complied, he pulled my sweater over my head. Before my shirt hit the sand, he reached over and cupped my breast. He pulled the bra's lace edge back and sucked my nipple into his mouth. I arched into him, asking for more and he didn't disappoint. He released the clasp with one hand and stripped me of the lacy garment.

Getting naked outdoors elevated the seduction to delicious heights. Fresh air skimmed over newly exposed skin like silk, and the threat of discovery heightened the sexual tension, not that it needed a boost.

We stripped off each other's jeans and I got to admire him in the sliver of moonlight. He had a beautiful body, his muscles sleek and taut. I especially liked the long smooth oblique muscles that ran down his abdomen, on either side of his belly button. He lay on his back and I traced those muscles all the way down. He loved that, moaning softly, and I loved his reaction. His erection was hard as stone when I took him in my mouth. He stroked my head, watching me with half closed eyes. At first, I was gentle, lulling him. But I knew James enjoyed skating on the edge of rough, so when his eyes closed, I nipped him carefully with my teeth and watched him fall apart. That I could undo him so completely was a heady rush. I fed off it, encouraged him and brought him up and over the edge of an abyss that left him breathless.

Afterwards, I crawled up his torso, settling into the crook where his arm met his still heaving chest. We lay in each other's arms until he recovered his breath. "That deserves a reward," he said, finally. He kissed my forehead and shimmied out from under me. He took a very sweet and languorous path licking and kissing his way from my neck to my hips.

He placed his hands on my knees and pulled my legs apart. The heat of his gaze felt like a warm caress. "Wider," he said, and I arched at the request. I was learning to love his bossy talk: it made me feel adventurous and sensual. I complied and he smiled, satisfied with himself. He stroked the inside of my thighs, from my knees to my groin, then back again, never quite reaching the apex that begged for his attention.

He enjoyed cranking up my libido, watching me, teasing me until I thought I'd scream. But he seemed to know my body better than I did, waiting until just the right moment to touch me. When he slid his fingers inside, I arched my hips to meet him, throwing away all pretense of modesty. When he lowered his shoulders between my legs and set his mouth on me, I gave myself to him completely. He was shockingly good at this and delivered a mind-numbing orgasm with rippling aftershocks. It was over far too quickly.

"Don't get comfortable," he said, when I melted into the towel. "We're not done yet. I have something special planned."

"Wait," I said, still breathless. "I need a minute."

"No you don't—you just think you do." He got to his knees and held out his hand. I looked at him skeptically. "Trust me on this." He was hard again and wore a condom that I hadn't even noticed him put on. He pulled me to my feet, steadied me then brushed the hair from my face. I looked around for uninvited visitors. Even without night vision, our pale skin against the dark cliff would draw attention. He saw me look around, and laughed, probably enjoying the threat of discovery.

"Ready?" he said, and I raised my eyebrows in question. He wrapped his arms around me and lifted me off the ground then broke us free from gravity. It was the last thing I expected from James; the James I knew didn't fly for fun. I liked this James. He held me close until we'd drifted to the top of the cliff.

We shifted to a horizontal position and he moved us along, looking for something in the cliff face. He found it in the sturdy clump of sagebrush. "Here," he said, positioning us perpendicular to the cliff face. He directed my arms up over my head and helped me wrap my hands around a thick clump. "Hold this and, whatever you do," he said with a daring grin, "don't touch the cliff." That took the smile off my face. I twisted around to get a better look at the sagebrush and surrounding cliff. I knew if I touched the earth my gravity would rush back, sending me plunging to the rocks below.

He squeezed my hands around the branches. "Lock your elbows and hold tight." He kissed me before sliding his hands down my out-stretched arms and supine body. He licked each nipple, leaving them wet to attract the breeze. I shivered with the cool kiss of the wind and the thrill of what we were doing. My legs fell open with a nudge of his knee and he drifted upright.

With a wicked smile tugging up a corner of his mouth he gave my hips a sharp tug. I gasped and tightened my hand grip. He leaned back, stretching my torso so I had to hold on, and then he plunged deep inside me, pushing all the air out of my lungs in a deep moan. He too traded words for guttural grunts. He was right; I didn't need more time. I held on tight as he pulled back then thrust forward again and again, taking up a rhythm that left me breathless. When my orgasm hit, the intensity of it frightened me. I bucked with abandon as what felt like a bolt of electricity slammed through me. James rode it, fed it with pumps of his hips until I arched, threw my head back and screamed. He abandoned his mind soon after, giving the reigns to the orgasm gods with a final pump of his hips and an incomprehensible utterance.

As he lay spent across my body, I pushed off from the cliff and set us adrift. We floated aimlessly while we came back to our senses. "You've ruined me for regular sex," I said, and felt the rumble of his laughter.

"Hmm . . . you enjoy zero-gravity sex, do you?" he teased.

"You can't tell?"

He laughed again. "I love what you do to me."

"Uh-huh," I murmured contentedly. "Right back at you, Mr. Moss."

We landed back by the big beach towel and lay down in a tangle of limbs, neither of us ready to put an end to the experience. I snuggled into his embrace.

Eventually though, the difficult questions had to be asked, even if they couldn't be answered. "What are your plans from here?" James asked.

"I don't know," I answered honestly. "Do you want to run away with me?"

He kissed my head and tucked it under his chin. "I'm not running anymore. Remember?"

"You need to work on your timing," I said, and then the quiet of the night settled around us again. After a time, I broke our comfortable silence. "I thought I'd call Sam and get his advice."

"I think that's a good place to start. I'll help if I can, but I can't leave here right now. I'm at the Tribunal's beck and call until this business with the Redeemers is resolved."

"Can I stay with you until I work something out?"

"Of course. Are you ready to head back?"

I wasn't, but we got dressed anyway and shook the sand out of the big towel. The tide had come in enough to force us to fly over the breakwater, but it was dark and there wasn't a voyeur in sight. He had the big towel slung over his shoulder as we made our way back up the narrow path to his small hut. He pulled me close when the path widened and I wrapped my arm around his waist. I felt safe in his arms and not so alone.

"Do you surf?" I asked, spotting the big board leaning against the hut.

"I do," he said, snickering. "But that board's just camo—"

I stopped abruptly and stiffened.

"What?" James asked, going on full alert.

"He's here."

Chapter Nineteen

W ho?" James stepped in front of me, shoulders tight, eyes panning left then right.

"Mason," I said with certainty. I even knew he was standing close to the surfboard. "He's on the porch." How the hell had he found me? We were ten feet away when he materialized, leaning against the wall. He posed with a casual air, but his narrowed eyes and stiff fingers betrayed his tension.

"What are you doing here, Mason?" I asked.

He looked from me and settled on James, but I could only see one side of their staring contest. Mason blinked first. "You were right about Jolene," he said, turning his gaze back to me. He measured his words. "She ran away from us . . . just like you did tonight. We thought she'd figure it out, or at least come back and let us explain, but she didn't. We put her in a terrible position. We failed Jolene. We don't want to make the same mistake with you."

"Let's take this inside," James said, reaching behind to pull me closer. He knew as well as I did that Mason would have his say whether we wanted him to or not. James valiantly put himself between Mason and me, and ushered me into the hut ahead of him. I immediately walked around to the far side of the room and stood with my back to the corner in front of the hot plate. James stood between the end of the bed and the dresser, cutting off Mason's path to me. Mason closed the door and looked around the room with interest. His eyes came to rest on Jeannette's crystal-case necklace then quickly flashed away. James reacted like lightning, snatching the necklace off the dresser. He turned the intricate crystal case around in his fingers then opened the clasp and let the crystal slide out.

"Be careful with that," Mason barked, but James wasn't interested in the crystal. He set it aside and examined the case, eventually twisting the bottom end. A conical piece the size of a jelly bean came off in his fingers. He tapped the open end of it against the dresser, and a small puck-shaped disc dropped out.

James set the necklace down and looked at me. "It's a bug: a tracking device," he said. He turned to Mason. "A little heavy-handed, wouldn't you say." James shook his head. "No wonder you were so quick to assure me she could leave any time she chose." I glanced from James to Mason. What? When had that conversation taken place? What else had they discussed?

"You assured me you'd let me know if she got in touch with you," Mason retorted. "Seems it wasn't a wasted effort after all."

"It's a moot point," I growled, cutting the argument off and crossing my arms over my chest. I glared at Mason. "Tell me what you came here to say, then leave. Please," I added as an afterthought. It never hurt to be polite, especially when your uninvited company could jolt you to oblivion.

Mason scowled at James for a moment longer and then spoke. "Ghosts are a rare commodity in our world. All the major players on the Tribunal are Ghosts and always have been. We're the only ones who can get in to do what needs to be done then cover the tracks. We erase problems like the Wrights. We take on scum like Manse and Dowling."

I knew I shouldn't interrupt. I should let him finish so I could shove him out the door, but I'd heard it all before. "The only reason Fliers like Carson exist is because of the Tribunal. The Flier community is scared shitless of you. Your brutal punishments, your dogged inflexibility—they'd risk their lives before asking for your help. Fliers don't respect the Tribunal, Mason, they're afraid of it."

"I'm sure that's true," he said. "It's a regrettable by-product of protecting the secret—something the Tribunal holds sacred above all else."

"*Regrettable*?" I repeated. "More like inevitable. The Tribunal is a self-appointed body responsible to no one. It holds power with violence and bloodlines—Ghost bloodlines. The Redeemers learned the Tribunal's lessons well. They're stealing gifts to get stronger—to turn the tables. Carson is merely facilitating what every oppressed group seeks— rising up against a malevolent and unrepresentative dictatorship."

"You think you understand what's going on, but you don't."

I spread my arms in welcome. "Then, please, enlighten me," I said, jutting my chin.

"When the secret of our existence is threatened, our lives are at stake, your life, all of our freedom. If someone chooses that path, they must be stopped. We can't sit back and hope they'll change. There's no room for second chances. Those who choose to threaten our secret, forfeit their lives to save the rest of us. But their gift doesn't have to die with them. Their gift helps us protect the secret. You call it brutal . . . we call it necessary to ensure our freedom.

"But now, not even that is enough. Twelve years ago we learned that the government suspected our existence. Since then, they've made tremendous inroads, mostly at the expense of captured Fliers' lives.

"My father and I have tried to change the Tribunal's thinking. We see what's coming. We can no longer hold our fingers in the dyke of change. Technology is improving rapidly, guaranteeing the exposure of our kind. Information—like your father's research—like cellphone photos—spreads around the world at the press of a button.

"What my father and I and a small minority want to do is control how and when that inevitable unveiling happens. If we can pull the Flier community together, present a united front, governments around the world will be forced to deal with our existence head on—not by locking us behind closed doors."

His revelations stunned me. It took me a moment to collect my thoughts. "What's stopping you?"

Mason slid back into carefully measuring his words. "Ghosts may hold all nine votes on the Tribunal, but the Reynolds family casts only one of them. This issue is contentious, and my father's and my opinion are in the minority. The majority have their heads in the sand, and no desire to consider, let alone plan, for our exposure. They're protected by a bubble of wealth and have been operating unopposed for so long that they've lost perspective. And now, with the Redeemers threatening, the old guard has closed ranks. Your presence could change all that."

"My presence wouldn't change a thing, Mason. I'm barely out of the Flier cradle. I'm so new, the tags are still on. They would laugh at us and spit the fact that I was gifted, not born, back in our faces."

"You're still a Ghost. You've got Jolene's speed and strength, and that's nothing to laugh at. Those who knew Jolene will recognize her gift in you. Ghosts play a critical role and because of that, our opinions carry weight among the founding coveys. Every voice for change counts, Emelynn. If you can sway just one or two others, we might be able to gain momentum to turn things around."

Maybe Mason was the one who had his head in the sand. "No one is going to listen to me."

"How do you know, Emelynn? How do you know if you won't even try?"

"Why should I trust you, Mason? You've been lying to me from the day you showed me my brother's grave. You could have told me all this right at the start."

"You wouldn't have believed me. I knew what you thought of us. Did you think we didn't know how much you despised us? You confirmed as much just hours ago."

"Hours ago, I learned that Jolene ran from you for these exact same reasons, and look what happened to her. Nothing's changed, Mason. You're still trying to manipulate me, just like you manipulated her."

"No," he said. "I'm not. We planned on having this discussion with you after you met the Tribunal—after you understood the depth of their convictions. We were giving you the time to see for yourself—to come to your own conclusions without the pressure of our expectations, something we failed to do with Jolene.

"The Tribunal families were Jolene's playmates, her friends. She'd never seen the Tribunal in action—we'd mistakenly shielded her from the ugliness of it. We pushed her too soon—forced her hand. We made the colossal mistake of pitting her against her longstanding, misguided beliefs and her friends, and she ran ... right into Manse's arms. We're responsible for that and we'll live with that guilt and regret for the rest of our lives.

"Please, Emelynn, give us the chance to redeem ourselves now. Jolene chose you; we want to protect you, but we're running out of time."

"What are you talking about?"

"The Redeemers may be the final straw: the undoing of our secret. They are sloppy but they're gaining ground. They're pushing the Tribunal. With no change in direction, the Tribunal will make decisions that are sure to further divide the Flier community. Each of those decisions carries with it the risk of exposing us in an unflattering light. If we're covered in blood and divided into warring factions when we're exposed, what do you think our chances are of convincing anyone that we're harmless?" Mason's eyes pleaded for understanding. "We need your help, Emelynn, and I'm asking for it now. We need to transform the Tribunal. You can help us do that."

I glanced at James. He leaned against the edge of the dresser with narrowed eyes. He had sucked in his cheeks and watched Mason with frightening intensity. I paced the small bit of available floor space, with my hands on my hips. Mason had betrayed my trust. Was I a fool for even considering his plea?

"I'm angry with you, Mason," I said. "Regardless of your reasons, you used me. I want to be angry and stay angry for a very long time."

"I'm sorry, Emelynn. Believe me, we never meant to hurt you. We're trying to do the right thing. Let your anger go and help us make a difference."

I thought about his words and decided to test their veracity. "If you want me to believe you, prove it. Release James and his family from this ridiculous servitude to the Tribunal."

James bounced off the dresser. "Emelynn!" he admonished from the sidelines.

"No, James. If he wants me to believe that he's being honest, he can prove it."

"Actually, Emelynn, I can't," Mason said. "Not until we represent the majority and gain control of the Tribunal. When that happens, I'd be happy to support releasing the Moss family. Maybe we could even come to a new understanding," Mason said, addressing James. "A collaboration that benefits us both."

James didn't respond. He stood stern-faced with his fists in tight balls as if he hadn't heard Mason. I wanted to know what he was thinking, how he felt about what we'd learned, but he would never open up with Mason in the room. It was time for Mason to leave. I needed to talk to James. "Let me think about it, Mason," I said. "I'm going to stay here tonight and I'll let you know tomorrow."

"We don't have that luxury," Mason said. "Manse killed Carrie this afternoon. Put a bullet through her head." I sucked in a horrified breath. "As it turns out, you were never his target. You were the bait. Manse was waiting for the Tribunal to show itself like he knew we would."

"What about Ron?" I asked.

"Ron's in ICU. He was shot in the back, but he managed to tell your friend Avery that Manse is now a Ghost. That's how Manse got to them. It means he was involved in the Vosburghs' disappearance. And if he stole one of their gifts, we can only assume that another Redeemer has stolen the other Vosburgh gift. We are at a terrible disadvantage until we learn who and where they are. Unfortunately, Emelynn, that means you're still bait and we can't protect you here. Neither can he. No disrespect, James, but these walls are like paper. A good jolt would bring the place down around you."

My body felt like it was crawling with ants. I paced back and forth fisting my hands, trying to shake the feeling of helpless dread. "What about Grace Shipley and Detective Jordan?"

"Fine. They're both fine," Mason said.

Thank god for that, at least. "I've got to get out of here," I said, and bolted for the door.

James moved aside to let me through, but Mason stepped in front of the door blocking my way. "Where are you going?" he asked.

I gulped suddenly unable to breathe. "I need some air."

Mason searched my face and something he saw there made him open the door. "Don't go far," he said, letting me by, but I was already halfway to the beach trail.

Debbie called my name. It made me stop in my tracks, but I didn't turn around. "Don't," I warned, but she kept coming. "I mean it," I yelled and she stopped.

"It's not safe out here," she reasoned.

"It's not safe anywhere." I rushed forward, calling on my crystal's power to blast free of gravity. It responded with an intensity that propelled me like a rock from a slingshot up over the beach path and straight out across the water. I screamed my frustration and hot tears escaped unbidden. I felt trapped in an endless, violent loop with Carson Manse as my dance partner. I flew hard, letting anger fuel my flight and poured on the speed Jolene had given me to wash away my fear and the feeling of impotence. A giant lumbering tanker forced me to veer north. At least no one could catch me out here. I took comfort in that, but it was hollow. There was only one path away from this nightmare and I had to come to grips with it. I'd be damned if I'd let Carson win.

I slowed my flight and my anger fell away. The night air blew through my hair reminding me of something precious: Jolene's gift. I may not have asked for it, and I'd paid a painful price for it, but I wouldn't trade it for the moon and all the stars. The freedom of flight; the miracle of night vision; the mystery of ghosting—this was my gift and it was worth fighting for.

James met me at the bottom of the footpath and pulled me into his arms.

"I'm sorry. I just needed to get out of there and clear my head."

"I know," he said, resting his chin on my head. "Mason and Debbie are waiting for you."

"Will you come with me?" I asked.

"Not to Cairabrae, but you should go. Mason's right; you'll be safer there than here."

"I wish you'd come."

"I can't. You know that." He took my hand and started for the path.

"Do you believe him? About changing the Tribunal?"

"Yeah, I do. I don't think he'd risk telling you or let me overhear the conversation if he wasn't committed to it, but you have to decide for yourself. Weigh their words carefully and don't be afraid to ask tough questions." He draped his arm around my shoulder when we cleared the path. "And never forget that they're Tribunal," he whispered as we approached his tiny hut.

Debbie was sitting on the rail. Mason stopped pacing when he saw us approach and stared angrily at me. "Are you finished?" he said, trying unsuccessfully to keep the snark out of his voice. I guess I couldn't blame him. I'd more or less thrown a temper tantrum. The thought made me smile.

"Did you bring a car or are we flying?" I asked and Mason exhaled.

"Debbie's driving," he said, and she quickly hopped off the rail and crossed in front of the porch to show us the way.

I turned and kissed James. No more hiding I thought and he obviously agreed, pulling me close. "See you tomorrow?" I said hopefully.

"You will," James said, letting me go.

Mason ushered me ahead of him and we followed Debbie to the car. Mason and I rode in the back. When we got to the highway, I broke the awkward silence with an apology, but he shook his head. "Don't apologize. It was a misunderstanding, that's all."

"Okay." I could accept that. "Where do we go from here?"

"We need to get you up to speed for the party. Tomorrow, we'll sit down with Dad and go through what we know of the Tribunal players and their politics. It'll be an excruciating conversation, so rest up tonight. You can test our theories when you meet the people and afterwards, we can discuss strategy. Does that suit you?"

"You've thought this out."

"I found myself with some extra time on my hands tonight," he said, flashing an indulgent smile.

"Glad to see you put it to good use," I said. "It suits me fine." Our love-hate relationship was giving me whiplash.

It was late when we got back to Cairabrae. I went straight to my room and texted James that I'd arrived safely. He replied with a happy face. It felt like a lifeline.

Sleep, when it came, was fitful. Carson haunted my dreams, taunting me with a whip in his hands. I dreamed I held an 8x10 glossy photo of Carrie lying dead in a halo of blood, her lifeless eyes still open.

I was lying on my back when the room grew light around seven o'clock the next morning. My mind was already busy replaying last night's conversation with Mason. I believed what he said about Jolene. His guilt about what happened to her was evident in his voice and on his face. I suppose he could also just be a good actor. But I remembered Stuart saying she was a gentle soul. A gentle soul wouldn't survive the Tribunal. Jolene had known that; too bad her brother and father hadn't.

I trudged to the bathroom. A swim would help, I thought, and tugged on a bathing suit. Derek was on duty downstairs and nodded to me as I passed through. The cool outdoor air raised goosebumps on my bare skin as I made my way across the patio to the pool. Mist rose lazily from its surface. I waded easily into water that was warmer than the air and settled into a float, happy to let the water muffle my hearing. I closed my eyes and let my arms drift away from my body. If only I could stay here in this comfortable, warm cocoon forever. A shadow crossed my face and I opened my eyes with a start, searching for its source.

"Sorry. Didn't mean to startle you," Stuart said. He stood in silhouette on the edge of the pool.

I made my way back to the stairs. He handed me a towel as I got out. "Thank you for hearing Mason out last night." He wore tan slacks and a collared shirt, which told me he wasn't working on the ranch today.

"I didn't promise anything, Stuart. I'll make up my mind when I've got all the facts." I dried off and blotted my hair on the towel.

"Fair enough. Come to the kitchen and get a coffee, warm up."

I wrapped my housecoat around my wet bathing suit and followed him to the kitchen. A folded newspaper rested on the table. Stuart poured me a coffee and I helped myself to milk from the fridge. I perched on the edge of a chair and watched Stuart. His moves were so well practiced it was like watching a dance. Cups, plates, cutlery. Toaster, butter, jam. He pulled out one after the other from the cupboards and set them on the counter.

"Would you tell me about your time on the Tribunal?" I asked.

He popped two slices of bread into the toaster. "I started as a bodyguard for my grandfather when he led the Tribunal. When the leadership passed to another family, I became an active member. Even back then, Ghosts were rare. We spelled each other off in five-year rotations for the most part. I spent forty-six years on the Tribunal before I retired. But you're never really out. It's more like the reserves."

"And Mason?" I asked.

"What about me?" Mason said, arriving fresh from a shower. His hair was slicked back and he was dressed in a light crewneck sweater and jeans. I felt distinctly underdressed.

"How long have you been a member of the Tribunal?"

"Since I was twenty. Why do you ask?"

"Curious, I guess." I stood and the housecoat fell away from my wet suit, leaving a cold spot against the back of my legs.

"Just curious, or are you skirting around something else?" Mason asked, turning his back to grab a mug.

"I don't want to be rude. I'll go change." I dropped my empty cup on the counter and turned to leave.

Mason didn't look up from pouring his coffee when he spoke. "I'd rather you be rude than have another *misunderstanding* like last night. What's on your mind, Emelynn?"

James's earlier comment about where their money came from had been on my mind. My imagined nefarious scenarios clouded my opinion of them. So even though it made me feel tacky as hell, I needed to understand. "Okay. How did your family come to be so wealthy?"

With a glance, Mason tossed the question to Stuart, who answered. "My ancestors were thieving rogues, but I suspect you know that or you wouldn't have asked the question."

"I don't know any such thing. That's why I asked."

Stuart flashed a cavalier smile. "All right. But before I explain, I want you to know that the Reynolds fortune was established before I was born." He took his seat. "You may want to sit down. It's a long story." I returned to table, and Stuart began.

"In the mid-nineteenth century, the Tribunal instituted a ruling that all Flier gifting be documented. It was a way to ensure the free will and integrity of a process that was rife with violent coercion. It was a prudent measure at the time. But like a lot of Tribunal rulings back then, there was another agenda in play. At that time, most families had a family bible of sorts that outlined the gifting ritual." He tilted his head to one side. "Like the one you so kindly returned to us. We call them anthologies now.

"Typically, those books also detailed the family's holdings. Whenever a family submitted their documentation to confirm a gifting, it alerted the Tribunal to the existence of another anthology. The Tribunal's Ghosts would ensure that the family's anthology quietly disappeared. Eventually, knowledge of the ancient rituals was lost to all but the Tribunal. But that wasn't all that got lost. The confiscated anthologies allowed the Tribunal to identify abandoned properties and untapped resources, which they appropriated with impunity.

"I don't doubt that somewhere along the line, the Reynolds ancestors filled our family coffers with stolen goods. That's where all this originated," he gestured to indicate Cairabrae. "And there you have it: the whole ugly story. We can't change it and we can't make amends."

It couldn't have been easy for Stuart to admit to his family's crimes. "Thank you for telling me." I stood to leave, satisfied they were telling the truth. James may have been right about the origin of their money, but I wouldn't hold the sins of their fathers against them.

"Our history is your history, Emelynn. I wish it were more noble."

"I'll get dressed," I said, and headed for the door.

"Bring the photos with you when you come back down," Stuart said, as he unfolded the newspaper.

I shoved thoughts of family wealth and confiscated anthologies to the back of my mind. We had enough going on without those worries. I showered and dressed in yoga pants and a running shirt. When I returned to the kitchen, Mason and Stuart were both buried behind newspapers. Crumbed-up plates sat in front of them. I dropped two slices of raisin bread into the toaster and refilled their coffee cups. A fly on the wall would think we were a normal happy family eating breakfast and talking about our busy plans for the day ahead.

"How's Jeannette this morning?" I asked then crunched into my butter-laden toast.

Stuart peeked out from the newspaper, folded it and set it down. "She had a good night. It's kind of you to ask."

"She came to see me," I said. Mason dropped his paper and stared at me, waiting. "The night I accidentally ghosted. Her nurse wheeled her in. I was stuck up in the corner, scared witless and she looked right at me and smiled. I think she knew I was there."

Stuart reached over and put his hand on mine. "I'm sure she did," he said quietly, then he stood and left the room.

"He misses Mom," Mason said in the wake of Stuart's abrupt departure. "The way she used to be."

"I've upset him."

"No. You just reminded him."

I reached for Stuart's paper and scanned the headlines while I finished my toast. We'd eaten by the time Maria bustled into the kitchen with her arms full. She dropped the bags on the massive marble-topped island.

"I'll take care of that," she said, as I started to clear the table. A buzzer sounded and Maria diverted to the service door. Two young women stood outside wearing chef's gear with leather bundles under their arms. "Good. Right on time. Come in—we have a busy day ahead."

Mason and I took that as our cue to get out of there. We walked the full length of the house to Stuart's office. Stuart was taking my Tribunal education seriously, if the sight of the room was any indication. Shutters had been opened along one wall revealing a large whiteboard. Stuart's sleeves were rolled up and he was busy adding names to lists scribbled on the board. The table was covered with sheets of paper and photographs.

We started with a review of the photos I'd brought. Stuart added photos and more details about the covey each member represented. I learned which ones supported the change, which ones didn't and which ones were on the fence. I learned which members represented their entire coveys and which ones only voted for themselves or their immediate families. He'd placed an asterisk beside the name of anyone who was a Ghost. Only about a third of the names had an asterisk.

I learned about the Tribunal leadership, which rotated every five years to another one of the nine founding coveys. Day-to-day business was managed by five active members under the direction of the leader. If a controversy arose, it was dealt with swiftly by the full Tribunal. The leader organized meetings when a vote was needed to decide a special case or settle a contentious issue.

Every year, a meeting was held for not only the nine-member Tribunal, but all of the Ghosts and other influential covey members as well. The agenda for the annual meeting was set by the leader. The only other way to get an item on the agenda was with the support of three Tribunal members. Anyone could speak at the annual meeting and discussion was generally robust and encouraged, but only the nine members of the Tribunal could vote. The leader voted last, breaking any ties. The Tribunal had never experienced a revolt, despite the differences among them. Their gift and its secret bound them together.

Stuart got up to answer the intercom on his desk. Mason explained that the leadership was slated to change at the spring meeting, when he would replace Sebastian as the new leader. Sebastian was staunchly opposed to any change in the Tribunal's status quo and Mason assuming the mantle was the opportunity they'd been waiting for.

"Escort him to my office," Stuart said, and disconnected. "We have a visitor." Stuart crossed quickly to close the shutters on the whiteboard. He signalled Mason and me to collect the papers on the table. I heard a rap at the door as I deposited the papers on his desk. They must have run down the hall to get here so quickly.

"Come in," Stuart called and the door opened. Sam barrelled into the room and glanced around. "Detective Jordan," Stuart said, calm as a mortician. "What brings you by this morning?"

I hadn't realized that Stuart knew the detective. I would've said it was good to see him, but he looked frazzled and he was a bear at the best of times.

He approached Stuart and shook his hand. "Stuart. Mason," he said, shaking Mason's hand in turn. The detective wasn't wasting words on greetings today. "Emelynn."

I stood behind the desk and smiled. "Sam," I said, mimicking him. He wore my favourite jacket with the visible bulge under the left shoulder. I wouldn't have thought he'd be able to travel with his gun.

"How can we help you?" Mason asked.

"I was in the neighbourhood. Thought I'd check out the security around one of our protected witnesses."

Ooh, he was in fine form this morning. I bit my lip to stifle a smile. Something had crawled up his butt and I had the feeling it was about to hit the proverbial fan.

"As you can see, she's fine," Stuart said. "Why don't you tell me what's on your mind."

"You can start by telling me why the woman who was killed yesterday in Summerset had your phone number in her cellphone."

"Carrie Marshall. Yes, her murder is tragic. She worked security for me. Ron Evans, the man who was shot in the back, is also one of mine. I understand Carson Manse has been identified as the shooter."

"Since you seem to know so much, Stuart, perhaps you can shed some light on why Manse went after your people rather than Emelynn's decoy."

"I wish we could help you," Stuart said. "We know nothing more than you do."

"Why did you send your security detail to Summerset?"

"We wanted to keep an eye on Manse. We didn't want him coming after Emelynn again."

"Something else is going on here, Stuart. I can smell it."

"Detective . . . Samuel." Stuart sounded exasperated. "Our record of cooperation with law enforcement is exemplary. Nothing is going on here. Nothing, that we're aware of."

"What's with all the fluffing up going on out there?" Sam said, flinging his hand toward the centre of the house.

"We're hosting a cocktail party tomorrow evening."

"Now? With Manse on the loose?" He shook his head like he was dealing with a wayward ten-year-old. "Cancel it."

"It's a small gathering of close friends—an opportunity for Emelynn to meet some people who are important to me. We know them all, so the risk is minimal and our security is, as you know, top notch."

Mason added his two cents. "The timing is unfortunate, but it's been planned for months."

"I strongly encourage you to re-schedule."

"She'll be safe," Mason said.

Sam's nostrils flared. "Emelynn, will you walk me out?" he asked.

Talk about putting me on the spot. I looked from Stuart, who looked ready to explode, to Mason, who nodded, then rolled my eyes, walked around the desk and led Sam out of the room.

When we'd cleared eavesdropping distance, he spoke. "I can take you out of here any time you want. Just say the word."

"Where would I go if I wasn't here?" I asked.

"A safe house. We have a few at our disposal."

"Are they as nice as this one?" I was only half kidding, but he was not in the mood for it.

He stopped walking and glared at me. "We usually choose based on security, not amenities."

"Why are you so pissed off?" I asked, sounding braver than I felt.

"I'm responsible for your safety—not the Reynoldses. What happened with Manse in Vancouver stinks to high heaven, and this party is a bad idea. The only reason I'm not pulling you out of here right now is because Moss approved their security measures, and I'm not sure we could do any better."

"I think I'll be fine. Really. They have alarms all over the property and security everywhere."

"My number's on this card," he said, handing it to me. "Program it into your speed-dial and call me if anything comes up. Any time. I've got some business in San Francisco before I head north again, so I'll be close by. And if you change your mind, I can have someone here to collect you within the hour."

"Thanks, Sam." He patted my shoulder and nodded to Derek on the way out. I watched him get in the passenger seat of an unmarked SUV and waved as it drove away.

Sam had been right about the fluffing up, as he'd called it. In the living room, Phillip directed the re-arrangement of furniture. Tall round tables, the temporary kind made out of cut-out plywood tripods, awaited placement. A bar area had been established against the wall beside the fireplace where a woman was loading bottles into a wine cooler. Liquor bottles already stood in a straight line on a stainless-steel cart, which sat at right angles to the cooler. Crates of glasses were stacked waiting their turn to be polished and placed.

Instead of returning to Stuart's office, I wandered in the direction of the heavenly smells coming from the kitchen. I pushed the door open and found what looked like a busy restaurant kitchen in full swing. The two chefs, who had arrived earlier, were up to their elbows in vegetables. Another man was butchering meat and Maria was stirring several pots on the big stove. She turned when she heard me come in. "What can I get for you, Emelynn?"

"Never mind, Maria. I can see that you have your hands full."

"No trouble at all. Was it coffee you were after? I can send Phillip in with a pot."

"No, don't bother him. He's busy in the living room."

"Nonsense," she said, dismissing my concerns. "I'll send him down with a pot in a minute. Is there anything else?"

"No. Thank you." I bowed out of there feeling like I'd taxed her already heavy load.

"Phillip's bringing coffee," I announced when I returned to Stuart's office. Mason and Stuart were poised with questions about the detective, but I had nothing to offer that they didn't already know. I, however, wanted to know how they knew Sam.

"The detective and his American counterpart on the task force were here asking about Jolene and her disappearance after your kidnapping," Stuart said. "We couldn't hide Manse's connection to her so we cooperated. The task force made several visits trying to connect the other disappearances." That discussion ended when Phillip delivered the coffee, but I wasn't done with my questions.

"I don't mean to be difficult, but now that I know how the Tribunal operates and what you're up against, what exactly is your plan?"

Mason answered. "The most important part is getting the idea of going public, onto the agenda. Even if they don't agree, it will get them talking about it and it will give us a chance to demonstrate the type of technology we're up against."

"What else?" I asked.

Stuart continued where Mason left off. "We'd like them to make the agendas available to all the Fliers in their coveys—to be more responsive to them. Some of the founding coveys know nothing about how we operate. The representative member either acts independently or only consults a small circle of family or friends. But what we do on the Tribunal impacts all of us. They have a right to know what's going on, and if they knew, they might support us."

"And what if you get it on the agenda and they still don't agree?"

"We'll have five years to keep the topic on the table," Mason said. "We'll keep the conversation going and prepare for the inevitable, because, unfortunately, it's not a matter of if, but when, we're exposed."

"What about all the other Fliers out there? The ones who don't belong to a founding covey? How will their voices be heard?"

"Let's not get ahead of ourselves," Stuart said. "We need to take one step at a time. Baby steps."

That baby better grow up fast, I thought and settled back. I picked at the photos and tested my memory. At one point, I retrieved my laptop and typed up the lists that Stuart had put on the whiteboard. Maria served lunch and afterwards, I continued my review upstairs in my room.

I talked to James later in the day, but we only had a moment. He'd been in and out of video-conference meetings with Detective Jordan and

the cross-border task force for most of the afternoon. By the time dinner
rolled around, the hustle and bustle in the house had died down. I made
it an early night and excused myself by nine thirty. Half an hour later, I
lay in bed staring at the ceiling thinking about the friends I'd left behind.
What were they up to tonight? Was Eden happy in Seattle? Would she
ever come back to Summerset? I wondered how Molly's pregnancy was
progressing and realized that tomorrow, while I was at a cocktail party,
she and Cheney would be getting married in Las Vegas. It wasn't right; I
should be with her on her special day. I missed my old life. I missed the
cottage.

That night, I dreamed of my father. He looked so proud watching
me descend a curved staircase. I was wearing the midnight-blue sheath
and his smile made me feel beautiful.

Chapter Twenty

The day of the party arrived with heavy fog rolling over the lawns in thick waves. I dashed to the pool for a brisk swim before dressing. The kitchen was off limits this morning but a chef, dusted white with flour, redirected me to the dining room. Stuart and Mason greeted me when I walked in. I helped myself to fruit salad and yogourt from the sideboard and joined them.

"Debbie and I are going for a run this morning," I said, sitting down.

"That's a good plan," Mason said. "It'll be hectic around here today. I'll be tied up with personnel and security for most of it. What about you, Dad?"

"I'm moving the horses to the barn on the north section. You should both be ready to greet our guests by five this afternoon."

"I thought it started at six?" I said.

"Humour me," Stuart said, standing to leave. "Carrie's family cancelled. We sent our condolences, of course. Unfortunately, their covey is sending her cousin, Dillon, to represent them. It looks like he may be her replacement." He looked over at me to explain. "Dillon doesn't support our position."

If I were they, I probably wouldn't support us either. I tried not to dwell on Carrie and her family. The guilt served no purpose.

"I've got to go," Stuart said, taking his leave.

Mason stayed and finished his coffee, while I finished my breakfast and then I too got up to leave. "Debbie's probably waiting," I said, gulping the last of my juice. "I'll see you later."

I found Debbie stretching outside my room in the hallway. "Come on in," I said, leaving the door open behind me. She picked up her knapsack and followed.

"Do you have everything you need for tonight?" she asked.

"I think so." I walked to the closet for another look. Dress, shoes, lingerie—no need for a purse. "Yup, all set," I said, returning to Debbie who hadn't moved from the sitting room.

"What about hair and makeup?"

"There's enough eyeliner and mascara in there to do the stage makeup for KISS *and* Marilyn Manson."

"What I meant," she said, laughing, "was, do you have someone lined up?"

"Lined up?" I asked, puzzled.

"Coming in to do your hair and makeup." She sounded exasperated.

I really was living in someone else's world. "That would never have occurred to me." Did I look as out of place as I felt? "I'll do my own hair and makeup."

"Let's go into Bodega Bay after the run. I have a friend I can call, who'll do your hair. He's good." Maybe my lack of finesse in the hair department had her worried. She raised her eyebrows, encouraging me to say yes. "It'll be a madhouse here today. You'll thank me for getting you out of it."

I reluctantly agreed, and she phoned her friend to make arrangements then we headed out for our run. When we arrived at the target range, the fog had thinned enough to shoot and I managed to nick more than an edge. I hit the ten-yard target twice and the fifteen-yarder once. That was good for me. Sad as it was, it was still an improvement. Though statistically, with the amount of ammo I went through, I was bound to hit one occasionally.

When we returned to the house, we had to dodge delivery men and the security people who trailed them everywhere. It looked like a florist had sent over its entire inventory and the temporary tables were now draped with white cloth. A thin-faced man stood behind the piano arranging sheets of music.

"What did I tell you," Debbie said, as we headed for our rooms.

We showered then met up in the dining room. The thin-faced pianist was now seated on the piano bench plunking random keys as if testing the pitch or tone or whatever it is you checked with a piano.

Debbie and I helped ourselves to sandwiches from the pile that lined the sideboard, and took them with us. There was enough food to feed a small army, which looked to be about right. I had never thought about how much organization was required to pull off something like this. It was no small feat and we were expecting nearly seventy guests. Seventy wealthy guests with high expectations, or maybe these were normal expectations in their circles.

Derek stood at the big front doors. He had a clipboard in his hand and a hands-free device in his ear. "Your ride's outside," he said, opening the door for us. A black Audi waited under the porte cochère. To the left of the door, a lectern was attended by an energetic young man who looked like he was still in high school. A valet? Really? He rushed to open the Audi's rear door and I slid in. Debbie walked around to the other side.

She greeted the driver as soon as she got inside. "Hey, Bill. We're going to Marcel's just off Harbour View Way. Do you know where that is?"

"I do. Buckle up."

During the drive, Debbie told me she often accompanied Jeannette to her doctor's appointments or Stuart to luncheons or meetings.

"I thought you were a bartender when I first met you," I remarked and she laughed.

"I tended bar in university and Stuart picked right up on that. I think he feels like he got a twofer."

We drove to a small house well away from the water on the eastern outskirts of Bodega Bay. Debbie's friend turned out to be a flamboyantly gay man named Marcel. They air kissed and Debbie made the introductions.

"No, no, no, no," were the first words the man spoke to me as he plucked at my hair like it was something the cat coughed up. "Did you let a blind man cut this? You'll need more than a set and blow dry, girl." I looked over at Debbie, who was using her hand to hide a grin that had swallowed her face.

It took Marcel an hour to wash and trim my hair and the entire time he quizzed us about the *shindig*, as he called it. Who was the party planner? What was the occasion? What were they serving? He was relentless and salivated over every detail. Debbie kept a good sense of humour about it, answering when she could and admonishing him when she couldn't. Marcel took another hour to arrange my hair in a messy up-do that left tendrils of curls around my face and the nape of my neck. He was no less relentless with his questions in the second hour.

When he'd tamed the last curl into place, he stepped back to get a better look. "You look fabulous," he declared. I had to agree. My hair looked ten times better than anything I could have done. I thanked him and before we left, I got my own set of perfectly matched air kisses. "You'll knock 'em dead tonight," he said with a wink. Debbie and I got back into the Audi and headed for Cairabrae.

It was almost four o'clock when we arrived. I raced up the stairs feeling pressed for time. Where had the day gone? I stripped out of my clothes and got into the lacy bra and matching thong that I'd picked for the night. The day had warmed up nicely, but the room had been closed all day and was chilly. I pulled on a robe and grabbed my phone before settling in at the vanity in the bathroom. I dialled James.

"Emelynn," he answered. "I missed you today."

"Debbie and I went into Bodega Bay after our run. I just got back. What have you been up to?"

"Reviewing security checks on wait staff, bus staff, cleaners and every other extra set of hands they've hired for this party. I promised Jordan I'd stick to you like glue tonight so you'll see me soon. I'm headed to the main house right now."

"Like glue—that sounds promising. I'm just getting dressed. I'll meet you downstairs." I hung up and stared at my face in the mirror. I'd need to kick-up my makeup routine to match the hair. I selected eyeshadow colours to match my dress and set to work. When I finished, a different woman sat before me. Someone who might just fit in tonight, I thought.

I slid the satiny midnight-blue sheath off its hanger and stepped into it. It was sleeveless and form fitting, with a zipper up the back and a slit from the hem to midway up the front of my right thigh. On the bodice, fabric draped between the tips of my shoulders plunging so low that I wouldn't be able to lean forward without providing a show. Maybe I'd do that for James when no one was looking, I mused, bending over to see the effect. He'll like that, I confirmed. I pushed my toes into the matching sandals and tested my balance. They weren't stilettos but they were plenty high enough for me. I hardly recognized the woman standing in front of the three-way mirror. "You clean up all right," I said to my reflection, then turned my fabulous self around and left the room. Nerves aside, I'd never felt more confident.

My heels clicked loudly on the marble floor. I was thankful for the slit in the dress. Without it, I'd be doing a Morticia Addams penguin-shuffle all night. When I got to the top of the stairs, I stopped in my tracks. A thick satin ribbon had been wrapped around the heavy handrail all the way across the atrium and down the curving staircase. The ribbon was the exact same colour as my dress. That couldn't be a coincidence, could it? I started down the stairs and caught glimpses of the same blue colour woven into two massive flower arrangements in the foyer. Stuart met me at the foot of the stairs and offered me his hand. He looked very suave in a black tuxedo with his shock of white hair.

"You look beautiful, Emelynn." He tucked my hand into the crook of his elbow.

"Thank you," I said, feeling a lot like Cinderella. "And you look very handsome, Stuart," I said, as he walked me across the foyer and down the stairs into the living room.

The massive room looked completely transformed. "Who did all this?" I marvelled. Stuart shrugged like it was nothing. The midnight blue of my dress had been added as an accent colour everywhere I looked. Sheer blue organza squares topped the white tablecloths on the temporary tables; blue cocktail napkins were fanned out on every available surface; and each crystal vase of flowers was tied with a blue bow. "It's blue," I said, dazed.

"Of course," Stuart said. "It's your party."

I'd been so distracted I hadn't noticed Mason join us. "You are stunning," he said, drawing my attention. He took my hand from Stuart.

"Thank you, Mason. You look pretty good yourself." Like his father, he wore a tuxedo, but with a more modern cut, narrower lapels, not as boxy. He also wore a black shirt instead of the traditional white and it looked great on him.

He kissed me on the cheek and released my hand. "You're missing something," he said, pulling Jeannette's necklace from his pocket. "I had this remade for you." He dangled it in front of me like a hypnotist. "A new beginning. Will you wear it tonight?"

I took it from his hands and let the chain fall between my fingers. Right away, I could see that the necklace was now attached to either end of the cylindrical case so it would sit horizontally rather than vertically. The case itself had been altered with a clasp midway and the whole thing opened up along the side instead of at one end. "There's no tracking device. I promise."

"A new beginning," I repeated, testing the words. "All right." The necklace was easy to put on; the chain detached from either end of the intricate crystal case so I didn't have to fumble behind my neck.

He and Stuart both smiled at me like I lit up their worlds. "Champagne?" Mason asked.

"Yes, please," I replied.

"There's one more thing," Stuart said. "I'll be right back. Pour a glass for me, son." Stuart left the room and headed toward the stairs.

One of Jolene's seascape paintings hung behind the piano and I walked over to get a closer look. I recognized her work, the way she captured the essence of the light in the waves. My father's painting was done in warm tones, but it was gone now. This one was done in cooler tones. Living on the ocean myself, I knew how the water could change from sky blue to slate grey with the pass of a cloud, and a storm could whip the water frothy brown or jade green in a heartbeat. Jolene obviously knew this too.

Footsteps alerted me to Mason's approach and I turned toward him. He held three champagne flutes. "First cork tonight," he grinned.

"Thank you," I said, accepting one.

Stuart came in right behind him and Mason passed him a glass. "To you, Emelynn," Stuart said, raising his glass.

"To Jolene," I added.

"To Mom," Mason said, and we clinked glasses. It was a tender family moment. Maybe we really could have a new beginning. We each took a sip then Stuart handed me a black box about four inches square.

"What's this?" I said, pulling my eyebrows together.

"It was Jolene's. We'd like you to have it." I didn't reach for the box.

"Don't look so suspicious," Mason chided. "It's not like either of us are ever going to wear it."

I set my glass down and reached for the box. Inside was a silver watch bracelet. The watch face was the same width as the links. It was square with a black face. Cartier. A line of diamonds adorned both sides of the watch face. They weren't insubstantial diamonds. It was beautiful.

I snapped the lid closed and handed it back. "Thank you, but it's too much."

Stuart hid his hand in his pocket. "We want you to have it," he insisted. "It was our gift to Jolene when she finished school. I'd much prefer you wear it than let it lay about here. At least wear it tonight. It'll look lovely with your dress."

"Go on. Try it on," Mason said. "It's inscribed."

They worked like a tag-team to wear me down. A suspicious corner of my mind wondered if they'd switched the tracking device to the watch. I opened the box again then took out the watch. I turned it over. The inscription read, *Time Flies ~ 1983*. I smiled at their inside joke, just as I imagined Jolene did when she first read it.

"Jeannette picked it out," Stuart said, and I finally acquiesced and slipped it on. "It's beautiful. Thank you." I leaned over and kissed his cheek then removed the lipstick smudge with my thumb.

"Stuart, Mason," James said, striding toward us. I hadn't heard him come into the room. He wasn't wearing a tux, but he didn't need to. He looked perfectly scrumptious in a black V-neck sweater and light wool slacks that hung suggestively, or was that just because I knew what was underneath? He was dressed in security detail clothes, not guest clothes. Would that ever change?

"Emelynn." He smiled, standing in front of me. "You look spectacular."

"Thank you." I took his hand and kissed him on the lips. Twice. Just so there'd be no mistake about the role he played in my life, regardless of his clothes. Then I reached down to reclaim my champagne flute.

"Gentlemen," James said, taking my hand. "Do you mind if I borrow her?"

"She's all yours until the guests arrive," Stuart said, his eyes twinkling. He left me with the impression he didn't have a problem with me and James.

James led me out the back doors and onto the patio. The air was still warm. I gulped the rest of the champagne. He relieved me of the empty glass then whisked me around the corner, out of sight. He put his hands on my butt and pulled me close. "I like the dress," he said. The warmth of his touch was immediately evident through the thin fabric and I purred in his arms.

"Did you see what they did in there? With the blue?"

"Yes, it's very impressive. I also saw the Oprah gift giveaway," he said, stepping back and reaching for my wrist. He whistled. "A Cartier. Thirty grand, maybe more."

"Are you serious?" I squeaked. "I could buy a car for that."

James looked me in the eye, suddenly grim. "What could *they* buy for that?" he asked.

I yanked my hand away. "James!" His insinuation stung.

"I'm sorry, Emelynn, but they're not beyond buying your loyalty." He fingered my necklace, as if making his point. "Don't let the baubles seduce you. You know how manipulative they can be. Make them earn your trust the old fashioned way—with honesty and follow through."

"You're a little jaded where they're concerned, James."

"For good reason."

"I know, but they also need room to prove themselves. I can't be suspicious of every little thing. But I will be careful. Their Oprah baubles can all be returned if the Reynoldses turn out to be the highly nefarious creatures you suspect." That, at least, got the frown off James's face.

"Just be careful."

"I said I would. Now stop being cranky and get me back to the party so I can show off this spectacular dress."

He took my hand and led me back around the corner and across the patio to the doors inside. I heard the piano before we entered the room and recognized Beethoven's *Moonlight Sonata*.

"I'll be close by," James said, kissing the back of my hand. "Have fun."

I watched him walk away then headed to the red piano. The thin-faced man had changed into a tux with a ruffled shirt. The tendons on the back of his hands moved like the inner workings of his instrument. His long fingers glided effortlessly across the keys. His eyes were closed and he seemed lost in the beautiful music.

Stuart sidled up to me. "Our first guests are arriving. They'll be here momentarily." He extended his elbow and I took it. He led me to the centre of the room and we stood waiting. "We'll greet the Tribunal members here. Mason will usher them off when the next party arrives. Are you ready?" he asked as voices erupted in the foyer. The sooner the better, I thought, as my nerves took up a game of ping pong in my stomach.

The first to arrive was Edward Kosikov. He brushed at the lapels of his tux and took the hand of a compact woman who marched along beside him. The woman's dress was lemon yellow with a heavy bodice and flowing chiffon skirt. "Edward, glad you could make it," Stuart said, clasping his hand. Edward had closely cropped brown hair and broad shoulders. He was about five foot ten with a ruddy, outdoor complexion. "You never met my daughter, Jolene, but I'm pleased to present her protégé, Emelynn Taylor." My face flushed at his words.

"Pleased to meet you, Emelynn. This is my wife, Carla." I shook both their hands and made appropriate small talk about their trip and the terrible fires south of Bodega Bay. Soon afterwards, Mason escorted them to the bar.

"That wasn't so bad, was it?" Stuart asked.

"*Protégé*?" I repeated. "*Really*?" I politely declined an offering from a waiter with a tray of appetizers.

Stuart smiled indulgently, like he was explaining something—yet again—to someone with short-term memory loss. "They need to be reminded of your connection." Before I could protest, he exchanged the indulgent smile for a benevolent one and introduced me to Ivy.

"I was so sorry to learn about your brother, Ivy," he said. "He'll be missed on the Tribunal." Ivy Adams had short grey hair and a brusque manner. Her brother had been forced to retire due to ill health and she had grudgingly replaced him. She was burly and her pale green dress put me in mind of Queen Elizabeth. Her shoes were the definition of sensible. "You remember my daughter, Jolene?"

"Of course, Stuart. We all remember Jolene."

Stuart inclined his head. "Ivy Adams, I'd like you to meet Jolene's protégé, Emelynn Taylor."

"Pleased to meet you, dear," she said, absent an ounce of genuine warmth. I smiled sweetly and concluded that Ivy was a cold fish. Maybe I would be too, in her boots. Stuart surmised that she was biding her time until her nephew was old enough to step up and take her place. Meantime, she was quite content to hand her vote over to Sebastian. Mason ushered her away to the strains of Tchaikovsky's *Swan Lake*.

Next to be introduced was Albert Vanderhoff. Albert walked in front of his timid wife and extended his hand to Stuart. He had a receding hairline and mousy, pinched features. He wore a gold cummerbund under his tux. A monocle wouldn't have looked out of place on Albert. I knew from my notes that Albert had recently replaced an older brother on the Tribunal. The Vanderhoff family were the elite of an elite covey. They didn't want any interference in Tribunal affairs by anyone not of their class. Albert and Sebastian probably belonged to the same polo club. Albert's wife, Eleanor, kept her well-coiffed head low and nodded a lot. Albert treated her like an afterthought. She wore a cream-coloured crepe dress with a princess collar. Albert offered me the tips of his fingers when Stuart introduced us, leaving me with the impression he wanted to keep our touch to the bare minimum.

I watched the Vanderhoffs walk away and noticed that the ambient chatter in the room had elevated such that the piano music was receding into the background. A scattering of guests I hadn't met milled about the room's perimeter. Waiters wandered among the guests, offering mouth-watering bites of pastries and decoratively cut cheese on home-made crackers. I didn't dare tempt my nervous stomach.

Lillian Spencer arrived next and was definitely the most elegant woman of her age at the gathering. Her chin-length grey hair was held back from her face with jewelled combs. She had sharp blue eyes and skin that only showed its age when she smiled. She had an ethereal quality that made me think of bone china so fine you could see through it. Lillian wasn't one of the five core members, but she was in no hurry to give up her vote at the table, not even for her grown children. She wore a black gown with a full skirt and deferred to her husband, Neville, who doted on her. It was all for looks, Stuart assured me. Lillian ran that show.

She looked me in the eye and offered a firm handshake. "Welcome to the covey, Emelynn." She then introduced her husband, Neville.

"She's sharp," Stuart said, when they'd cleared away. "She votes her own mind and avoids politics like the plague."

Rachael Warner and her husband, Marc, arrived on Lillian's heels. Rachael had big brown eyes and shoulder-length dark hair. She wore a turquoise-coloured dress with a lace bodice. Her husband's tux looked unique with a Mandarin-style collar. She was my height and her husband wasn't much taller. She was quick to offer me her hand and flash a smile.

Rachael came from the covey with the largest number of Ghosts. That may have been why she represented her entire covey and not just a select few. She'd been one of the core five for nearly five years and could ask to be replaced any time now. Stuart liked the way her covey managed itself and thought they'd be a good example to emulate.

Both she and Carrie had kinetic gifts; they didn't need to physically touch things to move them. I wondered if they had been close. A refreshing breeze swirled through the room from the open doors.

"How is Ron making out?" Stuart asked of the next man to approach. I pegged him for Gordon Evans, Ron Evans's brother.

"We're hopeful he's turned the corner," Gordon said. He wasn't as heavy as Ron but he was close; I'd put him at two hundred pounds on his less than six-foot frame. "You must be Emelynn," he said, taking my hand between his two big hams. "I've heard a lot about you." I cringed at the thought of Ron telling him I'd broken his nose. "You're a lot smaller than I imagined." He smiled and the corners of his eyes crinkled in a way that told me he smiled a lot.

The conversation in the room came to a halt with the loud rumble of a helicopter overhead. I looked to Stuart who rolled his eyes and leaned into my ear. "Sebastian likes to make an entrance."

It was a full five minutes before the rumble moved away and we could hear ourselves talk again. Then, sure enough, Sebastian waltzed into the room like he owned it. Trailing behind him was his wife, Kimberley, and daughter, Tiffany. It was difficult for me to keep an open mind about this trio after all I'd heard.

Sebastian's tux had shiny lapels and he wore a bow tie. He pushed his wife ahead of him, bypassing Stuart, and stood her in front of me with great flourish. "Kimberley, honey, this is Jolene's protégé, Emelynn Taylor."

"Emelynn," Kimberley said in a gooey-sweet voice. "It's so nice to meet you." An excessively large aquamarine pendant hung around her neck. It came off gaudy, mismatched against her pale blue dress. Her lipstick was sticky and bright pink. "Jolene and I were very close," she gushed. "She was like a sister to me." I knew that wasn't true, but no one was going to call her on it. Not here. I could see her building up to a hug so I thrust out my hand to pre-empt it.

"It's nice to meet you, Kimberley," I said, and then stepped back and changed the subject. "Is this your daughter?" I asked, looking to Tiffany.

"Yes," she said, nodding for Tiffany to approach. "This is my daughter, Tiffany Kirk."

"Hello Tiffany," I said, once again extending my hand. "Pleased to meet you." Like her mother, Tiffany was a bleached blonde. I knew from Stuart that Tiffany was my age, but she looked thirty. She also looked like a hooker with her substantial cleavage pushed up and on display in a red satin gown. She glommed onto Mason when he appeared, and he graciously ushered the family to the bar.

Stuart put his arm around my shoulder and kissed my cheek. "You did very well." I sighed with relief and checked my watch. It was after seven. The sun had set and I'd hardly noticed. "That's it for the formal introductions," Stuart said, and waved a passing waiter down. "You should eat something," he encouraged. I set a stuffed mushroom cap and a prosciutto-wrapped asparagus tip on a napkin, and scanned the room. It had filled up around the edges while I'd been decorating the centre. My relief fizzled. There were dozens of people I hadn't yet met.

Mason joined us with a welcome glass of wine. I took a rather unladylike gulp and Mason raised an eyebrow. "I thought I was done," I said. "But I haven't met half the people here."

"Don't be nervous. I'll introduce you around the room," he offered.

"I've got a better idea," Stuart said, walking briskly away from us.

"What's that all about?" I asked anxiously.

"No idea," Mason said. "Eat up and I'll take you around."

I popped the stuffed mushroom cap in my mouth and bit down. It was unexpectedly bitter. Maybe fancy pants canapés were an acquired taste. I washed the bitter taste away with another gulp of wine then cautiously nibbled the ham-wrapped asparagus tip. Even that tasted bitter to me. I discreetly abandoned the rest of it.

"Maria is magic in the kitchen, isn't she?" Mason raved. I nodded, unable to criticize the woman. She'd obviously done a huge amount of work, even if I wasn't enjoying tonight's culinary choices.

"Ready?" Mason asked. I took one more sip of wine then set my glass down and took his arm.

At that moment, the music stopped and I heard the insistent tinkling of metal on glass. I turned to find Stuart standing beside the piano, tapping a spoon against the side of a wine glass. I froze. He wouldn't, would he?

"If I may have your attention," he said. Heat rushed to my face, painting it in my embarrassment. "Your attention," he repeated as the room quietened.

"I know most of you have travelled a fair distance to join us this evening," Stuart said, making eye contact with our guests. Mason and I were at the other end of the room and he slipped a hand over the one I had on his arm and patted it reassuringly. "Thank you all for being here tonight as we welcome my beloved daughter's protégé into the fold. Emelynn, dear, will you please join me?"

I dug my fingers into Mason's arm and he smiled through clenched teeth. He jerked forward and began walking me toward Stuart. I felt like a sacrifice being delivered to the fire. This is exactly the type of thing I'd asked Stuart *not* to do. Sweat beaded on my back and between my breasts. I felt hot and clammy, and clung to Mason, suddenly unable to walk in heels.

Stuart deflected the daggers I shot him every few steps, and awaited me with outstretched arms, a tilted head and a benign smile. I was mortified and wholly unable to prevent Stuart from embarrassing me further. He reached for my cold hand when I got close enough and held me out at arm's length for a theatrical moment before pulling me close to his side. The room was deathly quiet. He placed his arm around my shoulder, so I was forced to look out at the sea of faces. I wanted to die.

Stuart's voice boomed clear and strong. "As some of you already know, Emelynn came to us rather unexpectedly." He gave me one of his benevolent smiles. I wanted to stomp on his foot. "But we're very glad that we found her." I smiled thinly in what I imagined was the expected response. He looked back at the assembled crowd. "Jolene may be gone from this Earth, but she left a precious piece of herself behind in this lovely woman. For those of you who haven't yet met her, this is Emelynn Taylor. Jolene's gift burns brightly in Emelynn, reminding us of our daughter every single day." Maybe I would throw up on his shoes.

A group of waiters, trays laden with tall sparkling champagne flutes, worked their way through the crowd. "We welcomed Emelynn Taylor to our family and now we welcome her to our covey. Tonight is a celebration. A celebration of this young woman and her very bright future. To Emelynn," he shouted, holding his glass high in the air. The crowd chanted, "To Emelynn," but the floor didn't open up and swallow me like I begged. I nodded appreciatively and poked Stuart hard in the back.

He actually had the nerve to laugh. "Again, thank you all for coming. Please enjoy the food and refreshments." He turned to face me and leaned down close to my ear. "There, all done," he said, and kissed my cheek. "I'm right about getting out of your comfort zone. It builds character."

"I'm going to be sick," I whispered. Stuart tsked dismissively, as if he thought I'd said it in spite, but I was trembling and in a full-on cold sweat. I pulled away from him and rushed across the room, feeling my stomach rise. James was at my side in a flash as I inelegantly lurched up the steps out of the living room, heading to the left toward the closest bathroom. "I'm going to be sick," I repeated as James rushed me down the hall. The bathroom door was locked. It was occupied. The other one was across the foyer full of guests and down the other wing. James continued walking me in the direction we were going, bursting into the kitchen, through the service door at the end and finally outside. I immediately leaned over the rail and threw up on a barrel cactus beside the walkway. I heaved until there was nothing left to come up.

I straightened up and when my balance returned, I bent to right the can of cigarette butts I'd kicked over in my rush.

"Don't," James said too late, as I caught a whiff of the can and heaved again.

When I'd finished that time, I stepped away and took the tissue that James offered to wipe my mouth. "That was mortifying," I said.

"What happened?"

"I don't know. Alcohol on an empty stomach? Nerves? Stuart? Take your pick." I smoothed my dress with still-shaking hands. "I wish he hadn't done that. I've never been so embarrassed."

"Emelynn, what happened?" Mason said, bathing us in a flood of light from the opened kitchen door.

"She'll be fine. Upset stomach, that's all," James offered.

"Do you feel well enough to return to the party?" Mason asked.

"Sure, I just need to clean up. Give me ten minutes."

"I'll send for Debbie," Mason said, and disappeared inside.

James fussed with my hair to put it right. "Wipe under your eyes," he said. The tissue came away black with mascara. "How about I walk you back to your room so you can fix your makeup?"

I took his arm and we headed back into the house. The kitchen staff was too busy to notice us. James gallantly shielded me from the concerned gaze of an elderly couple I hadn't met and ushered me quickly up the stairs. Debbie hurried to join us.

James stopped outside my door. "Do you want me to wait for you?"

"That won't be necessary, but thanks. Debbie's here. I'll clean up and come right down."

"Okay. I want to go out front and check in with Ryan anyway." He turned to Debbie. "I'll be back in ten minutes. See you downstairs."

Debbie closed the door and followed me into the sitting room. I explained what had happened. "Do you want help in there?" she asked.

"No thanks. I'm going to brush my teeth, fix my face and pray to the party gods to put an end to this night." I kicked off my shoes in the bedroom and walked into the bathroom. Now who looks like a hooker, I thought, staring at my reflection. My mascara had run and the eyeshadow lay in big creases in my eyelids. Crap! I'd have to re-do the whole thing.

Resigned to the chore, I tugged a makeup removal pad out of its plastic case and swiped at my eyes. They looked a lot worse before they looked better. I scrubbed my face clean with a washcloth and looked again. There, that was better. I slathered on moisturizer then set about brushing my teeth. After I gargled, I felt almost human and dreaded re-applying the makeup. I'd give up my first born to just crawl into bed and go to sleep.

But a thunderous crash below blasted all thoughts of sleep out of my mind.

CHAPTER TWENTY-ONE

I darted to the sitting room. "What was that?"

Debbie stood by the door. "Sounded like glass," she said, squinting as if that would improve her hearing. Then her face relaxed. "I'll bet someone's knocked over one of those big flower vases in the foyer. Stay here, I'll go check." She turned and left, closing the door behind her.

Reluctantly, I returned to the bathroom and re-lined my eyes with a thin black pencil. I retrieved the little pots of eyeshadow and opened them. A faint popping noise made me stop what I was doing to listen. A loud shout followed. I jumped up and rushed to the door. Bursts of popping thuds preceded panicked screams and breaking glass.

I yanked open the bedroom door and ran down the hall, skidding to a stop as a big man in camo gear and a balaclava breached the top of the staircase. I flattened myself against the wall to avoid being seen. He swung a big long-barrelled gun around like he knew how to use it. Chaos reigned below. With my back pressed to the wall, I slithered back the way I'd come. The big man slowly turned his head in my direction. With a sharp breath, I turned and tore toward my room, my bare feet inaudible against the screams coming from downstairs. I slammed the door shut and fumbled with the lock then ran for the balcony, closing its door behind me.

I danced around as if the balcony floor were on fire. The man with the gun must have seen me. What should I do? What the hell was happening? I felt useless. One thing was certain: hopping around on the balcony wasn't helping anyone. I squeezed my crystal . . . and ghosted.

My heart pounded in my ears. I drifted off the balcony, down to the back patio and along the folding glass doors of the living room. They were closed tight. A man stood in silhouette with his back to the door on the left. He was dressed in camo and a balaclava, and armed with a rifle just like the man at the top of the stairs. He held the party guests at gunpoint. Beyond the intruder, a mound of yellow chiffon lay in a heap. I searched my mind. Who wore yellow? Carla, I thought. It was Carla, Edward's wife. The man kneeling beside her with his hands clasped behind his head must be Edward. Why didn't he ghost?

I floated down the line of windows and saw the same scene repeated. Fliers and Ghosts alike were immobilized, impotent, their hands behind their heads. What the hell was wrong with them? Jolt them, damn it, or at least ghost, for crying out loud! Why were they just sitting there? I caught a glimpse of two other bodies on the ground, but whether they were dead or injured, I couldn't tell. I drifted farther along the row of windows and sucked in a shocked breath. Blood was sprayed across the end window like someone had thrown a paint-filled balloon against it. Inside, the pianist lay flat on his back, knees and legs curled over the broken piano bench. His arms rested akimbo over his head, his long pale fingers tangled in a potted palm that had tipped over. A deep crimson stained his white, ruffled tux shirt.

I looked frantically for James and Debbie. Where was Stuart? I scanned the room but didn't see them or Mason. James had said he was going outside—maybe he was still out here. Please still be out here, I prayed. I whisked on, passing Stuart's office windows, and rounded the end of the house. A breeze caught me and blew me backwards, momentarily scattering me. I couldn't afford to fight the wind tonight. The people in there needed help. I re-formed and shook off the last of my ghost then called on my crystal again, this time to fly. Breaking free from gravity felt like doing something. I surveyed the house from a height.

Relief washed over me at the sight of James. I spotted him crouched down behind the fountain with Ryan. A number of vehicles were parked around the perimeter and other people had sought cover behind them. I ghosted again then dove down to re-form beside James.

"Oh, thank god," he said, pulling me close. "You got out."

"I heard the gunfire. I ran, but there was a man at the top of the stairs," I blabbered as James smoothed the hair from my face. "What's happening? Who are they?"

"We're not sure yet, but we're thinking Redeemers," James said.

"It's too big for organized crime," Ryan added. "And covert government forces wouldn't take this kind of risk. Too messy."

"Have you seen Mason or Stuart?" I asked.

"I'm sorry, Em," James said. "They're inside."

"We have to do something. They're shooting people in there." I felt the unwelcome, but familiar pull of panic.

"We've tried. We can't get in," James said.

"The doors have been tampered with," Ryan explained. "They closed and locked automatically before the first shot was fired. The security codes have been over-ridden."

"Tampered with . . . but how?" I asked. How was it possible that this could have happened right under our noses? "Manny," I whispered, as a flash of his maintenance cart and his nervous smile popped into my mind.

"Manny Sanchez?" Ryan puzzled. "Couldn't be. He was cleared in the '90s. He's been here for years, like a damn fixture."

James glared at him. "Jesus, Ryan. A lot changes in a person's life in a decade or two."

"We can still get in," I said, offering some hope. "We could break the glass in one of the bedrooms or the library—get in that way."

"Won't work. The whole ground floor is fitted with bulletproof glass," Ryan said. "We'd have to go in on the second floor and the only access from there to the ground floor is the grand staircase. They'd pick us off at their leisure, if we tried that."

"I can get in. I'll ghost. I'll open a door from the inside."

"It's too dangerous," James said. "There's no telling what they've done with the locks. There's no guarantee the doors will open and they've posted men at all the obvious entry points."

"Well, we can't just sit—," a blaze of automatic gunfire cut off my words.

"Why aren't they fighting back?" I shouted, waving my hands at the building. "They're sitting on the fucking floor in there like stumps. What's wrong with them!"

"Emelynn," James said, yanking my arm. "Help is coming. We had a dozen men stationed around the perimeter. Half of them will be clearing their way in to us now. They're conducting a systematic grid sweep of the area. They'll be here in minutes and when they get here we'll know that all the intruders are in there," he nodded to the house. "Until then, we sit tight."

I steadied my breath. Off to my right, I caught a glimpse of a uniformed limo driver huddled behind his car. Beyond him, a woman I recognized from the kitchen crouched behind the questionable protection of a potted palm. They'd probably been outside on a smoke break. James rested a reassuring hand on my shoulder.

Within minutes, heavy footfalls could be heard as black-clad Fliers arrived at a run, spreading out around the house. They quickly dropped out of sight, laying on their stomachs and training their long guns on the house. Ryan and James finally felt confident enough to stand up. James helped me to my feet and then shook the hand of the Flier who approached. A large black delivery van pulled up on the far side of the fountain, away from the house. More security personnel got out and I watched as some spread out to reinforce the perimeter and others coaxed the people who were hiding, out from cover.

"What's the van for?" I asked.

"We'll clear these people and get them to safety," Ryan explained.

I watched his security detail gather together the people who'd escaped the house. They lined them up on the far side of the van. I spotted the young valet among the group and picked out a number of chauffeur caps, two waiter uniforms and a few white aprons worn by the kitchen staff. I'd bet they'd never quit smoking after tonight.

"Let's move away from the house, out of the line of fire," Ryan said. "It'll be safer near the van."

"Come on," James coaxed. We moved to stand in front of the delivery van. "Stay here. I need to hear what they've learned. I'll be right back. If anything happens, ghost. Stay safe." He kissed me on the forehead and jogged away.

Behind me, I overheard Ryan's men questioning the people who had escaped. Their names, birthdates and addresses were noted. They were quizzed about their jobs and who they reported to, and their responses were checked against a spreadsheet. No one was getting into that van unless they checked out. I breathed a little easier knowing how thorough they were being.

I leaned against the grill of the van and looked down at my filthy bare feet. My dress wasn't made for this, I thought, seeing the wrinkles from crouching and the stains from kneeling by the fountain. A man was being questioned behind me. He cleared his throat excessively, which is probably why I noticed. There was a quality to his voice that caught my attention. I straightened and cocked my head so I could hear him better. Something about his voice made goosebumps race across my skin. I closed my eyes to focus on the bass tone of his voice.

He replied, "I'm a car jockey. I've been out here all night." But what I heard was, *I have a gun, Emelynn. It's aimed at your head.*

Another question came. He replied, "My boss lined this up six weeks ago." What I heard was, *We call the boss every six hours.* I also recalled the rest of that conversation. *If he doesn't hear from one of us, he won't show. He'll leave you here to starve. You hear me? You need me.*

It felt like a switch had been thrown in my head. I was back inside that filthy trailer, blindfolded and chained to a bed. I swivelled my head. At long last, I saw the face of the man who'd held me captive and gotten away. This was the man who collared me like a dog and hosed me down like an animal; the man who left me at the mercy of a rapist and then left me to die at Carson's hands; the man who was going to pay a very dear price for those transgressions.

I fixed him in my gaze and pushed away from the vehicle. With measured steps, I made my way over to where Ryan's man stood with his clipboard questioning him. The guard didn't allow himself to be distracted by my presence, but my former jailer did. Did he recognize me, I wondered, in my pretty blue gown with my hair done up in curls?

"Excuse me," I said, interrupting. "What did you say your name was?" I asked. I stood beside the guard, three feet from the man who had held me prisoner, and studied his face. Male-pattern baldness aside, he looked pleasant enough. He was in his late thirties and trim. He had short brown hair, a solid jaw and smooth skin. He even had a dimple in his right cheek. He probably had a wife.

The man looked furtively from the guard to me and back again.

"Ma'am," the guard said. "Please, step back."

I smiled at him. "I'd like to know his name."

"As soon as we get these folks to safety, ma'am, I'll come find you. Give you his name."

I chuckled, "No, I don't think so." I felt strangely calm and the sounds around me faded.

"Ma'am," he repeated and the tone of his voice was a warning.

My former jailer stepped back from the guard—from me—bumping into the man in line behind him. "Keep her the fuck away from me," he shouted, pointing at me. I knew a wicked smile had spread across my face and I took great satisfaction in the terror it instilled in him. He stepped behind the man he'd bumped into, using him as a shield. "She's one of them!" he yelled. The line of people waiting to get in the van panicked at his accusation and scattered. I heard the guard call for assistance, but held my gaze steady on my former captor who tried to escape in the chaos he'd created.

He ducked low and scurried behind a row of parked cars. I walked unhurriedly in his erratic wake, watching his futile attempts to escape alongside a small group of fleeing workers who were beating a path away from the house. One by one, they dropped away from him as they saw me coming. I gave him enough room to hope he might get away. But he wasn't getting away. I wouldn't kill him. Not yet. No, he would suffer. I drew on my crystal, forming a jolt meant to hurt, not kill, and blasted it at his spine. He had gained about twenty yards on me, but, sadly for him, it wasn't enough. Not nearly enough. I watched him sprawl forward, landing heavily on his face.

Somewhere in my mind, I thought, ouch . . . that had to hurt, but I didn't let the sentiment interfere with the second jolt that I carefully prepared. Not as much juice this time, I thought as I steadied my pace. I'd hate to overdo it and end his suffering prematurely. Maybe a shot to his knees. Knees would be painful. I took my time closing the distance, savouring the inevitable. At ten yards, I heard him groan.

I'd have to flip him over, I thought, and then James dropped from the sky, distracting me. He frowned as if I were a puzzle he was trying to figure out. Ryan landed to my right and held his hands out, telling me he wasn't armed. I creased my brow at the gesture.

"Who is he, Emelynn?" James asked.

I looked in his direction. "No one. I'll deal with him." I wished James hadn't interfered.

"He might hold a key, Emelynn. He might be able to help us figure out what's going on in there."

"Help? No, he won't help," I said. "Leave us alone." I had to deal with the man myself and I didn't want James to watch.

Undeterred, James persisted, "How do you know him?"

"He's not a Redeemer," I said. "He's not even a Flier."

"How do you know that, Emelynn?" James's voice was soft, like a caress, and I swallowed a jagged breath.

"I recognized his voice. I'll never forget that voice." It taunted me, *No one will hear you . . . you're not getting out of those cuffs . . . you're not going to get out of here alive.* My confidence wavered. I looked at James's face and a shiver ran through me.

"Was he involved in your kidnapping?" he asked, but I couldn't answer him. Memories of the trailer flooded back, clouding my vision: the amber belt burning my skin; the smell of mould in the mattress; the promise of death hanging over my head like an anvil on a thread.

"Emelynn," James said. He'd stepped close enough that I felt his breath on my face. He put his hands on my shoulders. "Was that man in the trailer with you?"

How had I become this person? Someone who took pleasure in hurting another human being? I wanted that man on the ground to be nothing more than ashes in my hands. Carson Manse had done this to me. I'd let him turn me into a monster. "I'm not really like this," I whispered.

"I know," James said, putting his arms around me. It felt so warm, so safe, as if the horror would all just go away if I closed my eyes—so I did. James held me tight. When I stopped trembling, he spoke in my ear. "I need to touch him. Read his memories. Find out what he knows. Then I'll take care of him. He won't hurt you again."

He pulled away and studied my face. "Go with Ryan." He looked at Ryan and nodded.

In a flash, Ryan was at my side and draped his arm around me. He didn't say a word as he pulled me away from James, away from the man lying on the ground whose voice I'd never forget.

We stopped in the formal garden, well short of the van and away from the fountain. He brushed a gloved hand over the surface of a small stone bench and sat me down. He crouched beside me and settled in to wait. I should probably apologize, I thought, but words escaped me. I didn't want to dwell on what James was doing, so I looked at the people who had re-formed a line to get into the safety of the van. "Those people aren't Fliers. What are you going to do with them?"

He raised his head in question. "What do you mean?"

"They've been exposed. They saw your men arrive. They saw you and James out there."

"Most of them were on the ground with their eyes on the house when we landed behind them. They were panicked and scared. Not many will have seen us and whatever those few thought they saw can be explained away as a figment of their overwhelming fear."

I nodded, feeling a sense of relief.

"The windows in the van are blacked out. They won't see anything from inside."

"All your men, they're Fliers?" I asked.

"Yeah, it's SOP for these big gatherings. Each covey sends one of their best to supplement the host force." He hung his head. "It used to be enough."

"Ryan, Emelynn," James said, warning us of his approach. He was winded and crouched down beside us. "The food was contaminated. Ground amber. It was in everything: the food, the drinks, even the hand lotions and sanitizers in the powder rooms. They covered all their bases."

"No wonder they were just sitting around," I said, realization dawning. "They couldn't ghost. The amber prevented it."

"Yeah, and ingesting it is a lot quicker than just touching it. It'll be in their blood stream now, poisoning them from the inside," James said.

"It will weaken their gift. They won't be able to fly or even jolt." The horror was just beginning. They were defenceless. "It'll be a blood-bath in there."

Three loud shots rang out and I looked up to the roof in time to see a body fall from the rooftop. "One for the good guys," Ryan said with a look of satisfaction.

I turned back to James. "That's why I threw up. It wasn't nerves—it was the wine, the canapés." Avery had warned me I'd be more sensitive to amber after my extended exposure to it in the trailer. I'd expelled the amber. It hadn't compromised me. I'd ghosted, flown and even jolted since I'd vomited. My gift was undiminished. I could still help.

"What about the Fliers who aren't Ghosts? How will the amber affect them?" I asked.

"It'll slow them down," James said. "They'll feel sluggish. It'll dampen their jolts until the amber is out of their system."

We turned our heads to the roar of approaching vehicles. A dull-brown sedan slid sideways in a hail of gravel, stopping inches short of the van. Its front end was smashed. Two police cruisers followed, their overhead lights showering us with beams of red and white light. They too skidded to a stop about ten yards away, between us and the fountain.

"Shit! This night just keeps getting better," James cursed.

The police scrambled from their vehicles and took cover behind them. I watched Sam get out of his car and scan the scene, stopping when he saw James. He darted straight for us, crouching low. He took in Ryan and then me without expression.

"Moss. What the hell is going on here?" His face was a brilliant shade of scarlet.

Ryan began to answer but the detective shut him down. "I wasn't asking you." Sam swung around to James. "Get me up to speed. Fast."

James said, "A group of armed men rushed the house simultaneously from two access points: the main door and the service door on the north end."

"How many?"

Ryan answered. "We're not certain. Ten, maybe twelve. Heavily armed."

"Who they are?"

"That's unclear," Ryan said, answering again.

The detective glared at him. "You know exactly who's responsible. This is Carson Manse's doing."

Ryan shook his head. "We haven't seen him, but he's motivated. It's probably him. They're holding everyone inside hostage."

Temporarily satisfied, he glared at James. "Something wrong with your phone, Moss? If my men hadn't heard shots, we'd still be picking our teeth out on the road."

"We were outside when it happened. Just got back," James said, lying like a natural. I'd have to remember that.

Jordan looked to me. "Where are your shoes?"

"I had to run. I ditched them."

He turned back to Ryan. "How many hostages?"

"Seventy at least."

"Damn it! I knew this would happen." The detective dropped his head into his hand. "We need a hostage negotiator, sharpshooters and a battalion of officers." He pushed two buttons on his phone and turned away.

The scenario Mason had feared was unfolding before my eyes. Our world was unravelling—in the worst possible way. Ryan, James and the detective talked numbers and strategies. The only thing they couldn't discuss was the extra weapons the Fliers had at their disposal that the police didn't know about. Every Flier, inside or out, who hadn't eaten amber, could jolt. My jolt was lethal and I'm sure I wasn't the only one in this crowd who could say that. If there was any hope of keeping our secret intact, we had to make our move before the detective's reinforcements arrived to witness us in action. The rhythmic thump of an approaching helicopter stirred me into action.

"James," I said, hoping it wasn't already too late. "I can help. You know that. It's worth a try before this gets out of hand."

"No," Sam said, intervening. "You're under my protection and if that psychopath, Manse, is in there, then I'm getting you as far away from here, as fast as I can. Right, James?"

James hesitated. I could see him struggling between supporting my idea and wanting to protect me. The helicopter's search light bounced along the ground heralding its approach.

I let him off the hook. "It's not your decision," I said to James, raising my voice over the noise. I then turned to Sam. "It's not yours, either."

"But he's right, Emelynn," James said, moving in close. "Manse has out-maneuvered us and he holds all the cards: all seventy of them. He has the house locked up tight and until we can figure out a way in, anything we do will only get more people killed. Getting you away from here, out of his reach, takes one more card out of play. It's for the best."

The percussive thump of the helicopter became impossible to ignore. "That's your ride," Sam said, beckoning me to join him. The helicopter landed neatly on Mason's pad several hundred yards from the house, and I knew everyone in the house would be deafened by the noise.

"Please, Emelynn. Go with Jordan. There's nothing you can do here now."

I looked past him to the stone facade of Cairabrae. The elegant uplighting of the pillars and the welcoming glow of light from the porte cochère were fouled by the up-turned valet lectern and abandoned limousines. The darkened van, the flashing police lights and the thumping of the helicopter were all a prelude of what was to come. Tonight would change our lives forever, and James was right—it was out of my hands. "Be careful," I said, giving in. I held his face in my hands and kissed him.

"Cover us," the detective shouted to Ryan. "Let's go," Sam said, pulling me away. He took my hand and started at a jog across the property toward the helicopter. Covering shots rang out behind us. We broke into a run and charged for the helicopter. The noise was compounded by a stiff wash from the blades, the impact of which was disorienting and frightening.

We bent low when we got close and approached the far side of the chopper. Sam opened the door and helped me in. I scrambled to the far side to make room, but instead of joining me, he slammed the door and stepped back, giving the pilot a thumbs up sign. I scooted back across the seat and pounded on the window to get his attention. The helicopter inched up. Wasn't he coming with me? He shook his head then spun around unnaturally as if someone had pulled his start-cord . . . and then he went down.

The helicopter dropped and settled, and the pilot opened his door and sprang out. Sam rolled onto his back, clutching his arm. I couldn't hear the shots, but I saw flashes coming from the guns on the ground—our guys. I pulled the lever on the inside of my door and jumped down to help. The pilot and I got Sam up and shoved him toward the door I'd left ajar. He dragged himself into the helicopter with his uninjured arm. I jumped in behind him and closed the door as the pilot prepared to lift off again. Sam's face twisted in pain. I grabbed his hand and held on tight.

The noisy beast lifted then lurched forward, rising in a slow and erratic circle. I didn't know enough about helicopters to know whether something was wrong, but I thought we should have been arching away from the house, not veering toward it. We were headed straight at a gunman who stood on the balcony outside Stuart's quarters. We were close enough that I could see Jeannette's wheelchair flipped on its side. Her small lifeless body lay on the floor, tangled in the lap blanket. The body of her nurse was sprawled on the deck close by. The helicopter took a violent swing up and away from the house, tossing me back and onto Jordan's injured arm. He groaned and we swerved out over the field. I watched in horror as the pilot's head wobbled then fell forward. His hands dropped from the controls and the helicopter fell into a fierce spin.

CHAPTER TWENTY-TWO

I don't remember ghosting. The reflex had been automatic, like a sneeze. My body went on autopilot and slammed into self-preservation mode and I'd taken Sam with me. I felt his hand firmly in my grip and thanked the heavens I hadn't let go. He didn't struggle; he probably thought he was dead. I floated a hundred feet off the ground and watched the chopper continue its doomed flight path: nose first into the manicured lawn. The blades thumped into the ground and splintered, sending shrapnel in a wide arc. I fully expected a ball of fire to erupt, but it didn't. The fuselage just groaned and rolled on its side, like an elephant collapsing.

I scanned the grounds for a safe harbour—somewhere we could hide and Sam could get medical attention. "Don't let go," I whispered, knowing he could hear me even if he was in shock. He wasn't a Flier so if he struggled out of my grip now, he'd drop like a stone.

The big training barn was closest and it was bound to have a first aid kit. I moved toward it gently pulling Sam along with me. James said that Ryan's men had cleared the perimeter of the property. Hopefully, that included the barn. When I got close, I lowered myself and floated around the exterior of the structure looking for trouble. The vehicle bay was open, but the interior door was closed. I ducked inside, careful to keep us up off the floor, and then rushed the door, staying high and pulling the detective along behind me. I gripped his hand and drifted the entire length of the inside of the building. It was empty. I breathed a sigh of relief and dragged Sam to the small room with the cot.

When we got there, I pushed his shoulders down so he was sitting on the narrow bed. I tried to let go of his hand, but he wouldn't release his grip. "You can let go now," I said. He held tight. "Sam," I said more firmly. "Let go." He finally heard me and slowly peeled his fingers from my hand. I pulled back on my ghost and flipped on the light for him.

I'd ghosted with someone twice before, and it was a fascinating experience both times. The re-forming always started from the point of contact, so Sam's hand was the first thing to reappear. He held it up in front of where his face would be in a few moments. I settled on the floor opposite him with my back against the wall and pulled my knees to my chest, folding my gown around my legs.

I had no idea where this was going. He was injured and probably in shock. If I was lucky, maybe he wouldn't remember how he got here. I willed myself to re-form and waited for his body to come back to him. When his head came into view, he was white as a sheet and staring right at me. He didn't say a word.

"How's your arm?" I asked.

He didn't react. He just sat there wide-eyed. I moved my head to the right—his eyes tracked me. "Sam, are you all right?"

"No. I am not all right," he said. Then silence fell around us again.

"I'll go find a first aid kit," I said, then stood and scooted out of the room. I found a kit under the shiny stainless-steel sinks in one of the treatment areas.

I cautiously approached the room where I'd left Sam. How would I explain myself? Worse still, how would he react? He hadn't moved. I opened the kit and pulled out scissors, disinfectant, packets of gauze, and tape.

"We need to get you out of this jacket," I said, moving to stand in front of him. The left sleeve was stained red and torn. He'd have to break in a new one after this, I thought. He let me tug the jacket off his shoulders and he pulled his right arm out. I slid the jacket off his left arm and he winced.

He wore a dress shirt underneath with his gun holster strapped over it. "I'll have to cut the sleeve off." He didn't resist as I snipped away at the garment. Blood pooled and dripped from a crimson hole in his bicep. I ripped open a package of gauze and held it to the wound. "Hold this," I said. He placed his right hand over the gauze and I moved to get a better look at the back of his arm. An exit hole told me the bullet had gone right through. A trickle of blood ran down the back of his arm. I ripped open a few more packs of gauze and drenched them in disinfectant. I secured a wad of gauze against each hole with tape and then wrapped strips of gauze around his upper arm to cover both wounds. His arm was the size of my thigh and, I swear, heavier. I rolled the gauze around and around, and then tied it off. But despite my efforts, it quickly soaked through with blood.

"We need to apply more pressure," he said, and his voice startled me. He'd been nearly mute since we'd arrived.

I rummaged through the first aid kit and found a suitable length of muslin. He held his arm out with a wince and I wrapped the muslin around the wound and prepared the first half of a knot. "You ready?" I asked. He nodded and I reefed on it then quickly tied the second half of the knot. He didn't flinch. I would have been screaming. "Is that okay?"

He nodded, exhaling raggedly. Beads of sweat had formed on his brow.

I collected the bloodied bandages and dropped them in the bucket beside the bed, then busied myself repacking the kit.

"Are you going to explain any of that to me?" he asked.

I finished with the kit and moved it to the floor then sat beside him. Oh god, where would I start? Perhaps I could keep everyone else out of it. It was worth a shot. "I'm not like other people. I'm not *normal*."

"That much, I already figured out."

"The way I am—it's why Carson Manse is after me. He thinks I can make him like me. But I can't."

"This thing that you do—what is it?"

I sat on my hands to keep from fidgeting. "I ghost." The words echoed in my head. I'd never before uttered the admission aloud. To anyone.

"You're a Ghost?"

"Yes . . . well no. Not the way you mean. I'm not dead or anything. I'm still me—still flesh and blood and all. It's just that I can . . ." I searched for a word he would understand, ". . . vaporize."

"Vaporize?"

"It's called ghosting." It was just the tip of the weirdness iceberg, but he didn't need to know the rest. Not now. Hopefully, not ever.

I could feel Sam's gaze on me. "I've got to go, Sam."

He reached out to block me, forcing me to meet his eyes. "That necklace . . ."

Immediately I lifted my hand to my throat and covered the engraved case.

"It holds a crystal, doesn't it? Carson Manse's crystal."

"No. It's not his, Sam. It never was." I shifted forward and Sam removed his arm. "I've got to go. I can help them."

"They don't need your help. Stay here. My shooting arm is sound and I'm an excellent shot. I'll protect you."

No one, especially a police officer, wants to hear what I had to tell him, but he had to wake up to the reality. "Sam, you can't protect me. Not from these people. You don't know how much I wish you could."

He absorbed my words better than I thought he would. "Can you use a firearm?"

"Poorly, but yes."

"I've got a gun strapped to my left ankle. Take it."

I smiled in surprise and leaned over to kiss his cheek. "Thank you," I said, and slid off the bed to retrieve the gun. The metal was warm from his skin and felt good in my hand.

"It's a Pocket Glock. It's got 11 nine-millimetre rounds in it."

The gun was half the weight of the Berretta I'd been using and much more comfortable to hold. I slid the top back to check the chamber, popped the magazine and checked the load then slammed it back in. Debbie would be proud of me, I thought, and then chilled. If she were still alive. I pointed the gun at the floor and sighted down the barrel.

"I'll send help," I said. Voices in the building distracted me and I strained to hear.

Sam pulled his handgun from under his arm and shuffled to his feet. "Be careful," he said. I smiled then slipped out the door. He flicked off the light. He was clever that Sam.

I'd spent hours in the barn, so the space was familiar. The voices were coming from the vehicle bay at the end of the building. I couldn't tell if they were friend or foe or even whether they were Fliers, so I called on my crystal, broke free of gravity and floated up to the rafters. I drifted quietly along the hall in the direction of the voices. There were two of them. They didn't seem aware of me. It was pitch-black and they weren't using flashlights. That wasn't a good sign. On the other hand, they weren't keeping quiet so they weren't expecting company either.

They had left the big door open and sauntered in like it was a night-club. They both wore camo gear. I kept deathly still and aimed the gun at the head of the bigger man. When they were impossibly close, I fired. With nothing to hold on to, the recoil sent me sailing into the ceiling.

The percussion hurt my eardrums, but I'd hit the man and he dropped to the floor, lifeless. The second man didn't even glance around. He made a bee-line back the way he'd come and lifted off just outside the doors. Flier.

The detective called out, "Emelynn?"

It was too dark for him to have seen any of us in action. I answered, "I'm fine. I'm going after the one who got away." And then I took off for the open door. The man had made good speed, putting several hundred yards between us. I had nowhere to put the gun but I didn't dare ditch it. I held it in my hand as I took off after him. We were heading east straight toward the clump of trees at the crest of the hill above the house. He glanced behind once, but he'd topped out his speed and I rapidly gained on him.

I wasn't foolish enough to think I'd be able to hit a moving target with a bullet. Instead, I called on my crystal to generate a fatal jolt. I rolled the molten ball of power around in my mind's eye and poured on Jolene's speed, catching up to him in seconds. He didn't even see me coming. But he felt me. I released the deadly jolt and he arched dramatically like a ballet dancer, before crumpling and falling to the ground. I watched with detached fascination, as if it were happening on film in a blackened theatre.

Every Redeemer who fell was a victory for us; one less threat, I reminded myself and turned away. I made a U-turn and headed west back toward Cairabrae. I flew over the pasture where the cattle grazed, where Debbie and I ran and where ATV trails criss-crossed. I was probably lighting up a control panel somewhere in the house, setting off every vertical security alarm they had—if anyone was paying attention. I watched the ground carefully, ready to fire at the first sight of camo-clad intruders. But what I saw was much, much worse.

I drifted to a stop twenty feet above three ash circles. My heart thumped and I couldn't get enough air. Inside a circle of wood ash was where Carson did his worst damage—where the words of the incantations had their most potent effect. I searched for the candles at the four compass points, but found none. It was small comfort. Carson was preparing to steal the gifts from the captive Fliers: production-line style. They'd been stupid to leave their precious circles unprotected. Or maybe it was arrogance. I dropped down and dragged my bare feet through the circles scattering the ash as best I could. It might slow them down, I thought, but it wouldn't stop them.

I burst into the air again and took off at speed, circling wide of the main house to approach from where I'd left Ryan and James. From a distance, I could see that the black van was gone, but fear struck hard when I got closer. Bodies lay on the ground. The uniformed police looked like they'd just keeled over from their crouched positions. Sam's partner lay prone across the front passenger seat of the unmarked cruiser, his knees out the door, his radio just beyond his grasp. Were they dead? Twenty feet behind them, a man in a suit was splayed out on his back, covered in blood. That one was definitely dead. I didn't recognize him. I searched anxiously for James. Where was Ryan? I didn't see either of them, but I caught sight of one of Ryan's men and dropped down.

He had his eye glued to his rifle's sight. I didn't want to spook him, but how exactly did you approach someone under these circumstances? "Excuse me," I said quietly. He jerked his head sideways for a split second then quickly looked back through the gun sight. "Where's Ryan?" I asked.

"He's breaching the second floor. Stay well behind me."

I backed away from him. The balconies on the other side of the house were the logical place to try to get in. That's where I'd find them and they might be able to use me. I squeezed my crystal and ghosted, lifting up and straight over Cairabrae's dark slate roof, heading toward Jeannette's balcony. James and Ryan must have made it inside because a third body was now bleeding out on the stone alongside Jeannette and her nurse. I glanced across the lawn and spotted a few of Ryan's men in position. I dropped to the ground below the balcony and drifted along to the patio doors. I needed to see what was happening inside.

The crowd of guests had thinned; only a handful remained. Where had they all gone? The guard at the door was still there, but he'd lowered his gun to the crook of his arm, no longer on high alert. Another guard stood on the far side of the room, likewise relaxed. I could jolt them right through the bulletproof glass and they wouldn't know what hit them. Lethal jolts took longer to form, and distance took more juice. However, if I hit the guard on the far side first, it would cause enough havoc to give me time to recharge and hit the one closest. The only snag was I'd have to re-form to jolt. Someone might see me, but it was a risk I had to take. Hopefully, Ryan's men would recognize me and not shoot.

I moved into position directly opposite my first target: the second target was twenty yards to my left. I braced myself and willed my body back, forcing deep breaths to steady and calm myself. Then, I started building my jolt. The small spherical ball spun in my mind's eye and I poured on the power until it looked molten. I couldn't afford to miss and the jolt could be nothing less than deadly. With a snap of my head, I let it loose. The bullet-proof glass bowed imperceptibly. The scene inside unfolded like a cartoon; the man jerked up off the floor and smacked into a painting on the wall behind. He didn't slide down the wall; he bounced off it and landed face forward on the floor.

As predicted, the room erupted into chaos. The remaining guard, suddenly alert again, pointed his gun dangerously around the room, shouting orders and looking for the source of the trouble. I slid closer to him, careful to keep my movements fluid to stay under his radar. My second jolt was in the works, slowly building strength. Two more figures ran into the room. The guard moved away from the door, but I tracked him easily, biding my time. Just another moment. I watched him stop then hunch his shoulders and slowly turn to the windows facing me. I think he saw me, but it didn't matter now. I hurled my jolt and he lost consciousness before he hit the ground.

I raised my eyes beyond his body and sucked in a sharp breath, stumbling back a step. Carson! Chills shot up my spine. His beady black eyes darted around the room. Even from this distance, I could see the menace in his curled lip. His newest scar snaked in a red welt across his forehead.

This was my opportunity, the one I'd been waiting months for. Carson Manse was a dead man . . . he just didn't know it yet. I called on my crystal's power and began the process once again. I drew the energy I needed to form another lethal jolt: the most important jolt of my life. I kept perfectly still. It would take longer to prepare this time, coming on the heels of the two formidable jolts I'd just delivered. It couldn't be rushed though; it was too important. Carson had to be stopped and it would be my pleasure to do it. He wore a dark suit and gloves, just like the dead man in the driveway. Shadowed by a tall, gun-wielding bodyguard, he prowled the room.

The ball of fire took form in my mind. It glowed hotly, waiting for release. I took a step. Carson turned his head toward me. His eyes widened, and I whipped the jolt at his head. He jerked to his right and my jolt struck the guard behind him, sending the guard careening across the foyer. I'd missed! I sprinted for the nearest column and took cover.

I'd failed at the only chance I'd get to take him by surprise. It would be harder now. It would also take time I didn't have to recover my crystal's strength. I peeked around the column and saw him staring out at my hiding place. Hopefully, he wouldn't risk opening the doors to get to me. I pulled back behind the pillar and breathed, steadying myself.

I stayed put and built another jolt, praying I'd be fortunate enough to get a second opportunity to take Carson out.

Ryan had estimated ten to twelve Redeemers were inside. The man in the driveway was likely one of them. The guard on the balcony was another. I'd put another three out of commission, which meant their numbers had dropped by five. That had to help.

Loud voices came from inside and then I heard the click of a lock and the sweep of the patio door opening. I froze. My new jolt wasn't yet strong enough. I could ghost, but that would put me out of the game and I wanted to kill that bastard—badly.

"Emelynn." It was Carson's voice from inside the room . . . the cultured one he trotted out to conceal the monster beneath. "Emelynn . . . dear. Please come inside and join us."

Breathe, Emelynn, I said to myself. Don't let him get to you.

"Did that sound like a request, Emelynn? My mistake. Let me rephrase. Come inside—right now—or I'll kill your friend."

I peeked around the corner and my heart sank. I wanted to scream, but had no air in my lungs. Carson stood at the top of the steps to the living room. James was on his knees beside him. If James was conscious, it wasn't by much, but I couldn't see any damage. What had they done to him? Carson held James up by the hair, his head at a painful angle. In his other hand was a gun and it was aimed at James's head.

"I'll give you to the count of three. One . . ."

Unable to hide Sam's gun, I dropped it behind the pillar. I moved away from my cover and started toward the door. I had no choice.

"Two . . ."

With leaden feet, I stepped over the threshold. The door closed behind me. The floor was sticky under my feet and the room smelled of blood, stale wine and old food. Carson smiled triumphantly. He released James in dramatic fashion, displaying his empty hand as James collapsed away from him.

"Three . . ." Carson said, glancing at James.

Then he shot him. One earth-shattering shot to his chest.

I screamed and charged but before I reached Carson, he flattened me with a jolt. The pain was immediate and excruciating. I became the star of my very own cartoon. My feet left the floor and I sailed through the air, landing on my back. The room was suddenly very quiet, like when I floated with my head underwater. I blinked up at the ceiling, watching my circle of vision get smaller and smaller before it disappeared altogether.

I woke in the same position minutes later spitting water and gasping for breath. Carson stood over me with a dripping ice bucket. "Get up," he hissed. My chest ached like it had been split open.

"Help her," he sneered and a man grabbed my arm, yanking me to my feet. A faint light spilled to the floor beneath my gown and my feet looked like they were lit from within. Fear accompanied my crystal's warning. Cold water dripped off me onto the floor. I swayed, unable to hold myself upright. Whoever said what doesn't kill you makes you stronger hadn't experienced this. I couldn't breathe properly. The smallest breath hurt. It felt like inhaling and exhaling fire. I'd been stupid. I hadn't had my block up. He could have killed me, but he didn't. Not yet. I tugged my block into place. He wouldn't catch me unprepared a second time.

Carson's eyes landed on my necklace, Jeannette's crystal case. He reached for it, lifted it away from my neck and rolled it in his fingers. He shook his head and met my eyes then yanked hard, taking me down to my knees as the necklace broke free. I fell forward to my hands and stayed there, breathing short ragged breaths. Carson walked to one of the tall tables covered with a white cloth and a neat square of midnight-blue organza, and dropped my necklace into a pile. I focused on the objects he'd collected. Crystals. Of course; he'd need them to steal the owners' gifts. It meant the Ghosts who owned them were still alive—somewhere. Some of the crystals were bare, others were wrapped in leather or ribbon. Among the stash were gold and silver cases similar to mine. I looked from the crystals to Carson and a frightening thought occurred to me: the man who controlled the crystals controlled the Ghosts. The Tribunal was inconsequential without Ghosts, like a declawed lion, a toothless grizzly.

"Search her," he ordered, turning his back and walking away. "Thoroughly."

"Up!" the guard ordered, hauling me to my feet. He pushed me face-first against the nearest wall. "Hands on the wall over your head," he said gruffly. He raked his hands through my wet hair, ripping out bobby pins that got in his way until his fingers touched my scalp. He pulled my hair into a knot and squeezed. "Hold this," he said, grabbing my hand and slapping it against the crude ponytail. He ran his hands across my shoulders and down my back to below my butt. I stifled a yelp. He murmured his approval in hot breath against my neck and I cringed. He repeated the search up and down every square inch of the dress, paying particular attention to the front. Pig! I screamed inside my head. Heat coloured my face. With fierce determination, I defied the pain in my chest to inhale bigger and deeper breaths. I searched for the reassuring warmth of my crystal, the real one. The one not another living soul knew about. It was weak, but it was there. The glow faded from my skin.

The guard completed his thorough pat down and I dropped my hair. "Did I tell you I was finished," he growled, yanking my arm back into place. He unzipped my gown and I stiffened. I heard him laugh as he slid his hands down my bare backside, but the dress was too wet and too tight for him to gain access. He got his jollies feeling me up instead. I resigned myself to the assault. There was no gain for me in fighting him. The pain in my chest dissipated a little with every breath.

Finally satisfied, he zipped me up again. The cold wet fabric chilled me. But he wasn't done. He hiked up my dress and kicked my legs apart then proceeded to show me the real definition of *thorough*. Hot tears of humiliation ran down my face, but I didn't flinch—not once. "Now I'm finished," he said, laughing. I tugged my dress back down over my hips. "You can turn around." He smiled at me, wiping his fingers on a blue napkin.

I thought my humiliation was complete, but I was wrong. The room wasn't empty. I clenched my teeth and tears clouded my vision. Six or seven of the guests had front-row seats to my thorough search including Mason, whose blue eyes bulged from his bruised face. His nostrils flared above a twitching lip. His hands were restrained behind his back and blood ran from his nose. Gordon Evans averted his face. Carson wasn't averting his face. He looked pleased with himself.

Carson had my crystal and now he knew without a doubt that I didn't have another one hidden elsewhere. He thought he'd thwarted my ghost. It was best he continued to think that way. I let my shoulders sag and stared downtrodden at the floor. That's when I saw the small dart. It was almost hidden in the folds of the white table cloth, but I recognized what it was. Carson's crew had used darts in the trailer where they held me captive. That's how they were subduing everyone.

"I'm curious about something, Emelynn," Carson said. "How did you manage to jolt my guards? Three no less? Not one of your pedigreed colleagues managed that. How did you?"

I shrugged and my eyes drifted to James's body. I felt numb. Beaten. Tears welled up again and one after another dropped to the floor. I brushed them away. I'd cry for James later.

"Fetch Emelynn some appetizers, would you? She obviously hasn't had her fill."

The guard who'd searched me scoured the room and came up with discarded bits of pastry and a skewered shrimp. "Eat," he said, dropping them into my hand.

I looked up to Carson. "You heard the man, eat!" I lifted the pastry to my mouth and took a bite. It was bitter and now I knew why. Carson raised his gun. I forced the rest of it in my mouth and chewed, then swallowed. "Another," Carson ordered, waving his gun. I choked down the second and then the shrimp. It seemed to appease Carson and he lowered his gun.

"Just so we're clear, Emelynn. You're all done jolting. If I suspect you're even thinking about it, I'll kill one of your guests. We have more Fliers than we need, so it's no loss to me. Do you understand?"

I lowered my eyes to James's body and nodded my head.

"Good," he said.

A finger on James's right hand twitched. I swallowed and blinked. Then it twitched again. He wasn't dead—dying maybe, but not dead. Not yet. There was still hope.

"Did you hear me?" Carson said, and I jerked my gaze up. He'd been speaking and I'd missed it.

"Pay attention. I *said* . . . I could use your help with the guest list. This party was thrown in your honour—very nice party, by the way—so I'll assume you've had the pleasure of meeting the guests. I'd like you to help me identify the faces I don't recognize, so we can sort them accordingly. It can be your contribution to the cause. You can make up for Mason's lack of cooperation."

"Sort them?" I said, sniffling.

"Yes. Ghosts go to the north end of the building. They'll be going with me. Everyone else goes to the south end, the kitchen, unless they have a special gift in which case they'll also come with me. The new Tribunal awaits the Ghosts and their gifts with fevered anticipation." He rubbed his hands together like the greedy rodent he was. "The rest will be picked over by those with less money, but still faithful to the cause." Now there was a vision of the future: Redeemers hunched like vultures over a carcass. "So," Carson said, "Let's get started. Look around. Have I missed any Ghosts?"

I didn't dare look around for fear my eyes would land on Gordon. But Gordon was more valiant than I knew. I heard him clear his throat.

"I'm the only one left in here." I looked his way and he smiled kindly.

"Thank you," Carson said, and he flicked his head in a sign of some kind. I followed his gaze to a guard who had taken up position in the corner by the piano. He quickly aimed a small gun. I heard a pop and Gordon winced. It didn't take long for the drug in the dart to take effect. Two guards grabbed Gordon's arms and dragged the semi-conscious man across the smooth marble, up the three steps and off toward Stuart's office.

They returned moments later. It was obviously just a drop-off service. Carson held out his hand and one of the guards passed him Gordon's crystal. "Take the rest of them to the kitchen," Carson ordered. "Immobilize them when they get there." I could only imagine the horror those people, my guests, were dealing with. They shuffled out of the room at gunpoint, leaving me with Carson, Mason, and the guard with the dart gun. I didn't dare look at James for fear I'd draw their attention to him. I couldn't risk that they'd shoot him again, if they saw him move.

"I'm so glad you came back to the party. I was worried that you'd gotten away again and that would have been embarrassing," Carson said. "I'm going to save you for last, Emelynn. I didn't get top dollar for your gift, given the problems we had before, but this time I'll be available to supervise the exchange personally. We should have more success tonight, don't you think?"

Carson's arrogance edged out his ignorance. "What the hell did I ever do to you, Carson?"

"You? You humiliated me!" he bellowed, and then brushed his hands down the front of his suit, calming instantly. "That's what. You are a neophyte, completely ignorant of the power of your gift and you nearly cost me everything." He spit the words out with a sneer. "It will not happen again. Do you hear me? The Redeemers will prevail and I will lead them. I will not allow you to make a fool of me." He was shouting again, his eyes darting around. I think it scared his guard. It scared me. I stole a glance at Mason, but his anger overrode any other emotion.

Carson rearranged his face, smoothed his suit and walked casually to the table with the crystals. He carefully gathered the four corners of the blue fabric together and tied the pile into a neat bundle that he weighed in his hand with a satisfied smile. "Let's go see how your friends are making out, shall we?" He held his hand out, inviting me and Mason to walk in front of him. I helped Mason to his feet and felt my stomach turn. Saliva flooded my mouth and I knew I was only moments away from throwing up again. I swallowed, wiped my eyes and straightened my back, inhaling so deeply I felt my sternum crack in protest. I lifted my damp gown to get up the living room steps and led the way around the staircase toward Stuart's office.

CHAPTER TWENTY-THREE

One of Carson's guards stood outside the door to Stuart's office, gun trained on us as we approached. He waited for a signal from Carson behind me, then lowered the gun and opened the door. Mason entered first. I took two steps into the room, and froze. The disembodied animal trophies were no longer the most forlorn things in the room.

"Do you want them darted?" the guard asked Carson.

"No, but split them up. She's harmless now. Cuff her and if she causes any trouble, shoot her."

I looked around at the painter's palette of discordant colours that ringed the room. Ivy's pale green dress clashed beside the red of Tiffany's. Albert's gold cummerbund was bunched up in his wife's cable-tied hands, pressed to her face. Blood spotted her cream-coloured dress. A cold sweat bloomed on the back of my neck and once again I swallowed the gathering saliva. I couldn't hold off throwing up much longer.

"Over there," the guard said, pointing his gun in the direction he wanted Mason to go. Mason looked back at me, apologetic, seething and helpless. He walked across the room and knelt beside his father, then turned his back to the wall. Against the wall beside him, Stuart slumped, unconscious. Rachel and Lillian held hands, both bound, comforting each other. The black and turquoise of their gowns created a bold colour statement where the fabric intermingled. Directly across from them, Sebastian was regaining consciousness, shaking his head and fighting his restraints. He wouldn't fight for long. Behind the door to my right, I spotted Carla abandoned in a heap of yellow chiffon like a forgotten doll. Carla didn't need restraints.

Some of the men still wore their tux jackets, some were now in shirt sleeves. Like the women, they were in various states of consciousness. Most looked like they'd tried to fight, which I suspect is why Carla was dead and Eleanor had a bloody nose. It's how they'd subdued the men before they could dart them. They didn't dare kill them—not the Ghosts. Carson got top dollar for these people; he needed to deliver the goods. I wondered how the Fliers in the kitchen had fared.

The guard pulled my arms behind my back and I heard the ratcheting click of handcuffs tightening. Had they run out of cable ties, I wondered, or did I rate the real thing? He pulled me over and dropped me on the floor beside Gordon, who was out cold. I looked at Mason and held his gaze, trying to look encouraging. Stuart stirred beside him. Mason bumped his father's shoulder, attempting to rouse him. It worked. Stuart opened his eyes. He blinked slowly, trying to focus. He shook his head and straightened up. He looked at Mason and Mason directed him to me. I smiled as best I could. It was weak, but it earned me a return smile from Stuart.

Carson pulled out his phone and dialled. "Are you ready to roll?" he asked. "Excellent. Wait for my call."

"If you'll excuse me," Carson said to his captive audience. "I've got to check up on our other guests. I'll be right back." He left the room, cradling the cache of crystals. There were two guards left inside, one at the hall door and one at the outside door.

My stomach lurched. There was no holding it back this time. I turned away from Gordon and threw up. The guard at the hall door marched toward me with his gun poised, but he stopped short and put a hand to his mouth. I heaved again, and the last of the canapés came up. The guard cursed and retreated. When I was sure I'd finished, I sat up and rested against the wall, closing my eyes. Moments later the guard returned with a towel and threw it over the vomit. It helped with the visual . . . not so much with the smell.

I needed my crystal now, more than ever. It was there, thrumming and warm, ready. How much more could I squeeze out of it without risking the unthinkable? It had already glowed its warning once. Thank god for allergies, I thought, as I considered my options. The other Ghosts were useless, sorry to say, but without their crystals, they couldn't ghost, and the other Fliers weren't going to be much help either. The amber they'd ingested would make their jolts unreliable or weak, and no one was going to be flying any time soon. I could possibly get my hands on the gun I'd dropped outside, but that was a long shot. My best hope was to get Ryan's men inside.

Sebastian was wide-awake now. His lips were pressed into a thin line and his narrowed eyes seethed with frustration. His bow tie was up around his ears, as if someone had used it to drag him. He no longer looked smug or arrogant; he looked humbled, but he remained defiant. "Can anyone tell me where my wife is?" I wasn't sure if he was addressing the guards or the rest of us. When no one answered, he tried again. "She's wearing blue. Someone must have seen her." I knew where she was. Kimberley wasn't a Ghost. She would have been sent to the kitchen.

The guard closest to us approached him and smiled maliciously before he hauled off and kicked Sebastian in the chest, slamming his back and head into the wall with a loud thud. Sebastian grunted and stilled. "Shut up," the guard growled. Across the room, Tiffany whimpered. It was the first time I felt anything for her father. Under other circumstances, I might have been happy to see Sebastian cowed, but not today. He was one of only a handful of people who were capable of subduing this rebellion. And he was helpless.

I glanced at Stuart. His hands were bound in front, Mason's behind his back. I watched Stuart reach over and pat his grown son's thigh with a look of profound apology and regret on his face, and it broke my heart. I wondered if he knew that his wife was dead. Carson had rained unfathomable pain on this family and now he and his Redeemers were preparing the ultimate defilement of every one of the Tribunal families. No one would make it out alive. I had absolutely nothing more to lose and neither did anyone else in this room.

If I could take out one of the guards, I might be able to ghost before the other one reacted. Neither guard actively scanned the room. They had grown complacent, knowing their charges were now harmless. I closed my eyes. Fear tugged at my confidence and I batted it away. This had to work; there was no one else and there was no room for doubt. I focused on the vision of my crystal and touched it with the edges of my mind. Thankfully, Carson's jolt had done no permanent damage.

I began the process. A run-of-the-mill jolt was as easy to accomplish as blowing out birthday candles. This was different; this jolt had to be lethal. I wouldn't get a second chance. If I was calm, I could produce one in ten seconds. I wasn't calm, and it took an eternity. I kept my eyes closed and built the ball into a molten sphere. Once I let it go, it would take a moment to recover enough to ghost—not long, but three or four seconds is plenty long when guns are in play.

When the jolt was ready, I opened my eyes. I looked from one guard to the other. Eenie, meanie, miney, moe. I picked the one closest to the outside door and hurled the jolt.

He didn't crumple quietly, like I had hoped. He smacked into the window with a loud bang and fell sideways with a tremendous clatter. The second guard immediately came to life, shouldering his gun. Half the eyes in the room turned to me. I quickly looked away and didn't dare look at the other guard. I wrapped my metaphysical fingers around my crystal and held steady. The guard's eyes lit on each person in the room. No one moved. I glanced over at Mason. He'd hung his head, like those around him, but under his eyebrows, his eyes were fixed on me.

I nodded at him and smiled thinly. My crystal was our last hope but it was also my most prized secret, and I wouldn't reveal it if it could be helped. I misdirected Mason's gaze by jerking my head up and to the right, as if something on the other side of the room had caught my attention. The moment Mason turned his head, I squeezed my crystal . . . and blinked out of sight.

My cuffs dropped to the floor with a loud rattle. Mason immediately looked back, stunned. The guard swung around in the direction of the noise. His confusion was quickly followed by alarm. He assumed a shooter's stance and started a slow sweep of the room, sighting down the rifle. I drifted over to him and re-formed inside the reach of his gun. His eyes bugged out. I drove my knee into his jewels then grabbed his gun and swung the butt with a mighty wallop against the side of his head. He went down like a stone, but thankfully, a quiet stone.

Everyone in the room who could move, did. I pulled a nasty-looking knife off the second guard's belt and sliced through the cable ties on the first pair of hands offered up. The grateful man took the knife and set to work on the others. I ran to the outside door and tried the handle. It was locked. I shook it, stupidly, as if that would help, but it just rattled and I froze. The noise would draw attention.

I heard Stuart's voice say in a strained whisper, "There's a toggle under the handle. Turn it." I ducked down, turned the lock mechanism then tried the handle again. It opened. I sucked in a breath of fresh night air and prayed that they'd all get out.

I turned back into the room and ran for the hall door. Mason, now free of his cable-tie, cut me off and grabbed my forearm. I looked down at his hand then back to his face. He looked at me like I was a stranger. "What just happened here?" he asked quietly. I shook my head and turned to Edward who had joined us. "Where are you going?" Mason demanded. I saw Sebastian stumbling his way over.

"For the head of the snake. I'm going after Carson."

"I'll come with you," he said, stepping forward.

I stood firm. "No. You can't." All three men looked ready to explode. "The food was contaminated. You've all eaten ground amber. Every one of you. That's why you were all powerless. Your gifts are compromised." Anger coloured Mason's face. I pulled free of his grip. "Unless you have a gun or can outrun a bullet, you can't help." I held his gaze until he accepted what I was saying. "I threw up the amber; I'm okay."

He pursed his lips. "Go," he said. "I'll send help."

"Kill the bastard," Sebastian called after me.

I opened the door to the hall. It was clear. I tiptoed quickly to the south end of the house, toward the kitchen where the other Fliers were being held. Voices in the library stopped me. I pressed my ear to the door and listened.

It was Carson's voice. It sounded like he was on the phone. "I'm only going to say this once, so pay attention. In six minutes, two transport vehicles will approach this building. Do not interfere with them. If those vehicles aren't here in exactly six minutes, we start killing people. One for every thirty seconds of delay until they arrive." He paused and then a moment later I heard him say, "We're ready for transport," as if he were talking to someone else.

Carson slid back a slot on my priority list. I had to try to get those people out and I had less than six minutes to do it. I picked up the hem of my gown and ran flat out in my bare feet to the kitchen. The door didn't have a handle or latch; it swung open from either side like a door in a restaurant kitchen. I pushed it open a crack and peeked inside. Two guards were distracted on the far side of the room, allowing me to slip inside.

The copper scent of blood was thick in the air. Immediately to my left was the big six-burner stove. Maria was on the floor in front of it, her eyes wide and staring blankly into space. Another woman, a chef judging by her white jacket, lay across Maria's legs. The grey pallor of her skin told me she too was dead. I stepped closer and found the source of the copper scent in a puddle of blood under their legs.

The horrific sight struck me dumb until I felt the cold barrel of a gun against my cheek. I lifted my face and swallowed the bile that rose in the back of my throat. I hadn't seen this guard. He jerked his head, urging me to move toward the service door. "Joe, we got another one— you got a cable-tie over there?" he asked. I walked sideways, keeping an eye on his rifle. Fliers shuffled out of the way, making room for us.

My crystal hadn't failed me tonight, but I'd taxed it heavily. Without knowing if there was anything left, I called on it again. I needed another lethal jolt, and prayed I'd have the time and strength to create one.

The two guards at the service door yanked frightened guests to their feet and pushed them into a queue, preparing for departure. My crystal flared with a pulse of light. I looked back at the other guard. He eyed me quizzically, his gun trained on my chest. I counted to three. The jolt found its target and immediately, I ducked, losing myself in the huddle of bodies. The guard's eyes rolled back in his head and he dropped silently, like a rock star into an eager audience. The moment he hit the floor, the Fliers fell on him. Even with their hands restrained, they stripped his gear with alarming speed and brutality.

Shots rang out with a deafening blast and a rain of plaster fell on the room. All activity stopped and everyone cowered, covering their heads.

The door banged open and Carson entered with a murderous scowl on his face. He had a death grip on the bundle of stolen crystals. My own crystal was warm again, pulsing and I called on it yet again. I slowly rose and stood straight and tall. Carson looked at me and bared his teeth like a feral dog. "Shoot her," he ordered. But I had already squeezed my crystal, and I vaporized before his eyes. Two gunshots followed, splintering the cupboards behind where my head had been moments before. The noise hurt my ears in the confined space. What happened next was priceless. The guards practically hyperventilated. Carson ignored their frenzy and sensed the room for my ghost signature. He wouldn't find it. Jeannette was the only one who could, and she was gone now. "She's not here," Carson declared. "Get these people ready to go. The transport will be here in four minutes."

He left the kitchen completely unaware that he was missing a man. I glanced back at the two remaining guards. For the first time, I understood the power of fear from the Tribunal's perspective. Useful. Those two men were more afraid of my ghost than the fact that their prisoners had just pilfered their comrade's knife and gun. I crossed my fingers that it would be enough to get these people out safely.

I ghosted after Carson. He stood in the doorway to the dining room. "I don't care," he said. "Transport will be here in four minutes. Be ready to go."

Oh god. Were there more people in the dining room? I drifted under Carson's arm to get a look and saw a sea of frightened faces. They were bloodied and panicked, but keeping this group in good shape hadn't been a priority. Another body had been callously dumped behind the door at the end of the sideboard, but I didn't even look. I had less than four minutes to put a stop to this madness. I didn't have time for shock or indignation.

Then I spied Debbie. She was jammed in a corner with her hands restrained behind her back. The neat coil of hair she'd worn earlier was hanging in clumps. Her lip was swollen and split, and her brown satin jacket was torn. She looked fiercely determined, despite her predicament.

Could I help, I wondered? Two guards covered the room, one at the patio door, one close to the sideboard. They were mobilizing the guests. I drifted to the guard by the sideboard—he was closest—and scanned his body for a weapon. He had a firm grip on his handgun, but his knife was there for the picking and he was busy issuing orders. I pulled back on my ghost to get to the point where I could manipulate his knife, and reached for it. The large holes along its handle made it easy to pluck, and I timed my theft with his body movements so he wouldn't feel the loss. I drifted back to Debbie, who was on her feet now.

I moved close to her and whispered in her ear. She flinched. "The prisoners in the kitchen have a gun," I said. "I've got a knife." I pressed the knife blade between her wrists and tugged, slicing through the cable-tie. "Take it," I said, pressing it into her hand. "I'm going after Carson." She nodded and smiled, trying to direct the gestures to my ghosted form, but failed by inches. I had to trust that I hadn't just set her up to face a firing squad armed with only a knife.

I blew through the door and went after Carson, who was far ahead, having already crossed the foyer. I hesitated. I'd left Sam's gun on the patio outside the living room doors. I'd have a better chance of stopping Carson if I had it, but did I dare risk losing him if I took that detour? Happily, Carson gave me the opportunity I needed when he stepped into the bathroom.

I breezed across the foyer toward the living room and almost made it down the steps before a large puddle of blood stopped me cold. It was where James had fallen; it was James's blood. There was a frightening amount of it. No one could survive that. Had he died, lying here on this cold marble floor, all alone? The puddle was smeared, as if his body had been dragged through it. I searched the room in a frenzy, but in vain. My heart felt like it was in a vise. I slowed to a stop in the centre of the room. The pain was unbearable. I hung my head in grief. His body was probably the one unceremoniously dumped behind the door in the dining room. I hadn't even bothered to look.

I'm sorry, James. You deserved better than this. I tried not to cry. I didn't have the luxury of time to mourn right now, but the tears came anyway, materializing like raindrops when they reached the floor.

A burst of automatic gunfire erupted, dragging me back to the horror of the moment. I drifted upright, swallowing my grief. The gunfire had come from the direction of Stuart's office. I heard the bathroom door open and I raced to the hallway. Stuart's office door stood open, but that's not where the gunfire originated. Wood splinters lay like calling cards on the floor outside the library. Carson stood in the hall by the bathroom as if frozen to the floor. He looked back toward the kitchen, his eyes wide with shock. He chose that moment to ghost. Having seen him do it, I sensed him right away. I prepared to follow him, anticipating he would go in the direction of the gunfire. He didn't. Instead, he turned for the staircase and churned upward following the path of the stairs. I drifted straight up the centre and followed him. He threw himself through the big double doors at the top of the stairs. I followed on his heels, collecting myself on the other side.

I'd never been in Stuart's room before, hadn't even had a glimpse through the door. The room was large, but it wasn't grand. It felt homey and warm. One of Jolene's paintings hung in a prominent space above a fireplace. A thick, sculpted carpet in shades of warm yellow and pale blue lay on the marble floor.

Carson's ghost spun out of control near the ceiling. I recognized the motion, having experienced it myself on more than one occasion. It told me he wasn't yet skilled enough to control his ghost. He would tire soon and have to lie down to re-form, or he'd pass out.

I drifted around the room waiting for Carson to make a move. He dipped down and to the left of the painting, sifting without incident through the framed photographs on a pedestal table. He continued on that path, sliding off a curio cabinet in the corner before inching along the floor.

I sensed his ghost dissipating and for a moment I feared he'd find a way around me. I stole a glance at the balcony, shaken again by the knowledge that Jeannette and her nurse had met cruel deaths out there. Carson was responsible for that carnage; I couldn't let him get away. I swivelled around and found him struggling to re-form, fading in and out like a radio station. When he'd fully materialized, he dropped into one of two loveseats and abandoned his treasure of crystals on the table between them. He was a new Ghost; his activity would leave him tired and weakened.

I drifted behind him. A door slammed somewhere below and he turned his head to listen. "Doesn't look good for you, does it, Carson?" I said. My voice spooked him as I'd hoped it would. He jumped up and spun around the room trying futilely to sense me.

"Where are you?" he growled. "Show yourself."

I laughed, my voice a little too loud. "Now, why would I do that?"

"You're a coward!" he taunted.

I laughed again. "That's rich, coming from you." I drifted over to the balcony doors. Someone had closed them. I peered outside and saw the overturned wheelchair, the tangled limbs. Carson would pay for that. I moved in front of the curio cabinet to put a loveseat between us, then materialized and established my block. He no longer frightened me. I wasn't panicked or shaking. I wasn't sweating or having a crisis of conscience. I was in complete control. Better yet, I felt at peace. I had one mission and no illusions: eliminate this vermin at all costs.

"At least now, it will be a fair fight," he said, spotting me.

There wouldn't be anything fair about it. I'd been in his boots. I knew exactly how weak he was at this stage of his training. I formed a weak jolt, just enough to show him I cared and blasted it at him.

He inhaled sharply, but didn't move. His lack of reaction shocked me. Had I been wrong about his state of readiness? Had I made a fatal miscalculation? He should have been on the floor. He screwed up his face.

"You look confused, Carson."

"How is this possible? I did everything right with you. Your gift should have been mine and yet here you are. Why aren't you dead?"

"Are you disappointed?"

He stared back blankly. "Just curious," he said.

"You should have done more research. You know what they say, Carson: A little bit of knowledge is a dangerous thing."

And I shouldn't have engaged him in conversation, because it gave him enough time to recover. He hit me with a jolt and I didn't see it coming. My block was strong, but I felt the power of his jolt wash over me like a blast of heat. I staggered backwards rattling the curio cabinet. Light flashed around me then sputtered out. He smiled, pleased with himself. He was stronger than I'd anticipated. How? The Vosburg's gift must have been potent. Was he strong enough to ghost again? If he did, I'd lose him. I had to keep him in the flesh if I wanted to kill him, and that was the only thing on my to-do list.

He was arrogant. It was only one of his weaknesses but it was the one I could exploit. "Is that the best you can do, Carson?" He took the bait and hurled another powerful jolt. I immediately ghosted and the curio cabinet behind me exploded in a shower of glass. The more power I could get him to expend, the weaker he'd be, but it would cost us both. I rushed past him to the bundle of crystals and quickly stashed them out of sight under the sofa.

"I should have known you couldn't take a hit from *me*," he said, stepping in a circle, trying to sense me. When his gaze fell on the table where his prize had been, his eyelids began to twitch. "Get back here," he snarled. He dashed around the room, eyes darting to every corner, but he didn't find his treasure.

I spoke from behind him. "Did you lose something, Carson?"

He spun around and hurled a jolt that cracked against the wall.

His frustration was a good thing. My physical presence was the only thing he could lash out at, and he couldn't do it while I was in ghosted form. I re-materialized behind the sofa with my back to the hall doors and waited for him to turn and find me. He stopped when he did and glared at me. "Where are they?" he hissed. He stomped toward me. I took a step back to maintain my distance. He didn't have the look that preceded a jolt, but he'd fooled me once. He stepped toward me again. I stepped away. Perhaps he'd figured out how well matched our jolts were.

"Where are what?" I asked. It was the proverbial last straw. He dove at me, knocking me backwards. He was reaching for my neck when I blasted a jolt at him. He'd abandoned his block in his fit of rage and howled in pain. I struggled to get away from him and rolled out of his reach. He was on his knees. I fumbled to stand and he lurched at me again, this time tackling me around the waist. I reached behind to break my fall and trapped my arm underneath our bodies. I jolted him again, but missed. He grunted then smashed the heel of his hand into my jaw, snapping my head back. His hand found my neck and he squeezed.

I pressed my crystal into action and ghosted out from under him. I drifted straight up, coughing and sputtering. When I'd recovered my breath, I re-formed and drove the bare heel of my right foot into his ribs. He yelped and writhed on the floor. I ghosted to safety and watched him struggle to sit up in front of the doors to the hall. Light spilled out from my ethereal form, revealing my position and heating my skin. This time the light didn't fade.

"Why don't you and I make a deal," he said.

"A deal?" I croaked then coughed again.

"I have something you want." He sounded smug again. Why?

"You have nothing I want."

"I beg to differ. I've got buyers lined up waiting for a piece of these bastards. I'll trade you. For each name I give you, you give me a crystal."

I re-materialized, standing in front of him, but outside of lurching distance. He smiled a self-satisfied smile. It didn't last long. "You've mistaken me for Tribunal, Carson. I'm not."

He squinted his little rodent eyes, thinking hard. "You're not stupid enough to cross the Tribunal. The Tribunal wants those names and I'm the only one who has them."

"How unfortunate for you then that no one from the Tribunal is here. You see, I don't give a rat's ass about your names, all I want is you. Dead."

"You won't kill me. I'm too valuable. I know who the players are." He cocked his head. "And if the light you're throwing off is any indication, I think you're done here."

"Think again," I said, as I blasted another jolt at him. The light around me flared an ominous warning. He landed on his back with his knees in the air, groaning. I pushed aside the warning. "What's wrong Carson? Why aren't you blocking?"

He struggled up to his elbows then dragged himself backwards, toward the hall doors, trying to get away from me. The scar on his forehead pulsed. Someone rattled the double doors from the outside. It startled both of us. Carson's eyes widened with hope. He was just three feet from the doors and shot a quick glance over his shoulder to check.

"Police, open up. Right now!"

Carson kept me in his sights and reached behind for the door. He pulled himself upright and this time, when he re-established his smug smile, I wiped it off his face. I guess he thought the police would deter me. He was wrong. I barrelled a jolt at him that blasted him right through the double doors. Puffs of plaster and shards of light blew out around the door frame. He skidded along the marble in the hall all the way to the atrium rail. I followed him out, vaguely aware of the glowing spectacle I presented.

Carson's face contorted with pain. He rolled onto his side and groaned. I watched him struggle to stand and couldn't dredge up an ounce of compassion for him. He stood and wavered like a drunk trying to find his balance. I recalled a conversation we'd had on the night he tried to steal my gift. I'd asked him then if he believed in karma. He said he didn't. He believed that only the strong survived. I guess we were both right. My next jolt took him over the railing with a starburst of white light. I closed my eyes and awaited my judgment. Would I hear the satisfying thud when Carson hit the unforgiving marble floor below . . . or the eternal silence of a shattered crystal?

Chapter Twenty-Four

The house fell eerily quiet. I opened my eyes and drifted to the trail. Carson's body lay twisted on the floor, a halo of blood pooling around his head.

Close by, a man's gentle voice spoke. "Whatever it is you're doing . . . you can stop now." A heavy hand rested on my shoulder. I stared blankly at the thick fingers. "He's not going to get any more dead than that."

I lifted my face to Sam. He was filthy. I glanced down at his injured arm. Blood had seeped through the bandage I'd tied on his wound, and the way he held it told me it hurt. He pulled me into a one-armed embrace and I lay my cheek against his chest.

I listened to Sam's steady heartbeat and watched my light pulse. I felt numb. The enormity of what had happened—what I'd done—began to sink in. Sam and I stood in a protected bubble while people slowly began to stir around us. The scale of death and senseless destruction was staggering. How would we ever get past this?

I pulled back from Sam. "Will you help me find James? I don't want his body being mauled by strangers."

"You're too late," he said. "Strangers are mauling him right now— at the hospital. He's in surgery."

I didn't understand. "But how?"

"The tranq dart hit his wallet. He played along. He might have caught a break had Manse not shot him."

"But all that blood . . . I thought he was dead."

"So did they. He waited until they left, then dragged himself out the patio door. Ryan's men got him into an ambulance."

"What about Ryan?"

"He's sleeping off a triple dose of tranquilizers."

"And Debbie?"

"Touch and go. I'm told she got the people out of the dining room then headed back in. She was shot in the abdomen."

"Bastards," I said.

"And how about you?" Sam said.

I raised my arm and watched the pulsing light fade. "I think I'll be okay."

A woman who'd been lurking behind us approached with caution. She wore EMS gear and held up blue-gloved hands in surrender. "Detective?" she said. "I'd like to look at your arm."

"Emelynn?" Mason said, interrupting. I turned to his grief-stricken face. He held his arm out for me.

"Thank you, Sam," I said. His forehead creased in concern, but he let me go.

Mason put his arm around my shoulder and together we walked back into Stuart's room. An ambulance crew waited patiently inside the doors to the suite. We approached the balcony and I caught a glimpse of my reflection in the window. My hair was a wild halo. I looked down at the ruined blue gown and winced, thinking about the matching blue ribbon and decorations downstairs. How could it have all gone so horribly wrong?

Stuart sat on the floor of the balcony, his wife's head in his lap. My heart broke all over again. Mason and Stuart's grief cut me to the core, and I felt the loss of Jeannette as deeply as if she were my own grandmother. Whatever happy memories that may have lived within the walls at Cairabrae would be forever tainted by what happened here tonight. Stuart smoothed Jeannette's hair with his hand and spoke quietly to her. I turned into Mason's chest and we both wept.

EPILOGUE

When the temperatures dip below freezing for any length of time in Vancouver, the winter rain turns to snow and a quiet hush descends over the city. It's a rare treat. Even up on the eighteenth floor, I could hear the muffled difference. We were in the middle of an unusual late-November cold snap and the frozen ground guaranteed the accumulation would stick around for a day or two. Rumour had it that Vancouver owned a snowplow for these occasions, but it never made it past the main arteries as far as UBC's endowment lands.

I watched the fat snowflakes fall heavily onto the balcony beyond the glass door. The penthouse condo was as far removed from my Arts and Crafts–style cottage as it was possible to get. The condo held no memories for me. The furniture was new and modern. In fact, everything from the cutlery to the carpets was new, and I hadn't chosen any of it.

But there was a beach. It was across the road and beyond a narrow strip of parkland. It was sandier than the beach in front of the cottage and had fewer rocks. Come summer, it would be bustling with people seeking solace from the sea. Perhaps when the weather warmed, I'd try my hand at building sandcastles. I smiled recalling happy childhood memories doing just that. Back then, I'd always imagined that I was the princess trailing silk ribbons from a pointy hat. Who knew that all along, I was the dragon?

I cradled a cup of tea, letting it warm my hands, and watched the gas-fired flames lick stone logs safely behind the glass of the fireplace.

"Your mother Skyped me," James said, coming out of the office. "She wants to know what you want for Christmas. Any ideas?" James was my mother's new best friend. I'd settled into the condo a month ago but she didn't stop worrying about me until she heard he was visiting. It was only after he'd slapped his seal of approval on the security at the condo that she'd finally relaxed.

I turned to James and pursed my lips. "Pyjamas," I finally suggested. "The two-piece flannelette kind. It feels like it's going to be a cold winter."

"Pyjamas are fine, but how about I pick them?" he said, turning me around and pulling my back against his chest with his good arm so we could both look out the big window. "I love it when it snows. It feels peaceful, doesn't it?" I smiled at his words. They were the same words I'd used to entice him to visit.

James needed the peace. He tried to hide it, but I sensed his struggle. James and his family had been released from service to the Tribunal. For the first time in four generations, their lives were their own. James's vision of his future had taken a major hit and he was still reeling. He was starting to think about a family of his own. It leaked out in little remarks he'd make—small observances that other people might not notice. I noticed. It troubled me because I didn't share his vision of family.

But we had time. He wasn't ready to make any decisions yet. The bullet that I thought had killed him had shattered his shoulder blade and damaged muscle and ligaments. He worked himself into a painful sweat daily on his road to recovery. Nothing short of full motion in his arm would satisfy him. It would be a long recovery.

I sighed in his arms. The beauty of the setting didn't erase the horror of what had happened at Cairabrae. A few days after the carnage, Jeannette was laid to rest at Turner Acres beside my infant brother. It had been a warm afternoon. Mason, Stuart and I stood holding hands as the coffin was lowered. There were no tears. There was no dead dove. Sebastian offered me the "honour" of presenting it to Stuart, but I didn't have the heart.

Stuart returned each stolen crystal to its grateful owner in private. His grief hadn't dulled his political acumen. He'd extracted promises and acknowledgement of the need for change, in exchange for each one of those crystals. I wasn't holding my breath.

I'd accepted Stuart's gift of Jolene's inheritance. It was more money than I'd likely spend in my lifetime. James wasn't happy about my decision, but he and I often disagreed on matters concerning the Reynoldses.

Mason broached the subject of my crystal after his mother's funeral, but I'd side-stepped it. I knew he'd ask again one day, but I would side-step it again. After all, everyone had secrets. That one had saved my life so I would safeguard it.

I turned down the offer of an active role on the Tribunal. Mason wasn't happy, but he knew not to push. I knew he thought in time I would change my mind. I wasn't so sure.

Sam personally escorted me back to Canada. He never once mentioned the crystal or what had happened with Carson Manse. I was immensely grateful for that. And for him.

The physical distance from the nightmare at Cairabrae helped, but the memories were troublesome. It still frightened me how quickly I'd slid down that slope into unspeakably violent behaviour. Perhaps it wasn't the speed with which I'd made the descent, but the ease. It was much too close to Tribunal behaviour for my comfort.

Eden didn't come back. She and Alex decided to stay in Seattle. We talked on the phone, but it wasn't the same. I missed her sparky presence in my life.

I missed Molly, too. Her baby was due in June. I kept her at arm's length now. It was safer.

At least I had Avery. He and Victoria were still going strong. It was Avery who'd known someone, who'd known someone in real estate and in record time, with Gabe Aucoin's legal assistance, this penthouse was mine. I bought it sight unseen, shortly after I'd returned to Canada. It was Victoria who had furnished and decorated it.

The snow was long gone when I drove James to the airport on New Year's Day. It was difficult to say goodbye, but it was time. Demand for James's services in the States was bursting at the seams with his absence, and I needed to re-establish my independence.

He waved as I pulled away from the curb. I flipped on the windshield wipers and watched in the rear-view mirror as he turned for the departures door. Would he miss me? I wondered, as I stepped on the gas and steered the little red MGB south toward Summerset.

The cottage was never far from my thoughts. I hadn't been back since the day Sam helped me find Jeannette's crystal-case necklace. I slowed to a crawl along Cliffside Avenue and pulled into the familiar driveway. The tires crunched on the gravel until I came to a stop at the top of the loop where the cottage's blue door once stood. The skyline looked odd to me without the familiar outline of the cottage's rooftop.

At least the blackened pile of ash and rubble was gone. I'd hired a contractor to remove it and restore the grounds. Except for the garage, the two acres now looked like part of the adjacent park.

I stepped out of the car, pulled up my hood and walked to the edge of the cliff. My breath left me when I took in the view. It hadn't changed at all. I closed my eyes and drew in a lungful of briny air. Seagulls called to one another over the rhythmic wash of the waves below. Cold air billowed the edges of my hood and a fine rain sprayed my face.

Warm tears formed behind my eyelids and I swallowed a sob. One word . . . one thought . . . enveloped me. Home. The pull was so strong and unexpected that I felt overwhelmed. I let the tears run down my face. I was home. Even without the cottage, this place was still my sanctuary. Not even the horror of Carson Manse and the damage he'd done here had removed my connection to this place.

My life had been altered irrevocably—again—and yet here I was— still standing. In fact, I felt stronger than I'd ever felt before. My gift was intact, my crystal unscathed, and that place I called *normal* wasn't nearly as interesting as the place I called home. I'd protected my friends and defended my family. I was not a victim and I would not be pushed around.

Regardless, my world was changing. And I would change with it. The gift wasn't common knowledge, but we'd been exposed at Cairabrae. It was just as Stuart and Mason had predicted. Highly placed government officials on both sides of the border now knew about us and the secret we'd tried so hard to protect. In an effort to stem further exposure, James and I had both entered into an uneasy alliance with their appointed elite specialists. Sam agreed to be my liaison with them. To date, the alliance remained untested.

I wiped my eyes with the back of my hands and sniffled the rest of my tears away. The old arbutus tree that grew beside the deck had burned in the fire and the contractor had removed it. However, a bright green sprout with half a dozen leathery leaves waved like a flag from the blackened stump. A smile spread across my face. Like me, the old tree was a survivor and not even a chainsaw would keep it down.

I'm learning to live with the monster that Carson Manse created within me. Just knowing what I'm capable of is a sobering thought. I will eventually reclaim laughter and happiness. I try not to think about the Tribunal or the Redeemers, but it's a struggle. There were a lot of factors to blame for what happened at Cairabrae and neither group was without fault. I could say that I forgive them, but it would be a lie. I could say that I forgive myself, but that would also be a lie. But I'm working on it.

What I do know, beyond a doubt, is that redemption, like beauty, is in the eye of the beholder.

THANK YOU

Thank you for reading *Burning Lies*. If you enjoyed it, please tell a friend or consider posting a short review where you purchased it. Reviews help other readers discover the books and are much appreciated.

—JP McLean

EXCERPT FROM BOOK 4

LETHAL WATERS

The Gift has been exposed and Emelynn must pay the penalty for her role in baring the secret, but before her and her new handler, Detective Samuel Jordan, can establish a safety net, Emelynn stumbles into the middle of a drug smuggling investigation that has already resulted in two murders. Unable to extricate herself, she and the detective join the investigation and embark on a dangerous mission to find the criminals who hide in polite society.

Read on for an excerpt . . .

The concrete piers of the Burrard Street Bridge rose up from the False Creek seabed, its steel girders looming eighty feet overhead. My kayak felt inconsequential by comparison. I rested my paddle across the hull and drifted forward into the bridge's shadow. A weak sun struggled behind the overcast sky.

My breath condensed in white puffs. I loved these crisp, cool mornings alone on the water. It was peaceful. Out here, life seemed simple, uncomplicated. Almost what I imagined normal felt like. A light breeze stirred the chilly air. The kayak rocked gently, its yellow hull reflected in the ripples that lapped quietly against it. I gazed up toward the underside of the bridge deck, where car tires thumped over expansion joints.

In the distance, the rumble of outboard motors drew my attention.

Time to get a move on. I tugged my cap down over my ears and blew a warm breath into cupped hands. The dry suit that kept my body warm did nothing for my head or my hands. The temperature hovered around five Celsius and the cold was finally getting to me.

I gripped my paddle and continued seaward, cautious of the potential danger from the boats whose motors were growing louder as they approached from behind. Six strokes later, almost out of the bridge's shadow, the tandem outboards roared, drowning out all other sound. I darted a wide-eyed glance behind and then hunched my shoulders and braced for the inevitable wake that would follow.

The marine speed limit in False Creek is five knots or dead slow. They had the "dead" part right. They raced by on either side of me with their throttles wide open. I barely got a glimpse of them before I felt the powerful effect of their wake. My kayak rolled dangerously when the first wave hit broadside, but it was the second wave that swamped me. It struck from the opposite direction and lifted the hull, dumping me into the frigid water.

I flailed in the dark, trapped upside down in the seat of my cockpit, groping for the tether to my lost paddle. I'd practiced the Eskimo roll that would right me dozens of times, but all of those self-induced rolls hadn't prepared me for the real thing. It wasn't the sting of salt water in my eyes, or the frosty temperature of a February ocean that made holding my breath difficult—it was the clear memory of drowning. My drowning.

It's not something you ever forget: the desperation that compels you to inhale water into your lungs, the way the weight of that water sinks you more effectively than any anchor. It's the disquieting euphoria of finally letting go. The panic that should have compelled me to jettison instead froze me in place. A memory flashed by at the watery sight of my outstretched arm. Last summer that same arm reached for a surface that I could see but couldn't reach.

Precious seconds ticked by.

I felt my cap lift away in the current. It was enough to shake me from the nightmare. Latent terror ignited and galvanized me into action. I yanked on the paddle's tether and re-established my grip. In one adrenalin-fed stroke, I swept my paddle in a powerful arc and rode the momentum to the surface. The instant my face cleared the water into a halo of light, I heaved a ragged breath then coughed and choked in another gulp of air.

"I've got you," a man's voice called as his red kayak bumped against my hull. A dark beanie covered his head. I pressed my knuckles against my eyes to clear the stinging water. My rescuer steadied the kayak while I caught my breath.

"Thank you," I sputtered. The mother of all ice-cream headaches stabbed across my forehead. As I recovered, I took in the man who'd come to my rescue. I put him in his late twenties. A day's stubble covered cheeks flushed red with the cold. He had the shoulders of a weightlifter and a firm grip on the cleat behind my cockpit. He'd laced his paddle under the bungee cording to steady me.

"That was a lot easier to do in waist-deep water," I rasped, my throat burning. No wonder the instructor had insisted we repeat the Eskimo roll exercise each time we went out. She'd said I'd likely never use it. Yeah.

"You probably shouldn't have been out here alone. You did well, considering." He offered a conciliatory smile.

My natural impulse should have been to claw my way out of the cockpit. "I probably should've done a wet exit." I'd practiced those, too, and would struggle back into the kayak to pump it out. At least the neoprene spray skirt had kept most of the water out of the kayak.

"I saw you go under. Luckily, I was just across the channel."

"Thank you." I glanced around for his partner but was grateful enough for his help to not mention the fact that I didn't find one. A wave rocked our hulls, and he held us steady.

"We need to report those yahoos," he said with contempt. "They're going to get someone killed out here."

"You know who they are?"

"No, but I know where they rented those boats. Where're ya headed?"

"Back to my car. I launched at Kitsilano, but now I think I'd better find somewhere to warm up first." This outing was supposed to help me build the upper-body strength my new kayaking hobby demanded. Perhaps I'd been too ambitious.

"I know a place. Do you know Scuppers?"

"No. Where is it?"

"Not far. It's where I was headed. Want to follow me?"

"Yeah, thanks." I reached over to offer my hand. "Emelynn Taylor."

"Owen Cooper," he said, jutting out his hand to take mine in a fierce grip. "Nice to meet you, Emelynn." He offered a confident smile that reached up and crinkled the corners of his dark brown eyes.

Owen disentangled his paddle from the bungee webbing and swung around. "This way," he said, paddling landward back under the Burrard Street Bridge. Within minutes we'd slipped under the grey steel and concrete of the Granville Street Bridge. We passed a small marina with swaying sailboats and pulled alongside a dock parallel to the rip-rap shore of Granville Island.

"You can tie up there," Owen said, pointing to the end of the slim dock. He continued ahead while I secured my kayak. I unfolded myself from the cockpit and climbed onto the dock. My limbs shook from the effort, or maybe it was from the receding adrenalin. Wet hair didn't help. I needed to get warm. With stiff shoulders, I pulled my dry bag from the rear hatch.

I shivered as I clutched the bag to my chest and scanned the docks for anyone out of place. Constant vigilance was a heavy weight I'd gladly shed if I could. I walked to the far end of the dock to find Owen. I was halfway up the ramp when I spotted him and stopped short to stare like an ill-mannered child. Owen was operating an electric winch, which had just pulled him from his kayak and deposited him in a wheelchair at the top of the ramp.

He looked over and waved me up. I snapped my mouth closed and checked my footwear. I didn't know the man, but I could have sworn I saw him grin. I swallowed my embarrassment and continued up the ramp, watching him unhook the harness apparatus.

"Sorry for staring. You caught me by surprise," I said.

"I usually do." His grin widened into a smile. "Your reaction was stellar. Maybe one of the best. I wish I had it on film."

"Guess I'm fortunate you didn't have a camera," I said, feeling the heat of a blush warm my face. "It was rude. I'm sorry."

"Don't be. It's cheap entertainment for those of us easily amused. Come on; let's get warm."

He spun his chair with precision and set it rolling across the black-top with one push of his powerful arms. The chair had slanted wheels and a short back, similar to the type athletes use. We crossed a wide sidewalk and passed Scuppers' deserted outdoor deck. A brass porthole adorned the front door. Owen punched the plate for the automatic door opener, and I had another awkward moment: should I go ahead of him, or not? What was the proper etiquette? Happily, when the door opened, he swept his arm ahead of him, answering my question.

The warmth inside was heavenly, but it only accentuated the chill of icy water dripping down my scalp. "What can I get you, Owen?" the hostess asked. Her long brown hair was pulled into a ponytail high on the back of her head.

"Irish coffee for me, Caitlin. What about you, Emelynn?" He turned to me with an arched brow and lopsided grin that said an alcohol-free beverage would be unacceptable.

"Irish coffee sounds good."

"Ah, good answer," he said, and once again finessed his chair into a tight turn. "Caitlin, be a doll and turn the fireplace on, would you? We need to dry out."

"Sure will. The coffee's fresh. I'll be right over with your drinks."

"Thanks," Owen said, pointing his wheelchair toward the big stone fireplace on the far side of the room. Caitlin pointed a remote control in the direction of the hearth, and flames leapt to life along the ceramic logs behind a black mesh screen.

I trailed behind Owen through the mostly empty restaurant; it was too early for the lunch crowd. Too early for an Irish coffee, too, but I had a good excuse.

I dropped my bag on a chair near the fireplace. "Sounds as if you've been here a time or two," I said, rooting through my bag in search of a towel.

"My brother owns the place," Owen said, stripping out of his jacket. Everything about him spoke to his confidence, from the easy banter with the hostess to his quick smile to his decisive physical movements.

"That's handy." I blotted the worst of the dripping water from my hair. I unzipped my suit and peeled it off, grateful for the absence of customers, and hung it on the coat rack beside the fireplace. Underneath, I wore thermal tights and a long-sleeved shirt. In the dry bag I kept a fleece, which I pulled on and snuggled into. Much better, I thought, rubbing my hands together in front of the flames in an attempt to jump-start the warming.

Owen pulled off his beanie and I got my first good look at him. He had a broad chest, heavily muscled arms and a seriously bad case of hat-head. He followed my upward gaze and tried to smooth the tangled mess of brown hair. His smile revealed perfectly white teeth.

"Here you go," Caitlin said, setting our drinks down. "Can I get you anything else?"

"Not for me, thanks. Emelynn?"

"No, this is great. Thank you."

"All right. Shout if you change your mind." Caitlin turned with a flip of her ponytail and called over her shoulder, "I'm putting this on your tab, O."

"You don't have to pay for me," I said.

"Ignore her," Owen said, and then raised his voice to call after her, "She's teasing." He had a thick tracheotomy scar at the base of his throat. How had he ended up in a wheelchair?

"Not teasing," Caitlin replied with a giggle, and sashayed back to the bar.

"Do you live around here?" I asked, smiling at their antics.

"Not far. Over in English Bay. How about you?"

"I've got a place out by UBC."

"Student?" he asked, twisting his mug in rhythmic circles. He wore a heavy gold signet ring on the pinky of his right hand.

"No, I just live out there."

"Are you from here?"

"BC?" I asked, and he nodded. "Yeah. South of here. Summerset." My old hometown was a thirty-minute drive away. I still owned property there, where our family's old Arts and Crafts–style cottage used to be. *Used to be*. A man, whose memory still haunted me, set fire to it last year. I was inside it at the time. I closed my eyes against the memory.

"Still cold?" Owen asked.

I shook off the recollection and forced a weak smile. "A little." I took a sip of the Irish coffee. "This is helping."

"Summerset's nice. What brought you into Vancouver? Work?"

It usually took longer for the dreaded but inevitable *work* question to come up.

"I'm between jobs." If he pressed, I'd mention the bookkeeping I'd done for the Rumble sisters' bookstores. I'd learned long ago that if I had to skirt the truth then keeping as close to it as possible made the lie easier to remember. Besides, it wasn't entirely untrue. I was between jobs. Hopefully there would be another one; it just wouldn't be anything I could talk about. I changed the subject.

"You said you knew where those people rented their boats."

"Yeah, they're Oscar's boats. He operates out of the far end of False Creek. I'll talk to him."

"Thanks." I wanted the names of the boats' drivers, but if they'd targeted me intentionally, they wouldn't have used their real names.

I steered our discussion to kayaking, something I didn't have to lie about. Owen eagerly shared his experiences. His ingenuity in designing the winch apparatus and adapting his kayak was impressive. And kayaking was just one of the sports he enjoyed. He also raced wheelchairs and rock climbed. Those activities would have been a challenge for anyone. The fact that he took them up in a wheelchair said a lot about the man's determination.

"It was a skiing accident that put me in the chair."

"I'm sorry."

He dismissed my comment with a wave of his arm. "It was a long time ago. Most people I meet are curious; they're just too polite to ask."

"Polite is infinitely better than staring with their mouths open," I said, recalling my behaviour on the ramp.

"Polite's overrated." He drained his mug. "If you let it, the chair will run your life and stop conversation dead. I try to pre-empt that nonsense."

The muffled ring of my phone sent me searching through the dry bag again with apologies. I checked the call display. "I'm sorry, Owen. I've got to take this." I scooted out of my seat. Owen nodded.

"Just a minute, Avery," I said, making my way outside. "What's up?" I asked, bracing against the cool air. Avery Coulter was my doctor, but he was also a very good friend and the closest thing I had to a father.

"How quickly can you get over to Vancouver General Hospital?"

At the mention of VGH, a shock ran through me. "What's happened?"

"It's Sydney. Where are you?"

"I'm on Granville Island. I can be there in twenty minutes. Is she hurt?" Sydney Davenport was one of us.

"Physically, no. But she needs a friend and you're the closest. I'll meet you in Emerg. Twenty minutes?"

"Okay." I hung up and dialled Black Top Cabs. When I told them it was an emergency, they promised to send a car right away.

"Something wrong?" Owen asked as I scurried back to our table and began gathering my belongings.

"Sorry to rush off, but I need to go. Who can I talk to about storing my kayak for a day or two?"

"I'll look after it for you. Here," he said, fishing a business card out of his wallet. "Call me when you're ready to collect it."

I took the card, on which was printed, *Owen Cooper, Owner*. I pinched my brow and read, "*Goat Trail Indoor Climbing Gym?*"

He shrugged. "There's always a goat trail to hike before you reach the climb."

I smiled at his explanation and tucked the card into my bag. "I owe you one, Owen. Thank you." I shook his hand and rushed outside to my waiting cab.

ACKNOWLEDGEMENTS

Burning Lies was originally published as *The Gift: Redemption*. The title change is a result of overwhelming feedback from the books' readership. My gratitude goes to Elinor Florence, who was instrumental and supportive throughout the rebranding process.

When I started out on this writing adventure, I never dreamed it would be so much fun. I also never imagined I'd meet so many talented and generous people along the way. I am forever grateful to my editor, Nina Munteanu, who is also a writing coach and an author (https://ninamunteanu.me). Nina's insightful edits always improve the story.

My gratitude and thanks go to the best group of cold readers on the planet. Thank you Anna, Cathy, Colleen, Denis, Eleanor, Gee, Jean, John, Kathy, Sally and Sue. You do a tremendous job of checking all the nooks and crannies and sweeping out the miscreants. Your courage is duly noted. Thank you also to Bill, Isabel and Elizabeth for your invaluable contributions.

To the owners and staff at Abraxas Books on Denman Island, thank you for your early and continuing support.

Thanks to the design team at JD&J Designs for *Burning Lies'* enticing book cover design.

And because I always save the best for last, thanks to my husband, and Mom and Dad. Your enthusiastic support keeps me warm and cozy on the cruellest of days. Finally, thanks to my sibs, Kathy, Margaret, Sharon, Bill and Sandy.

Copy edit provided by Nancy Wills, ILEX *indexing and editing* (https://ilexindexingandediting.com).

All errors in the research and writing of this novel are entirely my own.

GLOSSARY OF TERMS

Covey: A group of Fliers who are geographically connected. Older coveys were and still are connected by family rather than location. All Fliers belong to a home covey and are expected to check in with coveys in areas they are visiting. Coveys are a source of information and are trained to protect their Fliers.

Crystal: All Ghosts need a crystal to achieve ghosted form. The two exceptions to this are Emelynn Taylor and the woman who gifted her, Jolene Reynolds.

Flash: Fliers can use the second lens in their eye to produce a flicker of light within the eye that other Fliers recognize.

Flier: A human either born or gifted with a mutated gene that allows him or her to shed gravity and take flight. The gene can also manifest with additional facets, such as memory reading and telekinesis. The mutation produces a second lens in the eye.

Founding families: The nine founding coveys are comprised of the oldest and strongest families within the Flier community. Centuries ago, these family coveys founded the Tribunal Novem to police the Flier ranks.

Ghost: A Flier with the ability to dissipate into molecules too small for the human eye to see. Ghosts are rare. The process of turning into this form is called ghosting. All members of the Tribunal Novem are Ghosts.

The Gift: The mutated gene that allows a Flier to shed gravity. The mutation produces a second lens in the eye. The gene can also manifest with additional facets, such as memory reading and telekinesis.

Gifting: The process of transferring the gift, in whole or in part, from one Flier to someone else. The receiver can be any human. The process strips the donor of the element gifted. When the entire gift is given, the process weakens the gift-giver and is fatal half the time. Giftings are strictly controlled by the Tribunal Novem. A Flier who has been gifted is considered a second-class Flier.

Jolt: Fliers can use the second lens in their eye to produce a wave of energy along a spectrum from sparks, which are like static shocks, to jolts, which are painful and can even be fatal. The degree of energy produced depends upon the Flier's particular gift and varies from weak to strong. A fatal jolt causes a brain bleed (hemorrhage or aneurysm), which is medically classified as a stroke.

The Redeemers: A group of Fliers who feel they have been wronged, or are not represented, by the Tribunal Novem. Their goal is to replace the Tribunal Novem. They are led by Carson Manse.

Rush: Fliers can use the second lens in their eye to produce a stimulative energy that falls within the low-end of the spectrum of energy they are able to produce. It's sexual in nature and used to heighten sexual arousal. Referred to as the/his/her rush.

Spark: Fliers can use the second lens in their eye to produce a wave of energy along a spectrum from sparks, which are like static shocks, to jolts, which are painful and can even be fatal. The degree of energy produced depends upon the Flier's particular gift and varies from weak to strong.

The Tribunal Novem: Judge, jury and executioner in the Flier world. They are comprised of one representative from each of the nine founding coveys. They are always Ghosts. Their identities are not known within the Flier community. The Tribunal's leadership rotates every five years. At any given time, five Tribunal members provide day-to-day investigation and enforcement.

Discussion Questions

Spoiler alert: These questions contain spoilers that will ruin the story for those who haven't yet read the book.

1. Jolene Reynolds's motives for gifting Emelynn Taylor are not definitively known, but Mason Reynolds believes his sister's motive was her own suicide. Is Mason's assumption reasonable? Why do you believe Jolene gifted Emelynn?

2. Mason Reynolds's mother is a stroke victim and rarely present in scenes with her son or husband. Do you think the author intentionally closeted her away, or might there be other factors at play? What might those factors be?

3. Ghosting is a skill Emelynn learns in Burning Lies. Is it a skill you wish you had? When would you use it? Are there circumstances where using it would be detrimental? Why?

4. Emelynn has had suitors from both of her worlds, Cheney and Dean from the normal contenders and Jackson and James from the Flier contenders. If you were her, which one would you pick, and why?

5. Emelynn rebels when she feels she's being controlled: against the gift itself, against the Fliers who taught her how to fly, against detective Coulter, and against the Reynoldses. Is she justified in her rebellion? Are there times in a free society when controlling measures are justified?

6. Mason confesses to having failed his sister which resulted in her disappearance and ultimate death. Do you believe his explanation? Why or why not?

7. If you were casting Mason's role in a motion picture, who would you choose?

8. When Emelynn discovers one of her kidnappers at Cairabrae, we see a side of her we've never seen before, a side with no compassion and a willingness to inflict pain and even death. Is her reaction realistic? Is this a turning point for her? Can you imagine a scenario where you might take the same actions?

9. Do you think Carson Manse's Redeemers had justification for their rebellion?

10. The authorities covered up what happened at Cairabrae. Do you think this has ever, or would ever occur in the real world?

11. If you could ask the author one question, what would it be? Would your organization or group like to arrange an author appearance in person or online? If so, please contact the author at jpmclean @jpmcleanauthor.com.

A printable version of these discussion
questions is available at jpmcleanauthor.com/extras.

About the Author

JP (Jo-Anne) McLean writes addictive supernatural fiction. She is an Eric Hoffer award winner, a two-time silver medalist in the Wishing Shelf Book Awards, a finalist in the Chanticleer International Book Awards and the Independent Author Network Awards. She is a B.R.A.G. medallion honoree and four-time Literary Titan Gold Award winner. Reviewers call her books *addictive*, *smart*, and *fun*.

JP holds a Bachelor of Commerce degree from the University of British Columbia's Sauder School of Business, is a certified scuba diver, an exploratory chef, and an avid gardener.

Raised in Toronto, Ontario, JP now lives with her husband on Denman Island, which is nestled between the coast of British Columbia and Vancouver Island. When she's not writing, you'll find her cooking dishes that look nothing like the recipe photos or arguing with weeds in the garden. She enjoys hearing from readers. Contact her via her website, jpmcleanauthor.com, or through social media.

 Sign up for her newsletter ~ jpmcleanauthor.com

 Find her on Goodreads ~ goodreads.com/jpmclean

 Like her on Facebook ~ facebook.com/JPMcLeanBooks

 Follow her on Twitter ~ @jpmcleanauthor

www.ingramcontent.com/pod-product-compliance
Lightning Source LLC
Chambersburg PA
CBHW061311190726
48288CB00002B/458